THE WOMEN OF WHITECHAPEL

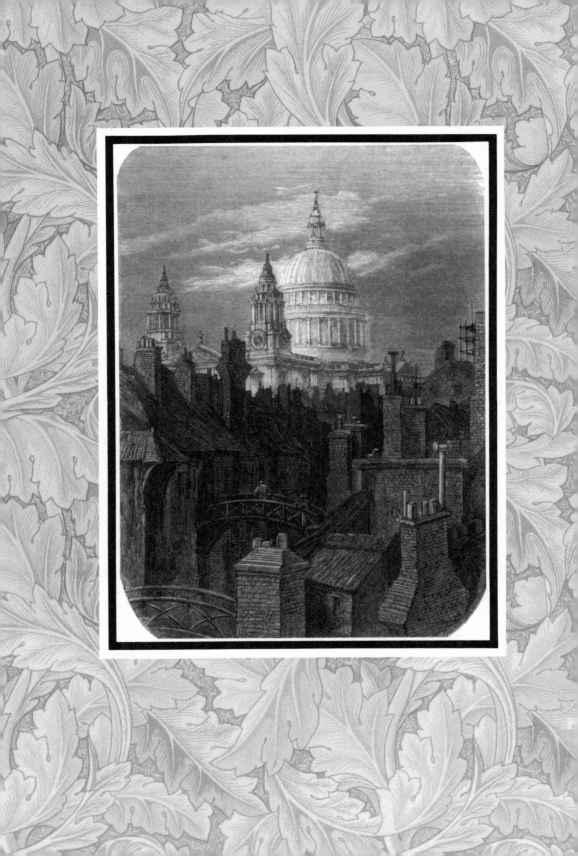

THE WOMEN OF WHITECHAPEL

and Jack the Ripper

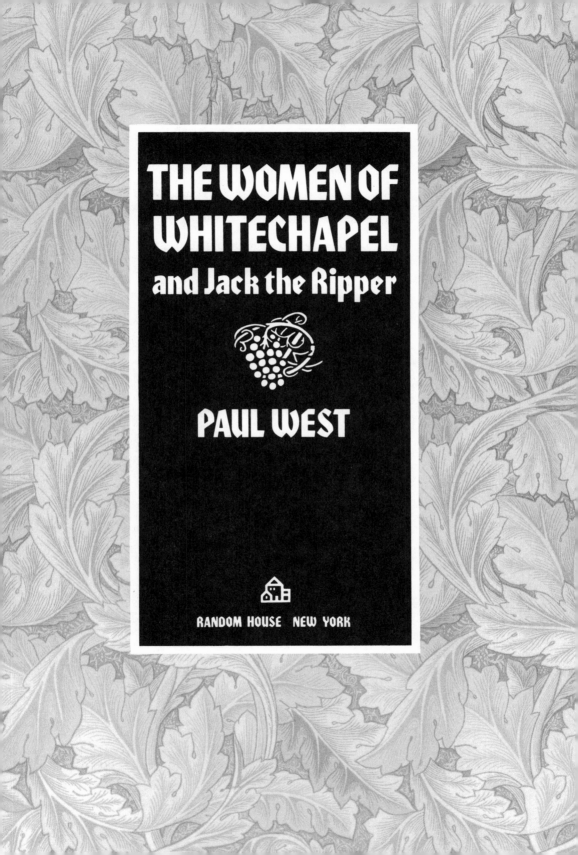

PAUL WEST

RANDOM HOUSE   NEW YORK

Portions of this work were originally published in
Conjunctions and *The Paris Review*.
Grateful acknowledgment is made to Harcourt Brace
Jovanovich, Inc. and Faber and Faber Limited for permission
to reprint thirteen lines from "Fragment of an Agon" in
"Sweeney Agonistes" from *Collected Poems 1909–1962* by T. S.
Eliot. Copyright 1936 by Harcourt Brace Jovanovich, Inc.
Copyright © 1964, 1963 by T. S. Eliot. Rights throughout the
world excluding the United States are controlled by Faber and
Faber, Limited. Reprinted by permission of Harcourt Brace
Jovanovich, Inc. and Faber and Faber, Limited.

Library of Congress Cataloging-in-Publication Data
West, Paul.
The Women of Whitechapel and Jack the Ripper/by Paul West.
p.   cm.   ISBN 0-394-58733-2
1. Whitechapel murders, 1888—Fiction. 2. London (England)-
-History—1800–1950—Fiction. I. Title.
PR6073.E766W47   1991
813'.54—dc20   90-9046

Manufactured in the United States of America
9 8 7 6 5 4 3 2
First Edition

Book design by J.K. Lambert

There is a gusto in the spending of the poor;
they are very close to what they possess.

Virginia Woolf, "Walter Sickert,"
The Captain's Death Bed and Other Essays

SWEENEY: I knew a man once did a girl in
Any man might do a girl in
Any man has to, needs to, wants to
Once in a lifetime, do a girl in.
Well he kept her there in a bath
With a gallon of lysol in a bath
SWARTS: These fellows always get pinched in the end.
SNOW: Excuse me, they dont all get pinched in the end.
What about them bones on Epsom Heath?
I seen that in the papers
You seen it in the papers
They *don't* all get pinched in the end.
DORIS: A woman runs a terrible risk.

T.S. Eliot, "Fragment of an Agon"

Although I based this novel on facts, I based it on few enough of them, having discovered that one Ripper specialist's fact is another's fiction. Each denounces the other's work as ballyhoo, which is an ideal starting point for a true merchant of the untrue. Years ago I found out, when researching the Nazis for my novel about Claus von Stauffenberg, that historians compulsively embroider and embellish; when I got to the facts, the fiction had already begun.

Never mind. The BBC television series, *Jack the Ripper,* and Stephen Knight's *Jack the Ripper: The Final Solution* beguiled my imagination no end and fed me some usefully preposterous *données.* Melvin Harris's *The Ripper File,* virtually a picture album, regaled my mind's eye and set it rolling. Perhaps the pitiful Annie Crook was not Scottish after all, as Donald Rumbelow contends, but born in north London; in my novel she is as I conceive of her, not just for my own convenience and whim, but for purposes of aesthetic development. Perhaps too she was a Protestant, not a Catholic; in these pages she is the latter. This is a work of imagination. It was Alban Berg's opera *Lulu,* in which the Ripper appears, that first set me thinking about him and "his" women. The net effect is surely more operatic than informational. Where nobody knows, we must invent, as the great religions do, giving the mind a ride, leading it a chase.

In the following pages, British speakers and musers get British spelling, but the American narrator otherwise writes in American English, except for certain moments of intense locutional empathy.

P . W .

Chapter 1

Born from a pelvis that was blue with cold, and later swept southward to the darker green pastures of the Midlands, Annie Elizabeth Crook had sometimes heard her name pronounced as Cook, she knew not why, but concluded it all had to do with a change in the wind from up to down. The dropped *r* was what happened when you left Scotland. Nobody rolled it then, although you could still go on talking that clipped antiseptic brogue. To her, who never learned to read or write, Scottish enunciation was a miracle, both audible and decipherable, and somehow linked to being clean-nosed and brisk. Having landed halfway down England, where it was less windy, being nowhere near the sea, she did not at first think about moving farther south, but contented herself with running small errands, and on her days off (which were many) treading in the local woodlands through enormous crops of bluebells, which she would gather in armfuls almost too heavy to carry home to the little hovel next to the church (two rooms up, two down, eleven people). Having brought home too many, she would take the excess, after being parentally scolded for overdoing it, and strew them beneath her in the earth closet

set atop a steep slope above the Ruthin River. In this pigsty-smelling hut she did her business through an oval hole in a wooden lid, after which she was supposed to shovel ashes from a heap outside. In time, thanks to natural drying and the tendency of mounds to crumble, the dung and ashes found their way down the slope, as if from some minor volcano of sulfuric refuse. She averted her unschooled mind from it, thinking instead of how, daily, she fruited upon the beauty and the intense pungency of the bluebells she had lugged home, pure as a woodland fairy. Her mind felt strong and lyrical, never more so than when she cast bluebells upon her droppings until all she could see was flowers and green stems. At these moments she desired to leave, almost more than anything else in life, but she had no idea of where to go, and would not have until she was several years older. She did, however, while delivering messages or fetching potted beef, dream about the color blue. She squatted over a piece of imagined sky or some very distant ocean, aware of the outside world only as a place where they strapped your new bosoms tight against your chest until you were almost flat, and bound your feet in similar fashion to make them small and demure. Having thus fused high fashion and China, she was ready to imagine streets paved not with gold, but with lead kept shiny by an army of urchins equipped with stiff metal brushes. The sun beat down and flashed and you could see reflections of your private places as you walked. It was like walking on a blade, and that was the city. Lying dozing in cow pastures after walking from Frecheton (an old French settlement) to Killamarsh, or from Spinkfield to Dronhill, treading where Normans and Vikings once had been, she made daisy chains, nettled herself on purpose (rubbing a dock leaf against the rash), learned to skim dehydrated cow manure through the air, and, eventually, began granting sexual favors to sundry butcher's lads, one of whom for novelty slipped his foot between her thighs and told her it was the normal thing to do. She would not mind if, one day, he raised her aloft on that foot, daring the heavens to strike her down. If this was all life was for, she decided, she would have been better off in Scotland, where people had no time to play. First she delivered milk, then joints of meat, followed always by dogs she beat off with a stick filched from a gamekeeper's cottage; he had seen her picking bluebells and introduced her to all his weapons, from shotgun to penis, always rewarding her with a rabbit full of shot or a floppy dead bird, its eyes already taupe and glazed. A career of sorts began as she went farther afield, in the butcher's pony and trap, each parcel of beef or whatever emblazoned with a convenient motif: a cross for the Jermins, who lived at the crossroads; a crude horse for the Staniforths, who kept a horse tethered on the front lawn; and an angel for the Gilbodys, who had a stone angel in front of their home, whose wings seemed almost to melt. In time, knowing the route and the usual orders of the customers, she needed these aides-mémoire no more; but twice the horse bolted, she was thrown, and she was blamed. She had watched lumps of meat, the bills skewered to them by something like small rapiers, soar through the air to an opportunistic dog. Elsewhere, she just knew, there awaited her some nosegay of invincible fragrance, and a bonnet to match—a life of ribbons, curtseys, and samplers, plus a few kind words, maybe a dozen a day. Life there would be better, she thought, than being marooned here among the uncouth loam-laden vowels of yokels whose vocalic output over an entire hour was often no more than a series of baa-ed ahs, these indicating profound and utter assent to whatever had last been said, as if indeed, among cattle meadows and with a fresh sprig of hawthorn between your teeth, there was never a need to think about anything. She determined one day soon to go to where gaslight burned all night, to buses and lemonade-sellers, to fast speech and the flash of unearned money. Scotland was long gone, with its twang like mother-of-pearl overheard in a seashell. To her, London was as big as all of England she had not seen. You could walk to it like Dick Whittington with his cat, asking for the Queen, who never sat in an earth closet on an ash heap. All Annie had to do was persist and somehow not get pregnant before leaving.

Gradually, from gabble and myth, she began to piece together an image of the longed-for city, where hotel rooms had outside them a little signal that went up and stayed up if the guest within rang for the maid; where Maypole Dairies confronted the shopper with vast marble walls and counters to give an impression of cold antisepsis; where flower girls cried "Who'll buy my blooming lavender, ducks? Sixteen branches for a penny." Perhaps London, or the South, needed a bluebell-seller, who would stand on a box in which parsnips had come to town. If she went, she would arrive without a character, and in that event she would have to become an unfortunate, a mott, or a dolly-mop, as whoring servant-girls were called. Only a recommended girl could work as a maid. In no time she would be found dead and afloat in a drinking fountain, obstructing a horse that wanted to drink. Distantly, she hoped she could become a statue, one of the human-looking ones that lifted up the floors of buildings, their places swathed in rags.

But she had reckoned all this without Walter Richard Sickert. She had only to get herself to London, walking and begging rides, gliding southward on barges that plied canals, and then maneuver herself into just about any public house in Camden Town, and a toff would do the rest; they were always on the prowl for some unfortunate who would take off her clothes for money. His eyes would begin it, noting that, although she was far from beautiful, she had a jaunty, effusive quality. For some reason people cheered up when they looked at her, even when she was severe of mien; it must have been something from Scotland, an essentially Scots vivacity that showed on her face under even the dourest circumstances. Never mind how bad the situation was, her features told the world there was still something to be lively about. She brought to conversation an appetizing sprightliness that won her drinks and offers, Sickert's included. He appreciated her thick eyebrows, her low forehead, the rather large retroussé nose, and the mouth, wide and slack from overuse. Something else drew him on, too: she never looked at things directly, but first canted her head sideways, then swiveled her eyes through a big angle to soak up the object of her attention. Her hair was dark and fluffy, growing back upon itself: enough to distract you from the willful, almost swollen jaw.

"So, sir," she told him in her fizzy, definite way, "it's to pose in the nude? I've done other things in the nude, so why not that. A girl—"

"A few pence, maybe a meal, would come of it." He did not want her to expect too much; he didn't want her to be building.

"With regular work," she persisted. "A girl can't live on that, sir. We don't wear out from being looked at, but the woman inside has to have her porridge."

"Oh," he said, with his best curl of the mouth and a hint of his French accent, "we can give you porridge by the ton. I think there are ways, especially on Cleveland Street, where I'm living." He had rooms in a large red-brick terrace house on a lively, quaint street that ran almost parallel to Tottenham Court Road. Cleveland Street was an island of art, with an artist's colorman, a picture-liner, and Landsbert the art dealer, all plying their trade among a host of other callings, from locksmith and hatter to engraver and cabinetmaker, from French-polisher to silver chaser. If London had a Montmartre, this was it, a place for the unrecognized genius to be a notable in, looked up to by rival and shopkeeper alike. It was also Sickert's laboratory, where he ran several experiments having to do with human relations: he liked to make people become more than themselves, and Annie Elizabeth Crook (or Cook) would do just that; he could see it already. Naked, she had what he sometimes, with almost foppish disdain, called "peasant amplitude." He fancied her, made the attempt, and had her, but realized there were limits to a girl who could not write or read. She was looking for a grand affair that would rescue her. Posing for Walter Sickert, she showed an uncanny ability to keep still, but he had no idea she was back among the mown hay or the bluebells in those deep woods. To turn to stone, all she needed to do was imagine that lecherous foot between her legs, out there among the cowflops, with her skirt down, and all the world could go hang. She had flawless skin like the softest bleached chamois leather, and she berated him in her soft brogue for painting her covered with bruises and molasses-like eruptions. He made her look scarred and scratched.

"You're unkind to me body," she told him, having already picked up some cockney. "It's nice."

"The shadows," he explained, "are all in my eyes. They have nothing to do with you."

"Then why don't you paint them *seprit*?" she said.

Ah, he mused, unanswering. That would be the day, when appearances would be nothing but appearances, and not appearances *of* anything at all. He would achieve it, he knew, courtesy of no Scotch-Midlands hussy; light would baste light with light. Darkness would form scabs over no wound. Love would float through the untrammeled air, being love of no one for nobody. He longed for purity of phenomenon, knowing that was what he saw behind his eyelids when he was dozing off or when he strained too hard at his bowels. The age of models would end, and all those whores in retirement would go back into business, and not during the Season only. Oh, he could paint the vestibule of the Metropole if he had to, when it opened next year, full of azure skies, mint-fresh arabesques, and festoons and amorini, all filched from the Gallery of Apollo in the Louvre. Oh, he could, but he would not. Better for him, while awaiting abstraction incarnate, to paint humans marooned in a blaze of woodchips (as somebody had said). Later observers would identify an expressionist buried inside an impressionist, long after he cared what label the morgue attached to his big toe or other parts of comparable heft.

"You paint skin," she was telling him, "as if the woman 'ad been lying down in a wet cowfield."

"I do," he said, amazed. "Paint is like excrement, isn't it? Oh. Shit, then."

She was wincing. "Be good."

"I'm never good. My friends cherish me for varying degrees of polished obnoxiousness."

Her mind was on ladies shopping without male escort, heading for the safety of Holborn's Grill Room; beeves with Lord Cadogan's name attached in big letters on a sheet of paper; butlers escorting a plate of muffins from below stairs to upstairs; the hell of Haymarket, where prostitutes competed (those who were not lucky enough to have been picked up by an artist gentleman); crossing sweepers who cleared the way for your white spats and your dimity dress when you made so bold as to cross the street, and horsedrawn omnibuses all placarded with signs for Nestle's Milk, or two soaps, Sunlight and Lifebuoy. What, she wondered, was a Gladstone Brief Bag? No, there were other soaps: Pears' and Sanitas. Was that what Dandy Dick Whittington, on at the Strand Theatre, used after his long journey southward? While she posed, she inhaled the reek of London and its open sewers; heard the whistles, one for a four-wheeler, two for a hansom; and saw, from somewhere within Sickert's crooked arm, the fuliginous orange of a street lamp. She felt most at ease in the mews, the alleys behind the well-to-do homes, where horses munched their oats and hay, and the coachmen and servants lived. Even the Haymarket smelled of hay. London wasn't that much of a city after all. Once she had regular work, it would dwindle into a village, just like home.

"Enough," Sickert was saying, allowing the curlicues at the sides of his mouth to ripple and pucker. He had been eyeing her flesh, but the leg he was painting belonged, really, to the music-hall artiste Emily Lyndale, the exact fit of whose tights occupied him a great deal. "I envy anyone, you know," he was saying, "who gets up after ten, has a beautiful maid serve him breakfast by a roaring fire, reads *The Times* from front to back in his slippers, then has a doze followed by a solid lunch with some port, then another nap, and here and there a bit of painting in a nice clean studio until it's time for tea and scones, toast and muffins, or a *café filtre*. Now that would be the life, Annie, eh? By the way, I have something for you. Opposite number fifteen, there's Mrs. Morgan's tobacconist's. Number twenty-two. Well, they need a shopgirl. How would you like to be a shopgirl? You'd have to serve sweeties, too."

Was it the humid fug of summer, worse than ever in 1884, that made her want to faint, or was it excitement tempered with relief? She tottered and fell, but was as swiftly picked up and placed on the couch, where all her London reveries came together in one panoramic idyll in which the river did not smell and the streets were no longer thick with horse droppings. Mr. Sickert would be able to see her from the front windows of the studio, he said. "Look." She did, and she exploded with mundane joy.

All of a sudden he saw something: she could not write a letter home, nor read one if one should come. She was landlocked, an atoll. He resolved to widen her range of acquaintances, sap it of its monotony—tarts and artist's models, painters and serving girls. What she needed was something of the romance that basked in her eyes when she modeled and recounted the tale of how London had lured her on across all those acres of England, swapping one dead end for another when, did she but know it, she wanted the Field of the Cloth of Gold, sun-treading argosies, the sword Excalibur, Crusaders and Arthurian knights and *belles dames sans merci.* None of this was Sickert's stock in trade by any means, but he heard the soul of Cleveland Street, where the Pre-Raphaelites had lived and worked, painting always into a wet ground, in the end creating portraits—prominent upper lip, red hair, gaze of unbreachable medieval solemnity—that were the plain girl's best friends. He saw Annie as the Lady of Shalott, afloat near the reeds, her hair clamped in by a fillet, and as Ophelia, being sucked down into the depths by her finery, yet unperturbedly horizontal. Annie was the girl these men never had a chance to paint. He vowed to give her a taste of heaven if he could.

To Annie the small world of Cleveland Street was almost cozy. She herself lived in the basement of number six, cattycorner from Sickert's place at number fifteen. She vaguely knew that directly opposite number twenty-two there was a male brothel, but she had no idea that "Eddy"—Prince Albert Victor Christian Edward, the future Duke of Clarence and Avondale—was a sometime visitor there, ferried in by his coachman Netley, who picked him up at a prearranged rendezvous where he transferred from the coach emblazoned with the royal arms that had brought him from Cambridge to one with no markings at all: most often the one that Netley, who rented it, had named the

Crusader. If the artists of Cleveland Street lived lives of introverted oblivion graced with taste, the homosexuals at number nineteen were destined to be discovered and exposed. Prince Eddy was not an artist, but he had artistic leanings fostered by his mother, Princess Alexandra, whom Sickert knew; both Sickert's father and his grandfather had been artists to the Royal Court of Denmark, from which Alix had come to London two decades earlier. There was a Danish connexion, which Alix exploited by writing a tactful, beseeching letter to Sickert, asking him to introduce her son gently to Bohemia. His father, Prince Edward, had virtually disowned the boy, bellowing that he was a dunderhead whom not even Cambridge could cure. One day Eddy would become king, and he should know much more than he knew. Could Mr. Sickert, Princess Alix asked, do something about bringing him out? So, in 1884, the same year that Annie Crook arrived in Cleveland Street, Prince Eddy turned up there too, to find art and men, to be weaned at once from his father's bluff ridicule and the Court's simpering routine. Sickert went one further, introducing Eddy around as his younger brother, twenty to his twenty-four, known to all as "Albert" or "the young Mr. S." Down from Cambridge during term time, and then during the Long Vacation, came Prince Eddy—not a painter, but a man with a gift for adoring those who liked him, and for effortless fraternizing—right into the arms of Annie Crook, who diffused about him an air of well-tempered maternality. Annie looked just like his mother, in fact, and he adored his mother, that gentle coaxer and intuiter who sent her adored but feckless son into the outside world with an injunction to Walter Sickert not to let him get into trouble. What he got into even he himself could hardly believe, wanting on the one hand to plunge his all into the mellow orbit of this milkmaid, knowing on the other that he would never be his own man, not even to the extent of being a watercolorist, a stamp collector, a closet deviant. He came to Annie, he told himself, with big infernal black wings behind him that would one day enfold and smother him; he would be swathed in royal tortoiseshell, as unable to kiss as to live. Better, then, he thought, to go sport himself with the bully boys of number nineteen, on the principle that, if you have to go, cleave to nothing you will miss. But he could not quite reason his way through the uproar in his glands. Why, if she could write, he would weep to see the exquisite tenderness explicit in her very handwriting. Her ornate cheerfulness moved him almost to tears as it was, and her garrulous adaptability made him feel crude and morose. Then, as he surely must, he made Annie pregnant and Sickert said to him "You royal fool, Eddy, you've done it now."

"I love her," said the luckless prince.

"You do not *love life,* though," said Sickert. "Your head's in a noose, and hers too. Play is one thing, but this is likely to occupy you the rest of your days."

Annie, of course, knew who "Albert" Sickert really was, and would perhaps have given her life for him if she had been asked to do so. To her, he was angel, prince, and playmate all in one, and Holy Ghost as well. She thought he would give up his all for her, even the furtive "uprights" across the road among men only. He was her savior and servitor; she knew now that she would never have to become a mott or go back to the Midlands. Eddy worked himself into a paroxysm in Sickert's studio, hurling himself against the walls and knocking down several wet canvases. "Ruin yourself, my dear Eddy," the painter shouted, "but leave my art alone."

"Who," Annie was asking, "said that? Soft and creamy. That's how *Eddy* sounds to me. He can be Albert too, if he wants. I don't care. He's more than one man now."

"Not in England he isn't," Sickert said. "He's been looking for trouble and he's found it. I blame myself. You two could have died natural and satisfactory deaths apart. Now you have to go to hell together. Imagine: a royal prince in the direct line of succession getting a shopgirl with child, and a Catholic at that. It's pure Amphitryon."

They both looked at him, confounded; their tutor could be arcane, every bit as much as he could be a bewildering headstrong friend. "Oh—the highest-born in the land disguises himself as an ordinary mortal and in that disguise goes to bed with a woman whom he makes pregnant. He has come from Olympus. He is Jupiter, king of the gods. Why do the gods always have to go slumming? *Issue,* my dears, that's the word that drives us mad."

All of a sudden, Annie knew that she was not going to spend much time at the Empire Theatre of Varieties on Leicester Square, promenading or standing in front of the refreshment bars, or watch Dr. Grace play cricket, his famous beard waving in the breeze, or attend a spiritualist séance and watch unearthly raiment floating in midair. She could see Prince Eddy receding from her already, off back to his randy chums, reciting for them the sum of her private parts, the thickness of her various lips, the experienced look of her hairs. As things turned out, however, she had a blissful pregnancy doing private and distant things by means of Netley's bouncy *Crusader,* sometimes accompanied by Sickert and his fiancée, Ellen Cobden, and occasionally Eddy himself.

Down to Yarmouth by train she went during the steaming weekends of 1884, there to paddle ankle-deep, squeak with exaggerated modesty in a bathing machine in which she was pushed a few yards out into the sea. A jollier-looking striped four-wheeler had never existed.

Chapter 2

When she looked back at Eddy she saw no Amphitryon unbending from his celestial perch, but the handsomest of ocean gods, his long, slightly corpulent face a blur of animal devotion, his oiled quiff shining in the mottled sunlight, his heavy-lidded eyes achieving an odd combination of candor and tender aloofness. He was never all there: the smile had been trained; the mustache turned a lad into a gullible rake; and the ears lay too close to the head, as if not wanting to provide something to hold on to him by. His demeanor was a house of cards arranged by experts who took their orders from Queen Victoria. Annie stared at him as the water crept up to her knees, wetting her dress, and thought she could discern the imprint on his mouth of men's lips, hear the scratch of men's nails in his hair, the secretest thought he had in which he did not quite know after whose body he lusted when he was most excited. At that instant she wanted to march off into the sea, turning her back on all cries to halt as she waded out of her depth. All she could do was pray that his wandering mind would fix on her long enough to know her name: Crook or Cook, she did not care. She wanted to put black lead on an iron fireplace that belonged to him, but she knew such a dream was sheer confusion; she could only be one thing to him, princess or drab. Then she cried "Save me!" from her two-feet depth, but nobody made a move, so she held her ground and let the tears dribble down.

There she stood, at sea among straw-boatered girls whose smiles were of the purest gladness. To Annie everything seemed slow-motion: people were savoring all they did, trying to act with maximum dignity in the presence of that enormous heaving meadow of blue-gray water. The urgency had gone out of so-called civilization. Everyone looked down to get their footing right. All clothing had risen to the thighs, around which it wrapped itself like so many ill-fitting turbans, and she half expected to see yards upon yards of petticoats and skirts fall all at the same moment into the water. She wondered at the variety of human expressions. Up to now, people had looked more or less alike, but by the sea they brought out of storage all kinds of faces she'd never seen before, from downcast perseverance to beaming paralysis, from suspicious relish to a grin that belied the wobble of the bearer. People were close together and that was surely so that they might help one another if the water got suddenly deep.

Not even Eddy had come to get her, so she started off again, letting the sea mount her thighs, wishing she were a passenger in one of those high-wheeled bathing machines, being tugged out toward the horizon, past the end of the pier that resembled a long ladder laid on its side. Cries of "Annie! Annie!" went past her like free-flying gulls and the water had risen to her waist now, cold and imperious. For some reason several youths rolled a spare wheel from a bathing machine through the shallows toward her, but it failed to advance and would have been a mere reminder of help denied if it had reached her. On she reeled, listening for Eddy's call, but what she heard behind her was a rumble, as of a farm cart starting up, then a *swoosh* and some grunts. He and some others had shoved a bathing machine, number nine, half way to her, but it had bogged down in the sand. Now he mounted the little forward platform, calling her from the doorway as if he stood on the tip of a departing train, the last train back to London, and she ignored him, able to think only of the heavy-featured women asleep on the beach, over-clad and ungainly, their hands arranged in odd retentive clasps around their possessions, not to hinder the thief but to make him feel guilty. How, she wondered, did one get comfy enough to doze off, with a flowered hat, two scarves, a long-sleeved velvet bodice and a thick skirt all the way to the ankles? That was how you kept the sand out, to be sure, but nothing kept the sun off their faces, now bloated and slack. What happened if all those hands touched during this most public sleep of all?

Still Prince Eddy, *her* prince, made no further move, but stood comfortably on the platform as if ready to declaim or even to give up. Annie looked at the mob on the shore, marveling that not one of them appeared in the least put out by the horror on her face. She was going to stumble and drown at any moment. She just knew it. It was one thing to be carrying a royal infant (her skin felt like gold leaf), but quite another to be a shopgirl out on holiday with a prince of the realm, whom somebody was sure to recognize. Was that why he hung back, disdaining to step from the bathing machine into the brackish shallows off Yarmouth? He should have been back at college in Cambridge, but he was never there anyway, whether the place was open or closed, and she had never been able to work out the difference. When the place was open, people left it all the time, and when it was closed they were always making little side trips to have a look at it. There he stood, the young prince, a pale-blue cap on top of the head it was too small for and some kind of pipe in his mouth. She knew enough to conjecture that, if he had been French, and this moment had been not now but earlier in time, they would have wheeled him away in that very bathing machine and taken him to the guillotine. She could see that he saw her as part of the seascape, in no peril at all; indeed, as someone to be talked into staying there because Sickert (who hated outdoor scenes) had said that the composition was good, meaning that the mass of people on the beach made up a pretty pattern. It was only then that she noticed, behind the ranks of slow-moving bathers, the farther horizontal stratum of strollers clad wholly in black, marching up and down the beach like people in mourning, glancing avidly at one another. It was as if they walked to unheard music whose beat they dared not miss lest their watch chains and tiepins and wing collars floated off and away. That was the realm of the dry sand, next to that of the wet and tousled sand, next to which was the tide, making its messy little inroads. Several of the men walked with their hands clasped behind their backs, their jackets open and curling even farther apart in the breeze, so much so that she caught a glimpse of armpits now and then and realized she was facing the land.

Then Eddy came, with a stylish plunge, as if going golfing. "Now then," he brayed, and her heart stirred at the sight and sound of him. "We don't want you out there."

"Anywhere you like," she said.

"Not in water," he said. "You'll rot."

"I'll rot?"

He took her hand and strained to land her.

"Come on in."

"I'm coming. I've been everywhere I'm going today."

"You can dry off."

"Oh my," she said, inside the bathing machine with him, out there in the slop where willing arms and shoulders had left it, "you can't cross the same river twice. You are a one. In here?"

"In here," he said urgently. "I love you and I have to make us one."

"We are already," she said. "Can't you feel it?"

In the gloom he held on to her frizzy hair, homed to the soft, inflated-looking lips, and entered standing even as a sea-salt aroma not Annie's came up at him, but in a few moments yielded to hers. For once, perhaps because of the setting (on wheels; at rest in the sea slop), she did not feel romantic about his thudding motions and his feverish clutching at her rear. Instead, she wondered about 19 Cleveland Street and the cleanliness or otherwise of what he did in there, and remembered a saying from up in the uncouth Midlands: *You'll eat a peck of muck afore you die.* Well, was this the peck of muck destined to be hers? Was *this* romantic? Had Sickert and the others any idea of what was happening inside the bathing machine? Did Sickert himself still desire her? How could she be both an easily taken woman, *open* as some said, and yet the high-toned darling of the prince? A new confusion grew in her heart, and she suddenly felt endangered, as if he were some deadly tree and to touch him were fatal. What was the name of that tree? The one that turned you into a leper with a single touch? Or the one that burned you with acid and then devoured you where you stood or fell? Eddy had finished and withdrawn, but neither of them was eager to leave, she thought, because this time people would see him and identify him, cooing, ahing, making signs.

And they did, either looking away with a giggle or staring so hard their faces seemed to putrefy. It was he. His face was known, and admired for its puffy staidness in which something raffish vanished into something dull. The saddest thing about him, she was beginning to learn, was that he was a sex machine with a tender soul. Often she found him in tears, moved beyond measure by something that she laughed off with Scots bravura. He seemed to fall in love with anyone who spoke half kindly to him, and, by the same token, anyone who was less than polite reduced him to a dither. Prince Eddy was hypersensitive, as one denied the basic coarseness that enabled most folk to get from day to day. This was his doting, unworldly mother in him.

Something blank and sheeplike in his face made Annie think he should always be dressed for football in a striped jersey, hair waved and oiled not to come adrift during Saturday afternoon's exertions. Netley, his coachman, told him what to think, and teased his lewd imagination with ingenious pranks that made him want to go to number nineteen and try them at once. Yet his heart remained gentle, his desire to be a father made him feel more adult than he ever had. He was happy in Sickert's Cleveland Street orbit. Compared to love, paternity, and the Bohemian way, sodomy, court, and Cambridge were so many dry exercises he performed almost as a sleepwalker. If ever, as he might, he heard himself called King Albert Victor Christian Edward, like the three kings of Orient plus one in reserve, he would have to thin out his rather ample style of living; until then, however, he could afford to fight on several fronts, as he put it, and have several by-blows. He was rehearsing, he said. He was reading widely in the book of life. He was, in fact, preparing to become much the rake his father was.

If any of this passed through Annie's head, as through osmosis it might have, she felt that, since she was doing something impossible, she might as well be doing something outrageously so. When she saw the Yarmouth bathers belatedly recognize Eddy and hover in his presence between bow and wave (between bowing and waving, that was), she felt him being sucked away from her. It was his shadow that awed them: not *who* he was, but *what*. Someone had told her that a red object had some green in its shadow, the two being complementary, and she found the very idea unnerving. If royalty were purple, what hue would his shadow be? What was it? Yellow or orange, she thought. It stood to sense. And she wondered if it was good that all she got wrong never came from reading; all her misinformation she received orally, from some liar or incompetent or knave. Had she been able to read, she would have been able to look in a book for the truth about the shadows of purple objects, for example, but when she asked people they thought her daft. Her illiteracy endeared her to Eddy, giving him the sense of being her custodian, as if she were a leper or a cripple. A woman who could read would have made a less feckless womanizer of him. Because she could not read, he sometimes treated her as if she were blind and deaf, too, which accentuated his tenderness in one way while, in another, simplifying it. She was a real and complex woman, but he was in love with a cartoon version of her; and in his mind's eye (oubliette, rather), she was as disposable as the seed he spilled at number nineteen. He was straddling worlds that could easily pull apart, and there he would be again, the rotten apple of his father's eye, the beloved runt of his mother, the butt of the Cambridge hearties, the fawned-upon popinjay of know-it-all courtiers. Truly he was a graft upon Sickert's world, almost an experiment in one color hidden beneath another.

Annie never quite forgot that apparition of him at the seaside: the man who could be king. Would that make her his queen, then? She doubted this, romantically gullible as she was. The toffs always had a way of taking something off you that rightly was your own. He was already, for all his peccadilloes, less of a man than he was a figment, a being semi-divine and hopelessly illustrious. What could he be doing talking to the likes of her, never mind fumbling up her petticoats, peeling her underwear aside? Practicing, no doubt, for someone else who really would be queen. Some Dane, some German, she guessed. Where then would she and the bairn be? Smuggled into Windsor Castle and supervised by nannies dressed in suits of armor? Why, they would probably not even allow her to feed her own baby, but would import a series of wet nurses with royal connexions. She began to have a vision of her remaining days, each one a golden shuttle that split open under the impact of sunlight and bared a furry, honey-coated interior tasting of custard and caramel. She had to treasure them as best she could, like the bluebells from the olden days. She had some grasp of how to make the most of a delicious thing, but not of how to retain it. Over a year, say, she could see how her love of flowers, of this particular bunch—Tuesday's and then Wednesday's—merged until her mind was full of brief, superimposed adorations. The flowers had withered, but the emotions they had stirred remained intact and fused. Her head filled with successive sprays, but she could no longer tell them one from another; what remained, the yield, was some gradual crescendo of attunement that enabled her to respond a little more finely each time, so that—perhaps in ten years—she might be able to revel in a bunch of bluebells without even seeing it. She was sensitive that way. Somehow, though, she knew that her life with flowers was going to be richer than her life with Eddy. God made bluebells by the million without waiting to be asked. They poured out every year. With Prince Eddy, however, there was no godlike guarantee, godlike as he was supposed to be (although not to a Catholic such as her). His crop was intermittent and irregular; she bore a bunch of his flowers in her belly even now, but he was already moving on, she could tell. No less amorous and attentive than he had been at first, he had about him the look of a man barbarically distracted—by lust, family, fame, death. But, when she saw them all ooing and ahing, almost in slow-motion developing new ways to fawn on him, she felt she was in the presence of some historical abstraction: a flag, a chalice, a very famous umbrella stand, not a sweetheart at all. It was like loving the pope from a distance and then having his hand up your thighs. She wondered how the break would come when it did, and she was left to bring up the royal bastard on her own with, maybe, a monthly pittance to keep her going (these folk, she knew, paid monthly rather than weekly; it was the upper-class way). Awed by the wonder of life to such an extent that it became almost an affliction, she was also afflicted by the banal truth, not so much waiting for the penny to drop as for thunder to start. She wondered how many of the seaside throng had thought she must be Lady So-and-So or the Honourable Felicity Stickydrawers of Bluebell Mansions, Bedfordshire. She wondered how many other women, cached here and there, had been occupied for the past few years bringing up Eddy's little by-blows: a few minutes' toil for him, and some poor slut had acquired a lifelong charge. Who could ever tell? Had these women abandoned their babes to the team of royal wet nurses, or what? Had the call gone out for women to give suck? What complexities a simple shudder below the waist could start.

Whenever she tried to speak to him about these matters, he deluged her with sloppy-lipped adoration, actually sealing her mouth with heavy kisses, then pretending to tickle her. She could hardly get a word out. What she did not know was that he had confided to Sickert how much he loved her. Increasingly drawn to her, he said, and to her tonic, succinct sweetness, he nonetheless felt something pulling him back, as if he were never his own man: surely enough his own man to wander into a male brothel or hardly put in an appearance at Cambridge during Term, but in other ways a mere pawn, a sort of royal remittance man as far from serious affairs of the heart as London from Calcutta. Muddle on, Sickert told him, as an elder brother to a younger. "Life has a habit of settling its debts when you least expect it. Don't worry about the child. We'll work something out. I have nothing against children." And he meant it, being one of those to whom class barriers meant little: a born mixer, he loved to have about him not just a ménage but an unruly tribe, a boisterous copy of the world he loved to go and visit, almost a little London for his pocket pleasure. Half the time he did not even harvest his canvases where they fell, so to speak, off the easel; they made up a chromatic spoor he left behind him, stuff for critics to clear up and sell. He lunged forward, as little fearful of fate's insolences as of the sun, the air, the grass. He was the ideal catalyst for an Eddy, who was in constant diffident flux, a man in high places yet doomed to triviality, while Sickert went from strength to strength, from good repute to real fame, from distinction to being almost a household word. Eddy almost saw himself following in Sickert's wake, except he had no gift, no will, no eye: on loan from Princess Alix, whose notions of life—of art, of the Danish court, of Sickert's background—were idyllic to begin with. She was no more in touch than Eddy, but she had intentions whereas he had none; he was one of those life happened *to*. All this Sickert knew and pondered, without, however, troubling himself. He had set things in motion, and he would soon have to add something to that motion, or it would interest him less. Spruce up, he said, and shoulder the wheel of history.

Chapter 3

If anybody had been alert, Mary Kelly would have been thought a comet, long ago calculated to be on a collision course with Cleveland Street, spawned in Limerick but fired outward by John Kelly along with seven siblings and transplanted to North Wales, where he found occupation in an ironworks, rising eventually to the position of foreman. The only person alert was Mary Kelly, however, and she counted the days and nights, all without privacy, which drove her to marry a miner called Davies, an ordinary and stock enough fate; she was still a long way from disaster, although, in her blunt and baroque way, she would not have told you so, with poor Davies crushed to death in a mine explosion three years after he married her. Illness, no doubt fanned on by grief, then landed her in a Cardiff hospital, after which she moved into the gravest, most awful period of her life, and lodged with a cousin for the introit to widowhood, at last letting something reckless mull and cook in her mind. The idea of London, where bears danced in the streets and Socialist rioters looted wineshops, began to nibble at her. She felt she had paid enough tribute to the fates, and wondered what might be worse than the way she was living then, in 1884. So off she went, and with not an hour wasted was skivvying in an East End Refuge run by nuns when a better idea struck, and she found herself selling tobacco at 22 Cleveland Street, handmaiden of black twist or navy cut.

Mary Kelly was not a sophisticated woman, but she had lifelong a dream whose dimensions kept enlarging. If someone were in pain, she thought, he might scream at length, and she persuaded herself she would be able to hear that scream; indeed, she heard it even when no one was screaming. Perhaps she heard it because, somewhere, there was always somebody screaming, in diabolical pain, and the sound went on in Mary's head for hours. By the same token, then, she decided, she could hear the noise of someone so happy he sang aloud, as at some of those highbrow concerts where they sang Bark. This Bark was not one of her favorites, but she unreservedly loved the idea of someone bursting into sustained song for the sheer joy of being alive, or in love, or rich, or pregnant, any of those. When she herself sang, it was less sustained and off-pitch, but it was singing nonetheless. Singing as an act of will impressed her little; rather, she construed it as an outright exclamation of the mind, something between a sneeze and a convulsion, but prolonged through an entire vocalic range, more birdlike than anything but in no way territorial. Sometimes when daydreaming she heard an entire parade of women singing on the march, singing not to argue or protest but to show what they were made of, and this was the inward pastoral that sustained her through her husband's death, then widowhood, and the skivvying, which never quite ended. Always in the same garb, linsey frock and a red knitted crossover on her shoulders, she knew that, one fine day, she would wake up from the tawdry dream of this life and find herself walking in a meadow equipped with stream and swarming daffodils, grass of uncanny emerald green. It was a dream of Limerick, to be sure, yet overlaid with randomly gathered delectables, from muffins and black stout to a fur coat and a Russian bonnet made from sable. She was able to go on with life because she knew this haphazard rhapsody was coming to her, perhaps in old age, but coming nonetheless, and so her entire life steered toward that point in front of her, not to be beckoned or solicited; one day it would surround her, leaving her no hope of an anticlimax or of going back to threadbare living. Thenceforth she would have no chance to become a cripple with an iron foot, or a leper, losing her toes and having her fingers retract into a painful bunch. Call it heaven: it was as far from orthodox religion as from archery, and sometimes there were cropping horses and nibbling sheep, eggs boiled to exactly three and a half minutes, slabs of butter with a prayer stamped on their flanks like the butter in the Maypole Dairy shops, on which something more pagan appeared. She intuited an orderly world in which she did not live, as yet, but she knew such a thing could be, and her move from the East End convent to Mrs. Morgan's tobacconist's on Cleveland Street was a step in the right direction.

"He'll have you by the drawers now and then," Annie Crook told her that first day, "and you'll have to toss him off, but he's a fast gentleman if you know what I mean. And having to sit for him, him being the painter he is, well, that's not too bad either. He talks a lot, but it's all wind. There's no harm in it, and just look what you get for your money. He's always picking girls up for this or that, in one of the pubs. He likes what he calls low life. Likes to paint it, see. He's funny that way."

Mary Kelly laughed her most abandoned laugh, tuned in to no singing at the time. " 'Tis all the same to me, ducky. I'd rather have a gentleman's jellybabies to jiggle than kneel for a whole morn and afternoon with a donkey-stone in my hand, whitening what was meant to be only grey. And a whole conventful of chattering nuns telling you to get on with it, they themselves *supposed* to be bound by the vow of silence. Never mind. I'll do what I have to, don't you fret, my duck."

"Well, I'm expecting," Annie said, rather self-conscious.

"Who isn't?"

"No, I mean really." Annie patted her front, not quite sure where to pat, so patting here and there like someone playing pat-a-cake, pat-a-cake, baker's man.

"Well," said the Irish girl to the Scots one, "you will hardly damage yourself, will you now, handing little packets of tobacco over."

"I," Annie said sternly, "am really a confectioner's assistant, by training. And suchlike."

"And you went to Trinity College, Dublin, I don't doubt. Look, lover, I know a sweetshop when I see one."

"Edinburgh it was," Annie said, "where all the clever-dick doctors come from. Then they come to England to make money. There just aren't enough sick folk in Scotland for them to make a living at it."

And so they worked together, each trying to outdo the other in gracious handling of the merchandise—not quite rivals, but

fellow-critics of the shopkeeping system: Annie more of a solemn one except for fits of falsetto giggling; Mary, the more
worldly, given to fits of incoherent song that piqued Mrs. Morgan, yet never to the point of protest. It was a quiet, soft, almost
profitable life for the two of them, and Mary soon realized who
Mr. Sickert's younger brother was, becoming unctuous and
maudlin in his presence. For his part, Prince Eddy liked the spicy
repartee of the Irish girl, recommending her (or her anatomy at
least) to several of his friends, but Netley took a violent dislike
to her, calling her an upstart and a conniver, contending that no
good would come of having her around: a spy, a gooseberry, a
meddler. None of this troubled Eddy, however, caught up as he
was in the slow-burgeoning mystery of creation, even though
he wondered what the future would bring, half hoping that
Sickert would somehow inherit the whole mess because he,
Walter, was the worldiest of them all and knew where to cache
people or things. Sickert was also good at losing things, having
no sense of money and little of ownership. When the time came,
Sickert would be the fairy godfather in a domain that forbade
the "glorious Captain-King" to have any traffic with Roman
Catholics, not to mention shopgirls and motts. Eddy lived in an
infatuated blur, hoping that his secret life as Sickert's younger
brother would never come to light, that one day his mother
would tell him he had at last passed all the social examinations
she set him. Approval by his father, the Prince of Wales (no
mean rake himself), and Queen Victoria would follow. For now,
he was happy enough, and he liked the look of Mrs. Morgan's
son, a beefy, faltering boy who breathed hard most of the time
and had pale-blue eyes, on the rims of whose lids small blobs
of fat formed and lingered, itching, making him scratch at his
eyes a lot without seeming to obtain relief. Eddy found him
tempting, both buxom and ethereal. Sometimes, he thought,
and without trying much, he could love everybody. As for
Annie and Mary, Cuthbert (Bert) Morgan set their teeth on
edge, not just for rubbing his eyes endlessly, but also for being
slow, bland, and sycophantic: too much wax in him, too much
breath.

———

"You're shutting the stable door," Annie was saying with the world-weary finality often used by women who work with their hands. "The horse has gone."

"Yes, darling, lover," Mary Kelly persisted, " 'tis the future I'm on about. No need to get your mad up. Get your darling back down again now, and listen. Just you look at this. If gin is Mother's ruin, then this is Mother's joy. Babe's ruin." In her hand she had a small guidebook, plucked out from under the counter where she kept all manner of contraband, and Annie saw a flash of yellow and red as Mary turned to the last page, then waved the inside of the back cover at her: hard cardboard bound in blue cloth.

"Yes," Annie said. "A library book. I know what I'm looking at."

"You don't then," Mary Kelly said, with a triumphant inhalation. "This is no library book. My God, imagine the fuss if you could get yourself a book like this at a lending library. Look again, me darling. It's clever."

There was no card in the little pocket that Annie saw, but there usually was not if the book had been taken out. In any case, the pocket was too fat. "Take it." Annie felt in and then removed a wobbly, fluttery tube of a thing, held it up to dry and inspect, then handed it back.

"In a book?" she said.

"Yes, lover," said Mary. "French letter made of animal gut. Now, where would *you* be with one of these? It doesn't come with the book now, not as I'd know, but there's clear catering for it. It's one way of keeping a gentleman clean, as well as of keeping his tiddlers away from where they can do most harm. He can walk about all over town and they see him and say, Oh, what a nice studious gent that is, he takes a little book with him wherever he goes, and all the time he has in it a little shiny suit for his Grenadier Guardsman. I think the world would be a better place if we had more gentlemen carrying books to bed, or into your back alley."

"Into your back alley?" Annie was horrified.

"Not that, silly. I mean, imagine London with these things on the go. You wouldn't be in the mess you're in, my girl, if your ducky little prince had worn his helmet. Like a policeman. Lumme, you'd be free as the wind. Now you're five months gone. I can see it, too."

"No you can't," Annie whispered. "There's nothing to see. Not a peck."

"We aren't dealing in pecks, my love, we're dealing in great gobbing mouthfuls." Annie was still trying to get used to the breezy, absolute way Mary had of talking, as if the whole world had asked her for advice during a storm at sea and all the wise men had drowned. Mary presumed, called a spade a bum-smacking bloody shovel, and talked right through customers' requests. When she was in the shop, everybody had to shout.

Mary had come to know Sickert well, better than Annie ever would, but that was because Mary was bumptious while being a keen listener. She had once told him that the men's voices in operas sounded *powdery,* and he asked her how she knew, how many operas—or indeed operettas—she had seen. None, she told him, but she had heard them practicing in hotels she'd worked in. She could have told him about deep-voiced nuns as well, but she couldn't be bothered. Out she would trot, telling Annie to watch the store, and within minutes, the time taken to cross from 22 to 15 Cleveland Street, where he set her on her back with her knees high, tasted her in languorous up-and-down slithers of his tongue, and possessed her with a series of abrupt disdainful movements. That done, he began yet another painting of the zone he had just enjoyed, from time to time mixing Mary's effluvia with his paints, not for realism but for excitement—afterward, when all was hard and dry, mounted on a wall, he alone would know. And she. Mary understood him as well as any woman was going to do, especially his sense that, no matter what happened, no matter what he saw, it would all go into art. There was nothing that was not allowed into Art. She understood this in her immoral, flagrant way, and didn't care. He babbled to her sometimes about the need for extreme experience, for life pushed to the utter limit, and she agreed, let him rattle on in his quick, captious way. Cock-talk she called it, just the sort of thing Prince Eddy had wanted to have with her; but she was too canny for that, she told Sickert. And Netley had asked her to participate in threesomes staged in the *Crusader,* but she had turned him down flat as undesirable, whereas Eddy, without an Annie (to whom she was loyal), would have suited her if only, afterward, she could have killed him off in a mine disaster. "I could make a thriving living, Walt," she told him, "as your royal whore, and never mind your shut-up stuck-up Queen. These Germans. I don't, though. We have to look after our Annie. We don't want that powder keg exploding before due time."

Sickert winced and said, "Aren't I enough?"

"It's not that," she said. "I don't want *enough,* only a bit of what drives me half out of my mind. Have you ever, me love, mixed a number two with your paints? From a woman, I suppose. It'd be ripe in a year, wouldn't it now? They would have to hang it underground and hand out masks to all the posh buyers."

"I will," he said eagerly. "That's the end of the spectrum that really takes me. Here."

"Lumme, Walt," she sighed. "To think it is to do it."

There was nothing to it, he thought, it was only another pigment, and he needed no Mary Kelly to instruct him in his own need to become the painter *maudit,* accursed, pushing *nostalgie de la boue* as far as it would go, indeed dabbling in all kinds of unspeakable experiences just to see what would come out at the other end in works of art. Let us be as *louche* as we can, he thought. I am a pioneer. One day they will heap me with honours for going this lonely, heart-wrenching way.

He no longer worried that he had involved Annie Crook in passions beyond her capacity; he always relied on his knack for improvisation, knowing that he and Mary Kelly could work something out, something just about adequate anyway. When Eddy sallied off, to pursue even more wild experiences with the abominable Netley, life as usual (or its household gods) would take over again, and then he could get back to his painting. To him a shopgirl, a model, a whore, and a mother were all the same, best expressed in one body, just as shit and pigment were both paintable-in. *Faex,* he learnedly interposed, telling himself that, when the Greeks wanted to make an unpleasant-sounding word for an unpleasant thing, they really did it. *Faex* sounded worse than *faeces,* didn't it? Whereas *merde* sounded almost English, fraught with crude little rhymes. No, *faex* had the authentic sound of revulsion in it, which pleased him all the more, bent as he was on letting nothing shock him ever.

Sickert felt less pressured when Annie came to sit with him while he worked; she no longer posed for him, although he asked her to. She couldn't keep still, she said, but she told him stories of her native village, of dogs that stole raw meat from the butcher's and turned savage; of one village notable who, for seventy years, said only one thing: "You get some grand young men on horses," an utterance so obscure that Sickert wanted to paint it. She told him about the veteran lispers, who tried to say "nice tart" and said it as "nithe thtart." He could tell that, although she hated the village for suffocating her, she also loved its rituals and mannerisms, its freaks and characters. She belonged there as she never would in Cleveland Street; and now, if she were ever to go back, she too would have become one of the eccentrics—she who had trudged to London, found her prince, got herself with child by him, and then come home to rue it. To cheer her up, Sickert marched around the studio, demonstrating what he called his Affable Arthur walk, in which he swung his arms curled in front of him with forced jollity, wobbling his head at the same time. It was the walk of chronic good nature, tinged with an obsequiousness wholly foreign to him. He said he was sorry for getting her into this mess, but she said oh no, it was a love affair all right, it was a match of hearts, they were truly in eternity together, come what may. Their different backgrounds had no bearing on it, she said, "not when you get two people in bed without their clothes on. It all comes clear then." It made not a jot of difference to her that Eddy went to the Cleveland Street brothel, plied Mary Kelly with his lusts, and in general behaved like that royal stud his father, the Prince of Wales. No, Eddy had left a sacred presence behind him, and there was no way he could suck it back from her, she a Catholic who called the growing baby a "remembrancer," from which imposing and final word Sickert shrank, knowing what he would eventually have to do, unruly custodian of them all as he was turning out to be.

"Leave the tobacconist's," he said to Mary Kelly the next day, "and be the nanny."

"The what? Me with sperm on me hands?"

"With sperm up your bum, my lass. There will be a need. You watch. We can hardly expect Eddy to take the baby off to his mother and grandmother. Another little Sickert it will be. After all, the father is my so-called younger brother. How do you like imaginary families?"

"Better," she huffed, "than imaginary money, old toot. Just so long as—" She halted herself, a roaring falls of blood in her mind's ear. "No midwife stuff. I can't handle that." She was slurring words again with gin, but sometimes she sang out clear and loud, a rococo elf:

> Oh, dear girls, I love you more than honey.
>   London is a funny place.
>   It costs a lot of money.
> Yes, London is a funny place
>   Where rummy things get done.

Each day as she went from her lodgings at number six to Mrs. Morgan's shop she bore with her a cardboard box of what she called "Gentlemen's Wares," from guidebooks with condoms in those discreet little pockets to "artistically" posed photographs of prepubertal girls, whose hairless mounds of Venus were made to appear enormous. Sickert himself had trafficked with her for some of these wares, although he disdained condoms, preferring to varnish his member with linseed oil and turpentine if in doubt. Not that Mary Kelly cared. She doted on danger, needed it, and was getting a little bored with Annie, tobacco, and Cleveland Street in general; she wanted Sickert to take her off to Dieppe on one of his trips.

It was Mary who brought to Sickert's sometimes inflamed attention the true bond between Annie and her Eddy: not so much romance, though the canny Mary allowed that romance sometimes flitted in where nothing else held sway. "No, me darling brush-and-paint man," she told him, "neither a one of the darling pair can *read.* Only the other day I showed him a piece of what I'd call Provoking Literature, one of my under-the-counter specials you might say, and he looked at it as if he'd just come from Tibet. He likes the naughty little girls in the photographs, them that has no curly on their dooies, but he can't read the naughty things about them underneath. I'm a bit of a Royal watcher myself, and I know his surname must be something like *England,* see, but he couldn't write or read it for the life of him. Why, he wouldn't even qualify as an Irishman. Also, me toot, he is deaf as a post, like his Denmark mother, pretty soul as she is, and the only thing he takes much interest in is between a pair of legs. Romance, you say. Well, *I* say he has the brainpower it requires. You know why he smokes all those Turkish cigarettes all the time? So they can't see his long-drawn-out face. I love him as I would an eft, but what future has a man with gout, the clap, and lord knows what else buried under his skin? His brother now, he has an honourable degree from Cambridge University, but I can't imagine what good old Cambridge makes of Eddy. The Eddys of this world get ploughed under, you mark my words, for fertiliser. He might as well be happy while he's marking time, poor devil. Catholic women are what he likes, maybe because they let the seed splash home without giving a tinker's cuss. Nothing unnatural about Eddy, oh no. *We* know what he's good for, don't we now? And that poor soul who loves him so, what on earth is *she* going to do with him? And with his kiddie? Nothing, I tell you. Lovey-dovey they might be now, but you watch Lord Arthur Somerset whisk him away for a quiet weekend's turd-stabbing now and then. That's where our lovely Eddy belongs. Take it from me. Stripe me, Walt, I'm right. Honest I am."

She spoke speeches as if they were brief asides, and Sickert had to shake himself free of her oral spell. When she spoke, she seemed to compress time into something like froth, but her froth had a hard basis. She watched the entire street, she knew where everyone went and what they did with whom for how much. Whereas Annie in her feckless, effusive way remembered exactly what her tobacco customers came in for, so well that they never needed to be specific, she had no idea what else they did or wanted. When Mary served them, her smile was total. She saw them undressed, *in flagrante,* across the street or up it, or halfway across London. Even if she had not been able to put together the jigsaw puzzle of gossip, she would have imagined the truth of their doings. Perhaps she was one of those psychics, Sickert thought, as he examined her eminently paintable face by the mellow light of afternoon. How mobile the mouth; even in repose it seemed to be talking, and when she was asleep it moved as if she were privately devouring some salacious tidbit. What was it about this face? The slightly Roman nose spread wide, giving the whole face a coarse, reckless air. Was that it? The eyes were never still, as if she could not bear to miss the latest bit of scandal just heaving into view over the horizon even as she spoke of another. It was a predatory face, he thought: hearty, jolly, affable, all those estimable things, but also smug and devious. None of his affair. Well, no, not quite. It was he, after all, who had hoicked her here from the Providence Row Women's Refuge. All it had taken was Mrs. Morgan to ask for someone, and the solicitor Edmund Bellord, one of the Refuge's founders and officers, had brought Mary Kelly into their orbit. As soon as the baby was born, Kelly would give up her job at the tobacconist's and move into Annie's basement as nanny. Sickert had planned it this way, although Mary Kelly made him nervous. Why did they all trust her so much? Because she blathered? She provided an eiderdown of raw and random chatter on which they could all repose. She was not innocent, and thus somehow instantly available. Conference, he knew from reading Bacon, made a ready man. Or was it conversation? She always seemed to be ready. Her mouth was always marking time, ready to maneuver at the drop of a syllable, almost as if the woman (in whose expert clasps he had felt the acutest physical delight even while waiting for the black widow to sting him) never needed to think before spouting off. This was what he had tried to capture in his painting of her, a preliminary thing; he had gone for that primed, voluble, forward look of the madam *manqué*, and the way she had of looking down slightly when talking to him. Her face seemed always to have a whisker-burn from someone else, or her blood was too hot or thick. Perhaps she ate too much rich food, too much meat; there was always a blemish on her chin, around her mouth, maybe a clue as to where that mouth had been. He found her intensely desirable, yet dangerous, and he could not quite understand why he kept inventing new things for her to do in his vicinity.

"Say the word, my old toot," she was telling him, as if he had not been listening, "and Mary's your girl. At least until the day I find a prince of me own, and all that. What do you need? I'll not be after going to the shop today. I have me goodies all with me here." She tapped the box and, like some conjuring druid, brought forth for his scrutiny the usual guidebooks ("Cundum Classics," he called them), then other bits of sheepgut plastered with feathers and thorns, miniature cutthroat razors, those postcards of hairless and adroit-looking nymphets, vials of what she said were aphrodisiacs, tins of nerve-dulling ointments, spicy underwear that always looked used, and tissue-wrapped dildoes made from a light wood imported from the tropics. There was even an electrical gadget filched from a surgeon's operating room, but he could not remember the name of it. What a still life all this would make: stuff that had come in from Europe or had been manufactured in the hovels of Whitechapel for toffs to tweak themselves with. At the moment she had no whips or clamps—there had been a run on them—but she did have a group of ebony balls from Siam. She *catered.* That was the word he'd been groping for. She knew what people really wanted to do, and she brought them the wherewithal. She was going to be famous, but she had not quite established herself yet; she lacked capital, that was it, and a wider set of acquaintances ranging beyond artists and painters.

"Well, Walto," as she sometimes called him, "what'll it be

today?" Even in his sleep he heard her asking him what his night's rampage required. She was of course offering herself too; but how could he be thinking of that and getting ready to marry his Ellen? Every canvas had a back, he thought. Every *honnête homme* needed a slut with whom to be his basest self. He bought a postcard of a blithe-looking nymphet and stood it on the mantel shelf, clear now about the memory it stirred. When he was little, he had seen a commercial traveler arrive at the door with a big bulging case, whose contents had tumbled onto the rug: brushes, combs, shoe trees, brooches, hair curlers, tie-presses, potato mashers, crumb brushes and crumb trays, all of which the poor devil had had to scoop back into the case and then lug to the next door. He had always wondered at people whose life, whose living, was to carry pieces of the world about with them all over, hoping one day to have sold the very last thing and so be saddled with an empty suitcase no one ever wanted.

"Not very eager today," she said.

"Painting today," he said. "And talk."

"I'm always going to waste," she said. "It's me fate."

"Until you find your prince," he told her. "And *then.*"

"And the darling lover," she said with frothy fervor (almost saying *loover*), "will be having none of the clap to give to me."

"That'll be the day," Walter Sickert said, wishing he could paint her while she was sleeping.

"They won't see Kelly for smoke."

"By then they won't be looking," he said.

"Long time off, you think, Walter?" She sounded dejected and somewhat truculent.

"You need more clientele, like the Prince of Wales. Well, if not him, then some well-placed politicians."

"They do say," she pronounced, "that the Prince, he has worn it away to a thistle, a *t*istle, not with his darling Princess, the gaunt and bony one, but with ladies of a more—cushiony sort."

"Like the whores of London," Sickert said without meaning to, talking to himself. The ones he loved to paint as well. "I'll none of your bony ones myself."

She was watching him for the first flicker of desire, ready to come closer to him with hand or mouth, like a reptile of the desert as aware of him as of the sun. But what he wanted today was an internal rhythm on which to paint, not an orgy.

She did not budge, but he could feel the vitality of her attention waning, then withdrawing from him. He showed her the oil sketch he had made of her, and she pouted, told him to finish it, then do another: a nude, she pleaded. "While me thrumps is still creamy, Walt."

He had never heard of thrumps from anyone but her, but he knew what they were, more or less, and he wanted to paint them with clay splattered over them, and bird droppings and pieces of dust mice, trying to pin down the element of menace in her: not Mary Kelly as Mary wanted herself, but Mary Kelly much affected by terminal moraine or, if not that, then the muck of the London streets. She was his Limerick cat, that's what she was, who came to purr while he was engaged in selfish acts of thought, intent not on women but on what weather and disease and death could do to them. As if, he thought with a wan grin, he were always on the side of the destroyer rather than of the celebrator. What an odd thought for an impressionist. She was silent now, having stowed her wares away and fallen into a dyspeptic-looking reverie as she stared out at Cleveland Street, where her future was not. He made tea for them both, grunting with every movement as if he had rheumatism, but he had only been holding his breath while he pondered: an old habit that often made him gasp without apparent cause. She heaped the sugar in, and he knew then what all her spots came from.

Chapter 4

Pleased to have found the answer, he got up and did an Affable Arthur around the studio, loving the semi-military swing of it, the fluent motion that evoked tubas and trombones. She laughed her Irish laugh at him, all ribald derision, but he swaggered on, careful not to set his foot on lumps of paint sitting on soup plates. Then he went back to his tea, feeling all of a sudden the fatigue that hit him daily at this time, as if his blood had been watered down, as if the air he breathed had no oxygen in it (or was it nitrogen he lacked?). He had come to Earth from some other planet, and, after long training out there, he could manage most of an Earth day until about now, when he would feel frail, dizzy, helpless. This was why, he told himself, he needed to be concerned with extremes; he was making up for these doldrums, or whatever they were. While he felt all right, he had to do things with more than usual intensity. Twenty-eight, he was also fifty-six, having lived at twice the normal speed.

As for flesh, he was always thinking about it, and had learned to prefer buxom because, if there was much flesh, then they had less chance of being able to control it. On the other hand, he didn't want them so fat they had only the impetus of gravity. The way he saw it, the Princess Alixes had a higher bone-to-flesh ratio than, say, the whores hereabouts, or Queen Victoria, or Mary Kelly. And they weren't as likely to let themselves get carried away, whereas the well-upholstered ones he reveled in had built into them the suffocation of will by flesh. It sounded too simple. What then of the gaunt nymphomaniacs? Surely it was as much a matter of the responsive nervous system as of *fat*? Was he right or wrong in thinking that a woman with big bosoms was more a *thing* than a woman with small ones, and therefore more prey to impersonal, automatic stimulus? After all, lust travelled along the flesh, not along the bone. Thin whores were not to be plunged into. It was obvious. Plump ones, however, were both anesthesia and aphrodisiac. He almost wanted to write a book about it, but it would be better to paint images of what drove him. The visual always seemed closer to venery than thought. He yearned for France, for Italy, where art had heart and fat, unlike the perpetual waiting room that England was: draughty and proper and bland.

Sickert slept poorly that night, prodded from sleep, his head full of a preposterous universe in which teapots reproduced Queen Victoria's head (their lids were the crown) and Victoria herself worried that Alix's head, topped with exquisite blond curls, was too small. Victoria had already had her own effigy carved in her exact measurements; it stood ready, stored nearby, to join the white marble Albert in the mausoleum at Frogmore. To Sickert this was the era of heads, and he wondered if he too, like hundreds of his contemporaries, should invest in a walking cane whose knob was Victoria's head. When he painted Mary Kelly, he did her first without a hat, letting her matted-looking hair ride high; but he wanted an effect more regal or imposing, so he painted in a wide and exaggerated headgear that looked like basketwork, sucking up the light and nestling it within. There was more light, leaked and reflected, in the hat than there was in Mary Kelly's face on this occasion, not least because the big hat shaded her eyes completely, so that she became all nose and mouth: almost a caricature of well-fed rapacity. It was a face of garrulous truculence all right, but he was not satisfied with it, and, lighting his bull's-eye lamp, he stared at it for a while, then set it aside, allowing his real thought to surface.

Ellen was twelve years older than he, and he adored her because she was his complementary opposite: cool, withdrawn, demure, whereas physically he needed the Kellys and the Annies, most of all the West End courtesans, those caravanserais of scented fat with whom all his inhibitions fell away. His urge to paint low life in the raw grew strong and fierce. He wanted to make it even rawer than it was. For this kind of painting he wanted to use petroleum on canvas: it was not sticky like turpentine, it remained wet, and it did not soak in. His physical desire he understood, even in the sweltering summer-night heat of 1884, but not why he was contemplating marriage, that protracted exercise in masochistic stability. He should live for art, and its hiatuses, its horrors. He should have been happier, sensing that Ellen's resistance was weakening; she was going to say yes, he could smell it. Yet he felt like someone who, while remaining civilly infatuated, had commissioned an exquisite marble fireplace and seen it in his mind's eye without ever wanting to imagine himself lighting a fire in it. Bored with the Annie-Mary duet, and with the limp vagaries of the ineducable

Eddy, now down from Cambridge for the Long Vacation and free to run the gamut of Cleveland Street, Sickert thought it better to fetch and carry for Whistler, as he had done at St. Ives last year, with the Master shrieking at his panels and grey paint and the notebooks with Dutch paper in them and his slugabed habits. Better to don the jersey and top boots and go mingle with the local fishermen, who watched him do half-a-dozen canvases a day and then made him presents of fresh fish.

What did his life lack? What was he waiting for, with all his senses primed? Surely not something wholesome. He would have to go to Dieppe to find out; it had always been the rug on which he frolicked. His mother had gone to school there, and his father had worked there. But he did not need Dieppe to tell him that he had meddled in others' lives, getting Bellord to remove Mary Kelly from Providence Row because he, Sickert, fancied her, as indeed he had fancied other women but had given them only part-time work sitting for him. This Kelly was already at the heart of his world, spinning and manoeuvring, already acquainted with the darker side of him which did not want to do good for the Annie Crooks, but to take the blackened and rancid lard from an old frying pan and rub it all over a child's pillow, then paint that and call it, oh, *After a Bad Night*—one such as he himself was having amid the reek and heat of London, on a street that was really an island in the West End, of culture and perversity.

He was still young enough not to have learned much about life; there was no need to be knowing. He knew, though, that, as people aged, their eyes became squintier, harder to see into, not that they saw less with them. It was just harder to watch their eyes in the act of seeing. He could see the Mary Kelly of many years hence, her eyes reduced to slits from having seen and known too much, tightening as her entire face began to droop. His own eyes would do the same, so that people would never again look into them to see if he were honest, but would look away in relief that here was somebody no longer penetrable: pinched in, all scaled over, a mature pachyderm of witness. By then, of course, prolific painter that he was, he would have expressed all his witness on canvas, and whether or not he told the truth would be a matter of judgment on paintings, no longer an attempt to intuit the man who did them. He wanted that time to come sooner, the time when a man, an artist, vanished from view behind his masterpieces, and even if he stood alongside them at an exhibition would go unnoticed, as if he were some nurse, some attendant. To have achieved this inside-outness, this swathing of oneself in one's soul, this assimilation into the unreachable centre of one's most trivial externals, was the desired state, almost as if (and to hell with Whistler) the butterfly at long last had gone back into the caterpillar.

Marriage, which he both dreaded and yearned for, would have no bearing on these mutations of his person. It would no longer be a matter of dressing up to play a part, as he once had done to be Demetrius in Edward Saker's 1880 production of *A Midsummer Night's Dream* at the Sadler's Wells Theatre, required to repose upon the mossy bank while the fairies tramped heavily about him, making the boards rattle. If he were to marry, really go through with it, he would be playing another role, and his reward (*their* reward) would be that Whistler would design the interior of their house. Was it worth it? He sensed he would weaken and marry; if so, he would encourage Annie and Eddy to go through with a farce of their own and make a Catholic marriage.

It was not that he wanted things tidied up (as he did in his own impromptu, haphazard sexual life); it was more a matter of creating a sensible context, or frame, in which the child might have a chance, and Annie too. Eddy occupied his thoughts little, knowing as he did that Eddy was a moth, and he sometimes wondered what on earth went on when Eddy met with his tutor, as he infrequently did, trying to be a good Cambridge man, but unable to decipher the title of a book he was required to read, or breaking down at the first two-syllable word on the page in front of him. In the kingdom of the blind, he thought, the unlettered man is king. Would this unlettered man, his own private charge, his pseudo-brother secreted with him by a princess who pleaded with him "Don't let him get into trouble," ever be king? The powers behind the throne would kill him first, dump him in the Cam one starry night, or somehow speed up his venereal disease. Sickert wondered if he himself were not ringmastering some debauched circus in which, at his bidding, the diseased and the unlettered multiplied incognito under the gaze of the worldly Kelly. It was just another play, and that was why he, Sickert, the most promising impressionist of his day, did not always take seriously the fate of the actors. They would go away, the play would end. There was always a curtain behind which the shadow-play dwindled into thin air. Almost, he felt, he was playing God with these people, helping one of them into a culpable disguise, pulling two women into his unprofitable circle, both to go to the dogs instead of continuing as surly but dutiful skivvies elsewhere, bucket and donkey-stone in hand.

In a word, why did he meddle so much?

And why did his charity often take the form of meddling?

Sickert did not know, but he knew his bad habits well enough to recognize that this was one of them; it was as if people were pigment and all he had to do to change their lives was to take his brush or palette knife and move the soft receptive paint, blotting something out to make a new life. He was not in charge of Annie, Eddy, and Mary, but close to it, having brought them together: A. to himself, as he thought of her, then A. to E., then M. to them both, now three. With a blabber like Mary Kelly in the triangle, all London would soon be in the know, and then what? It was worth marrying and going off to Europe just to be rid of the worry, for a time at least.

Why had he not been more prudent? Had he done all this aligning and arranging in the strict interests of a disaster to come? What was he asking to fall down from heaven upon them? Or from Buckingham Palace? Or from elsewhere? Was he tinkering with suicide, which was to say the suicide of others? Had all this been in the cause of seeing what wild and preposterous thing would happen? Had he been trying to prove that, with a little effort, humans could bring about untold suffering? With no effort at all, they achieved every bit as much. How much effort did it cost him to be able to think of decapitation as hairdressing gone too far, or of conscience as the piled-up sediment of faintheartedness over uncounted generations? Something evil swam through his benign system, now and then surfacing to the tunic of his eye: a mote, a fleck, a spot of itinerant fat, to be seen only as a shadow, invisible when he approached the mirror with magnifying glass in hand. He knew only that a man such as himself should learn to leave other people alone and not play chess with them; yet people were his métier, greasy and palpitant, and he could see no way of doing without them.

Sooner or later, he just knew it, he would have to cry wolf about himself, not as if he were the wolf advancing on the fold, but the wolf unfolding from within. He smirked at the glibness in his putting it that way; if only he could be so adroit in French when he was in Dieppe. In all seriousness, he was a dangerous man, another variation on the theme of the man of good will, him of the good intentions, but not to be trusted, not even to do something thoroughly. He would charm people loose from their proper, and quietly assumed, stations in life, then ply them with hopes they could not survive. That was what he had done with both Annie and Mary. Bad enough. But worse was the business with Eddy. He could hardly blame Eddy's mother for sending her son to Cleveland Street; all he had needed to do was tell her what might happen and explain the appalling risks. He had done nothing of the kind, alas, and here was Prince Eddy in his hellward plunge, alongside Sickert, the debonair devil. No, he was only Sickert the meddler, but was there a connection (perhaps even a partly ennobling one) between the man who meddled and the man who backed into marriage like a skittish horse into a blazing shed. Was he a meddler with marriage too, going into it to sharpen the tang of compulsive adultery, whose bite was keen only when someone tied to you got hurt? Profound attachment was one thing, but casual snatch-fondling was another. In London he yearned for Dieppe, and vice versa. In bed with Mary he craved Annie, though he could not have her unless he really wanted to push Eddy over the edge. When he walked the streets, he wanted to be at work in his studio. He was a born floater, he told himself, a man who needed a coxswain. And marriage would only multiply his problems. Here he was, behaving like a man of wealth whose hobby was "adopting" others' lives, and most of the time he did not even have two sous to rub together. There was a time to come when he would have to settle down, but he could not imagine it, he knew he would be dead before it arrived.

It was not only, however, that he was a tactless and garrulous blunderer even while being the man of good cheer; what sickened him was his hunch that his bungling, and all that went after it by way of amends, was merely the prelude to another side of his behavior, cruel and gross. That it was there within the weave of his being he was certain; how it would come out under pressure and provocation he was not yet sure. Perhaps, quite simply, he wanted to destroy, but knew he could not destroy until he had his hands firmly in his pockets. It was something paradoxical. All of a sudden he saw Annie, Mary, Eddy, and Ellen (his Nellie) lined up before him, fingers outstretched in accusation. Could there, he wondered, be such a thing as dapper malignity in a man? Was it in him, like a worm or a cancer? If so, how could he remedy it? Did he even want to? He needed someone to take him in hand, not Mary, but some *domina* who would see through him and thrash his ambivalence. That was hardly Ellen. No, she would have to be French, he thought, and have been appallingly mistreated within the last few years: someone with a noose to soap, a whip to knot. Someone might yet knock it out of him, he hoped, but at the same time he wondered if it was altogether bad in him that he wanted to see life at its worst and help to bring the worst into being. All he wanted was knowledge; he wanted the facts that came from harm. It was a French, not an English, notion, based on some honorable idea of perversity, and it was Roman too. He could feel himself reaching out across the centuries to Catullus and Propertius, to Juvenal and Ovid, ah yes, to the Inquisition, the Terror, and the compulsive exoticist Lord Byron.

Constantly trying to catch himself at the onset of an evil move, he saw what he wanted to see, and he always saw a man not quite gone over to the enemy, to the bad, but in need of only a short intense stimulus to get him on the move toward it, to a place where noses bled, loins dried and flaked, dead babies rolled in slush along the gutters, angels ate feces with neuter zeal, and loved ones turned into charcoal before one's eyes. Sometimes he heard a sustained scream coming from the East End, and he knew something dreadful, yet commonplace, was afoot, and he continued on his way home from the music hall, wondering if the death scream was an art form. A paddle steamer had come to a halt in mid-Thames, its wheel fouled by a female corpse no one had yet been able to remove; he had not seen the steamer, nor was he going to look, but the image dogged him, making him wonder how many corpses floated on the river before they sank below.

He felt he had a family that was not his, as if he were Old Father Thames himself: sucking his energy and wasting his time. If he went on this way, there would soon be half a dozen who depended on him, begging a crust or a sovereign, a bed or a sitting—Netley's crippled sister, if he had one, or Mary's favorite tapster down on his luck but eager to be painted in bright colours on a barrel's flank. One way of breaking away from all this was to become respectable by cleaving to Ellen's crowd: her father, the radical M.P.; Margaret Burne-Jones; the daughters of Sir Walter Raleigh. One of Ellen's sisters had married Unwin, the publisher. With these he would be safe from what he had come to call his leprous altruism, safe in the chaste light that shone from Ellen's taut and tapered face.

To marry while whoring, he thought, would be like learning Esperanto while speaking the French he had always known. Or would it? Which was older: marriage or whoring? Well, marriage would be new to him, so it was a kind of Esperanto, new-fangled and tricky, whereas French, that taut, impatient language, was indeed like the itch in his trousers, the stone-ache he complained about and cherished. Always, he had instructed himself, he must take on more than he could manage, because doing so was to scramble the mind, make it vulnerable, at the same time demoralizing it and making it alert to combinations it had never known. Only on the brink, he thought, when your mind is all tatters, do you get anywhere near the dishevelled shamefulness the artist needs in order to be the true pariah of his genius. Marriage, to Ellen or anybody, was a way of shattering his preconceptions, like using a newborn lamb as a footstool, or, on a bad day, a tied-up baby as a bookend. As long as he made life stretch him, he could marry *and* burn; he needed the pain of monotony, the stimulus of spurning someone's love.

He knew that nothing for better or for worse would happen until Annie had her baby in April. Eddy would stay put, fondling and cooing, and so would Mary. There was going to be a welcome doldrum, at long last, and he just wanted to go and marry—touching the beastly thing, getting it over and done with, licking the icing sugar off its caustic and pretty rainbow. Or, if none of that, he would go and swim in the brisk sea off Normandy, strut along the dunes with the walking cane that reached his nipples, and, above all, relive that fabulous journey of 1883 when he had taken the portrait of Whistler's mother to Paris for the Salon, going by packet-boat from Folkstone to Dieppe, where the small deal box swung from the crane against the stars and the shut-tight houses of Pollet de Dieppe, a masterpiece in flight. He had stayed in Paris with Oscar Wilde. Would his life ever be that keen and good again? He saw before him half a century of brutish work; a quarter of a century, then, and entanglements ruinous yet having nothing to do with painting. Almost like Eddy, he could not resist people, even when they offered him nothing, it was as if he were a specimen hunter, not a man who imagined his way into the universe with introductions from powerful friends. In those days, when he first met Degas, whom in his ignorance he wrote down as Digars, Degas-Digars had said to him at the door, *"Monsieur, je ne peux pas vous recevoir. J'ai une bronchite qui me mène au diable,"* only to be told brashly in French that he, Walter Sickert, had other things in mind:

"I do not like conversation. I have come to see your work. I am the pupil of Whistler." That had worked, and he had been let in, his teeth locked tight in painterly awe. Would he ever feel so proud to be himself again? He sensed maturity riding up close behind him like a swamp on the move, or a volcano, warning him with advance fumes that he would have to earn his old age by not scorning love.

I am a *man,* he coached himself: I have dignity, gifts, and hope. Why must I always go in fear of some eruptive demon whose fodder is the cheeks of babes and the heads of princes? Perhaps, because I am more sensitive than most, I am harsher on myself, and what most normal men tolerate within them drives me daft? *Me mène au diable.* All I need, really, is to perform; I am a poseur born. No more than that. If I see a blue sky, I want to be just as comprehensive and rinsed-looking. If I see a fog, I want to crawl along just like it, with a furry mouth and sulphur leaking from my pores. All I am, truly, is a copycat. I do impressions of people and things. I also tend to think all behaviour is bogus, done to entertain, and I forget that, with most, behaviour is a matter of impulsive seriousness. I must learn to be serious when others are, not just about art. Death is not the biggest toothbrush of all and pain is not the cheapest disinfectant. Once he had sketched a blue girl, actually taking the mix of pigments off Whistler's own palette, and that was what he would have to do with life, painting in the hues that others saw, delving into the same serious pigment they all expected to be buried in, six feet under in burnt umber. When bores came after him, Whistler had told him, with armfuls of tedious information, all he had to do was say the word "stocking," and that would settle their hash. But Lord love a duck (as Annie said), what good did saying "stocking" do when people came after you bleeding and convulsed, with headaches and the shivers? It was quite different then. If you mocked them, you became a homemade cad, and by that token an artist on the fringe of the race. The human race. He had to-ed and fro-ed thus for years, always trying to take a stand, unable to reconcile his high spirits with the vision of things at their worst—which he was finally working his way toward, as to the palette that matched them. An exuberant fatalist: was he that? Or was he a euphoric radical? Pessimism mingled in him with high energy and took him out of himself in the direction of shame. A rotting brussels sprout was a small plane to him, but the joy he showed on even wondering about painting it sorted ill with his numbed recognition of what it was. He wanted to set the sprout on his mantel shelf, to symbolize certain kinds of art, or some phases of history, but he never did, somehow knowing that it would serve him better as a mental talisman. A heart was better at one's core, was it not?

Such haggling with himself he called *controvertings,* fervently wishing his other self were more like another person, with whiskers and rheumatism and a paunch: more real, more capable of being reduced to helpless giggles by a bon mot. He had begun to draw things at speed, eager to finish before the satanic caught up with him and broke through. This had made his work uncertain and freakish, ever on the hop, or toppling away from unpretentious sublimity into a raffish daub. Once, of the painters he despised, far back in history, he had thought, *archaic;* but we can have archaic and eat it too. Never mind how many times he tried out the pun at dinners, it never had the feckless-seeming gleam it had had on that first occasion, when he had gone to watch himself in the mirror, laughing with flushed cheeks. He wanted to have come up with it in company, not to have exported it, with slight laboriousness, from private to public. He was suffering from what the French called *l'esprit d'escalier,* when a riposte came to you on the stairs as you were leaving a party, and you wanted to race back up and regale them all with it, then descend again, smug and sated. Only the French would have a phrase for such an event, such a turn of mind. A wiser Sickert than he would have fixed his mind on his work, neither playing the social popinjay nor the careless altruist; he would have given a thought to the safety of his own gift, making sure it got recognized and praised.

As for his intended, the intractable Ellen, she remained the permanent property of those who had brought her up and coaxed her into unyielding gentility. The image that matched her best was one of his own devising, executed, he thought, with the tip of a brush sucked so sharp that no human lips could have teased it to such sweetness. His Ellen, he knew, was of best

Britannic Majesty North Ocean Steamfaring stock, her decks flawlessly swabbed, her portholes chamois-leathered as monocles, her funnels painted in stripes that showed no wobble of a wavy line. Yet she put in to the most appalling harbours, where corpses rotted and human waste floated about like a crop from the devil. Then she sailed away again, and the ceaseless plash of the ocean washed her clean. In time, her wake got pure. And those disposed to pay her price—a high tone, a starched voice, a middle stance in all matters affecting morals and art—might lounge in the immaculate chairs on her decks, their knees wrapped in blankets of uprightest flannel: no flea, no weevil, no moth, no ant roosted in there, for below decks an entire regiment of the unwashed pounded away with carbolic soap and caustic lime, just to purify the wrappers of the pure in heart.

He was no more interested in being pure than Prince Eddy was; he cared only to apportion the nonartistic side of his being to some safe human resort, a sexual Brighton, say. He had always persuaded himself that having an illegitimate mother, as he had, gave him a developed interest in seeing people suitably knotted together, and then displayed in a reliable place. All his life he had retained an image of the perpetual and permanently entrancing childhood: the Theresienwiese district of Munich, almost a village, especially at Christmas time, when the cobbled marketplace grew caverns of darkness in between the lit candles and lanterns on tin trumpets. The Christ-child lay in a drift of sugar that looked like snow but did not squeak half as well. In this grown-up nursery of gilt gingerbread and resounding imperfect trumpets they ran and ran, he and his sister Helena, Robert and Bernhard his brothers, to whom his mother, Eleanor, sang in her crisp, bony contralto. It was these mellow, ruby lights he tried to create in one studio after another, aiming not merely for coziness, but for mystery as well, as if invisible siblings, true masters of the world, would suddenly emerge from within the walls to claim it, and the perverse, wayward, baby-faced Walter would join them, leaving all his paintings behind like so many depressing Christmas cards.

For several years now, fired into emulation by hearing an

Argentine guitarist speak to women after a performance, he had been practicing and polishing his skills at the *piropo*—the spontaneous and hyperbolical compliment man paid to woman, perhaps uttered with some pragmatically lustful intent, but most often floated onto the air to cause a surprised smile, a slight change in a woman's gait. His first one had been in a theater lobby, said more for practice than for anything else, although, being Sickert, he always expected the unexpected and was ready to profit by it. "Your eyes have scalded me," he said, following up with "There is no ice for my heart." Thrilled, the woman he had addressed smiled, almost bowed, and moved away. The consummations of rhetoric were not crude. He had learned that. Surely, though, there was something lacking in a man who spent his evenings uttering such bombast, intent upon chivalry as he was. Only someone implacably drawn to the sordid needed to say such things, to proffer his own mind a nosegay of words; to go abroad mouthing preposterous compliments that boasted more about himself than they paid tribute to the receiver. It was a gutless way of expressing desire or a bold way of expressing next to nothing. Yet Sickert continued to do it, construing the habit as finesse in action, a touch of French or Spanish where English hung back. He enjoyed the confected quality of what he said, its histrionics; he knew what kind of figure he cut, with his barley hair, his almost uncouth hypersensitivity behind the quick-trigger mouth that looked sucked-in as if ready to spout or to spit. Bland, his features had a quarrelsome look, a touch of ill-curbed bossiness, and he knew it—it had been there ever since, as a child, he had bossed his mother's servants about and, when she was most tender with him, had taken the occasion to try riding roughshod over her. People were amazed when his apparent grimness evaporated into high-pitched jocularity, as if for months he had needed such a release and did not anticipate another for ages. An addict of the seamy, he nonetheless doted on the shining patter of Park Lane and Mayfair.

He knew that God Almighty had dirty, bloody hands, his own equivalent of which he vaguely detected on the horizon, but without knowing clearly with what raw materials he would work. All he knew was that some vast and lovely experience awaited him, out there in the steam of the future, like a slavering bison with matted flanks, some lump of quartz coming to life and turning into a host of sea-sirens. He had seen men of talent look forward to something monumental, then have nothing at all, and the undeserving inherit miracles they could not savor. Neither was going to happen to him, if he remained patient, did the decent thing by those near and dear to him (Annie included), and worked hard to improve his painting. When moral questions arose in his head, he wondered about Eddy, who had clandestinely made a total stranger his elder "brother" while turning his back on his real younger brother, George. Was that right? Eddy had no choice, his whole family having chucked him over, but Sickert dwelt on the geometry of the pattern, on the prince's choice of the fake over the true, and he decided they had that much in common: they both lived in a fabricated world where being brave was easier, although the eviction from paradise kept looming—a worse fate than soldiering through the tedium of daily life could ever be.

So Sickert kept trying to make himself over into a bon bourgeois, but was spiritually too raffish to come close. If only he had been able to take Eddy's place alongside Princess Alix, say, or at Cambridge, he might have prospered in an undreamed-of role: Prince Walter, whose dark and surly works lined the faded walls of many a palace. It was not to be: the prince did not wish to be a prince and had not the gift to be a painter, while the painter would merely go on having a small connection with the court, a connection that demanded more than it gave. In a sense, Alix had boarded Eddy with him, and grace and favor—both abstract and uncashable—were his rent. Sickert marvelled that he felt so comfortable with both feet in the mud of London and his head in the lower reaches of the royal clouds, a combination he half recalled as recommended by Pico della Mirandola, philosopher of the Renaissance. Or perhaps Pico discerned the contrast rather than recommended it, he could not remember.

On a thousand fronts, he was arriving—but he was also going nowhere; the big plunge was missing, the flamboyant master-stroke that made him a household word, and not merely among painters and draughtsmen. If you were royal, and had inherited that mystical divine right of kings, you went ahead automatically, to greatness or ignominy; but the genius or the hard worker had no guarantee at all, which was no doubt why monarchs and royal families had presumed so much in the first place, leaving nothing to chance, more eager to risk the block and the headsman than the whim of a rabble. High stakes, he thought. Can't the layman, the commoner, play for them as well?

If the chance came, he knew he would take it, in a strictly Faustian spirit, bartering his soul for power and knowledge, for the unique privilege of this or that. He saw his life as utterly his own, to squander or exalt. That was why he had fagged and toadied for Whistler, had gone off to kneel at the feet of Degas, and had taken Annie, Mary, Eddy, and others into his circle. Inasmuch as all or most things were available, he knew he had squirmed his way up to the surface of the planet to have them. If Ellen had known him intimately, she would have sent him packing; she had no idea what a monster of direct trajectory she had in tow. But the well-to-do, like the poor, took what they could find, sternly converting the man of the moment into the man of the hour and thus into the man of their dreams. It shocked him, but he meant to profit by it, having Ellen pay his bills and Annie or Mary be his sitters and pleasure him as well. In a word, he found the world useable, all of it, and lamented that nobody ever lived long enough to exploit it to the full. "Beggar on horseback, you," Mary had murmured to him during their more intimate passages, and he had thought she meant he was getting something for nothing, but she referred to his arrogance, his peppery volatility, the soaring hubris of his sense of humor—the one thing he kept locked away tight lest it endear him to her before he was ready. To him, her flesh had seams and folds just like the linen on a bed. She was often more interesting to him as a thing than as a person, but to her he was always a person, never the thing he wanted to seem.

So they settled in for the long wait as summer dwindled into seething autumn and people began to brisken up, take more notice, and the foul smell of London began just a little to taint itself with fog. London reminded Sickert of himself: he and the city had many disguises. One day he would sport hair long and curly, evoking the young painter who once had worn perfume and set his hair in ringlets, for Alix. The next, he would have had his hair cropped short and his body encased in somber charcoal gray: another, older, less optimistic man. To and fro across the Channel he went, between London and Dieppe, drawn thither by some siren call of how much more interesting the English were when abroad. After all, he was a European born. His sights were set on Venice, where a painter succeeded or failed in his profession, and he had an abiding sense the English lacked of what was absurd in life. To him and his European siblings the absurd was something basic to being, as he had discovered from Georg Brandes's book on Kierkegaard, whereas to the English it was a deficiency in the social system, to be put right by reform and debate. In a word, Sickert saw himself as more serious than the English, and certainly than the Americans; therefore he was more at home in Europe, where life was at the same time less trivial and more ravishing. The English punished nothing more than they did an idea, and Sickert fancied that he had quite a few ideas to propagate, including one filched from some author or other about being always at one's own disposal, open to opportunity and all things impromptu, which you then went ahead and did, full of glad gratuitousness, without a shred of guilt. It was hardly a system, but it was a stance; it justified all he had done with regard to Annie and Mary and Eddy, all the way from acquiring a rate payment book for Annie to becoming Eddy's surrogate brother.

To be sentiently in the thick of life was all he wanted, to feel it swilling and billowing about him as it issued from the sluices of God. He cared deeply about the impersonal abundance of life, seeing it, in an almost German way, as *process* transcending the surface differentiation between bodies and identities. An artist, he was convinced, needed such a sense of the remorseless copiousness of things, and, lacking it, would degenerate into a suburban pit-a-pat expert, an orthodox butterfly.

Chapter 5

Did Sickert mature between 1884 and 1885? Not really. He worked hard, watched Annie bulging and fretting, and Eddy becoming more and more aloof in that sentimental way of his, and Mary achieving more and more control over her demeanor as the quality and tone of her customers improved. Life was on the move; he and his friends rode the flux of Christmas, New Year's Day, Valentine's Day, all of them harping like addicts on seasonal time rather than on the drab passage of numbered but insignificant days, Annie like someone condemned to the ax, Eddy a more and more frequent visitor to number nineteen with Netley (who had become more arrogant over the months), and Mary ever on the point of a knowing smirk that spoke not volumes but whole libraries. She knew all about the underwear of upper-class England, but she still had not found a way to make much money—most of her clients for tobacco eyed her other goods and bought them elsewhere, away from Mary's knowing looks and prying eyes. And what she did not know she assumed, not having read Kierkegaard, but just as much aware of fear and trembling as Sickert was, and with good reason.

"You marry, my Hotspur?" she had said to him. "Pigs will fly, me old cock, but you had better not, not unless your lady darling be one of the sloppy-sluice lot. To lead you a dance, my dear. You haven't the character for a bride. Honest you haven't."

Was she challenging him? Or was she right? She had been married. She knew, and she had a full knowledge of all the people who, rather than marry, burned. He was one of those burners. "Lord lumme, look," she would say, "any respectable lady would be downright astonished at some of the tricks you requires of the woman with you. She won't be willing, mark my words. They don't know about such goings-on where they come from. You know what they say, old Walter? They say, 'Oh-ho, oh-ho-ho-ho, that's the sort of thing them *prossytutes* do, using their mouths for it, and giving him the—proper fuddle, as I have heard it called.' That's what they say, Walt, and they will say it to you. Come back to Mary, my old duck, and leave the virgins to their violins. I'll see you right, if not with me, then with a just-as-lively other. Same rates." For the first time he saw that her mouth was like a calceolaria, the lower lip a full round bleb, the upper rather incomplete and sketchy. Why the disparity? Why the large, inflated, bedroom-slipper shape below? That was the difference between the higher and the nether lips, and on the whole he liked the symmetry of the nether pair. Oh, how, these days, clefts and crannies, gashes and pleats drew him on and in, as Mary knew in her uncringing way, as if life were a delicious wound and all one had to do to achieve heaven were to enter it. So, was marriage to a frost-piece (poor Ellen, he thought) the way? Was marriage the wound? They could take an extended honeymoon in Italy and Germany, say, and he wondered what Ellen would think of his whoring away after all kinds of low life and then returning to chaste middle-class repose with her? From the stews to his angel? He needed his bills paid: exactly what Mary Kelly kept saying. She was drinking too much, she would never be a nanny, but who else? He almost vomited at the thought of Ellen as nanny to Annie's child. No, if anything, Ellen would write a book about the experience and let the child choke to death. She was not brought up to serve. Mary Kelly did nothing else, and with submissive fastidiousness.

One day before she gave birth, Annie left the tobacco shop and sat in her basement room, waiting, while Eddy sought oblivion farther down the street and Mary served in the shop. Next day, April 18, 1884, Annie entered the St. Marylebone Workhouse and, like someone not wishing to give others trouble, promptly gave birth, willing the bulge beneath her to cringe away and vanish. It did not. Here Annie remained, in astounded bliss, until May 5, when she went back to work and Mary Kelly looked after the baby as agreed, chiding Eddy, when he came to see, that she, the baby, was not an it, but a she, an Alice Margaret as it happened. Those were the names Annie had picked, but if he had others. . . . He had not, but he thrilled at the new morsel of life, cached away here in Cleveland Street, on the brink of the cesspool farther up, not even that far from the home of the new Prime Minister, Lord Salisbury, in Fitzroy Square.

"What now?" he said vaguely, sipping a sherry.

"Keep it alive," she said. "Begging your pardon, Alice Margaret. *Her.*"

"She can't stay here for ever, in here."

"Pending transfer to Windsor Castle, milord?"

He meant in a basement, under the false name of Cook, as the rate payment book said: "Elizabeth Cook, Basement." It was the perfect disguise, but when had Annie ever needed one? There was already a birth certificate from the St. Marylebone, describing Annie as a confectionery assistant (wielder of the toffee hammer and the boiled-sweet scoop), but leaving the father's name and occupation blank.

"Cute little hands, they all have them." Mary Kelly was a genuinely doting nanny, even if the worse for ale on an empty stomach.

"She has to go somewhere," Eddy said, trembling. "Brother Walter will know." Actually, Brother Walter did, having some time ago decided that, once he had had his honeymoon and taken a European bath, so to speak, they would all be better off in Dieppe. He was tired of Cleveland Street, but would return to it refreshed by a different diet, a different language, different ways. "Two baptisms," he said. "Anglican and Catholic. This is a princess we are all staring at." It was done. Then, with Mary Kelly and himself as witnesses, there was a Catholic wedding ceremony at the chapel of St. Saviour's Infirmary between Annie Elizabeth Crook and Albert Sickert, Annie signing herself once more, as on the birth certificate, with a cross, whereas Eddy daubed his fake name with furtive jaggedness, eager to be gone. His love made him stay put, however, whatever else he did on the side with Bert Morgan and Netley, the three of them sometimes driving halfway to Cambridge and then parking in a quiet dell before stripping nude inside the *Crusader*.

A peaceful time began, during which Sickert committed himself to marriage, in June, with a honeymoon to come in Scheveningen, Munich, Vienna, and Milan. He wanted to see if Mary Kelly's prophecies would come true. What she had not foreseen, though, was that her Walter, many years later, would come back to Alice Margaret, the princess he had identified with such ingenuous awe, and find her full of wasted days.

It would have been a pleasant summer but for the incessant flies, like clots of damp pumice being blown from infirmary to river, from dustbin to kitchen. Alice Margaret was born into a hail of flies; Sickert proposed to his Ellen in an open carriage while disorganized squadrons of flies came for his mouth and eyes; and Eddy, Morgan, and Netley, having a chicken and ale picnic somewhere in between Cambridge and London as the Long Vacation began, found themselves consuming almost as many as the open-mouthed dogs of London did. It felt as if some spiteful power had decided to humiliate the lovers of the outdoors, making them sense an itching film descend upon them and then lift away, only to return seconds later with tiny pinpricks. Faint, incisive feet set the whole population swatting and flailing, and each in the course of talking to others exhibited the familiar shiver of revulsion at those weightless little bellies coasting over their eyelids and lips, as if this were one of the worst parts of Africa. Was it a plague, would it end, or would the flies get worse, becoming bigger and wetter, developing stings and louder buzzes? The slaughterhouses and open-air butchers' windows seethed black with the morass of resting bodies; all red meat seemed on the move, shuddering or quaking, and many a butcher's lad smashed a score of ethereal, glossy bodies deep into the marbled surface of the Sunday joint. It was not a time to be fastidious or to undertake sustained gestures; the flies interrupted everything, like rubbings aloft, the worse for seeming infatuated with the human or animal presence, making constant overtures with the frailest impedimenta imaginable, and always being rebuffed, yet with only an *idée fixe* in their negligible heads, making them try and try until one human relented and let them have their way, and then the swarm moved in to roost. On kings and commoners alike they stood and squirted, heedless of the slimy totem poles that grew in living rooms, as scores of flies found a final resting place on sticky paper spiraling down from a thumbtack pushed into the ceiling. From any one of these, the noise of the bluebottles and lesser breeds, stuck fast, was like that coming from a football match heard far away, a strange muted medley of utterly human cries superimposed and garbled: ecstasy upon indignation upon incredulity upon fury, as if some malevolent deity had parodied the fly's compound eye in a compound human, whose main noise was a cacophony of indecision. On the sticky paper in thousands of ill-ventilated rooms, the flies buzzed their last, and then a new paper went up to honey them to death all over again. It was as if some new curly, golden plant dangled from every ceiling in London, yet never enough to sate the unswattable invaders from the domain of filth.

Surely, Sickert thought, we will never be clean. There will never be enough washing for us. We should start again, under-ground, not up here among the manure heaps and the drains, the cesspools and the latrines. Wasn't it the great Goethe who said it is all very well to go on building sublime architectural monu-ments, but as a race we have enormous trouble disposing of our excrements? Are we entitled to dote on the angelic while hold-ing our noses? London reeks in every season, but spring is the worst. What was this? Showertime? A wen, a plague, a midden. Then he knew he was not really thinking about the foul smell of London; he was, but only indirectly—his mind had blamed the city for something of his own doing that haunted him. Two things, in fact. First of all, he had somehow managed not to feel much when, to have her baby, Annie had had to go to the workhouse, away from her comfy if shabby little basement room, as if she were being punished—not as if she were going to hospital—for wanting to have the biggest, most emphatic bowel movement in the world. He was astounded at his callous-ness, or his lack of awareness. He had said nothing beyond a sentence or two to report that the arrangements had been made; they were the best he could manage. "Best thing all round," he had said. Or "best thing in the world, Annie." Or "You'll be safer there. They understand these things." Sanitary? He wondered, his mind on carbolic soap and skin-rending scrubbing brushes. Annie had gone to a place of shame and humiliation, a place of last resort. It almost seemed the inevitable punishment for a woman who had presumed too far, and Eddy had agreed like someone in a dark trance, shaking with dismay, blinking his tears sideways in great big gouts, sniffling a few perfunctory words, mainly "Well, yerrss, yerrss, we can't—no, we can't have that. It is the best course, Walter, oh by far." It would have been kinder, Sickert, thought, to shove her into a cage and put her on view in Piccadilly, exposing to passers-by the slithery and blood-hot working of parturition as the little stranger came blundering out, like some greasy plug removed from a polar bear. Was this what the blithe lass from the Midlands had come to London for? He determined to set her up in the South of France somewhere, to make amends, with servants to command, gold-buttoned waiters to bring her restorative fizzes and warm douches, the tenderest of blotting papers. He had had little idea of what happened to her when she gave birth, but he realized now that it appealed to some instinct within him for carnality spread wide. What he wanted—what all men lacked—was an experience like this, basic to life and indeed love, that was slimy and unstoppable. The idea of the afterbirth appealed to him as a mass of God's will. Forbidden to be present, he had nonetheless bribed an attendant and peeped at the birth of Alice Margaret, shocked by the torrent, the pain, the convulsive momentum of the whole process. He had almost vomited, wishing he had come into the world by some other route. How Annie toiled and writhed, letting out with what sounded like curse words but were really appeals to God, Christ, her mother, the Virgin Mary, Mary, Mother of God, her pronunciation slewed and twisted. He found his mind forming questions that outstripped his will. Did women, he caught himself wondering, always link this kind of suffering to the so-called deed of kind? When they let any man, never mind a prince, "have his way with" them, did they always have this horror in mind as a possible outcome? And were they always prepared to pay for a moment's pleasure thus?

What about the act when it was not even a pleasure and this was the penalty? He heaved, then called out "Help her, for God's sake," and they fussed and clucked him out of there, urging him by the elbow and from behind. *"Sir,"* said the attendant he had bribed, but he was thinking of things more visceral, appalled by the secret red sponges of life yet utterly rapt by them as well, as if the innards of men did not count at all but were truly no more than a sewage works, whereas this smithy of fecund membranes was a miracle hard to look at, certainly when it was churning, as only just now.

Was it for this that he had moved to the sullen, dull end of the spectrum and to scenes of low life, of life reduced to its grossest minima? In his unhinged yet responsive state, he saw the insides of women as an array of tender little bugles made from liver, mucous onions that peeled away to reveal looms of blood, and corms or bulbs of infinite complexity, all purging something like amber. He wanted no flies near any of it. He tried to tell Eddy something of this, but Eddy fled to the brothel up the street, and Mary Kelly was already too busy to listen, one of those women who knew about hot water and clean sheets *when the time came,* as if birth were some ghoulish table setting or superlative feat of laundry. There was no one to tell about his most private discovery: that he was learning Woman from the inside out, and feeling himself in familiar terrain long denied him. Not babies, oh no; what sang to him and called to him was the magic in the tripes, and he said to himself, I never felt any of that when I was having my way with any of them. It's having *their* way too. It isn't just we that relish the act. You have to think hard where you are putting it when you put it in, and especially of what lies just beyond the slippery walls, left and right, and above; you are never ramming a tunnel, just like that, but an entire landscape of divine bulblets, little cruising soft pearls, and glossy orchids fraught with future life. It would surely halt many a tupper in his heaves to think of what a precious little nursery he was thrusting toward. It even sickened him, though, because it was all alive; so, after the fashion of Leonardo, should he then contemplate the same wonders when they were dead, in the dissecting room? He thought not. He was going to have to get on nodding terms with life raw and bubbly, or he would not be qualified to paint the mysteries with true reverence. Annie had shown him her all, almost enough to humble him into squeezing in *his* belly the babies that were deep inside.

"I hate the very word," he told Mary Kelly, "it sounds like what it is: *Work-house.* Like work-horse."

"No, it's not, old Walt," she answered. "There's nothing wrong with work, only to you artist blokes. Nothing wrong with workhouses that a bit of candid thinking won't cure. Where else will you send out-of-work women?"

No, he saw workhouses full of pregnant women at term, being delivered by other women in bonnets, with tubs and buckets and chamber pots all around them, big fans of steam rising and blood on the institutional sheets on which someone with nothing better to do had written in India ink the name of the workhouse in letters the size of a thumb. Or he saw workhouses as homes for the idle and the vagrant, where they got what was called indoor relief, but also as prisons of a kind for pilferers and tramps. Lunatics found a bed there too. Each parish was responsible for its own paupers, and its lunatics as well. There was no migration; the flavour was local. It was all right for them, he supposed, but not for Annie Crook.

"You're worried because they're keeping her there," Mary Kelly said. "It's usual. A woman can't just rise up like Lazarus and go back to work. Her insides might fall out like Tuesday's washing." He saw that image only too clearly and tried to think of something else.

"Why Tuesday?"

"Because," she snapped. "Tuesday's the day, see."

Yes, it made sense. He saw that. A woman could not just deliver and walk. He wanted Annie back where she belonged. He wanted Annie in Dieppe, and her daughter too; but here he was, at a loose end, waiting while her organs worked their way back into place after the upheaval that had moved him so much. Make plans, then. Plans were a snap, he told himself. He and

Mary Kelly would just go. This was April, and he was due to marry in June. Well, they had time to play with. Having proposed marriage in several ways to Ellen—jocular, solemn, in the open carriage—he now proposed Dieppe to Kelly. It had taken Ellen almost a year to warm to him, to take his miscellaneous proposals seriously, but it took Mary Kelly only a minute to answer him. A quick trip. They took it in April, and they were back before Annie Crook came out of the workhouse with her baby on May 5.

It was a time of striped awnings, boisterous winds, wine-fuddlement, drawing patterns on the sand with their toes, and long afternoons of desire piqued then sated. Their few days together in Dieppe struck him as the epitome of the perfect life, but who wanted to live for ever with Mary Kelly? The very idea made him tremble. On the one hand, he found her irresistibly voluptuous, on the other a dangerous plaything. Below the waist, she was imperative to his well-being, but the mind was too busy and adroit, not really connected to the impulsive motions of the rest of her. At meals she had already begun to command the waiters with loud, imperious waves, and execrably uttered French; she said *garçon* as *GAR-son,* and otherwise embarrassed him with her ugly table manners. But she adored France and pretended to be French, styling herself *Marie* Jeanette, determined (she said) to spell her name *Quelle-y.* He let her forget this, but made a mental note that she, unlike Annie, was no back-street illiterate, and was not to be trusted with anything. In that case, he wondered, in that paradoxical way of self-vexing he favoured, what was he doing here in Dieppe with her? Some lure, some drug, in her sucked him on; she had no inhibitions whatever about gratifying him in any way conceivable. It meant nothing to her, whereas being "abroad" with a toff did. "You *are* a gay gent," she said again and again. "You put people out of your mind like closing a book. There's no Annie and there's no Alice Margaret just now, is there?"

She had a point, Sickert conceded. It wasn't that he had

turned against Annie or Cleveland Street; he just needed a change, and he always would. Any man of the world needed his *congé* from time to time, from *Kinder,* wife, and work. He came here to paint, too, in a different light, to different background noise, the sound of French included, and the bracing air of the coast after the stagnant estuary of the Thames. Oh, he had cause to be here, he knew, and he would be back in time to greet Annie on her return from the St. Marylebone. Perhaps Eddy could be persuaded to take an interest in his baby princess, even if only a clandestine one. There would surely be money, Sickert thought. Not even the Royal Family would let the child starve; and that was a view of things, he thought, right up Mary's (or "Marie" 's) street. He could see it now: Marie Jeanette working hard on Eddy to fatten the purse to get them all off to Dieppe, or even to Paris. That would be better than eking out an existence in the slums of Cardiff as a widow.

In the end they stayed in Dieppe two weeks, in the course of which he developed a working rhythm. He was sorry to go, but she seemed fidgety, as if the strain of being on approximately good behavior had been too much, and she wanted to slink back now into her old habits, with a wink proffering her beneath-the-counter novelties. They arrived back the day before Annie left the workhouse and declared herself ready to work. Sickert felt dazed, lost mostly in the trance of inspiration that had come upon him in Dieppe, as it always did if he stayed long enough and curbed his appetite for wine.

He lived less in time than in a little bubble that floated aimlessly, in which he made sure of his eighteenpenny stall at the music hall, always on the stroke of eight; ordered some pastel glasspaper and sandpaper canvases; and dreamed of one day buying an oak *secrétaire* to write at. The daily need of other human beings he considered only now and then, which was all he asked of them. He thought of himself as the Intermittent Man, warmed to the conceit, and did a couple of Affable Arthurs around the room to celebrate.

Chapter 6

Already Sickert could sense the almost seismic changes brought about by Annie and Kelly, and the presence mentally offshore of some vast floating mass, pachyderm or geological, that was going to change their lives irrevocably. A medley of minor shifts had brought it into being (mainly shifts he himself had arranged), and now there was no stopping it. Neither marriages nor births nor journeys abroad nor royal blood could halt it now. All he had ever needed to do was to invite Annie Crook to work at Mrs. Morgan's tobacco shop, and that was that. He had initiated some tragedy whose exact countenance he could not fathom, but the bleak mood of it had begun, and all he needed to know now was when it would start. It was no use saying life was tragic. It was both tragic and not tragic. It was a muddle, but it was so only for people, never for stars, icebergs, and waterspouts. Life could seem tragic only to those who made mistakes. It was no use hoping to be like an inkblot or a daffodil.

Of course, he could readily see Eddy disappearing, washing his hands of the whole affair, and himself going off to spend a season or two in Dieppe, deep in the thicket of his marriage; even Marie Jeanette Kelly, as she now fancied herself, marching away to ply her trade. None of this would alter the presence in the world of Annie Crook and her royal-blooded baby, about whom, surely, the word would soon be out, and then what? Sickert knew he would not be able to paint Alice Margaret, because to paint her he would have to look at her, and then he would want to do more about her than paint her, yet he knew not what. She seemed a quiet, unresponsive child, almost a caricature of the kind of baby called "good," as if she had inherited from her mother the same inclination not to be a nuisance, not to get in anyone's way. He stared at her and some force dragged wild horses kicking through his bowels. He wanted to explode or drown. Some horror latent in that quiescent, oval face tugged at him, wanting an answer, a prophecy, a word in time; but he had nothing to say or to give, it was too soon for that. He just knew, however, that some drear and carnal web hovered over them all, could they but see it and evade it, presided over and mended by some ghastly beast whose origin no one knew, but it had come together from a thousand unguarded acts allowed to stand and so infest the bright promises of yet another swollen summer.

This baby did not flinch, not even when he approached her closely, and he took to gazing at her as if he were outstaring a sundial or the head of a chess piece. Surely this child was the very model of radiant calm. Why, she was queenlike, or as queens should be. This is Alix's grandchild, he said; she is part Danish, part Midlands. I have seen them fidget and blink, and slaver and bubble, but never one who did not seem to wish I were far away. It must be the auburn yellow of my hair. This is the only baby to whom I am not some kind of devil.

"I do not scare her," he told Annie.

"*Shush,*" she told him. "Don't talk into the baby's face." Annie looked pale and drawn; birth had made her less hearty, less bonny, and she seemed a woman consecrated to the silent life, wanting to hear nobody, see nobody, take no praise and, if blamed, to have it pressed upon her in submissive silence.

"She's a peaceful one," he said.

"With as much future as *she* has," Annie told him with slow bitterness, "you'd be quiet too. Her father just stands and stares at her as if she was some kind of Christmas toy. He wants to wind her up and play. At least when that nasty Netley lets him. He's married to Netley now."

"Oh, Netley's all right," Sickert said from within his dream, vaguely recalling some new scandal about Netley and the man who managed the Prince of Wales's stables—Lord Arthur Somerset. Was *that* where he had got the idea of an Affable Arthur walk? Surely not. "Netley's like a watchdog. Leave him alone and he won't bite."

Annie, shaking her head, gestured at the empty room. "Look at all the visitors she gets." Marie was upstairs, serving in the shop, the clang of whose bell they could plainly hear. Business seemed brisk. "Wasn't she supposed to be looking after Alice Margaret while I—"

"Not yet, my darling," Sickert said. "There has to be a decent interval, hasn't there now?"

She did not answer, but plucked at her baby's moist cheek as if trying to remove some foreign object invisible to all eyes but hers. When Sickert made as if to pick the child up, she did not cry, nor did her mother make the faintest further motion. Sickert was unused to seeing mothers allow him to do anything with their infants; he was too imposing a man, he thought, too volatile-looking. All Annie did, however, was sigh and loll, then slightly open her arms to receive Alice Margaret back again. For a moment, Sickert wondered if Marie Jeanette Kelly had been drugging the child, but dismissed the thought. No, he had just held a placid, equable baby, and was learning from the experience. One day, perhaps soon, he would have babies of his own, draughtsmen or painters, to be sure, but by then he would not be living on Cleveland Street. He saw his future in a more rural part of London, in which city *his* impressionism would be the dominant mode, and he would never go away for so long, not even to Venice or Dieppe, as to weaken his hold on taste. This day would come as certainly as it would rain or go dark before morning, an expression he had picked up from Marie Kelly, the Gallic Gael. Respectability would be a catalyst, would it not? No, he knew better than that, but it might become a salve for an overexercised soul. He often wondered why he had been so willing to take Eddy on; it was not that he felt an intense compassion for Alix, whom the Royal Family snubbed, or that he felt a certain sexual attraction to her, which he did. It was more that Alix had come from Denmark, the land of his grandfather, Johann Jürgen Sickert, who painted easel pictures and ran a firm of decorators much called upon by Christian VIII. There was an old royal connexion, made firm by his father, Oswald, who at the age of sixteen had painted a masterly portrait of Christian, who promptly conferred on him a royal purse to Copenhagen. In those wonderful old days, before Christian died and the gluttonous Frederick VII succeeded him, Sickert's father had been a frequent visitor at the Yellow Palace among the beech trees at Bernstorff, where Alix was born in 1844. Sickert knew the facts by heart. It was as if a sunny myth had moved through their family, and continued to do so, bringing with it blessings of a nostalgic sort: at nineteen, Alix had married Bertie, the Prince of Wales, and five years after that Oswald Sickert had arrived in London too—one of the few Danes available to her for homesick reminiscences and misfit complaints. Poor Alix, abandoned by her husband for women of riper physique, had formed an intense attachment to the young Walter, sixteen years her junior, treating him partly as a son, partly as an exquisitely compatible lover. He had waited for her to put on weight, but she did not, so he often felt like a second Bertie, dodging away from a woman he adored spiritually and facially, but found of no carnal appeal. Indeed, in deciding to marry Ellen, he realized, he was really marrying Alix by proxy, and seeking to cure himself of his indifference to women of an angular type. And, when Eddy went to orgies or paraded his flesh in other ways, Sickert always felt he was somehow exorcising the family skeleton.

So the coming of an Alice Margaret meant a great deal to him, and in some ways he thought of her as his child, by complicitous extension. He had managed to undo a bit of the social fabric, helping to produce a creature whose brave new world included crowns and donkey-stones. That he had created an insoluble problem had not occurred to him, for he saw the solution in poetic terms: pigment, Dieppe, a change of venue, all manageable but no more than temporary. He thought of human life in images, not in long impromptu parabolas.

Just once or twice a year a dreadful slate-sharp feeling would drive through him that told him he was living a life altogether wrong, and his bones would ache, his eyes would pour, and his mind would seem to tumble, full of shards and cinders. While he had been thinking about art, his techniques for living had fixed themselves; he was to remain a prisoner of them, twirl as he often did to escape. Much too early, he decided, Sickert was said and done.

Wandering about in the Hampstead house one evening and trying to school himself out of the supposition that the house was partly his, he heard sluicing noises coming from the bedroom. Was it a leak, or Ellen drinking heavily? He had no sooner walked in than she began shooing him away with little, packed-sounding yelps that rooted him to the spot, aghast at what he saw. She sat astride a portable bidet he knew had not come from Dieppe, manipulating a black rubber syringe with a ninety-degree curve in its neck. It was as if she had found the thing coming out of her and had sat there in the bidet to wait for its birth, wondering what to do with it. The smell was of carbolic, although with a sickly component unknown to him. A bottle stood on the floor beside her, its contents masked in dark brown glass. At last he managed to speak.

"What on earth . . . ?"

"Precautions," she said, dreamily. "Disinfectant. It's for something I got from you or from myself. How can one ever know? It appears and has to be dealt with. A rash of sorts. We're not even married, but look what happens."

Was this, he wondered, the way to deal with it? As if she were a man? She would certainly not confide in any doctor, that he knew. If he asked to look, she would begin to scream; and, if he asked to help, filling and squeezing the syringe with proprietary zeal, she would sail into a frenzy. He did not belong in this scene, he knew, but was unable to wrench himself away from it, feeling responsible and therefore entitled to view. She looked quite regal squatted there, her head bowed, her hands ever at work, plying and ladling.

"A little visitor," she said grimly.

"But not a little stranger," he told her with a grin. "It isn't, is it?"

"No it damned well isn't," she said. "Nothing so wholesome, Walter. Not that I'd expect anything wholesome from you. It's a wonder leeches aren't crawling out of the water, just to get away from me to you, where they belong." Odd, he thought: dealing with Ellen and her insides changes the way I am with other women. If I didn't have her to cling to and moan about, I'd be a different, maybe much nastier man. She's my deposit with the bank of sexual respectability, and here she is washing her thatch and its foyer with the same disinfectant they use in schools and pubs. It's as if she's marched out of a public institition right into the house. Nothing will survive all that ammonia and carbolic, with alcohol and ether mixed in. God, the stuff we have to use on ourselves, just to keep the creepie-crawlies at bay.

Ellen herself, accustomed to self-imposed rigors of the mind, had already dismissed him from the event, whether or not he was the cause. Simply, it had nothing to do with him. It was a private plumbing matter, one of those maladies that women inherited. It had happened to her before she met him, and it would happen again. Against her better knowledge, she *almost* subscribed to a theory of spontaneous generation: the germs were born of the deposits in there, she supposed; better that than some germ ferried home by Sickert from one of his nightly escapades among the sluts, whose innards and orifices—she abandoned the thought, slaughtered it with biting slop and caustic aroma. If only, she thought, women had tighter *zones:* less open, less prey to rubbish; but that would make them less open to men, which in the end would defeat all purposes. It had to be so, but she often wished she were a man, able to cut off all traffic with the outside world by simply trapping the end of it in a clothespin or squeezing tight between finger and thumb. Nothing entered *them. Their* troubles came from the surface and lurked in the cheesy folds. She did not shrink from the facts of life, but she wanted them revised.

"Trouble in the works, my darling, eh?" He was being jocular now, unable to cope otherwise. He still had not moved, his eyes unblinking on the bidet, whose water was now offwhite. "I'll change the water for you."

"No you won't. Be said. *Go."*

"I'm useful," he said. "Let me wash you out. Damn it, woman, I'm a painter. I'm at home with oozy things."

Always shoving his nose, she thought, well—where he shouldn't. "Walter, I would like to be alone. Private."

"Then put up a sign. People on intimate terms don't always have to be in each other's pockets, or anything else."

"Please don't," she told him, now trying to be be gentle and diffident. First make him tenderhearted, then he turns tractable. "Please go and look at the rest of the house. It's not as if we lived in a kennel."

"We don't *live* here, my beauty, we *use* it." It would make a lovely whorehouse, he thought, with a bidet in every room and inhospitable liquids ready poured. Already the disinfectants were developing a venereal appeal for him. In a year he would need a bucket of the stuff at bedside merely in order to achieve erection. No doubt of it, he was interested in the plumbing aspect of sex: it was all a gigantic waterworks, put together before rubber was discovered. Sickert loved to watch, to ogle, to savor; he was the muse of the unsavory, and here he was peering at his beloved affianced, a pagoda among women, his Nefertiti of the nether lips. This was just like marriage, he decided, but better: he could walk away; but what he needed was something that made him weep in private, so binding its hold on him was, all the way to the grave. He needed something to chafe against, not a state that, fluid-like, accommodated every contour of his self-assertion. Like Catholicism. Oh, not that, not quite, he thought. Better to ape the druids, and the Aztec priests with their stone knives.

Now she stood, liquid streaming down her calves, brawny in her tautness, and he desired her at once and prevailed even as she protested, there on the expensive rug beneath them. "Walter, at least let me dry myself." No, he wanted that tang of caustic in the air around his gasps, no doubt as he put back into her the very germs she had in vain tried to scald, or their relations. She fought against it like a demon, but she always achieved a vast, quaking climax that puzzled him, in the end confirming his theories about catalytic aversion and contributive pain. I really am, he thought as she squirmed and he pushed, very French indeed. I have this twisted side to me, but I wouldn't if the world as I find it didn't somehow match me in it, tat for tit. We are alone with our germs, who surround us ever. Why bother to keep clean? We take them to the tomb with us. They are God's footmen, the silent sentries of our parts. God be praised, she's in splendid form today. What a wife-to-be.

Already relaxing from his latest onslaught, Ellen nonetheless needed to abolish him mentally as soon as it was over. She couldn't bear him, she told herself, but she couldn't often bear to be without him, and she was thinking, with lethargic vengefulness: I was wrong about the difference between the sexes. There's a tiny bloodsucking catfish in Brazil, the *candiru*, is it? The thing swims up and into men and then expands, giving them terrible pain. It even has spines. Surely it goes after women too, but perhaps it needs tightness to make it feel at home: men only. Walter will know. She asked. He snored. She answered herself, *pleasuring* herself, as she sardonically noted, with the answer, idly noting that women were so good at pleasuring themselves they hardly needed men at all, not for that. The sperm-bearers, she decided, are full of redundancies: that's why they go whoring off to make more of sex than it really is, adding filth and frenzy to something that's, for them, over in a trice, and, for us, easy to do at home, in a hammock or just about anywhere. We need their seepages, that's all.

Advancing into marriage, then, he was the superfluous swain walking nobly into the slaughterhouse, doing it to chasten his spirit, willing to listen to Ellen explain to him over and over again how she organized her ideas when all he ever wanted to see was people's ideas blown askew by a tornado. Why bother with her, never mind with how much decorum and man-about-town finesse? Not for money alone, but for something to fight against—to see if he could be faithful, as indeed he had been faithful to Annie and Eddy, although in a wholly different fashion. He wanted to see if Ellen, the weaker of the two, could break him, and yet he knew it would never happen. He recognized he was being perverse, but perversity numbed his common sense. He was going to a *domina* who, he pretended, would tame him and deprive the whores of Whitechapel of much hard labor. It was as silly and as deep-seated as that, and he woke up laughing, knowing that he would soon qualify as a bad man, a ne'er-do-well, remembering a French phrase, *elle avait les fesses profondes.* She had a deep ass, into which, et cetera. The phrase came from Dieppe, lovingly garnered: no *piropo,* but in the right language for erotic polish, and quite unuseable about Ellen, whereas Annie and Marie, oh yes, oh yes. Beyond the flesh he sometimes could not go.

Now, of course, although Marie Kelly was more than keen to babysit, Annie hated to go upstairs into the shop to serve. She was what, in her Midlands village, they had called a *wittler,* a worrier, who could easily get *maddled* (mixed up) and one day might even go *scranny* (off her head). Being in London had made her worse. It was not just the noise or the smell, it was the upside-down type of life she was living, skulking away in a basement with a slumming prince. It was what she had dreamed of, but she wanted the dream to remain a dream: in some ways the moody, impressionable Eddy was too real a man to be dealt with, an imposing presence with a soft inside. Had he remained more of a figurehead, she might have been happier; after all, she hardly knew how to address him. She would use words from the Midlands, which amused him because he used an altogether different vocabulary.

"She's nesh, this one," Annie would say with a tremendous, almost chiding love; her baby felt every breeze and was vulnerable even to breathing, especially heavy breathing such as Eddy's.

"His Nibs, jolly cute, rather," Eddy said in what he hoped was praise.

"No, dopey," she told him. "It means, well, *nesh.* She'll catch cold easily."

"Then by all means let's keep her warm," Eddy said, chastened, willing to believe that people somewhere spoke in such a fashion. Sometimes his Annie sounded like a new-grown Viking, as uncouth and uncourtly as the drabs in the stews. "Have Netley bring some eiderdowns."

"She's a lovely babby," she said, uttering the word as her mother uttered it, "with soft white tabs. Look at them. And her gob's always shut."

"Pardon," said Prince Eddy, flummoxed, even though she had tried to teach him village talk.

"Nice ears," she explained. "And her mouth, see, it's always shut. Like Fletcher's chimbley. Oh, never mind, it doesn't matter." Sometimes, when she saw the incomprehension mount in his face and his hands begin to mate and wring, she gave up and made every effort not to talk Midland.

"She'll be after the men soon, mark my words."

"Well, I'll go to Trent," she said, shocked.

"What?"

"I'll get shut of you, Eddy my lad, if you talk like that in front of her face. I'll clip your tab on my way out. Don't you be so forcey."

Now he was truly lost, floundering, reduced to a half grin, a little crouch that almost overbalanced him, and he felt he was falling into a nest of wet leaves mired with animal droppings, birdlime, cuckoospit, things he had heard about only down at Windsor, at least until he met Annie the woodlander, who had told him all about bluebells. "Now she has to have her snap," she was saying, exposing a breast that she then cupped away from him, as if shielding the spout of a teapot.

"Her snap?"

"Her sup, you daft bugger. Why, you're a right ha'p'oth, a right Herbert you are. She needs a drink. Then she'll grow big and fat."

"Jolly nice baby," he said. "Imagine, we made her together, we did."

"She didn't blow in on the wind," Annie said. "And she wasn't delivered in no royal carriage neither. One of these days I'd like to see you cleaning up her business, like, with your bare royal hands. What goes in must come out."

"Where did Walter go?" Anything to change the subject. To get wed, she told him. Off to foreign countries on his honeymoon. He felt nervous when Walter was not there, for Walter was his protector, his go-between, the connoisseur of all the social zones, even the one that Annie came from, and the formidable Kelly woman.

When Walter was missing, Eddy felt that his mother and father could see everything he did and thought. He adored the way Walter could pass things off, defusing their menace, puncturing their grandeur. It was easier to make fun of backsides, queens, and babies when Walter was around, almost as if Walter took nothing seriously—except art—and his attitude was ragingly infectious. He would never have that suavity, he knew, that fine tuning of the copiously gifted autocrat; if he could, he might squat on the throne after all, and make a mess of both England and his life from there instead of scuffling around the streets, the brothels, the tiny mildewed basements where the rate payment book was king. Some days he felt he was ambling into paradise with Annie, hand in hand, she in her most radiant finery, he in his naval uniform, his mustaches freshly waxed. Other days, however, he felt they were making an exhibition of themselves, trudging through the rank and unwashed of the East End, some Dorset Street of the heart.

"She doesn't half like mammy-pap," Annie was saying, talking to herself. "Pull it out and listen to her chelp. Gets her little gob on it and she gobbles it up. Oo, my little princess, thou're a gradely little beast."

Eddy could hardly believe his ears. Sometimes Annie's speech seemed thick as porridge, thrown into a register that mules and donkeys would have spoken better, almost as if baby-stuff, as he called it, from milk to vomit, had developed a voice of its own: *mam, sup, goz, gob, clart,* and *nesh.* Now, what did *clart* mean? Dirty, perhaps: all clarted up. Tempted to take on the same idioms himself, he always backed away, telling himself it was women's prattle, and what he needed were words for horsing, whoring, gambling, and politicking.

"She's not a mardy one," Annie was saying, "even if she is

a bit nesh. I gen her all I had, and then she wanted some more. Why, she's right forcey, not one of your force cats, like, but throng once she gets sucking. See. She spews a lot back, but some stays put, and then she grinds it all up. It's like having a little factory in my arms."

"Just so," said Eddy. "She's a real nip."

"She's not then."

"No, she's not. She's a bobby-dazzler."

"Ah," Annie sighed into her baby's hair, "now you're talking, Eddy. She's champion all right."

"Champion," he echoed, wondering what his mother and father, not to mention Queen Victoria, would say when they found out, as they were bound to. They just might be proud of him for once, for having seed in his loins, though the whole Royal Family seemed full of nothing else. He had proved himself as a man now, had he not? "Always fetching spunk," Annie would say to him in their erotic transports on the gray-sheeted bed she slept in. "You must live on eggs." Then she would school him in Midland if he promised not to school her in Palace. "Say it like this, Eddy," her head on two bolsters sewn in hard-faced curtain cloth with a raised brown pattern. "Say *antla.*"

How on earth? What did it mean? It meant *haven't I, haven't you, hasn't he/she.* He made no effort, so she plied him with *Gerooamwithee,* meaning Get off home with you, for lack of which expletive he would surely perish on his first day if he ever ventured north, where the men were fierce and the women ate the men. By the end of this particular lesson, feeling like someone whose mouth had been filled with curds and whey, he managed to say *Mester* twice and *thrape* once, these being the words for *mister* and *thrash.* The phrase *nithe spithe* (nice spice), meaning nice sweeties, he could not manage at all, being wholly unequal to the fake lisp of delicacy required, to be said only through a surfeit of spittle. If this was how the lower orders talked, then the sooner the Socialist revolution brewing in London came, the better; the sooner it would be stamped out and lit with hellfire. He was beginning to see the good in Cambridge after all, where a man might rehearse an acquired lisp for three years even if only to seem exquisite when he had to. *Edda* they would call him up north, or in the north Midlands, she told him. Imagine that. Yet their language classes, especially when she was in charge, had a bumbling, cuddly glory to them. A tarted angel was teaching him how to be down to earth, and he doted on the extra range of primitive emotions the new words brought within his reach. "Yes," she told him one day, as coup de grâce, "if somebody's *thee*-ing you, as they do up there, and you don't like it—you'd rather be called *you*—you just say *Don't thee thou me, thou tharrer,* and they'll shut up. They'll shurrup, see." He laughed out loud, said it six or seven times, and then they both said it, at speed, loud enough to wake the baby, but it did not wake. It never woke up. It never cried. It was the best-behaved baby he had ever heard about. Up there, she told him, an afternoon was *an after,* just like that, and he warmed to that one, saying he loved their afters together, for afters was what they mainly were, while Kelly sold upstairs, on her face a look of mutinous disdain.

The day of reckoning, according to Mary Kelly, could not be far away. She was not going to be nanny for long, not once Buckingham Palace had the news. How could Eddy and Annie imagine, for a minute, that they would go on having their little sessions undisturbed?

The world felt different, less starched, with Mrs. Morgan in charge rather than Sickert, who had been a stickler for routine. She ran a sloppy shop, Kelly did, whereas Annie was altogether more rigorous and deft. Eddy kept getting sovereigns changed in other shops so that Annie could have a ready supply of cash, whereas Mrs. Morgan now paid Marie Kelly who, after all, did most of the work in the shop. Things had changed somewhat, but not that much. Nobody was on the streets yet, and even the tart-spoken Marie elbowed the counter and dreamed dreams about dreams undreamed; dreams in outline, they were, quite empty of lofty plumes and gallant princes and serving-girls in crowns, but replete with gamblers and jockeys, princes with chancres, and men-women in rustling shirt cuffs of blinding white. During this lambent interim, Annie learned to say "Don't you know?," "Charmed, I'm sure," "Extra-ordinary," "Chin-chin," "Tophole," and "Old Bean," all phrases she was going to find useful as she rose in society, even if only as blanks to say to Eddy at boring receptions where her loam-laden vowels would cause a fuss.

Chapter 7

Wordless almost, with Netley coming back for them in two hours, they lingered in the countryside by a chirping spring, the baby firm in her arms while he plunged his hands to chill a bottle of champagne. They were both feeling emotions they could not express, but blissful all the same, knowing that paradise once entered could never end. Instead, she told him the grass had just about stopped growing for the year. Should they gather bluebells? Better, he said, to listen to the birds, some of whose calls he recognized: thrush, linnet, skylark; his boyhood had not been a total waste, though he was never bookish and never would be. One of these days, somehow, he would take his degree from Cambridge, no matter how badly he did in the examination. "Always an—" he stumbled— "an *aegrotat,*" he said, naming the degree they handed out when illness prevented them from assigning one of the classifications.

"Lovely," she said. "If you go to the workhouse to have a baby and you don't get a baby, then they give you a baby anyway, so you won't feel disappointed. It's like that." Perhaps there were no bluebells left.

"More or less," he murmured, his mind on an imaginary woman who lost her wedding ring in a fountain and would let down her hair to envelop her lover's naked belly. No, that was not Annie, but he knew that one day he and she would enter an old, dilapidated country house with a high veranda, set in the middle of a vast garden run wild, with not far away a rather sluggish river upon which sat a barge full of hay. There would be snow on the distant mountains and the sound of cowbells trickling down into the valley. They would steal the barge and make their escape toward a big lake, in which the old barge would eventually sink, hay and all. He was given to these morbid fantasies of their life together, but he never told her the details. The images scalded and wounded him, but he could not express them in words, even when nuzzling her swollen bosom, as now. When she held him, one-handed with the baby in the other, she did not know she clasped a whole internal opera gleaned from conversation, nights out, and the jabber of the ambitious Netley, who made a habit of picking up bits of cultural dialogue with which to grease his way upward. Eddy knew that Annie and he would have no chance of a life together in England. They would have to go abroad, or part, and he left it at that, as unwilling to sacrifice his wild oats in Cleveland Street as give up his lover and their child.

Whenever he had dithered, someone had always intervened and settled his problem for him, and he was sure the same would happen with Annie and himself. He was not the type to seize the initiative, but he *was* the type to hope that Sickert, on his return, would have the answer. Indeed, he was blithe enough to think that Sickert had gone abroad himself partly to think one up, which was untrue. Eddy had never recovered from the constant image of Bertie, his father, who ignored both Eddy and Alix in favor of chorus girls, whores, duchesses, and all manner of social butterflies. Gutterflies, Eddy had once called them in a slip of the tongue that ranked as one of his few puns. Ironically enough, what he admired in Sickert was the same kind of promiscuity, but Sickert was an artist, not a husband and father— well, he was a husband now, Eddy remembered, and therefore respected him less.

"Talk Midland, lass," he said to Annie, to get his mind away from such vexing themes, and Annie, ever willing to walk backward, treated him to a confected mouthful of almost incomprehensible rusticisms. "Sithee, Eddy, shee-ap," she exclaimed, and to him it was as if a sheep had spoken. "Ah," he brayed in his baritone, as he knew he should. "Yon's a grand rooad, int it?" He had become good at the accent, not quite so good with her dialect; it was as if, always on the fringe of English, he were babbling in some asylum, talking to God or to himself.

"Where are we going?" she said.

"Staying put, my love. We are not the roving kind." He kissed her, the baby, then held them both tight. He was attired for tennis or cricket, all in white, with some regimental colors in the V of his sweater. She looked very much the part of his partner, at least until she spoke; something radiantly decorous occupied her face and made her, if not exactly royal or imperious, like someone faintly accustomed to splendor. They made a seemly couple there on the quietening grass, and Sickert might have wanted to paint them, although in more somber colors. The baby was a mere speck of life, a scrap, who did not complain. Sometimes both he and she felt at her gums, in between sips of champagne, but of course she had no teeth yet; she was only pulp and juice, as defenseless a human as either of them had ever seen, reminding them of their own vulnerability. One, two, three, he sometimes counted, and Annie followed along, mouthing the count; then nothing happened, and they knew the reckoning was not upon them yet. Why, they would be able to count up to three a million times before then, surely. Perhaps they would all three be dead before it arrived, or in America, where nobody cared where you came from or what you had done so long as you—what did Americans have to do? They had to believe in America, that it was really the land of the free, where the free became wealthy, and those free who didn't were the freest of all. They were huggers, these two, at least when not being watched. They *applied* kisses to each other, selecting the *point d'appui* (as Sickert called it) with exaggerated care, anxious not to repeat themselves in any given bout, ear rubbing against ear, nose against nose, and attempting blurred eye-to-eye confrontation. Their hair got entangled, and sometimes their eyelashes. Now that they were three, it was still the same idyll, the same mellow oblivion, the same preposterous daylong doting. They were less lovers than extensions of each other, as apt to cry out in the night without doing anything about it as to expect more than a few months together. They wept to be together, they wept when apart. They could have found each other by smell on a deserted heath in Cornwall, if they had had to, and their romantic imaginations might have been interchanged without mishap. Different, they were affectopathic twins, and never more fused-looking than when they lay back and let their naked feet link up and part, sometimes playing slapping games with them or building a tower of heel to toe, toe to heel. Fops of affinity, they did better out of doors than in the Cleveland Street basement, whose baleful light only Sickert loved.

Netley, whom Annie loathed, would be coming soon to ferry Eddy back to his fleshpots, about which she never asked, content to add a second subordination to the one she had learned in the Midlands. Girls did not object or they got thraped; and girls of her station were hardly entitled to quibble about the foibles of princes. In her straitjacketed way she was content, but she blazed privately when she thought of the licence he took, the Bertie way of living that Eddy had acquired. Eddy was only partly hers, but did that mean the rest of him belonged, as it were, to several others, or only to himself? Was hers the only part of him committed? She loved him, and she was certain he loved her, but she was the monopolized monopolist and he was sometimes no more than an idle shopper turned effusive client. It was better than the Midlands, though; a woman's destiny was to be fruitful, so what better fruit to bear than royal fruit? Surely something magical would come from it. Surely it was not nothing. A wiser woman than she would have left Eddy without a bun in her oven, whereas this way it was better: there was something to hold and fascinate him, beyond the allure of a passing fancy. There was flesh, a face, a drawstring from one body to another, permanent in the eyes of the Lord and those of biology too.

Annie had never had much cuddling at home, having to compete for it with four siblings all younger than she. No wonder she had cut loose, fueled with approximate dreams of London's magic. Even she had known that dreams they would remain, yet here was one already coming true, so why did it make her shudder, never know which way to look? When they two hugged now, as they obsessively did, there was a keener edge to it. He was aware of having called out for her, with a cry all the way from his stomach, in deserted alcoves of palaces, far from equerries (he hoped), whereas she felt her very skin summoning him daylong—a cry would have been too selective, too episodic. No, he was not his father, short and fat and popeyed, but actually a good-looking young devil, as the phrase went, a bit of a Turk, and Annie was still vivacious, though calmed by motherhood. She yearned, however, for another striped bathing machine to wheel them away, float them off, to where they would never again have to account for their behavior. It was what she sometimes called her Kelly mood, but it did not last, she was too commonsensical for that. No, whatever had to be done had to be done in London town, with or without Eddy, Alix, the profligate Bertie, or anyone else. After all, she had managed this far; surely she could manage a bit farther: from nowhere to confectioner's assistant, from that to who knew what?

Champagne made her cough, but she grappled with its prickly tickle, feeling lightheaded and vaguely attributing that feeling to all those bubbles, each one a messenger of disarray. Eddy drank it all the time and so floated through his days. By his standards, he loved anyone who treated him better than his father had. For Annie, it was as if Mrs. Sarah Winslow of the chandler's shop, George Endersby the bookseller, Isaac Lyons the linen-draper, Henry Mowbray the hairdresser, and Henry Fletcher the greengrocer, all of Cleveland Street, had become objects of infatuation for treating her with a modicum of decency as a friend of Walter's, which they did. She liked having a neighborhood, especially one in the West End, but it did not keep her from her sleep, whereas Eddy was a wholly impressionable booby hungering for kindness, of which Annie had given him more than anybody else. Hence his fixation on her, but not to the exclusion of crushes on others. London knew of him, as of his father, but in its worldly way said of him "wild oats," as it said of the father "oats even wilder" (but more discerningly done, with ladies of deep consequence). High government in Whitehall had not yet begun to take Eddy seriously, as eventually it began to do, once it got wind of Alice Margaret Crook.

Chapter 8

There followed a three-year interval of peace and stability, in which Sickert, failing to discover in himself a man with a gift for marriage (too much of a roving eye, too keen for novelty), did discover himself as a family man. Central to the small tribe of Annie, Alice Margaret, Eddy, and Marie Kelly, he told himself he was gaining on the roundabouts what he lost on the swings. As paterfamilias he had ample confidence, and he actually looked forward to Eddy's protracted absences, glorying in his role in London or Dieppe, with Ellen trailing along as part of the harem, wondering why he got on so well with women of the lower orders. With all three of them he had been on terms of sexual intimacy, and he wondered if, in the fullness of time, he and Alice Margaret might achieve something comparable. In Dieppe they became festive and fizzy, even Ellen, by far the most serious person of the group.

"You're surrounded," she told him. "It's exactly how you like it. All women."

"We really must try to get Eddy over next time," he said. "He balances things out a bit. One of these days he will quit Cambridge, and then the rest of the world will be in trouble. At least their wives and husbands and sons will. He doesn't molest little girls much, not yet. I imagine he's saving them up for when he turns thirty, in ten years' time."

"Oh, *Sickert,*" she said, as she often did when deploring what he said, or how, as if he were an institution. "I can well imagine that Eddy will come to his senses."

"Come to them? He's long past them, my love. Eddy was at the senses a long time ago, champing to be off."

"I didn't mean that," she informed him, with an agile, searching look. "I meant he'll stop fornicating around."

"You speak more frankly than you used to," he said, with a not altogether appeased smile.

"I've been living with you on and off, in case you haven't noticed."

"So it was you all the time."

"I sometimes wonder," she said sternly, "if you know, or care, which woman you're with at any given time. All you need is a pelvis, and there you are. A woman's body is a workbench for you."

"Nothing unique, you mean? I thought so."

Ellen was always asking if the things he did with her were the things he did with other women, and he always told her that every act of "coalition" was different.

"Honest," he said. "Apart from some common-or-garden anatomical analogies. Anyway, what other women? *Me?*"

"But for Eddy," she said, "no hope of that?"

"Eddy," he scoffed, "wouldn't know the difference between Cleopatra and a loaf with a greased hole in it. Eddy's primitive in all ways. All the energy that belongs in his brain is in his private parts."

"So," Ellen said, primly final about the matter, "all this business about his being up at Cambridge is bogus. It's just window dressing."

"Eddy," Sickert pronounced, "nice chap and all, is your ultimate dunce. There's a use for him somewhere in the world, but up to press nobody's been able to think of it."

"And *they* rule *us,*" she murmured.

"They tell us where to get off."

"And they're not even English."

"They're not even human, half of them," he sighed.

"With divine right," Ellen said abstractedly.

"Fit for the slaughterer's knives," he said. "They bring out the natural-grown regicide in me, they really do. Some days I'd like them all stood up against a wall and shot to bits. I'd shoot at them myself. Parasites. Leeches. Lice."

"Your old friends."

"*My* old friends," he said with tender laboriousness, "are folk of far lower social standing. I get on best with sluts, tramps, beggars, arse-wigglers, dung-sweepers, borrowers, pariahs, and thieves. The royals, as I call them, are only so much coal, lard, and whitewash. They try to make life have a better tune, but they accomplish nothing. Oh for 1789."

"And what, pray, am I?"

"You're the missus," he said boldly, "when you're at home. And, when you're not, you're the hoity-toity lady they saw me with—*wiv*—the *uvver* night. See."

They trod the quaint, worn streets of old Dieppe, clad in clothes rather more raffish than the English wore when over: whiter whites and starker blues, with more ribbons and ker-chiefs (Sickert himself reserved his biggest red one for exclusive Dieppe use). They drew attention to themselves, as they did not at Yarmouth, a lopsided family group with Sickert towering over them and leading them now and then in little snatches of song or showing off his Affable Arthur walk with big body twists and enormous looping swings of his arms, touching his right thumb to his left shoulder, and vice versa, and putting all his weight on one foot, then on the other. Sometimes Marie Kelly imitated him, but she lacked the height that made the walk both alarming and gainly. Sickert looked like a distin-guished young barrister all dressed up for a day's sailing in his green-peaked yachting cap and double-breasted blazer with a large, ornate coat of arms on the breast pocket. Something Nor-dic in him came to the fore at Dieppe. His mustache bristled more. His eyes looked severer. His voice coarsened. He became the captain of their souls, urging them forward as he marched on some invisible captain's bridge that moved along with him. "Avast," he liked to say to the backs of their heads, although when he did so Ellen would halt, come back, then walk at his side as if trained. She did not much care to walk on ahead with Annie and Marie Kelly, feeling that socially she did not belong with them, with The Women, trundled ahead like some uncouth advance guard, speaking an idiom both slovenly and crude. The trouble was that Sickert said little to her, though he was free enough with his hands, tapping and steering her almost as if she were blind. So the most usual formation for them was two and two, Annie or Marie wheeling the perambulator with Alice Margaret in it. From behind, Sickert mused on perambulators, on how large they were for the tiny body within, how arrayed in valances and flounces, fringes and veils they were, so that neither sun nor wind, perhaps not even the air itself, could get through to the coddled lotus-eater there. As he watched, noting the sprung wobble of the hull, like some fairground swinging-boat deprived of its rope and frame, the pram (thus abbreviated) seemed less a container or conveyance than a blatant emblem of extravagant delicacy; the infant did not need all the piled-up finery, but the persons wheeling needed the rest of the world to know how much they two cared about their child. It was advertising, he told himself: We are delicate, we are gentle, we do not bump our spawn.

What he liked about Dieppe was that they were all four *perambulating*, ambling through the streets again and again, as if taking possession: a quartet in pastels and nautical-looking contrasts, making even the English stare at them and painfully conclude that the flamboyant quartet were a toff and his lady, with two skivvies tending their baby, whereas the baby was a royal heir of England and the missing member was a prince of the realm. It amused him to know the truth behind the deceit, and then the truth behind the truth (that bisexual Eddy was fertile, could hardly read, but at this very moment was grinding through the Lord's Prayer with his Cambridge tutor in a vain attempt to honor the gods of required theology). Here, in Dieppe, the English had come and gone before they came as tourists; they had been thrown out, but now they were back, taking their revenge, making Dieppe more English than it was

French. Should Eddy ever become king, Dieppe would be his already, his own heir having been wheeled through the streets in some weird laying-on of hands, or of wheels.

If only the pink and yellow stucco could talk. "Bear left there," he cried forward, quite without needing to; they had traveled this street a hundred times, with parasols and shooting sticks. Annie and Marie went left, as if obeying, Annie quick and high of step to Marie's more dogged, lumbering gait.

After a while, news of the ménage began to circulate. The pieces of the puzzle could fit together in various ways, but the way most often confided to Lord Salisbury, the Prime Minister, was that Sickert had adopted a by-blow of Prince Eddy's; indeed, he had entered into a somewhat arid marriage with Ellen Cobham in order to do so. Salisbury, who knew Sickert, wondered at such altruism. It did accord, however, with one of his views of the world, for Salisbury had been a bookish, introverted boy who grew up into a bookish, not altogether extroverted man, and he wished people would leave him alone, choose a lifetime's books, then their one and only bride, and get on with the terrible chore of living. Sickert envied him, but not for having to be the recipient of yet another tale of royal scandal, leaked over the mahogany in his club, or even at Fitzroy Square. Salisbury hated hearing about bad behavior at a high level. Princes nowadays had no standards. It was as simple as that. One would rather look the other way. For months he averted his gaze, almost as if dreading contamination by what he listened to. Perhaps the whole thing was lies. Prince Eddy was surely not the ample scoundrel his father was: just a boy, up at Cambridge, an adequate university for a halfwit, and inspired by a good and lovely mother. Lord Salisbury got on with the job of running the country, for as long as he had to. The monarch was in disrepute, of course, but he was not going to raise a hue and cry for a dunce in his twenties. If the tale were true, then *measures* would serve. "Windsor," he murmured. "Foster mothers. The colonies. The power of money. One of these days I must have a word with Sickert about it. About painting, of course. They do say he excels." He could see that, with a mere baby to deal with, there was no great problem; but babies grew into upstart pretenders, and sometimes clandestine marriages tied both the royal family and the higher echelons of Whitehall into a Gordian knot. It would all be so much easier if people, having had their taste of honey, would go away, amply bribed. He summoned all of his poise, his placid stoicism, his insight into the least commendable of men, and held on, waiting for something to turn up. The baby might die. The mother might kill it. Prince Albert Victor Christian Edward might deny the whole thing and fall for a different charlady or shopgirl. Why were people so histrionic? What a relief it would be if the whole pack of them went off to France and stayed there; Eddy too. Was it, perhaps, merely a matter of money? Salisbury made inquiries and was glad to have done something other than lend an ear.

Alice Margaret grew, a cheerful child, but partially deaf, like her grandmother, Alix. She learned to walk on the beach at Dieppe and had some French among the babble she spoke. Sickert had already considered several not too well-to-do families there for the job of looking after her and her mother. Annie, unlike Marie, refused to learn French, and therefore was not that employable. Eddy never came to Dieppe anymore; it was as if Sickert were his jealous rival into whose terrain he never wandered, but the Prince and Annie kept up their trysts in Cleveland Street and occasionally ventured out for a stroll with Alice Margaret dangling between them or, as she went from one to two to almost three, twisting to escape in her favorite playsuit made from a tricolor flag. It was as if time had frozen or was going backward. Sickert had a jubilant sense of having managed to get away with something. Life, after all, could be a steady process of growth and fulfillment; all that happened was crescence, maturation, onset of age. His marriage was a hoax, but he and Ellen were on speaking terms, although living apart. She had accused him of "dirty talk," and that had been that, distressing to her but not to him, whose head was forever on paint and art. He was becoming known. Those in high places had begun to eye his work—perhaps a development that would in the end make him independent of Ellen. He painted on, absentee husband, proxy father, genuine brother to a fake one.

Then Salisbury came out of his sophisticated delay, provoked by an angry note from his Queen instructing him to sort the whole business out; Victoria had at last got wind of her grandson's indiscretions, and she wanted the affair terminated, the whole thing hushed up. In a way, all that followed, and much did, was a direct or indirect result of Victoria's fit of fury in 1888. If her horror was personal and familial, Salisbury's—so slow to be born—was political. She felt snubbed and defied, as by the inordinate sexual appetite of her own son Bertie, and she sometimes wondered if all that ailed mankind were not a surfeit of tumescent flesh. She, however, might be mollified, whereas Salisbury, once tweaked out of his patrician trance, got his nimble mind to work and reviewed the odds: The British had a German royal family and they did not like it; Victoria, for all her *réclame,* had done nothing about the condition of the poor, working or otherwise, or indeed about Ireland; the Republicans were loud; there had been attempts to assassinate her, and Bertie's sex life was an open scandal; dynamite had gone off in Trafalgar Square on November 13, 1887, where rioters had charged the police on what came to be known as Bloody Sunday. Salisbury had been in office for only three years, but already he could sense the beginning of the end, the end of the notion of monarchy. A rabble full of justice was one thing he abhorred, whereas a comely young prince too young to be corrupt and too stupid to be devious pleased him very much. Until lately, Eddy had been the high hope of those who favored a monarchy, but if he too now slid into the moral and erotic cesspool all was lost. Already he had been meddling with Catholicism, which the British public hated more than they did a German queen. What might be done forthwith? He pondered the night away, opening his Tacitus, then his Suetonius, taking huge handfuls of his bulky beard and worrying them like a terrier, twisting and tugging. If something were not done about Eddy, he might well blunder into a revolution that would fell the already toppling queen and irrevocably damn both Eddy and his father.

Socialists and Republicans be damned, he thought. This is a pickle that gentlemen can manage, and on behalf not of the Queen but of government itself. We do not wish the last years of the century to be an elegy for decent polity. The Prince has gone on long enough. Of Eddy's bisexual side he knew little enough, but was not immediately concerned with it. "After later," he said quietly. "First, his bicycle, then his omnibus."

What he did next was easy, inasmuch as there were always on hand more thugs than he needed, even during days of uproar in Trafalgar Square. It was merely a matter of delegating something far enough down the line for it ultimately to seem none of his doing at all. He had a way of saying mildly things that others championed with eager force; and often gave orders in an almost wheedling, poignant fashion, seeming to plead without much pragmatic grasp of things. He thus grafted the initiative onto others, letting his mind dawdle instead with the fact that, when he took a rest, he tended to take it in Dieppe, the very place where Sickert conveyed his ménage. Aware of Sickert's link with Alix, he decided Sickert was a useful man to know, especially if he could be dealt with off the premises, so to speak, although the British Prime Minister was as well known in Dieppe as in London—more so, in fact, owing to the nature of Dieppe's clientele: top drawer and well connected. Yes, Sickert would be useful later on, after the dust . . . later on, certainly, and he could be, what was the phrase, *vigorously induced* to serve his queen.

Sickert was not thinking of Lord Salisbury at all on that afternoon in 1888. It was late and he was longing for tea as he strolled down Maple Street and then turned right into Cleveland Street, but not before looking all the way to the other end, where a bunch of rough-looking characters were lounging against a wall. The area was going down, Sickert thought. It was time to move on, and never mind the place's honourable associations with Pre-Raphaelitism and eternity. Looking diagonally down the street, he paused, wondering which shop they were going to bother, but his mind was on Venice and the not-too-preposterous notion that he himself was a *literary* kind of painter, the painting equivalent to a belle-lettrist author. Then, to his amazement, he heard the manicured tones of Eton—or was it Oxford?—coming from these toughs. Had the street been noisier, he would not have picked up such languidly exaggerated diphthongs. A jape, he thought: a practical joke, and the actor in him, never far beneath the surface, began to guess and participate. Was this one of Eddy's quasi-brotherly escapades? Suddenly the well-spoken, loafing oafs began to shout at one another and a brawl began, soon filling the far end of Cleveland Street as customers and tradesmen came out to watch. At least the trouble was not at his end; Sickert could walk home and forget the whole thing, which was just as well as he had a headache and an awful sense of having failed Ellen, who had called him a man with no gift for honesty or fidelity.

Again he looked down toward the heaving mob, none of whom were cursing or yelling in exquisite accents. Uncouth profanity was all he heard (dark brown language he called it, and rather enjoyed it), and then, all of a sudden, he saw the street empty, cleared of all those who had come running. For some reason he began to worry about Eddy, who had been a frequent visitor of late, so off he went at what he thought was a brisk military clip to number fifteen. As he did so, two hansom cabs came round the corner from Tottenham Street, raced past him and drew up at his studio; then one moved along and crossed over to number six. Two rather well-dressed men in brown tweed went into his studio, while a portly man and a massive tall woman went down to the basement of number six. They looked, these four, like plainclothes police or nurses from some lunatic asylum.

When he should have run, he dwindled to a halt, mesmerized and appalled. Instead of going to see, he guessed, as if he were in no way involved. Could he have prevented it? He doubted it; the staged riot at the other end of the street had deprived him of both witnesses and aid. He was the only one watching when, first, the two husky men in tweed came out with Eddy between them, strongarming him forward as if he were a trespasser or a rioter. From Eddy's mouth came an awful sound, part scream, part bray, as if in some invisible way he were being disemboweled. When he saw the other couple dragging Annie up the steps, Eddy let out a different cry altogether, in a different register, more palpitating and hysterical. He cried her name and she his. In Sickert's head the known world seemed to split and rot. Annie was not screaming; she had winded herself by fighting her abductors, and all she could do, as they dragged her to the hansom, was beat with her lower arms against her own trunk, as if to punish herself for being taken. Those with Eddy shoved something into his mouth to stop his sobs, but his eyes picked up the lament, and Sickert, cold with shame, watched and watched, knowing it would be useless to intervene; he knew too that he would do himself no good. Where was Alice Margaret? Where was Marie Kelly? He looked for a third hansom to draw up, but nothing happened. The two cabs rattled off in opposite directions, and Sickert still heard Eddy's scream. The street was full of it, not an echo but the full-blooded thing: a cry from the heart and the poor, bludgeoned brain. He knew what it all meant. Eddy's days of love were over, at least with Annie Crook. His Queen and grandmother would scold him with her dreadful German temper squeezed to dithyrambic pitch, and then relent, provided he behaved himself—or misbehaved according to family tradition. Annie's thoughts were more for Alice Margaret than for herself, for once; Marie Kelly had taken her out shopping. Half an hour later, Annie would have been in the shop and Alice would have been in the basement with Marie, and perhaps Eddy too. Lord Salisbury's Cleveland Street spies had almost got it right.

Sickert never saw Eddy again, and that last apparition of the clown-white face with the gruesome curving scream was to haunt him many a night. Why had they waited three years? None of it made sense, but he had known nothing of Lord Salisbury's temporizing ways. The Prime Minister had lulled them. And he would wait for Marie Kelly, letting her percolate the various ways out of the London system, knowing that she would eventually show up again. Sickert needed a drink, several, and these he went and found at the City of Hereford pub, almost ready to vomit from what he had seen.

For some reason he did not understand, he did not go and check his studio until he had had several brandies and was too pickled to care. He knew that, quite soon, he would be called upon to do something to help or to impede. He waited at his window, watching for Marie and Alice to return, but they did not, and he knew that his world had ended. A vital piece of him had snapped, never to be repaired, never again to meddle in the lives of others. There were a dozen things he might have done. Why had he never carried a pistol? A big man, he might have impeded them, overturned the hansom cabs, made the horses bolt. Yet he did nothing, as if his role in all this had been decreed eons ago. Fair-weather friend was all that he had been. He had not even shouted or spoken. It was as if he had never been there, just as Marie Kelly the voluble and canny had not been there, and Alice Margaret, the partly deaf royal daughter. It was no use going to the police; he knew that much about the workings of Whitehall, and it was no use looking. On a nice afternoon he had irrevocably defined himself as one whose role had been to watch, in spite of all his interferences, and he felt as moldy and shabby as if someone had rubbed his entire face with a big rotten lettuce leaf. Sickert was debonair no longer; Sickert smelled, Sickert was not brave.

Chapter 9

When they hauled Annie through the big doors, she was almost unconscious, one of them having thumbed her throat hard just before she left the cab. Until then, she had been ready to make her mark, + or X , her signature, just so as not to offend them, one of whom smelled of mothballs, the other of wet heather. When she came to, she was being frogmarched through a vast green hallway full of screams and clanging pans. She smelled burning meat and wondered if she was in a butcher's shop. It was cold, but she thought she saw columns of steam rising. Perhaps it was a kitchen. There were

rolls of white paper, or were they bandages? Every now and
then a whirring sound came and went, followed by a long,
languorous *suck-suck* and there was the sound of laughter. People
in green masks walked past her, bearing laden buckets and pans
full of what looked like beef liver. She was going to be made to
cook, she could see it now, and it was a come-down from serving at Morgan's tobacconist's. Then they shoved her into another hallway, this one whitewashed and even noisier, with
windowless doors at wide intervals and an occasional wooden
bench. A buzzing, sawing sound came from behind several of
the doors, as if all that was locked in there was a certain univer-
sal noise, not human, yet not unwelcome.

"I want my babby," she whispered, unable to muster breath
as the fat man and the enormous woman haled along past the
doors and the sounds, digging their fingers and thumbs into her
arms. Then she smelled disinfectant, a creamier smell than ammonia, but could not establish where it came from. They thrust
her into a rusty little room with only a box to sit on, a tea chest
she thought, and stood alongside each other at the door, more
than blocking the doorway. She could hear clanking, rattling,
and screams again, as of someone small. Was this a place for
children? She wished she was back in her basement room again,
with Eddy, modelling for Sickert: anywhere but here. No one
came, no one went, and Annie began to feel the needs of nature.
They gave her a bucket and told her to get on with it. She did,
her mouth beginning to do an involuntary stammering twitch.
There was disinfectant in the bucket, something like whitewash; it was a workhouse, then, or an infirmary.

In fact it was Guy's Hospital, and across the hall from where
she sat a small confrontation was going forward. On the metal
table lay the body of a quite young man, poor and already
forgotten except by his sister, who stood looking at him. On the
other side of the table stood a tall, burly man with aggressive
eyes and a jowly face. He wore a brown smock of superior cut
and spoke with a slightly obscured rustic accent, as if he were
a market gardener who had come up in the world.

"For the sake of knowledge, madam," he was saying. "If the

dead are not allowed to help the living, how shall we get on? Do you agree?"

"Only if nothing be taken away," she said, her voice all congested trouble. "Nothing. Leave him intact."

"For the worms?"

"For me."

"I understand," he said heavily, "and so will you. I thank you for your understanding." With that he leaned over the cadaver, maneuvered a knife, and, barely grunting, began to cut. She did not look, vaguely aware of having consented to his exploring the body in this fashion. When she looked back, he had her brother's heart in his hands and seemed to be trying to fold it or compress it, and then with a shrug and a half smile stuffed it into the pocket of his smock. "For knowledge," he sighed, then had to catch her as she reeled and almost fell. Seated, she heard him say "I trust to your honour not to ruin me, madam." How had she known it was her brother's heart? She half expected the body to rise up from the table and follow its heart into the man's pocket. This was Gull of Guy's, the most famous vivisectionist of his day, so she and her brother had got off lightly. Or so Gull thought as he bowed and left her to it, the gaping cadaver and the dead-looking room with pulleys and weighing machines lolling in the draught. In a terrible access of grief and indignation, she hurled herself on the body of her brother, dead at only forty-seven, and bloodied her face while explaining. Dr. William Withey Gull had already crossed the hall, dismissed the male and the female thug, and fixed his gaze on Annie Elizabeth: another weeping woman, whom he then made as if to comfort, he the baker of live dogs, first patting her on the back where she sat on the tea chest with the bucket of her leavings by her, then tapping her on the knee. "Have a grape, Annie," he said. "We have much to talk about." From another pocket of his smock he withdrew a handful of black grapes, smiling to himself about the heart in the other one (had he been careless, he would have squashed his grapes). "No," she told him, "I'm not hungry."

"Wet your whistle," he said, proffering them again, having

labored on them exquisitely, hollowing the centers and loading them with hyoscyamine, his one concern being its slowness to act (slow for him, anyway). He himself had peeled the skins from other grapes to stitch back together around the poisonous ones. Tradition told him that hyoscyamine (henbane) should be decocted into the ear. Too messy, though. "Try one," he whispered to Annie. "Finest quality. Don't be shy. Just try one. You can have them all if you wish. Here." Unresisting, she blinked her tears away and sampled the first grape. It was good, although tart and a bit gritty. "How do you know my name?" He seemed to take forever to answer.

"We were expecting you," he said. "And we regret the rough-and-ready way in which we had to bring you here. It was an emergency. Do you remember Marie Kelly? Don't alarm yourself, please. Out shopping she was. Yes. Well," he went on improvising, mainly for mental exercise, "she had a slight mishap."

"My daughter was with her," Annie said from within an incandescent fog. "You can't mean—"

"Not a bit of it," Gull said, stretching his back and so easing his ample paunch. To Annie there seemed acres of it bisected by his gold watch chain, but it was receding from her. They were not taking her upstairs or along the hallway to where Marie and Alice Margaret awaited her, the worse for wear or— Two nurses entered the room and began to examine her while Gull stood, preparing to escort her out. He was having a busy day, but he was a law unto himself at Guy's, almost a legend; he had been a student here, had won all the prizes, and had now come home to roost, no longer discharging his duties as Lecturer on Physiology and Comparative Anatomy, but undertaking special enterprises, some of these for the Royal Family as Physician-in-Ordinary to Queen Victoria and regular physician to the Prince of Wales, Eddy's father. Not only was he a power in the land; he was one in the next world too. One of his favorite interests was a small asylum for twenty or so insane women, within Guy's Hospital itself: a madhouse within a human warehouse. None of his royal patients came here, of course; he tended them in the sumptuous bedchambers of Windsor Castle, or the Palace, but to him it was all one: berserk hags in canvas shifts or royal ones in silk under elaborate canopies. Humans, dogs. The body ached and broke down. The Gulls of the world intervened. No, there was only one Gull. He always told the truth to the dying—"Yes, you are dying. You have but a few hours. You are half dead already," but he had been known to slip a few guineas to the very poor when he saw that they were going to survive, almost as if to reward them for testing his prowess so well. He glared and glowered, but he saved lives, and these days, after what happened last October in Scotland, at his country retreat, he was even more sensitive to the flesh's frailty: walking in the garden, he had suffered a mild stroke that lowered him to one knee, but within minutes he had been able to walk to the house and announce the event with a slight slur in his speech. A powerful man, he had recovered speedily, but thenceforth began to shed his practice, saving himself for Senate work at the University of London and such special assignments as the Throne sent his way. "I have been warned," he liked to say. "The Furies are gathering. They mean to reward me with something I will not be able to treat. Let me be a hobbyist from now onward, please."

With a fresh heart in his pocket and an Annie in his charge, she already groggy, he seemed hardly an invalid, and he was not. It was just that he felt a little closer to the lugubrious bourne of the irrecoverable, to maladies that even a senior Mason such as he might not rectify. "I feel another man," he said. "I *am* another man. I must distinguish myself again now, if I intend to achieve anything further." He wanted to be an examinee all over again and be found outstanding, just to prove to himself that he was. He was seventy-two, and he wanted all that old applause anew, making him blush, the bargeowner's son who had made good, the youngest of eight, taught everything he knew at his mother's knee, and delightedly reciting a rhyme he had picked up:

If I was a tailor
I'd make it my pride

The best of all tailors to be;
If I was a tinker
No tinker beside
Should mend an old kettle but me.

Once again, as in 1837, he paused in front of Guy's for the first time, wondering whether to enter the front courtyard between the ironwork pillars of the gateway or through either of the adjoining entrances left and right, each flanked by a sentry-boxlike column. Damn it, he thought, a bargeman, Thomas Guy, founded this hospital, and here comes the son of a barge-owner to work himself to death in it. He strode in, noting the triangles and hemispheres that adorned the upper façades: mystical, Masonic emblems urging him in and on. As he walked into the courtyard, he murmured "If I was a tailor" in full, then recited the Lord's Prayer to cover his bets. It had been an astringent, sunny December day, dedicated to the promotion of intelligence; stimulated by the weather, he saw himself advancing upon the putrefying inmates of Guy's as a tender scourge, a soundless snowstorm of caustic chemicals, willing almost to kill in order to cure. At home, this being Friday, his mother would be cooking fish, and rice pudding, for both of which all of a sudden he yearned.

"You know," he was telling the recumbent, insensible Annie's head, shoving the rods home, "we had a strict Christian upbringing, by George yes. Never missed a saint's day. My mother always wore black during Lent. And she fed us on rice pudding and fish on Fridays. It wasn't an easy life, my dear, and I'm sure you know about lives not being easy. You had a good ride. You will be calmer after this, and want less." He still heard the voice of Lord Salisbury, urging him to do what was necessary. "Nothing drastic now. Just use your own discretion."

"I never use anyone else's," he had answered. "Fear not, sir, I have the very place, comfy as Red Riding Hood's cottage."

"No physical modifications," Salisbury had said, knowing his man well, though he might not have believed it about the heart in the pocket of his smock, still there as he lobotomized Annie

Elizabeth Crook even while Sickert was drowning his sorrows at the City of Hereford.

"I used to want to go to sea," he was telling Annie's brow as Salisbury's voice half chidingly insisted "Nothing outlandish, dear fellow. The whole situation has to quieten down, and then it may be appropriate—if you think it so—or if not. Use your judgement." Salisbury hated the cocksure directness of surgeons, though Gull, he reminded himself, was a physician, not a surgeon; he specialized in paraplegia, in ailments of the spinal cord and abscesses of the brain. Salisbury too had been to sea, all the way to Africa and Australia, after his father had withdrawn him from Eton, where he was being bullied so much that he couldn't get any work done. While at sea, he had read the works of the early Fathers of the Church, having always excelled in theology. In South Africa, stuck at the Cape waiting for a ship to Australia, he had tried to go up Table Mountain, but had had to come down when he was halfway up, with a ferocious headache and a pulse of 120. Never mind, he had always hated "scenery," much as he had always hated aggressive climbers such as Gull. Once, when Gull was tooting away about having won the gold medal with his M.D., Salisbury had decided to shock him.

"*You* had a Fellowship at All Souls, Prime Minister?"

Yes, Salisbury told him, he had, although at the time he thought he would never get it. "There were two vacancies and seventeen candidates, six of whom were formidable. The chance against me was three and a half to one. Why, Sir William, since no marquess had ever been elected, my real chance I rated at seven to one against. Amazing, when I look back on it."

"They all," said Gull in his tempestuous, insistent way, "had Firsts?" Authentic language of the parvenu, Salisbury thought. "Actually"—he smiled—"*I* took a Fourth. An honorary one, on medical grounds. My doctors wanted me out of Oxford as soon as possible, so I took my degree after only two years—the so-called nobleman's privilege. I was much happier roaming about the countryside looking for botanical specimens, with a sandwich or two. I was once arrested as a poacher until a search of my person and specimen tin brought no rabbits to light."

"*I* could give you some specimens," Gull had said with a lugubrious yawn. "I too was a boy botanist, with a tin."

"No thank you," Salisbury told him. "Prime Ministers are not allowed to accept specimens."

Usually their conversation, of which there was coming to be a tedious amount, was sterner, mostly because Salisbury and he were serious men, the power behind the throne, or like the curious power in Greek myth that told the gods what to do. The Napoleonic thrust of Gull would always deliver a full-blooded version of any hint that Salisbury left dangling; the man was brilliant, dangerous, and quite without conscience. In 1888 he was complaining about having lost some little shreds of memory, thanks to his stroke, but he was quite capable, as he put it, of clinically discouraging the Annies and the Maries. "Although not necessarily or desirably all in the same place," he said. "Separate quarters seems advisable."

"*When* you have the Kelly woman," said Salisbury. "She will turn up, have no fear."

If he had read his Gull carefully, and he was not as good at this as his wife, he would have seen. Here was a man who had just relinquished a famous Brook Street practice, who was tapering things off, and had only his work at the Senate to keep him busy. Nonetheless he had an entree to several hospitals and asylums and had already served Her Majesty well. He was no stranger to discreet abortions and opportunistic sequestrations; indeed, if he had known about Annie's pregnancy in time . . . When a zealot went downhill a bit, and a boaster to boot, he usually made a fetish of going too far. So Gull would more than accomplish what Her Majesty had insisted be done. Having ousted the Royal Physician, Sir William Jenner, when the Prince of Wales had been struck down by typhoid, he had stayed top dog ever since 1871. Pushy, Salisbury thought him. Thereafter, Jenner had been merely a second royal opinion. Ah well, such miracles are wrought by Masons, he thought; it is the nature of society to be swayed by the potent societies within it. And it was Gull who had first said something about Sickert's usefulness, calling him "This busybody painter fellow—we must save him, save a thought for him, for he has the strings of the marionettes in his very hands. He is not only with them, and has been so for some years. He is of them. I think we might gratify him even further."

With two knurled rods stuck into her eye sockets above her eyeballs and beyond, Annie Elizabeth was unlikely ever to hear talk so genial as this. She would come round, of course, but sea-changed into something dull and serviceable—hardly a fit wife for a prince, if indeed there were any degrees of fitness worth considering for a woman who could neither read nor write and had strayed so far from her native mental heath as to upset the Queen herself. Gull sighed, and with a self-conscious, pudgy flourish, applied an ether pad to the slightly stirring Annie, almost as if wiping her face. The pad rested against her mouth and nose, a gentle, thorough thing, and then he raised it. Now he tried on her another of his so-called transorbital manoeuvres, humming dully, the only snag being that, near the fibers he wished to sever, there ran some large blood vessels. What he did in his improvisatory and callous way was to draw some blood from the patient's arm and then inject this into the fibers. The blood was good because it was viscous, and the brain itself tolerated hemorrhage well. Injection of the blood split the tissues along the fibers rather than cutting across them. It was preferable. When Gull did this, he felt he was discovering America, and heaven and hell as well, alone in the misty dawn of science, like someone riding a bicycle whose whirr could be detected without the cyclist's having been seen. Only when he meant to did he shove the rods in deep, far beyond the frontal lobes, deep into the midbrain and the basal ganglia. When he used the mallet he had to be careful; sometimes the bony orbit was thin and could be penetrated with a shove of the hand. When this happened, the patient did not regain consciousness.

At the very least he was making her more tractable, of course, scrambling her mind, her brain, enough to keep her from such complex acts as selling sweeties or tobacco. Anyone more enamored than he of the little bright pouches of lyricism within the human head would have been unable thus to rummage about almost at random in her brain, but he had done this dozens of times by now, for one cause or another (sometimes even the cause of unpremeditated experiment—doing something he knew would be a failure). And there had been nothing clandestine about it, any more than now: he was a law and no one questioned him, Knight of the Royal Victorian Order, neither sister nor nurse nor colleague. In the open he murdered the brains of those who did not fit someone's notion of society, so in a way he was a reverse saint, despoiling life for banal reasons, pushing people over the edge far enough for him with some plausibility to give them bogus certificates of insanity and a padded room. Gull was the silencer, one of life's more questionable addicts, a lover of the half light and in-between states, an infernally wound-up doer of lofty commands. Hippocratic oath be damned; his Queen was not Hippocrates, and he had taken an oath to Victoria and to his fellow-Masons.

So it mattered not in the least to him that, with even so little as a half-thirty-secondth of an inch's motion, he destroyed in this humble woman's head a memory of bluebells, perhaps, or that she reverted to the most uncouth tastes of her childhood, such as the longing for a jam butty, which was jam smeared on bread and doubled over to make a hollow wing of bread, or a chip butty, which was fried potatoes neatly arranged crisscross (or all lengthwise) between two slices, or even a bread butty, which was bread between bread, homogeneous acme of the semidestitute diet. Or, if not that, she might be craving toffee apples with the merest pinpoint of brain matter, cherishing some game with top and whip, some atavistic memory from an afternoon spent in an old laundry basket, her first feel at the slippery belly of a minnow. He knew the records of a life lay couched in there, in unspeakable casual radiance, invisible yet final, but he ploughed through them all, as if reviving the mode of ancient Greek ploughing, *boustrophedon,* that had lent its ponderous name to a fashion of writing in which alternate lines went left-right and right-left (to save the hand the chore of moving leftward to start a new line?). The hand is not a ploughhorse, after all. The reader had to be patient and adept, the problem being not to get intercepted while moving the eyes west-east by something moving east-west. Thus, perhaps, give or take a few, the scrawls in Annie's brain.

As well as a heart in one pocket, he should have had a brain in the other, for coat of arms, for the most heraldic version of himself, but he was untidy and only grateful that as he plied his ghastly trade, his own body remained intact, apart from the stroke.

Yet he was a physician rather than a surgeon, a treater and a reasoner rather than a delver and slicer. It was simply that he knew where to go and had a captive population of the poor, none of whom had any rights once under his hands. Convicts, the mad, the poor, all made grist for his devil's mill, especially now that he had given up his practice and was free to move about the human body according to whim and fancy, severing and wrecking in the very spirit of the berserk demiurge, say Goya's Saturn, not so much devouring his creatures as blighting them. That he needed a thrill this keen was beyond doubt. The Annies had lived their elementary lives for many years before coming under his ruinous spell, but all the time he had been lurking there, waiting for them, a truer destroyer of delight than one who guaranteed death, whatever that automatic anonym might be. He was Gull, devoted husband and father, burning to live with a gemlike flame until the next stroke. He had to serve his queen, his prime minister, but he also reveled in the helpless pliability of human stuff, its openness to harm and hurt.

Anyone wondering could have gone back to his pronouncements, written or otherwise, on such matters as vivisection, on which he testified before the Royal Commission in 1875 and published a sixteen-page article in *The Nineteenth Century* in 1882: "The good we may obtain," he argued, "to ourselves by physiological experiment should outweigh the immorality of the process" and "Our moral susceptibilities ought to be bribed and silenced by our selfish gains . . . *Baking dogs alive! How horrible and disgusting!* would be a natural exclamation. What purpose could there be in anything so cruel? This we shall see directly." He had never made a secret of his flagrant views, but no one in the profession ventured to take him on, perhaps because, as Salisbury in his smug way noted, an upstart's capacity for outrage and revenge easily exceeded the mellow sense of injustice to be found in those who, like kings with their divine right, came naturally to power and deployed it with civilized ease. Salisbury never thought about how arbitrary it was, back in the good old days, for a king to snatch land and hand it out in irrevocable parcels to his cronies. That even the doughtiest and most famous wielders of power began as pirates and freebooters, he never took the time to remember; but he should have when he saw the rabble in Trafalgar Square—Republicans and Socialists—for he was witnessing the age-old longing to have landed estates, huge hunks of the irredeemable chthonic handed out like slices of Bakewell tart. Deep down he wanted that rabble not to prevail, or to come even near his exalted monarchy. He was not only a Conservative, he was a custodian, a lightning rod of power, keeping the poor in the same ghetto as ever, where a Gull could slice them up for fun or practice, or for gain, with heroic impunity. If Gull thought of himself as the agent of something sanitary, Salisbury tended to think of himself as an archbishop *manqué*.

When poor Annie was done, and the thing like a narrow nutcracker removed from her forehead, and her head restored to its unthrown-back position, and all her ordinary joys made null with simple puncture, Gull gave her a pat on the cheek before she came partly round, said something about a brave Scottish lass ("It's to Killiecrankie we gae ourselves"), told the nurses "I'll sign the certificate tomorrow," and waddled eagerly back across the hall to look at the heart in his pocket, none the worse for wear. He wanted to know how bad the necrosis was. He loved tissue and muscle, flesh and skin, and felt like someone reading poetry while all the rest of the world read prose. He and Sickert had this in common.

No one lobotomized Eddy, but his father thought him lobotomized to begin with, so he did not mind the abuse heaped upon his son by Queen Victoria, who slammed him with such words as *imbecile, fathead, dolt,* and *swine,* none of this worrying Eddy more than routine—groveling praise irks the Deity. Indeed,

Eddy felt rather lucky to have been rescued in so summary a fashion, saving him from making painful statements and having ghastly, heartrending scenes with Annie and Alice, who had come to know him as a father. Alice was developing with granitic slowness; she was deaf, like Eddy's mother, like Eddy himself in part. It was a time for lying low; Victoria, he could sense, was angry not on political grounds—because he had imperiled the Realm, et cetera—but *because he had not confided in her,* consulted her, allowed her to veto what she had now quashed. Little did he know that she had Gull behind her, the pistol who functioned as a cannon (as they all knew, save Eddy), or that his Catholic, illiterate wife was now fitted to do nothing at all save moan and twitch, a poor creature this side of epilepsy. Oh, he sobbed and fumed, but he stayed where they had put him, under virtual house or palace arrest. Something soggy about Eddy always came to the fore in emergencies; his deepest emotions were optional, all of which suggested to Salisbury and his cronies that he might make a very manageable king indeed, should he be put on. So Eddy spent his next few weeks staring down equerries and planning another sortie into the brothel in Cleveland Street, for his homophilic needs had not died with the kidnapping. Several times he had asked about Annie and Alice, only to be told that they were both being cared for *befitting their station,* a statement he did not review too closely. He did not know that Marie Kelly had escaped with his daughter. All he knew, inasmuch as he knew anything, was that his working-class wife had a *superior* station awaiting her, and his child a more suitable nanny than the worldly Marie.

It was time to be a prince again, at least to go through the motions of it. Cambridge did not start up until October, but Netley would come and get him sooner or later, he was sure of that, and then all would be almost as well as it had been. It did not occur to him how badly the poor were treated in his precious England, or how severely, in that massive group, women were dealt with just because they were women—vessels of slop, as he had heard his father refer to them, whereas the tonic tone of the time was to be closed, sealed, upright, dry, and aloof. Women, he had been taught, were a disease, and one he rather enjoyed catching; but he could see that his own choices were unwise, to say the least.

One hesitates to call Gull headstrong, but he went ahead with little thought to the remedying of his own condition. Had he had a hemorrhage up in Killiecrankie, or a blood clot? Either way, he saw himself as having received a rebuke, a curse; the curve thence was downward, he thought, and fast. Anticoagulation was unknown, and he was right. He did have time, and indeed superlative occasion, to interfere with the mass and atoms of others, but he wanted all he did to have that gold-medal gloss, a Promethean stature. It was too late to become more distinguished than he already was, but it was never too late to achieve, in private, some new intensity, some unrepeatable grandeur. All the time, the situation was becoming more and more propitious. Not only had his fellow Masons called him out of what might have struck others as stoical retirement; his Queen and Premier had put their trust in him to rectify an embarrassing mess, about whose causes he had known little enough, apart from the fact that Sickert meddled and Eddy fornicated and the mother and the father hardly spoke. It was enough for him to know that the state of the nation was at risk, as it had been when the Prince of Wales had contracted typhoid and he, Gull, has risen to the top of the medical ladder by healing him. So, penultimately, this little service to his Queen, a cleansing of the royal stables; he asked no more.

Chapter 10

When Annie came fully to on a rough mattress, she was not quite sure who she was, but she knew she had a three-year-old child, for whom she began an instant howl, unable to speak but sensing that vacancy, that hole, in her remnant being. Her cry, contralto before her throat began to work and cleared itself, became higher and higher in pitch, powered by fuller and fuller lungs, but no one came, no one even looked her way. Her head was pounding, her eyes smarted, and her eye sockets throbbed. On she screamed, but only as one among several. She was one of nineteen now, not all of them screaming, but hating the condition in which they had been put, mostly by Gull. When she paused, to gather breath and look about her, she felt thick-headed and suspended, nothing like the woman who had gone in there only hours earlier. And it did not come back to her, where she had been when kidnapped, or what had happened to Eddy. She thought only of her Alice and could not remember where Alice had been. Where had she, Annie, been taken *from?* No memory of Sickert came to her, or even of Marie Kelly. When she tried to speak, her lips would not obey her, and she seemed to be making involuntary blurting noises like those of someone having a fit. Still no one came. She realized she was strapped down, as if she were a threat, and then came to the recognition that her mind was working after all, but slowly. Now she remembered the fat man and the enormous woman who had come to get her. She remembered the hansom cab, the horses, but not Gull or the grapes.

Next thing, someone with her mind on something else came by and roughly slipped her bonds, then left. She was in a long, dank room with no chairs, no tables, only two beds, on one of which she had been lying. There was no window, no door, and some of the other women in there were pointing at her and laughing. One of them came up, tapped her, and shrieked as she sprang backward. Annie felt at her face, which seemed encrusted (as it was, with blood), and began picking at the crust, looking at its maroon hue and tasting it with revulsion. She had never heard of Guy's Hospital, but she had heard of workhouses, so she made the obvious assumption. After all, she had had her baby in a workhouse; she remembered that. She tried to connect memory with memory, but found nothing but loose ends, nothing to connect with; she felt at her breasts, her stomach, her loins, all of them still there, but sensing a woodenness in her hands as she did so, and sensing too that her hands were not moving as fast as her mind would like them to. Little that she knew it, this was the way she was always going to be. William Withey Gull had worked his obscure miracle upon her, and England was presumably the safer for it.

Now she felt able to cry for "My babby, my babby," but the filthy-looking women in there just laughed and made baby sounds as if they knew only too well what she was going through. They had survived it. Her head was full of light. She felt dazzled without, however, needing to blink. Her jaw seemed wrongly anchored and her mouth did not seem to close correctly. When she walked, she skewed, and when she took a deep breath she felt a neat, clawing pain in her left chest. Henceforth, she would be direct, practical, and uninspired, not that different from what she used to be, except for one thing: Gull had cut the effusiveness out of her, the gaiety that always preceded whatever attitude she formed about someone—the thing that Eddy had loved in her from the first and had been unable to damp down, whatever he said or did, in London or Dieppe. Whether or not she remembered things from long ago no one could tell, she being real and therefore immune to all guesswork save the farthest reaches of narratorial conjuring. No one was taking notes on her, observing her as only a beloved object can be observed, which is to say that her life became one of the most lost things in the universe: beyond her own ken, or concern, and inaccessible to anyone else.

Back in the gloom of what was in fact a cellar, there was indeed a door, but she did not see the peephole in it, at which from time to time several expensively coated people came to peer, making surprised or approving sounds. She was the only one on her own, easy to pick out; for the most part, the others huddled together and made brief sorties toward her. All the women wore canvas shifts with big numbers on front and back: Gull's Girls, they were called, 1 through 20, brought here from all parts of London to be made different and/or to be studied further. Gull had certified all of them as insane, whatever their true condition both before and after treatment, and he often thought how wonderful it was that one man should have at his disposal so casually run a clinic, for both scientific and social convenience. That the whole place needed fresh whitewash did not occur to him, nor that whatever hygiene it had was primitive. He thought only of the intactness of the little congregation, as he called it, and, when he promenaded through, felt the family man all over again. Whatever crimes these women had committed, they bore their lobotomies rather well, even trying to curtsey to him when he arrived, although apprehensively shielding their heads with their hands. Sometimes they vomited on him or spat, and for that he had them belted to rings in the wall. Sometimes he took one of them away again for another bout with the leucotomes, but that was unusual; usually he got it right at the first try and the women were no longer troublesome. Indeed, those who remembered his procedures liked him too much, actually fawning, and he thought of several eminent social hostesses whom he would like to install here after first puncturing *their* brains. That would raise the standard of small talk in Brook Street and elsewhere.

Slowly, Annie became used to these squalid surroundings, to the damp, the noise, the stench, and the big stone slab, always wet, on which their food was put, soup in the white bucket, bread and turnips in the gray one. Each of them had a big tin mug to scoop with. There was no talk, not really, although the basic units of talk, uncoordinated, could be heard nonstop. No one seemed able to finish a remark. The talk was all interjections and echolalic raves, and sometimes the only way the women had of expressing themselves was to shuffle all together from one wall to the other at the far end. Annie had lost her high-kneed, chopping gait, once a thing jaunty and fetching. She now shuffled like the rest, rather more slowly, in fact, and so collided with them as they turned, like a wave bouncing, and came back. They walked right through her as if she were not there, and their smiles were not for her but into vacancy, their true dimension.

Justifiably raving against men and their brutal ways, Marie Kelly had made a beeline with the bewildered Alice Margaret to the very place she had come from, Providence Row Women's

Refuge, run by the nuns of the convent. It sounded like the right place to head for, but of course she had gone there by foot in a state of shuddering nerves. She had no idea if Sickert had played her false. She just knew that, dragooned away or not, Eddy was the cause. How easy it would have been to have himself conveniently marched away from the scene of his most recent disgrace, which he wanted to be quit of anyway. When a man forgets to come and celebrate his child's third birthday, something is wrong. So she told herself, marching toward the East End from the West End, as if the whole of London were on guard against her, ready to inform and seize. The nuns had heard it all before, they loved to see a child brought in, and clearly Marie was in such a demented state she would have to be found room for. She was back where she began, but encumbered, as they eventually would report to Bellord, who had offices in Cleveland Street. Bellord told Sickert where Kelly and the child were, and then it was up to Sickert to do something or nothing. He knew, as Marie did not, that Lord Salisbury paid rent to Perkins and Bellord for his house in Fitzroy Square, a link that might or might not yield extraneous information by way of everyday gossip. The link was enough to make Sickert even more nervous, of course, but it was no use blundering over to the convent until he had a plan. Would the two of them be better off there than in either of the rundown rooms he rented in the East End, to draw lowlife in—mainly prostitutes of bent physique and limited trade? No, the convent was better for Alice Margaret, he was sure of that. But where was Annie? The child needed her mother, not the volatile, grasping Kelly.

For as long as he lived, he would regret having done nothing to impede the kidnaping, and then having gone to drink away the memory of it. Tall and strong, he might at least have got in the way enough for Annie to make a run for it. Had he known her much altered condition, he would have been even more chagrined. Gull had wasted no time. He had actually got to work while Sickert was getting drunk, but that was something Sickert was never to know, not in detail. It was as well; he might have gone into a total funk of ineradicable shame, something he felt badly enough as it was. He was still on the board, so to speak, his moves guessable-at (Dieppe, Bath, where he had studios), but in no condition to play himself to maximum advantage. And his moves would soon be more limited still.

As for Annie, after a much broken night in the kind of surroundings that even she, of workhouse experience, was not accustomed to, she saw the dawn in an almost trancelike condition, full of feelings that tried to surface to her mouth but fell back neutered: wool-gathering, that was the word. Only old women. Not she. Then who? What? In a place like this? For what crime? Babies. Baby crime, it was. Where were these women's babies then? All be out and away soon. Back to daffodils, no doubt. Where the gamekeeper let the birds perch on the end of his gun. The treetops curled over together and made a roof. There had been a baby, of what name? Headache. Not a name. A hurt. You came here to be hurt. Warm water with potato peelings in it and bread with green corners. Had she come from better? She must have. She had been. Oh, she had been. Now she was a was. Would somebody come for her? Only to hurt. A man with a knitting needle. That much. This was not Scotland, still clear in mind, heather and crags. Nothing like this could be in Scotland. Nor was it in that village she had lived in, the bluebells. It was not a where. Vestigial thought could not help her, even though, as she tried to think consecutively, she felt things drowning, but shoved back down again, to where all died. She wondered if she had died and this was the punishment for the life she had lived. What had the life been like? Had it really been hers?

Sickert had an unsatisfactory interview with the nuns, who told him to leave well alone what even they could not understand. The child was welcome to room and board. Kelly would work as before, a skivvy. He would do his best to sell some paintings, he said, and they did not answer him, whereas Kelly, in the brief talk allowed her, could not shut up, reviling him and telling him never to come back. "All your flaming fault," she yelled. "All we need is help from men. Women are women, and men is what kills them off. All the time." Alice Margaret hugged him, however, and laboriously asked about her mother, about whom he knew nothing.

He said yes and took his leave, heartbroken late in the game, resolved to do right, but powerless, knowing now that he was too involved to be left out of the reckoning, whenever it came. He was no spectator, watching love triumph but a semi-pander, an arranger, an interferer. He said a private, candid thank you that the age of torture was past, but was it? He had much to reveal, even at the hands of the foul-looking pair who had come to Cleveland Street on that atrocious day: the heavy-set man in the dark suit and bowler hat, the enormous woman with exposed muscular arms heavy as billiard-table legs. He had not done an Affable Arthur since the event, and he probably would not. Nonetheless, the actor in him made his legs and arms move as that dreadful two had moved, and he found himself naming them, against his will, as the only way to defuse their horror, the ghastly bloated quality of the threat they brought. Ogres of righteousness, they haunted his daydreams, and he knew that one day he would have to deal with them, with—in vain he rummaged through the German of his childhood—Slerch and Senna, Slerch the muscle-bound man with caterpillar eyebrows, Senna the costive-looking woman with the truncheon umbrella. Where did they find such ogres? Of those who had ferreted out Prince Eddy, he had not a thought. Eddy was a goner, he knew, but the Eddys of the world always floated back to the surface, to tell, to be lionized, to open somebody else's trouser buttons.

Sickert had reached such a point of impotent despair that he no longer cared what he did, or why. It was no use painting people, urging them around on a palette and daubing them into places they had never thought of going. Beyond color there was another realm, of incalculable deeds, where lives fell apart and lovers saw each other for the last time. Not even a night at the music hall could clear his mind. Ellen was back with her family, as he had known all along she would be, and all he had left was the need to sell some work, soon.

Which he did, but not as he had intended. When he got back to Cleveland Street from the nunnery he entered stripping his clothes away with almost hysterical relief (it was hot), only to be brought up short by the heavyset man sitting there patiently on the rocking chair, moving ever so slightly as if blown by an indoor wind. The man stood, not tall, but stocky without being portly. His eyes glared into Sickert and past him, the pearl in his cravat caught the mellow indoor light, neither of the hands moved forward. Did he, the man asked without preamble, have a sketch or painting of one Marie Kelly? He had heard that such a thing existed—not that Marie Kelly interested him in the least. The work had been extolled to him by a fellow doctor with rooms in Brook Street, like his own. So this was how Lord Salisbury went about his business. Not even getting Netley to come and steal it. The point of the visit was not the painting, it was to tell Sickert that the eye of God was upon him already. Without flickering, he said yes, it was somewhere here, and he unearthed one of his sketches of Annie, mainly chiaroscuro and browns. Five guineas, the man said, still without introducing himself. "Any others?" "I'll look in the mess," Sickert told him. "My card," Gull said, then reached forward and seized a fold of cheek flesh between finger and thumb and waggled it, much as a headmaster might with an erring boy.

Sickert had heard of Gull, the famous saver of princes, but was wholly unprepared for his physical impact; he was a man sheathed in suit, immaculately turned out, but with a seething quarrel in his burly face, in the eyes a look of staggering arrogance. Sickert had no idea where those hands had recently been, with what, but he sensed in the man something overbearing and masterful. It was not that he was intuiting the doctor with the heart in his smock pocket; he was detecting the Napoleonic self-assurance of the man, his utter imperviousness to criticism. He was the best, the best-known, and no longer human. He was one of the Olympians, much more famous than even Sickert wanted to be (yet), and he had nothing to say to painters. He shuffled through the stacked-up canvases, grunting and fidgeting, but said never a word. "We shall meet again, Mr. Sickert," he said with gruff formality, and left with the drawing of Annie Crook. Had he noticed? How could he know? It was the only sketch of Annie he had made, and the paintings he had given to Eddy, although not to keep. So they were after Kelly. It made sense. But why Gull? What had Gull to do with it? Gull, he did not know, was not an observer of faces so much as a piercer of skulls, and he had not really seen Annie's face. For a man whose practice was no more, the Pudding Club was an interesting diversion. He dismissed his cab and walked round the corner to Fitzroy Square.

Why, Sickert was wondering, didn't I make him pay? Funk and panic. Why didn't he ask where Kelly was? No doubt he already has a good idea; these people always do. Only if she were in Australia or Mesopotamia would she have a chance. Was he looking for the child too? Poor Alice, caught up in the web of violence, had little chance to be a child. Clearly, other people than Gull were scurrying about London doing the hunting. Gull had shown up at 15 Cleveland Street only to show him, Sickert, he was not going to get off as lightly as that. It was Salisbury's way of showing *his* hand. It was also, he presumed, a way of saying We have her, she has been sequestered at a high level, and she is not going to come out. Could she be at Sandringham, or Windsor, he wondered, or in Victoria's retreat on the Isle of Wight? His distance from the crude and brutish truth did him credit, of course; and so did his feeling that, if the Establishment were going to hold on to Annie, then surely they should reunite mother and daughter. Could not even Eddy, the scapegoat, insist on that? On that, even if on nothing else? With all his heart he wished he had stuck to painting and worked hard at his marriage. A few tears fell, then more, and he let his grief plunge out, as on so many subsequent occasions, mortified by the insolence of accident and the dumb, material nature of cause and effect. Into his red kerchief he shoved his brow, almost as if trying to rub the tears home, and not away. He resolved to sell as many paintings as he could, for however little, for Kelly and Alice, and for Annie too should she reappear from the clutching bosom of the Royal Family.

He had no idea that Gull had paused on his way to the Prime Minister's house to buy half a pound of black grapes at a fruiterer's, to restore his vigor and supply the minerals he too easily lost. The difference between Gull grapes—not only sedative but analgesic and antispasmodic: *three good things,* he thought—and grapes untampered with made him smile. The further idea of hollowing a grape and loading it with enough hyoscyamine to kill (or with any other poison at his command), and then sewing it back together with human hair, struck him as cozy and original. It was as if he had discovered a new life form that would love him for having coaxed it, fiendish and fragile, out of Creation's night.

Chapter II

Sickert was still struggling, though he had powerful and imposing connexions in both England and France. What he lacked was money, otherwise he would probably have gone and bought the house he fancied in Dieppe. Now he had handed Gull a sketch ostensibly of Mary Kelly; could the enigmatic doctor of herculean ambition be a genuine art-lover after all? Like the Prime Minister? What Sickert was tempted to do, as if to fuse his public and private maneuvering, was to send Marie Kelly and Alice Margaret off to Ramsgate, on the south coast, where Ellen was. This would perhaps give her and Sickert something in common, something that might bring them back together. But he doubted it: Ellen understood him too well and always lifted her nose from what she called his "plebeian" friends. Buried in the general frappé of her personality, there was a wild streak that ogled free love and fancied breast-feeding other people's babies, but you had to catch it fast when you sensed it, and lure it into the open, then fan or lick it into life before her ancestors clamped down on her again. So far, Ellen had refused to sink money into a house in Dieppe, or anywhere else outside England, much as she had liked the idea; if he had bought one, she would have consented to live in it, playing the grande dame, or the half-pint belle. A better idea was to ask her if she would care to receive summer visitors—it was almost May, and surely people became more receptive the better the weather became? It was time for things to go right: no more kidnapping. He was sure that Eddy had his Annie stowed away safely somewhere in the grounds of some castle or other, gathering flowers, learning to read or write, drinking afternoon tea. Was it a hopeless dream? Sickert believed in lovers in the most abstract, German way; they evinced God's basic humanity, His aberrant tenderness, the side that did not guarantee to kill every human born. He was not looking for divine intervention, but for a little spasmodic favoritism on the deity's part, and, if not that, then a little slip in the divine hauteur, a flicker of incompetence such as one found in the best of people.

But his timing was somewhat off. Two weeks later, as Ellen replied saying she *might* be induced to sit the child and her nanny under her umbrella down in Ramsgate ("The season has hardly begun yet, but everybody else seems to be here; why not two more for a while?"), the royal cabal of Eddy, Alix, Victoria, and Bertie decided it was time to inspect the three-year-old child under proper circumstances, so Slerch and Senna went forth again, properly briefed, to bring Alice and Marie in. They got Alice, but not Marie, who had seen them coming and hidden herself behind the altar. The nuns were unhelpful—after all, this was England against Catholicism—and bowed to the letter empowering them. Alice cried, but that was nothing new, and off they went to Windsor, leaving behind them (until the nuns assaulted it with carbolic) an odd scent of mothballs and tobacco. En route, little Alice got the birthday she had missed: just a few simple wooden toys and a rather royal-looking doll based, perhaps, on Alix, having the same long mournful face and big noble forehead. Thus, as the lanes and fields swam by, Alice got the full benefit of their simple side, neither Slerch nor Senna (Arnold and Hetty Drury, truth told) being that bad, but zealots of performance whose sheer physical bulk had suggested to Victoria that they would be hard to knock over or dislodge.

They had not been briefed to drown Alice in a keg of malmsey, or just to lose her in the East End (which would have been easy), but simply to bring her, preferably with the Kelly woman, who had already scuttled away from the convent into the deep East End, certain of finding a bed, a niche, but cursing royal whim. She was convinced that they now had Annie and were staging a reunion under proper auspices. She saw herself as utterly unneeded, which was all right, but why searched for, then? It was she, not Alice, who would go into the Thames on a dark night. As she understood things, and she was constantly having to make uneducated guesses at royal caprice, it made no difference either way: drown Alice and her mother, they would want no survivor to tell. Or set them up in secret style, in Southern Rhodesia, say, and they would not want a survivor to tell about that either. They had nannies galore, they did not need a Marie Kelly; what she could not count upon was their good will. With everything settled, it did not necessarily follow that they would leave her alone. Indeed, with a good outcome in prospect, she was a bigger threat than before; and it was at that point she reconciled herself to prostitution, if she had to. It was no good hiding out with nuns or Sickerts, or tethering herself to a child. An awful hell opened up of exposed loins conjoined into something like seaweed with a thousand hairy animal tails lolling forth, and she almost shrieked, but it would have to be. If only Sickert, her fancy man, had had real means; but a toff without a bank was a toff manacled. If only the nuns had shown a little more gumption and fitted her out with a habit; she would have gone through the motions, she might even have taken the veil, properly instructed. There was always room for an obscene book or two in a nunnery, or an unusual implement. She wasn't born yesterday, but the nuns and Sickert were. So, even on the run as she was, she mentally reviewed the names of the women she had come to know in the East End—Nichols, Siffey, and Stride—and vowed to throw in her lot with them, wretched as their lot so often was: gin, beer, bread and potatoes, and a good singsong at the pub in between bouts of vomiting and sex. After a while, she reasoned, whores (like nuns) all looked the same;

indeed, of the ones she knew, though not that well, Rose Mylett was Lizzie Davis and Martha Tabram was alias Turner and Annie Siffey was alias Chapman. And, she smirked as she hurried along, face down, wasn't Mary Kelly also Marie Jeanette Quelle-y? It would never come to that. She aimed for a certain public house, The Britannia at the corner of Dorset and Crispin Streets, known to regulars as Ringer's because of Mrs. Ringer who ran it. Even the pubs had aliases here. She would have been amazed to have known that Sir William Gull now had a sketch of Annie that he thought was one of Marie Kelly and that, because of him, Annie Crook had virtually no human face.

Yielded up to her royal hosts, Alice fell silent, even in the presence of Eddy, who limited himself to a combination of bow and strut, walking up to her and then crouching as if to speak but saying nothing. On the way, she had moaned now and then to Slerch and Senna, unresponding if asked "Are you comfy?" and unable to tell them that she had a full bladder. They had a potty (Alix's idea) for her and emptied it out of the window as the cab made its way through the thickening greens of England. All Alice saw when she stepped out of the cab was a lot of bulk near the ground, trews and long dresses, but she could see that the lawn they stood on was sunken; even she sank into it. Alix broke the ice, taking her hand, even while thinking *My forehead, my chin, whatever they say,* and taking her apart, instantly noting that the girl heard poorly and therefore did not respond. She had a battery of utterances, none of which, however, anybody could provoke into being. I too am deaf, Alix brooded, as the small finlike hand made a slight plucking contact with hers. It is like walking a puppy. Already the potential nannies had lined up at the far side of the lawn, and, as the Queen and her son withdrew, having graced the occasion, they all walked across to Alice and Alix in a broken line, each intent on ministering to the child. Alix, however, shooed them away, made the child look her full in the eyes, and asked "Your mother, do you miss your mother?" Alix knew only that the mother was ill, in the care of Dr. Gull, one of the very best. It was a matter of coaxing the child through the interim, then. A little slum grandchild, Alix was thinking, knowing the child could not detect (or if she could could not construe) her smarting face, her big open Scandinavian eyes full of pain. She could not get over the likeness, the tiny face cut in soap, mimicking her long-drawn-out one. Over came Eddy with some of the nannies, one or two of whom had misinterpreted the call and had offered themselves as wet nurses and were now astounded to see a rather large child on the grass. "Yours, without a doubt," Alix hissed to Eddy. "Just look." "Yes, Mama," he whispered. "At least London is not *full* of them."

"What about the mother, then? Annie."

Eddy almost exploded, not having had the faintest idea what to say or do for the past several weeks. He was broken-hearted. He had been in love, and he loved the fact of it. He also wanted the Morgan boy and more time with Netley. He did want to be a father, but not of a child, if that made sense to her. It did not. She scolded him aloud for all to hear, but they all feigned inattention, tapping the child, prodding and caressing, kneeling and fawning, all wanting the job and assuming that Alix was watching them to size them up. Alice stared them down with her silence, then cracked a small smile to see what would happen. They all smiled back at her, on cue, clucking and exclaiming.

The queen had called them in, had seen them, and now the future queen, Alexandra, went among them, planning the future, and the future of this child. The canniest of them, such as Mrs. Shrewsbury, thought the child's future might be long; she had come this far and had stirred Alix's goodwill. The child was interested only in something she did not know how to articulate: the birds were closer to her than they had ever been in any other place, Yarmouth or Dieppe. They were tame, from friendly thrushes to placable doves. Crumbs fell and sparrows pounced. The child liked this, was wholly unaware of Eddy as he loomed, wondering how to get through to her and say something when his mind was on something quite different and more urban. But it was he who, as his grandmother Victoria Regina had told him with sardonic hammerblows of Teutonic intensity, had begun the whole farce. The mother had been *seen to,* whatever that meant (he shuddered; back in April he had thought the toughs who came for him were going to kill him). Annie did not seem likely now to figure much in Alice's future; he could tell. She was no doubt back in the Gorbals or wherever in Scotland she had come from. Potentially, though, the child was a threat, and Alix in her open, thwarted way was all for having her sent to a secret school. Why not Denmark, even? As ideas went, it was not bad; it was not a day for ideas but for airing a human curiosity, going through the motions, setting Eddy's mind at rest (while stirring up Alix's). Nothing might come of any of it.

As Salisbury had said in some military connexion, buccaneers had to rough it, and Eddy was by way of being a sexual buccaneer. It had been Bertie who brought this tidbit home to the palace, and it had also been Salisbury who provided a couple of lines for Bertie to use against Eddy his son: "He is a man who is likely to render much more distinguished service if he is at a distance from his native land" and "X has reached that pitch of eminence at which a man becomes imbecile." Why, Bertie wondered, could not Eddy acquire a little discretion? No doubt it was highly indiscreet to have this three-year-old bastard traipsing about on the lawns of Windsor, but that experiment was under control (Slerch and Senna were in the constant offing), whereas if Eddy had organized it there would have been trouble already—some bit of buggery in the greenhouse, a coupling with a horse. "Can't we," he said to the Queen his mother, "just *kill* them all? Kill him?"

She gave the quick little bend of the head that for him was the epitome of her regality. "There is no need. Most people, Bertie, kill themselves. Eddy is already doing it. Can't you see it? His life is a *Totentanz. I* want *Verständnis.*" Her face sank. The regality melted away. She was looking at herself in the pool of ink exposed by the raised lid of the silver inkwell, as if she were drowning in a Prussian eye, and she was watching herself watch it happen, immobile and helpless for the first time in her life since her husband's death. How could liquid and optics shrink a face so much? A queen? She saw no future in the blue, just a fluid (like a century, a reign) that would accommodate her face for as long as she hovered over it and would then, never mind what abomination had taken her screaming and struggling beneath, smooth out and seal up its mandarin surface for the next comer—with not the slightest favoritism or compassion. Beneath that blue meniscus lay the horrors of her reign, of her family, the incompetence and lustfulness to which she had been a reluctant witness, wishing in the end that no one ever bred; look at the disgusting commotions of the act itself—who could expect anything decorous to come from all that gasping and tupping? Yet it was all her son and grandson could think or do. She wanted to let out a long, royal, Empire-sundering scream that would carry over London and last from breakfast to dinner as her tiny, puckered hobgoblin face with its hooked nose and bulbous, runny eyes said yes to the inkwell as if it were the Thames and slid beneath.

Alice Margaret walked on manicured grass. Or rather she tottered. Perhaps she thought she was again in Dieppe, though Windsor was less festive, less chromatic a place. She must have missed the pinks, the scarlets, the luminous teal blue that only the French use, and only for work pants. She must have missed the sea, as well as her mother, and the walks through the ancient town, she in her pram or pushcart. She kept coming up against earthen walls as the lawn ended, or wandering into what seemed mazes but weren't; she was in arbors, gazebos and pagodas, ever plied with toffee apples and cold lemonade, led about by Alix, who had taken rather a shine to her and, because she was deaf (family-deaf), felt a certain honorable bigotry about her. Alice was ruining her teeth with sweets, a habit begun when her mother worked at Mrs. Morgan's, and encouraged by Sickert and the others, who did not quite know what to say to her or do with her. Even Eddy had fed boiled sweets to her out of parental unease. Everything went into her mouth, and she appeared to have substituted taste for hearing: bird droppings and snails, spent matches and used hankies all found their way to the same place between her worn-down teeth.

Once she had her bearings, she ran at speed, even staging little races against herself (or Alix), and she let out an uncanny warble like a yodel mixed with bird imitation. This was her sound of delight. She never mentioned her mother, or showed any sign of recognition when Eddy came near, even though he tried to play with her and brought her all kinds of the wrong things (lead soldiers, for instance) from his boyhood toys. She liked a doll best and kept it by her, from time to time trouncing it severely for some offense, and they all wondered where she had seen such behavior. The mother? Eddy said no. It must have been the Kelly woman, then. Alice hugged the doll better and put it to sleep, usually in a bed of tulips although she liked to leave it out in the sun on one of the sundials, where the blade seemed a constant threat, ready to sever it.

A game little trotter, then, she began to adjust to the cushioned, remote life available there, as visibly thrilled by the long bath and its hot water as by the big bed in whose center she refused to lie, insisting wordlessly on lying near the edge, as if that was where the lifeboats were. And who could blame her, cosseted by temporary infatuates, led through the day by buxom women from Queen Victoria's list of devout handmaidens, and ministered to intimately by Alix, who was glad of a child to fuss. The whole experiment (i.e., something designed to fail) was precarious: it could either never end, depending on whim, or it could end in the next five minutes, again depending on whim. At least the weather was good, for tents and daisy chains, kites and tea parties with dolls, not the sort of life Alice had been used to; and not one of them had any idea that the suppressed hinterland for all this delicate play-acting was the affronted, sagging face of the child's mother, now certified by Gull as insane and to be kept in Guy's Hospital indefinitely. Had Lord Salisbury known this, would he have gone to the "Chalet Cecil" in Dieppe with quite so buoyant a heart, determined not to see those foreign dignitaries the Queen was always trying to make him look up, or contrive an accidental meeting with? He knew where the child was, and he was all in favor of children having country houses to grow up in; he himself was a walking specimen of the breed. But he was not going to sleep on this matter until Kelly turned up, as she was bound to; such women always did, once they had been put under enough pressure.

In the end, Alix sent a note to Sickert explaining what was

going on, asking if he would take the child under his wing should the Windsor experiment fall through, as it was bound to, and no Sandringham or Balmoral sequel came into being. She offered the money. He said yes, he knew of a quiet family off Cleveland Street, a greengrocer's, who would be glad to have Alice, being childless themselves. Alix had made him feel useful again, but nothing was going to redeem him, he knew, and he would soon be asked for other favors, of a different sort. Of that he was sure. He felt he was fixed in somebody's sights, for ever.

So: the beguiling Alix invited him to Windsor, and he went; but it was no use his staying there, lovely as it was; he had his career as a painter to think about. He had artistic work to do. He mentioned Ramsgate as a possibility, Dieppe as another. "Alice *has* a mother, Your Royal Highness. Eddy may never function as a father, any more than he did as my younger brother, but Annie is devoted. She was kidnapped, as I told you. The only new developments are that Gull appeared in my studio and Marie Kelly ran away. I know no more than that."

"Gull," she whispered, "has a practice at Guy's Hospital. Or he used to. I will ask."

"You look more regal than ever," Sickert said, trembling, reminded of an early infatuation, doomed.

"I have suffered more," she said. "I am like a woman in an iron maiden. You know what *that* means."

Of course he knew, but he thought she was sometimes more like an iron maiden in a woman. Out there on the lawn they sat, watching or pretending to watch the grounds staff scythe long grass beyond the wall. Not quite knowing what to say to her, he tried his old opener about the Royal Family's usually requiring several previous and widely recognized failures of anyone appointed to high office. "There have been times," he joshed, "when they ended up with somebody almost competent, just because there was nobody else available. On tap." He kept adding suffixal variants out of nerves or thick-headedness. "I hear some people manage to secure high office with only one or two failures behind them. What's the country coming to, Alix, when they turn to rubbish like that?" He was thinking dimly about All Souls and Lord Salisbury, wondering if the Prime Minister was a flop or not. Could such a man be rated a failure? All Souls, he seemed to remember, was the college that had no students: all was Thought there, hard and lofty. Was *that* where the nation hid its introverts? Without warning he was talking to Alix about his fits of depression, when he knew there was nothing for it but to go to some barren place and sit on the crocodile-infested shores, quite fatalistically waiting to be eaten.

"Now," Alix asked, "how would you get crocodiles on a barren shore? Or the other way round? It's not that easy, Walter. Nothing is. Look at the life of your Alix, if you will. It is I who am among crocodiles." The very image seemed to recharge her as she said softly "Infidelity, the thing that goes on all the time in my private life, as the nation knows. Here I am, married to a prince of the realm, as the saying puts it, I a foreigner like you, and there's nothing I can do about him. *Quel viveur, mon vieux.* He has to ride them all. There, I've said it aloud."

Chapter 12

Vehemently silent, she tried to quell the image of Bertie at Kettners or Rules in a private dining room where all he had to do was tap a button for the ornamental paneling to divide and reveal a double bed made with military strictness. Did they do it before or after dinner? Against this image, she kept in her own bedroom something that vulcanization had brought into being: crepe rubber, domesticated in the shape of condoms, upon the lids of whose boxes Queen Victoria and Mr. Gladstone glared, each daring the other to use (or not to use) what was inside. It was as if both of them were the permanent guardians of hygiene and taste, as if nothing used under their auspices might ever seem lewd or crass. If it was royal, if it was prime-ministerly, it could not be all bad.

There lay the mysterious box, whose contents, like rubber underwear for the drowning damned, would keep Alix from the poxes of whores. Just so long as her husband, taking her in her (pretended?) sleep, put on his armor first. Alix of course worried about spillage already lurking in her Bertie's pubic hair, but no prophylactic was going to shut that out: a lady had to take her chances. A sound sleeper, and deaf as well, she could not always be awake to be ready for Bertie's late-night onslaughts, and she could hardly tuck snakeskin into herself to await his plunge. So there she lay, sleepless, hoping to check him in time and make him dress for the occasion. Too often, though, he arrived, blundered about with pyjamas in hand, and spread-eagled her without a glance. Whenever he found Alix awake, she managed to remind him of what to do, and then she lay beneath him wondering if he and his paramour had flung themselves upon each other, earlier, with the same degree of protection. She thought not, and tried to suppress her vision of what might come home to roost. No wonder the Gulls of the world remained on call. She knew that, one day, Gull would tap at her chamber door with his chalice of mercury, opium, or whatever he used, his hands enveloped in crepe-rubber mittens, just to be safe when greeting her, never mind manhandling her most open places. The day would come, sure as houses, when her own face, or Bertie's, or Eddy's even, would be on the lid of the condom box.

On she talked, her realm of worry opened wide. She thought she knew why Eddy was a dunce, just as much a *viveur* as his father—"Although Bertie was no dunce, was he?—"

"At least you haven't forgotten your French." Sickert smiled, trying to ease the atmosphere between them. "Most folks don't know the difference between that and a *bon vivant.* They say the English think the difference is that a *viveur* eats with his mouth and a *bon vivant* with cutlery. They may be right."

Alix winced, reluctant to pass any of his witticisms by without a mental curtsy, but anxious to air something much worse. "I often think about it," she said slowly. "Very rarely, we have *relations,* and then off he goes and puts himself between the limbs of some floozy, spreading the—well, my flux, far and wide, mixing my flow with hers, then mixing them with some-one else's, until he has become a sort of sexual pastry chef to the whole country. I worry about what he brings back. I feel it enter me and—forgive me—I wonder where it has been, in what syrup, slop, slime, or rubber shift. Unless he washes himself off with remarkable timeliness, he's bound, isn't he, to, mingle us all together? Here I am, Princess Alexandra, and my royal hus-band treats me like a poultice, a washwoman's bucket. It isn't the morality I'm talking about, it's the lack of hygiene. He may not love me, but does that give him the right to *soil* me?"

"Ah, promiscuity," Sickert sighed, remembering Ellen douch-ing herself in Hampstead, "thou art a mixing bowl."

"Just think," she said, "if *I* were being unfaithful to *him*. What a fuss there would be."

"Ah, that is different," Sickert said, wishing he could melt down all the royal coats of arms in the world into one holy grail of average caliber: ploughman's model or the sort of holy hope you could find in Whitechapel or the Minories. He was tired of well-to-do folk with lawns and innumerable high-born nan-nies. There ran little Alice among them like a rented animal, tolerated and indulged only because the order had gone out; with equal aplomb they would drown her or hold a pillow on her face. He knew how the system worked.

"Tell me," she said. It was a royal command, uttered by a woman who knew all about her Prince's escapades with Lillie Langtry, the Misses Stonor, Tennant, Duff, and Chamberlayne ("Chamberpots" to Alix), and at Le Chabanais, his favorite Pari-sian brothel *de luxe*. She wanted him to lay out for her in full the landscape of depravity amid which her husband moved like an effigy of simmering brisket. She knew he had the words, but all he would tell her, while she roamed around the idea of retaliat-ing by becoming a street woman, or even a whore of the paddle boats, her face and loins smeared in fresh ripe mud from the low-tide shallows, was "I'll tell you anything."

Alice was staring at them, doll in hand, as if to memorize what they were doing, perhaps at some time to attempt a moment of it herself. Probing her nose without picking, she responded to the movements of their mouths, just possibly picking up their voices as attenuated boom, much as the hearing person, with some surprise, at first registers the sapped, cavernous voices of certain German women, honed down deep by liquor, smoke, phlegm, and hormones: a voice almost too deep to be spoken with, but ideal for nightclub chanting. Alice moved her own lips, making a match without being in the least attuned, to English or to talk.

Never again did Sickert want a woman to come and discuss her intimate life with him; he would rather wonder about how they got the poor drowned sluts or princesses out of the paddle wheels in the Thames, first running the wheel to dislodge the corpse but only managing to tear it into large chunks, then setting convicts to cut the remains away smaller, passing piece after piece up to another convict with a sack. That was the place to be for such a realist as himself, as unafraid to peer as to sniff. And there were men in the Thames too, harder to cut up, to cut away from the wheel that no longer spun and pounded. Would they allow an itinerant painter to go and watch, make his sketches, answering their disgust with his pet theory about *worstness*, filched from some ancient Greek or other. He always wanted extremes, even if only to paint what was middling and middle-of-the-road. "Otherwise, gentlemen," he'd always say, "we have no north, no south. I am groping for directions. I keep looking for the horizon, trying to reach it." They would never see. He doted on the prospect of green marrow-fat remnants— human sirloins—afloat on the river as toiling convicts dropped them and watched them settle to a suitable floating depth, their eyes on what they now had to fish out of the water. These men had not hardened to their work, but hosing down the paddle wheel would school them in the perishability of the human form, as perhaps no painter, not even he, Sickert, could.

He felt his stomach rumbling and struck it with a fist, half anticipating the heaves.

He thought of Alice, doomed to a series of Windsor chairs with high spoked back, out-slanted legs, a crossbar beneath, her belly full of dark brown Windsor soup, her entire body redolent of the lavender in Windsor soap.

The cuddle-hungry nannies of Windsor took turns with Alice, nestling her on their laps, one hand against her waist, one over her right knee, velvetly clasping her while Alix, surrendering her for a while, strode the lawn with a look of daunting sensitivity. These ladies had their hair parted centrally and brushed back hard, giving them an air of preternatural tautness. Eau de Cologne came off them at all angles. They looked like penguins, all in white and black, and the black ribbon forcing the starched white collar against the throat was tight. Alice was content to sit with her feet off the ground, her head in a muslin cap topped by an enormous white doily of a crepe flower. When she was not being watched too carefully, she ran a ribbon from side to side between her lips, trying to make it vibrate, but it rarely did; she needed a length of elastic, but she did not know. The nannies were rather pleased that a girl so big had so undeveloped a personality, one which made few demands and created little fuss. They preferred their charges somewhat deaf, and could manage two of Alice to one of almost all others. None of them had Alix's deferential elegance with children or understood it; Alix, acutely self-aware, understood full well that a lonely foreign woman will fix upon children, her own or those of others, almost to the exclusion of rational activity. Toss deafness into the sum and you have a formula for slavish empathy. She would have given a great deal, she thought, to have been transported by giant eagle back to Denmark with this child, to bring her up in a Scandinavian way, with a different language and a less Germanic tone to everything. Eddy had given his mother nothing but trouble and love, but now, almost in spite of himself, he had given her this, a child, to cosset, even if one somewhat aloof and unyielding.

Every day at Windsor was a birthday for Alice, unannounced of course, but tangible and full. After a week she had become accustomed to it, and the sight of her enjoying it—so gradually beginning to unbend and risk a smile—would have broken her mother's heart, broken as it already was by the lethal ministrations of Gull. Each day there were more and more flowers, both from abounding Nature and from those who tended her, choosing the language of flowers over that of words, perhaps, having her smell them and get the pollen on her hands and face. Alice enjoyed this, finding the domain of flowers smooth and aromatic, ideal to be wrapped in; some petals she ate, and some she just chewed, lackadaisically, too lazy in that stoked-up summer to spit them out. She was finding her way into nature, as if sensing the mother vanished, ineligible to return. She liked her stay best when Alix took her for stately, patient walks, pausing at every object not made of grass, and sometimes even approaching a small table set for tea with no heed of the people there. Alice would savor the wicker table as if it were a bush, the tiny three-legged stool with the spare toast rack on it as a plant. At these tables the nannies sat, waiting to be called back to duty, their demeanors mincing and overt. This was when Alice formed her fixation on biscuit barrels, quite often hooking her wrist through the bamboo hoop and taking one away to her private cache behind a stand of gladioli. Alix returned one or two, but always left enough to keep the peace; if Alice liked biscuit barrels, then she should have them. Surely the royal family, having done her so much ill, could do that, with or without an alleluia.

The queen, still dickering with Salisbury about Prince Bismarck's intemperate behavior, had not forgotten that Alice was still on the premises, but was not giving her the full monarchical attention. Could, Alix wondered, a child of three be bewildered, or did everything come at them in a big glorious kaleidoscopic wave? Would life with a greengrocer off Cleveland Street sort well in Alice's head with life at Windsor? It was all grist for a tot's mill, she thought, but someone was going to have to tell the mother. The grandmother was ready and willing, having already in her mighty and tangential way having alluded to the abundance of insects at Windsor: not inching or scurrying through the grass, but invading the castle to be scrunched underfoot or swatted down. There were flies and wasps galore, no corner without a reigning spider, and ants and caterpillars behind the cushions, almost as if royal occupancy were a thing of the past. Windsor might indeed, she said, become one of those elementary colleges for the people Mr. Dickens had taught to read, but she was not going to give up without a fight. She found abhorrent the thought of a mere child among such wildlife, testing her minute shoes on the smeared innards along the vast corridors, brushing bluebottles and beetles off her mouth in her sleep. Thus did fanatical nicety open up the world again for Alice, and the double muslin curtains Her Majesty had installed against the open windows only provided scant and billowy hindrance to whatever flew through and in. There was not enough muslin to keep Windsor free of buzz, never mind what slunk in on the ground.

Chapter 13

On this same day Annie, marooned with mostly comatose women in the ill-lit cellar of Dr. Gull, half-thought she was back in the Midlands village of her childhood, among the quavery-voiced "mesters" who said "ah" repeatedly, but sometimes made histrionic reference to their tonsils, making themselves even hoarser for the occasion, then floating off into loving reference to things not "redla," or to other people, about whom they kept asking rhetorical questions: "He's went and died antla?," meaning *hasn't he?* These were the sounds that choked her spinning head as she did her business into the stone trough shoveled out once a day, tried to get enough potato peelings from the murky water in which they were delivered, and shoved and budged the other women's eager fingers away from her. She no longer looked well-fed or well-slept, and her face had developed the Pudding look, just right for Gull's purposes, especially when he signed her away to limbo. She had to look the part. She kept trying to recall a lovely story once told her, about a princess who fell in love with a prince, but the high priests gave him a foul disease that made black worms fall from his nose, smelling of rotten cabbage, and she never again wanted to kiss him. The two of them had had a child, but it came out covered with fish eyes and feathers, hardly a human child at all, so they had agreed to part for ever and had given the child over to an old doctor who lived in a cowshed in the Midlands, where he shoveled cow dirt and shaped it into bricks that could be burned instead of coal. That was the usual version, but the story varied from day to day, and the slowcoach women in there with her began to get into it too, mostly as a herd of cows who never gave milk. Annulled, Annie nonetheless occupied what remained of her mind and used what she had of memory. Had she known where Alice was, she would perhaps have recognized the ironic ending to her story. Right, she told herself, imagining it: she would work in the washhouses at Windsor, thumping and twizzling the pegleg in the washtub, then mangling the wet clothes in the mangle, later known as a wringer, and pegging them out on the line, hoping hard to remember a nursery rhyme about just that activity. Once a week, on Saturday, she would be allowed to see Alice, walk her around the vegetable garden and give her a lollipop, which of course is when Alice would show her the latest biscuit barrel filched from a picnic or an unguarded afternoon tea. Then they would tuck into short-breads, digestives, arrowroots, cream centers, gingerbreads, fig layers, oatmeals, and the rest, not nibbling in the genteel way but cramming their mouths, cramming the giggle back between their teeth as it formed, and saying good-bye with their mouths full.

Now that, in the barbaric real world of the Pudding Club cellar, Annie had discovered certain hospitable concavities, she sat and slept better, even knowing that, if she got into position early enough on the stone slab, she could place her cheek against the wall in such a way that her cheekbone would find a place to rest. Then she would not spend the rest of the night rolling her face in vain across the whitewash. She had to sleep in the one good position, having found it, but that at least in its spasmodic way was sleep. Part of her knew now that she was willing to say or do just about anything to be let out of here. She had done her time and would never behave badly again. Already she knew too much about the texture of whitewash and stone, about wetness and damp. Her joints had a new ache quite apart from the one in her head, and her eyes, like those of a pit pony, had begun to reconcile themselves to the gloom. She was no longer able to trust her own mind, which had worked quite well when exchanging, for a halfpenny, Mint Imperials, Pontefract Cakes, Humbugs, Jelly Babies, Dolly Mixtures, and all kinds of other sweets whose very names, when they came to her, seemed those of friends. She could remember school and being given a tiny violet cachou for Good Behaviour, never for penmanship or reading because she had not stayed at school long enough to get to serious business. But for folding her arms well and keeping them so until the blood almost stopped she would get a few pretties. She had not even had a chance to impart good arm-folding or sitting still to her daughter who, as daughters always did, had a greater chance of rising above her station, nay soaring, being plucked from the soil by a big hand from the sky that was not God's hand, but kingly.

She had never detected the irony of sweet rewards being given to little children for being inert, for being the best at being inert, with their legs tucked neatly and politely out of sight behind the legs of the chair, and those real dangers, the arms, being clamped hard together, right-hand fingers on the left upper arm, left-hand fingers down below, inside, hugging the right breast—except for left-handers, who did things opposite. To be born and then hugged tight, that was nice; and from it followed, as far as she could see, having to sit still while sort of hugging yourself. Where, she wondered, in a panic, was the brainpan? Where had *that* come from? Did everyone get one? Were they issued? If so, she had missed getting one, and that meant that any leakage from her brain would dribble onto the floor, not into its brainpan, which she had reckoned similar to a drip pan for roasting in. No, *you* didn't roast, your joint did. No, not your joint, your *beef*. If you had some. Otherwise it was Yorkshire pudding in beef gravy, preferable sometimes to the meat itself so long as you had the eggs to make it with, otherwise it was just a floury pancake in powdery gravy. She yearned for such delicacies, trying to pretend that what came in the bucket was delectable, had taste and bulk, but it was no use. Stronger than the other Puddings, she managed to get more than her share of turnip and potato peelings, but it was never enough. And she knew that rat dirt got mixed into what she ate. The rats came in to join them at night, but she and one other were the only ones who screamed hard; the rest had lapsed into a giggle a little bit indignant. When they were dead, the rats would bite them good and proper, but until then the rats came in for a frolic more than for anything else.

What Gull liked about the Pudding cellar was its utter freedom from time. Nothing had to be accomplished. He had become the proprietor of a human state at once an absolute (it needed nothing else) and a self-perpetuating secret, whereas with spine disorders and paraplegia you were always trying to determine the future. Oh, he could envision the day when some zealot of a reformer came along and said "Down with Pudding Clubs," and a vital freedom would have gone by the board; there would be forms to fill in and charts to keep. Until then, however, he was able to dote on his domain, although, because of hospital rules, not feed the inmates on roast dog from other experiments. The Chinese did it all the time, and even selected the dog from a pack in the window beforehand. So far as he knew, not even the archvivisectionist Claude Bernard ran a little café on the side, as well he might. Somewhere in the back of his head, Gull knew that an experiment was possible in which all the components dovetailed: there would be no waste, no loose ends. He would feed the vivisectionist's dogs on the women who had died, who had been troughing on roast dog—like that. Economy. The closed system recommended in the Holy Bible. But the squeamish among his colleagues would never consent. Why, some of them had denounced his Pudding Club, but he was a power in the land, in Brook Street as at Guy's, and that was as far as opposition had gone. He kept all his results to himself, knowing that, if he published them piecemeal, they would soon no longer be his own.

He liked to go and survey his women, those ghosts in calico, marveling at their endurance on reduced brain power, like galley slaves in the olden days, with no future but to row and row. Sometimes the women exchanged shifts and the numbers got mixed up, but it hardly mattered since the women were intended to overlap until they did not know where one began and the other left off: "experiment in fusion," he called it. He had begun to wonder who, after him, would recognize the purpose of the Pudding Club. Could it be deduced from the spectacle of the women turning and turning, stopping and seeming to think? After his fifth stroke, he told himself, he would go in there and join them, stark naked, with just a few surgical knives, for one last consecration. By then he would not care, any more than any other pioneer, what became of him. Perhaps the women would even turn the tables on him, seize his knives and needles, and even as he lay *in extremis* lobotomise *him* and sever his member, as if in sacrifice to some underground goddess of damp and stench. He would not mind, not by then, because he would probably be just a turnip himself, although still having the eyes of a beholder. He was hoping to achieve even finer results: what could he reduce women to, those vessels and nourishers? How far could he push their hold on life? Someone else would have to write up the results: perhaps Acland, his son-in-law, who after all was his own doctor, and Salisbury's too. Gull and Salisbury ran this land, as any fool could see; one did not have to have been a Fellow of All Souls College, Oxford, to be eminent in Victoria's domain, thank goodness. All you had to be was willing to serve.

Annie was remembering tea. They never had it in here. Almost a sanctioned drug, it was never quite only a drink, it had too much ritual for that. She longed to warm the pot, scald the leaves, put the pot inside its tea-cosy, pour it, make it thick with sugar and milk until the spoon, as they always said, stood up of its own accord. She wanted the soothing warm pot, the little tile it stood on, the brown-veined mug that received the tea, the tannin taste, almost bitter as if a sheep had washed its nose in there. The mere presence of the pot on the table had reassured her. Just a spot would do it, the noises—tinkle, crisp foaming, the gentle swill—were themselves enough to do all the right in the world. You didn't really need to drink it or smack your lips when you had the first sip, the addict's homecoming sigh. The very idea of it, that's what pulled you through the worst. What bucked you up, in tea's presence, was the idea that you could be bucked up. She herself always liked it in a jug, which was how she carried it out to the fields, slopping a bit here and there on a grateful mouse, an ungrateful wild rose; but there were also those tapered cans, blue and white, with little wire-hoop handles and tight lids. Tea-cans. You could take it with you anywhere in those, you could, even to bed, and the warmth of the can under your pillow or bolster, or down where your feet froze half the year, was worth losing a month in paradise for. Oh yes. Hand-warmer, foot-warmer, sock-warmer, glove-warmer, could be rolled about it instead of an iron. There was many a workshirt ironed with a can full of hot tea. The miners, now, they carried one swinging in their big jacket pockets, of the jacket they never buttoned up, so many a passer-by had been struck by a full or empty can as the bearer hurried home or to the mine. She lingered on what she could not have, not even sure enough of herself now to ask for it. What was the word? *Ee,* she cried, that was it. They could bring a bucketful for her, she would down it all, then give it back:

> Okey-pokey, penny a lump,
> The more you eat, the more you trump.

It was the only song, such as it was, she had remembered. She tried it, standing with her arms aloft as if beseeching, but the words came out all wrong although nimble as skylarks in her loafing mind. She hauled her shift up and off. Nobody even looked. She felt cold, so she tried to get it back on, but somehow could not work out the proper moves. It stayed off and she carried it about with her like a wet dishcloth, screwed up and foul, tempted to suck the water out of it, something of hers given back to her on the quiet. Annie was becoming less and less herself, and a cup of thick sweet tea would unhinge her quite.

Hardly knowing how to do it, and doing it with initial full apprehension that the writing hand was that of a woman who was going to be Queen, Alix wrote to Sickert—something she had not done for a long time, and the doing of it made her feel younger, as if she were sucking some hitherto untractable nipple. He was an *old friend,* that was it, and she had got him into trouble; if she had kept Eddy to herself, as a mooncalf in brass buttons and waxed moustaches, all might have been well. Instead she had fobbed him off, and Eddy had meddled with his role of castaway and turned it into that of graft. Now there was a seedling, a shoot. Alix glanced outside, from indoor stifling heat to its outdoor version, amid which Alice was scampering in pursuit of a ball that did not bounce too high, of course. There was a decorum even for three-year-olds; but, she wondered, was there one for fully grown sons? Only when the heavens split open, she thought. Only then.

Dear Walter, she wrote, for the fourth time. A letter was not the way to do this, but she had little social occasion to talk with him nowadays, and her duty was here at Windsor. Little Alice needed her; Sickert did not. She tried again, mustering all her disused rhetoric to convince him that things might be worse, although they could be better. Annie, she urged upon him, was the worse for her ordeal (she wrote it down, but she wondered which ordeal she thought she was writing about); any woman with nothing wrong with her, then maltreated, will be the worse for it. What then did she mean? Annie, she told him, had been sequestered, as she knew he knew. Then why was she writing him? In the end she wrote, quite bluntly (for her):

Annie Crook is beyond reach, I fear, having been seen by the cream of the medical profession. Full accommodation has been provided for the meantime. Her child is here, and settling in well, although I have no idea, dear Walter, how long she will be allowed to remain. I do not read minds, as you know. That is better than Eddy, who reads nothing at all. I was never able to write to him, as you know. He lags behind in all ways but one, and I wish he would somehow wear himself out, but he is his father's son. Only I wear out, with hives, pimples, midnight chills, headaches and earaches, various kinds of rheumatics. For the time being, Eddy roves not. His grandmama has put the leash on.

What am I telling you? Nothing much. I wanted to tell you that the subject is on my mind all hours. The fruit of all our stupidities is running around on the lawn and endearing herself to everyone, even the grey tweedy ladies who have come in to nanny her. Paint, do not fret. This is the English you taught me. Forgive it and wring its neck. The child is well.

When he saw the word "medical," Sickert thought at once of Gull and then of Guy's Hospital, though surely it was likelier that Annie would be in some workhouse or refuge. He decided to go in disguise, wondering whether he should get himself up as the French soldier whom Pistol captures in *Henry V,* a part he had played on the stage. In the end, drawn as much by nostalgia as by the practical, he walked down Cleveland Street and hired himself a naval officer's uniform, his mind on the court-martial scene in *Black-Eyed Susan,* in which he had been the foreman of the jury. One of his old acting names back then had been Nemo, and he determined now that he would go off to Guy's as Captain Nemo. Tempted to do an Affable Arthur, in spite of the bulky package he carried, he nonetheless refrained; life had become altogether too sad and awful for games, but perhaps a game was what he needed to find something out. How could Alix write about someone's being seen by the *cream* of the medical profession? Curds and whey, yes.

An hour later, affecting a slight limp for which he bore a stout cane, he marched out and hired a hansom cab, to go in style. How they sirred and captained him. It was almost not worth going through life in mufti. Could there not be a painter's uniform, all gold braid and navy blue? His natural jauntiness came out; he recognized it, and slapped it back. This was not the occasion. In truth, his spirits were low: he expected to find nothing out and to have to go on torturing himself day after day, wondering about Annie's whereabouts. Into Guy's he stalked, bowing and hurrumphing as if indeed on the boards, and then he risked asking for Annie, but no one knew anything until he said the name "Gull" to a venerable doctor more whiskered than Lord Salisbury himself and was directed downstairs to the cellars, where the smell was of rotting meat, laundry steam, and oceangoing sewage. Well, it was just like being on board one of Her Majesty's rat-traps, was it not? He peered and pried, but found nothing, although adding to his retinal store of pathetic sights, at least until he found his way to the door that led to the door with the porthole in it, and was halted there by a vast hand, or so it felt, coming from behind him. "Well, Mr. Sickert, ah, Captain Sickert, what have we here? Care to look?"

He did for several minutes and almost convinced himself that he had seen an Annie in a canvas bag, her face white and shiny as painter's putty and her expression one of poleaxed misery. "I think I see her," he exclaimed.

Gull himself looked, shook his head. "Very like, to be sure, Captain, but that was Nelly Pridgeon, who on an off day looks like Mary Tedstone. They're all off their heads in there. Annie Crook, you say? Well, she *could* be in there. Look again." Gull had never felt so bold.

Again Sickert thought he saw her, now looking green and seeming to be screaming quite silently, with her mouth wide in the roar. "That's her," he said. "I'd like to go in."

"Too dangerous, Captain," Gull said. "Why, man, they would tear us to bits in a trice. You'd better come back another time. Anyway, it is against the rules."

"Whose rules?"

"My rules." Again that Essex accent.

"*You* make them?" Captain Nemo very much himself.

"I did. For safety's sake. This is a hospital, sir, not a workhouse or a refuge. Investigation and experiment. Take it from me, if she's in there, she's there for her own good, to be all the better when she comes out. It's for her own good, for the best. But let me show you something else."

Across the hall, seated, Sickert watched Gull do a blood injection on a handsome young man, all the time droning on about this and that: "Impossible to call upon a person who has undergone operation on the frontal lobes—for advice on anything vital, you see. Their responses are direct and hasty, rather child-like in their ingenuousness and openness. They have to be protected. Not that they lack insight. They remain direct, deliberate, and uninspired." In his mind Sickert again saw the white turnip of Annie's face as it skittered past the porthole, then came back into view, her look that of someone after first turning cannibal. She looked albino, dried, numb, nothing like the Annie of old. As he looked at Gull, his mallet and needles, and the face of the poor youth on the table, Sickert wanted to weep, and only his uniform, some nominal constraint, kept him from it.

Gull seemed in an even more reckless mood, perhaps because his patient was male and did not vex him as the women in his Pudding Club did. "Sad case," he said, as if the stricken man were not there. "This is young Stephen, Prince Eddy's tutor at Cambridge. The cover stories are already out, of course. Something sticking out from a train struck him as it was going past. Or, while he was riding at Felixstowe, his horse shied and put Stephen's head within reach of a windmill vane, which struck him as it approached the ground. Bizarre accidents for a classical scholar, wouldn't you say? He talks fluent ancient Greek, as if that were useful. Comes from a famous family, too. It is very sad. I have to do my best, but it's going to take forever." Why, he wondered, am I showing off? I can easily recruit him to the cause without making him adore me.

Sickert found himself unable to assimilate all that Gull was telling him, but asked for Eddy's whereabouts. "Oh, the Tenth Hussars, I think because their tunic has a high collar like the starched ones he wears in mufti, to hide his long and swanlike neck. He was gazetted some time ago, I believe. Just the thing for him, the Army. Much better for a young fellow than licking his tutor's trouser buttons. There was a bit of that going on, you know." The one thing Sickert had not anticipated was gossip, although if gossip it had to be it would be such gossip as this. The reclining young man, Stephen (his surname, Sickert realised), made not a murmur. Presumably he had been Gulled beyond making further trouble. Two nurses took him out on a gurney, and Sickert presumed that was the last the civilized world would see of him. Vaguely he wondered if Eddy too had been in here for Gull's ministrations and was already on his way to India or Australia, port outward, never home. He asked, but Gull knew nothing, he said. He was virtually retired, yet the work kept coming in, and who was he to refuse Her Majesty?

It was as if a whole generation or class were cleaning up its attic, taking the reprobates and making them socially palatable, filing off their edges and corners, filling in the grain before sandpapering and veneering. And Alice Margaret was at Windsor, being vetted no doubt, for membership in the same debauched tribe; his mind, as it often would, lingered on the image of the strict-faced child among the turrets and cloisters, the barren chambers and the long ornamental halls, as if she were a ghost brought there to inspect the venerable old pile for tenderness.

Eddy would surface again; he always did, mainly because, wherever he was sent, he did badly and had to be evacuated from the scene of another failure. So he would probably see Alice Margaret, if he chose to; if he wanted to. Perhaps, Sickert thought, he won't and I am the father apparent. You never know. He had begun to divine a world in which exact relationships of a formal kind did not matter, so long as compatible people kept together. Never mind who was whose whatever, the main thing was to be someone's anything, if you were devoted to them, as he had been to Annie, whose fate did not square with the rest of his notion. He found it hard to believe that Annie was a permanent loser, never to surface like Eddy. Surely she did not deserve to be hidden away with only Gull to tend her. He asked, and Gull without a moment's pause told him that, of course, it should be possible to speak with her, if she wanted to be spoken with. "It doesn't follow," he sighed, "that she will *want* to. The treatment sometimes takes them that way. *Mens sana . . . ,* you know." It had done him good to show off a bit today.

"But she wasn't insane. She was in the pink."

"Not *my* information," Gull said sternly, "nor my *finding.* Now look, if you want to be helpful, just put her out of your mind for a while. I do need help. If, in return for visitor's privileges, say, you were to assist me in the search."

"The search?" Sickert felt his face flush, his hands begin to tremble, as if he had been gripping brushes too hard all day and now the reaction had set in.

"We need the Kelly woman to tell us what went on," Gull was saying, even as Sickert thought he saw a black ocean closing over Annie's beleaguered face, her colorless shift. "What you gave me was not a good likeness, sir."

"Why don't you ask Eddy?" Sickert burst into the conversational open with a reckless lunge; anything but that engulfing sea, deep as the journey to the moon was long.

"Have you," Gull blustered, "ever tried to have a serious talk with Prince Eddy? The man is inarticulate, and that may well be a cover. We asked him about his affair with young Stephen, who was just here and comes from a good family, but he couldn't get it out into the open. Not the explanation anyway." He laughed. "For a man who had a mild stroke last year, I'm not doing too badly, am I? All of a sudden I have most of the Royal Family round my neck, wanting this, wanting that. This will be my last big case, I assure you. I don't mind how much I do, but I sometimes get tired. Pardon but I am due at the University senate in half an hour. I have to clean up and go." Captain Sickert let himself be escorted out, then saw Gull to a cab, told him he would rather walk, and watched him out of sight, amazed by how much he distrusted his portly joviality. One day, Sickert thought, he will have the lot of us in shifts in cellars. He is going to put the intelligentsia of London into the sewers, and we are going to be like the poor, fighting over the stuff in the rubbish bins for bits of bone, roast chicken skin, and pork fat. Even though the entire mess had been soaked with disinfectant. In Guy's he had seen huge bags of lethal refuse being humped downstairs; destined for the river, he was sure; but so much of it went into the bellies of the poor instead from remaining on the street. London was a dunghill and the royal family stood atop it crowing, amassing fine artworks from Europe, oh yes, but letting the dregs go to the dogs. I, he thought, am among the dregs, and Gull is going to flush us all away. Even if I had not taken sides, my side has been chosen for me: I am among the unwashed, the down and out. Where else should a painter be, anyway? Grabbing with the mob for a pannikin of skilly. We have to get rid of these royals and their Gulls, Sickert was thinking: their Slerches and Sennas. It's not how we behave that wounds them, they have no morals themselves—look at Bertie, damn him; it's that we are poor, that *our* ancestors didn't have enough initiative to seize thousands and thousands of acres of land on which to plaster the family name. What this royal stuff comes down to, all this fawning and pretending, is who's the more blatant pirate? Those who did it first, on a scale so vast it's no longer recognisable as a crime, have ruled the roost ever since. *Why* should the poor of London bow the knee, touch the forelock, to the likes of Eddy and Bertie? Why in heaven? I am a radical. As if I never knew. What we need to do is kidnap Annie all over again, though I fear he has done something to her we will never undo. Sickert felt the courage draining into him, and then from him. He was a mere beholder who had interfered and now could not withdraw. When, he wondered, would Gull's needles pierce his own frontal lobes, to make him more cooperative, a puppet of velvet with a brain of soap?

Chapter 14

Again he heard, as so often, the cry of London's poor, beginning as a murmur, then pitching itself higher until it wounded his ears, almost as if it were the scream of someone being savagely assaulted. It was, of course, but the scream came from uncounted mouths, from those who had had to make a familiar of the rat for life, whose crime had

always been that *they never did give nothing though they did speak kind.*
He knew why he painted in such somber colors; he was emotionally in the same slough of despond as they. He wanted to
get that low, that hungry, that uncared-for, that far from The
Bank of England, The Royal Exchange and The Stock Exchange,
down there, in Aldgate and Whitechapel, where a child might
lie untended, dead, on the floor of a room that slept ten people.
He knew, not all but somewhat, about it, the huge clusters of
creeping things pulled out from behind the rotten wallpaper, the
twopenny rope stretched across a room for men to lean on while
they tried to sleep standing up, and the walking to the hop fields
of Kent and Sussex every summer to make a few pence: half a
crown a day if you were over twelve years old. He had not, as
it were, descended yet to matchbox-making (buy your own
string and paste) or pea-shelling, but he knew the going rates:
a shilling a day if you did as many as twenty hours. None of this
goes on at Windsor, he told himself; little Alice will be flourish-
ing there. It wasn't far away.

Then Sickert remembered one of the tirades of Marie Kelly,
discomfiting the man of good conscience even as he was about
to proclaim that poverty drove the women to it—to the trade,
or whatever they called it. "Mostly by inclination," she said.
"Don't be sentimental, my old lad. Don't you forget that what
the ladies have between their legs is every bit as bad as what the
gentlemen have. Just as hot to trot, my dear, mark my words.
Just as wet and wobbly when the moment strikes, so much you
don't rightly know what you're a-doing of. So long as it gets
what it wants."

Well, he didn't know, Sickert said, but he'd heard tell that
penetration, not to put too fine a word on it, rarely happened
because the ladies were a dab hand at popping the upright
gentlemen between their thighs and clamping hard. It was almost as good, especially if the gentleman was eager. She knew.
She always knew. She told him how women of her acquaintance
(which was vast, it seemed) would whine and moan for something they wanted, and then go out and find it. It's normal, my
old cockchafer," she told him. "Don't you go feeling too sorry

for the girls. They like it like they like a tot of rum, a piece of fried fish, a good go in a water closet whenever they can find one—the sound of the water trickling about makes them want to widdle even more, see. All this is women's knowledge. They doesn't always do it for doss money, they does it out of devilment, that's why."

All the same, he preferred what Marie Kelly liked to call his sentimental view of the London poor, of London's harlotry, much as he liked to think of Alix, some years back, as the mother of a dimpling brood, with not only Eddy and his younger brother George to see to, but Princess Louise, Princess Victoria, and Princess Maud, then eight or nine, the third one nicknamed "Harry" after the "little Admiral, Harry Keppel," famed for his courage like little Maud. He preferred *this* Alix to the Alix whose mind was a doll's house of wide-eyed mediocrity, who read aloud to her children from such things as *St. Winifred's* or *The World of School,* who doted on the violet scent she wore, while fussing that it might be too strong for everyone else. Who am I, Sickert had wondered in his day, mentally in love with a Danish princess, married to an English highbrow, and talking things over with a whore and cynic of the streets? I must be a patchwork man, aching to have several of me killed off so that I can be constant to myself. He could never quite dismiss from his heart the Alix who longed, eventually, to find a quiet, safe room in which not to conduct an affair in vengeance on her whoremastering husband but to arrange her watercolours.

How hot under the collar he could become, how vehement in a cause. Was it that he genuinely cared about the downtrodden, or that he relished a convenient altruism? An inconvenient one would not have inspired him at all. He loved being serene, and the only way of staying serene while involving himself with the lives of others was not to expect too much. Otherwise he was as well off as God in France, as the saying went. If Gull was Salisbury's demon, as it appeared, and Eddy was really his father's son, then who was Sickert? What? Somewhere he had put a foot wrong, although settling it with a courtier's daintiness.

He could see his immediate responsibility as Annie no longer, but Alice Margaret, backward at three and bound to have been unhinged by Windsor, the glowing fuss made by Alix, the sheer size of the rooms, the big draughts of air indoors, the omnipresence of echoes, ghosts, and armor. He was indulging himself, he knew, in an adult's version of a child's experience, and she was much more likely to have formed an incurable craving for cream buns. Part of him just hoped she would never come back, for relegation to the greengrocer in Cleveland Street; but another part of him longed to play the lightweight father, *any* role vaguely paternal, if only to prove to himself that a lapsed husband need not necessarily be a rotten father or an incompetent uncle. To sate the parental side of him did he have to get in deeper, did he have to take even further risks? Did he have to go and involve himself all the more with Gull, who clearly had more power in the realm than was good for anyone? If Gull could do that to Annie, then what might he do to Kelly? To Alice? To Sickert even? And on and on? Should he go and try to talk to Salisbury? What he did not know was that Salisbury regarded the conversation between him and Sickert, that reprobate painter with French cravings, as already over. The man was bound to be of use, if only he could be induced to serve. And Salisbury was a great man at waiting. A born dozer who to keep himself alert at vital junctures during Cabinet meetings had purchased a wooden paperknife shaped like a dagger, he would press the point against his thigh, under cover of the big mahogany table, and, when things got dull, ram it home hard, confident that his look of calmly mastered agony would pass muster as one of excruciated attention. Sickert had also heard that Lord Salisbury had high fun at home with privately rigged telephones, maintained an electricity laboratory all of his own, and liked to refer to himself as a degraded voluptuary, mainly because he loved to sleep. When Sickert thought about this man, his charms and foibles, he knew, he just knew, he was not living in a country in which unspeakable things happened, sanctioned by those in high office. No, those up there, or even off-duty in Clubland, were eccentric but not vicious; they had taken no interest in Annie and Marie, or in Alice, and had certainly issued no orders to Gull, to Slerch and Senna, to kidnap and maim, to jail and maltreat, to hunt down. England was theirs—Salisbury's and Gull's, but they had not turned it into a Roman bear garden: not yet, not quite. There was hope so long as gentlemen ran the world in their impromptu schoolboy way.

No sooner had he thought it than he recognized it as something no gentlemen would say. Very well: he was no gentleman, he was an observer, a snapper-up of unconsidered trifles. That was what made an artist of him, when, without even trying, he absorbed a hundred thousand disparate particulars and, in a flash or years later, returned a few of them to currency sea-changed, or paint-changed, into something that broke the heart and healed it all in one gaze. Who else knew, as he did, that the River Lea, upon which Gull's father had sailed bargeloads of ironware and coal, supplied Lord Salisbury's estate with electricity by means of a sawmill that cut wood all day and served as an electromagnetic machine at night? Did it matter that he knew? No, but his knowing it changed him fractionally, and it changed his attitude to the two men. The bargee in the one's background and the love of light in the other's had to be taken into account. Two men with a river in common, they held sway over different areas, but their sways overlapped, not neatly (the one man supplying what the other lacked, and vice versa), but more or less usefully. His task was to learn them, these two men, and allow for them, keep them jointly in mind day and night, since they held his future in their hands. They would use him, he knew. He just wanted, if possible, to be one step ahead of them, so that he had a breathing space, a time for maneuver, and so might not only solve the Annie-Alice-Kelly problem, but do himself and his career a modicum of good. Was that hypocritical? He thought not: good old Sickert, all of twenty-eight, would never wrong those dear and near to him, whatever the cost to his career. True, he had cultivated Wilde and Whistler and many others, both in England and France, but he was none the worse for that. A man had to get on, whatever demons barked at his heels, whatever snakes curled in his bed.

So Sickert listened to gossip, regarding it as the breadcrumb obbligato of great societies; those who ignored it were missing the texture of daily bickering, and those who spent their lives on it had found the most delicious narcotic of all. Sickert's problem was to make his information serve him, especially with Gull, who might be regarded as a man with a sword of Damocles over him. By dint of asking in his daily round (everybody knew somebody who had had a stroke), Sickert established that the mildest strokes seemed to recur within the next three months, if they recurred at all, which was something that few doctors told their patients, lest worry bring the event about. Now, Gull had suffered his funny turn last October, so, this being midsummer, he must be feeling rather pleased with life. And indeed his demeanor was that of a man whom the Furies had tweaked and, without quite letting go, had let continue almost unimpaired. Sickert did not know the tiny details, but Gull had made no secret of them: his memory faltered somewhat, his speech (he felt) was slightly slurred, his eyes were not quite as keen, and the muscles about his lips were sometimes erratic, not always allowing him to speak with the promptness he wanted. The main thing was that the attack had not recurred, not yet; Sickert told himself he was dealing with a man, albeit of seventy-two, who had an incipient Lazarus complex, whose way with the world was characterised by a domineering euphoria. Tripped once, he would never trip again, at least until he was destroyed, and he would not waste his energies on gratitude but drive forward with colossal pride to make his mark upon the universe. Treat him as such, Sickert said, and you will do no wrong. Treat him gently, or with affable understanding, and you will end up floating away in the River Lea. Deal with him as you would with an adder fanged, he quoted with a smile. And live to love.

Gull was Salisbury's torpedo.

And Salisbury, whose children said he treated them like ambassadors, was Gull's pharaoh—aloof, donnish, sharp-mindedly gentle, yet for all that the keeper of the keys, the man to whom that caravan of princely riders traversing history was paramount, to whom the flashing blue and scarlet of the military escort surrounding the one little figure in black, their *Queen,* was

the purest poetry. Nay, *Poesy,* Sickert whispered. If what survived was the status quo, all would be well, certainly with the
Queen and the Prime Minister, whereas Gull was one who
believed in energy for its own sake; much as Victoria believed,
ultimately, in the magic of people's doing what she told them
to do. Gull was the risk, the threat, a man whose quintessential
mystery was mayhem. Now, for nothing, he had a Sickert of
Annie Crook, immortal icon of a perishable woman. The tears
formed, and Sickert began to think he could not take the strain
any more of a life that had suddenly turned political and harsh.

What had once been his natural morbidity, his love of the
gutter as a subject and a theme, had now become a trap, no
longer optional. A style had turned into a footprint of fate,
wished upon him as ineluctably as a port-wine nevus on his
hand at birth. It felt different. It *was.* He no longer had the
luxury of an evening's tasteful melancholia, almost as if he were
some variant of Salisbury's homegrown "depraved voluptuary."
He woke up in tears and went to sleep to be rid of sadness. God
was leaning over him, he was certain, getting him ready for the
next great wound, apprising him that his former gaiety and the
dignified flippancy of his old manner were going to have to yield
to something much more miserable, not as one of those poor
filthy outcasts squatting by the abyss, but as a man marked for
singular and awesome degradation, no longer a matter of choice.
He would feel the eagle peck at his liver, and then he would be
thrown out of the human race, and his lugubrious works after
him, for having tampered, meddled, for having failed. Gull
would be his butcher, he could tell, and all those refined people
in high places, mouthing tribal diphthongs and regaling themselves with the vision of plundered territory, would write him
off as one who paddled out of his depth, beyond his means, one
who could not tell a taboo from a royal inkwell. Sickert was a
marked man.

In that case, he decided, he might as well go on painting as
usual. That would be stoicism, would it not? As well as common
sense. Under whatever pressures, the artist should maintain his
routine, letting into his everyday work whatever happened. A

creative man was like a river; he always flowed, if he could, and then big happenings had something to topple into. He could see the sense in never letting success or failure, good luck or bad, deflect the creative impetus. It was a good way of domesticating things too big to cope with. Could he, Sickert, do it now with what had happened, irrevocably or not, to Annie? Was there any uncallous way of getting on with his own life? It was no good cracking up over what he could not remedy; but how opportunistic and callow that sounded. Again and again he wondered where the paperwork was, the signature and the memorandum, requiring Annie's kidnap, the breakup of the lovers, and so forth. He wanted to know what to blame: Salisbury's vagueness or Gull's draconian determination? As often as not, whatever brought some event about remained hidden in a clubby consensus of kindred minds, hidden away in the cuckoo clocks of history. And now, with the telephone, everything would be even harder to pin down, though it had always been something such as "an enhancement of zeal into which we will not inquire too curiously" or "an honourable bigotry whose repercussions even the Angel Gabriel might never be able to calculate." He knew how things got done, how one old boy shaded his preference into the other's pragmatism, and something happened, although nobody quite remembered why, such was the onrush of events, the terrible Niagara of Empire. That was not Sickert's world, but he was not wholly averse to one fellow's putting another up to something, in the vaguest terms; he had heard it could be done, and one of his fainter acquaintances, a young but old-looking solicitor (he was thirty-two but looked sixty-five) had explained how it might be done through passionate vicariousness, telling a man who knew another man what you wanted; then this second man told a third, important man, who at once had the first man look at your credentials. This young-old solicitor, with whom Sickert had formed a habit of taking short lunches at a tiny restaurant in Soho crammed with doves in cages was named Peregrine Straws-Cuthbertson, but Sickert out of irritation with the English habit of portmanteau names had amplified him into Peregrine de Explicit Ridgeway Ffoulkes Straws-Cuthbertson, Grine for short.

"Are you taking notes?" the solicitor asked. "Good. This is tricky. Concerning the hypothetical I refer to as Prince and Slut, Her Majesty would be sanguine in that the Royal Marriages Act would invalidate the marriage on two grounds at least. First, from what you say, the Heir was under twenty-five at the time of the marriage. Second, he married without the Queen's consent. If only *private* life were as discriminated for. After all, dear fellow, the marriage of Augustus, Duke of Sussex, for instance, was quite easily quashed, in spite of the birth of a second child. He could have fathered a regiment of royal bastards without altering the case a jot. I take it, however, that your interest in this is not wholly legal. I will simply add that" (this was their third lunch, the second time he had explained things, but the first time he had added anything) "the Act of Settlement, going back to 1700, expressly prohibits from inheriting the crown anyone married to a Roman Catholic. Watertight as a nun's eyelid." Clearly fish was improving his brain; but it was not this parchment-and-statute artillery that interested Sickert; he cared more about the moods of people, from the Queen to the venomous toady Netley. The law was one thing, but how people worked themselves up was another.

Downing a wine so pale it might have drained from the pancreas of a corpse, Grine explained further, although redundantly. "Imagine, Walter, a twitchy general in an utterly impregnable fort. No need to worry, but he has an apoplexy because he feels insulted about even being attacked."

"Stunning," Sickert said. This was the final lunch.

"I think it *is* an ainalogy," said Grine, mispronouncing.

"It is nothing else," Sickert told him, wondering why he had paid for three lunches with money borrowed from Ellen.

Eddy had offended everybody by pleasing himself, and, although Victoria would eventually come out of a rage (having stormed for several weeks like a woman scorned, not to mention a monarch snubbed), Salisbury would remember, even if only a little more vexed by It than he wasn't. That leftover bit of vexation would direct his animus and feed his prudence: It must not happen again; Its having happened at all must be effaced; and the execution of remedy must go to someone whose way of doing things was so erratic that nobody quite realized what he was up to. Lost in the Byzantine excesses of that steel-toed personality, the original motive would wither and crumble; once again history would have been written by an idiosyncratic self-server, no more to blame than Peter the Great when he knelt under the table and felt at the private parts of his courtiers through holes he had had specially cut in their chairs. *"Foramen,"* he cried, whenever he felt a pudendum. *"Foramen habet!"* More historical gossip, Sickert chided himself; but history was made of such stuff.

Chapter 15

If only, instead of plopping into textbooks, such things settled into the still-soft pigments of art instead, not as events but as pomegranates, thrushes, frogs. What was he trying to tell himself? If only such things helped a Sickert, say, to fortify and increase the keening-mourning tenor of certain works in hand. What he meant was that he wanted the emotions of history without the chapter-and-verse *and then*s with which they had been involved. Joan burning. Robespierre foaming. Peter the Great fondling. He wanted, mainly, the sadness of things—some temperamental bias, he supposed—but he wanted to arrive at it without having to journey through the daily structure of mishap and the regular shift to stoical acceptance. The greatest work came about, he was convinced, when you went to his old friends, Those Without Hope, whatever their economic condition, and took them down in browns and ochres, mildewed greens and sour greys. Some day, he thought, he would like to get it all on canvas without spelling things out like

The Illustrated Police News; and the way to do this was perhaps apocalyptic: a combination, in his habitual colours, of allusion, cryptic hint, and full-blast portrait—not for the squeamish, he supposed. He dreaded becoming what he called a society painter, but he knew he needed society to make his blood run cold.

"Once they marry you," Polly Nichols was telling Marie Kelly, "they reckon they've got you for life. Iad five by him before I said toodle-oo, Bill, I'm not a whelping bitch any more. They treat you like a lavtrie. Bung you up and off they go to squirt into somebody else. Sproper painful, ain't it, ducky?" When she spoke, Polly, who was forty-two, released a fine sibilant spray, being short of teeth both above and beneath. She had a wide Teutonic jaw and long, oval eyelids that in some lights gave her an Oriental look and added to her seductiveness. She and Marie Kelly were downing enough rum to keep the world at bay, at least until tomorrow morning. "Yes," Polly said, "what with him being a printer, see, I ends up with black ink in all my entrances, almost as if he was some kind of chimbley sweep. Sooty-butty, that's what they should have called me. Even me nips was sooty. Suck them, and you gets a tribe of little black uns, if you understand me, Mrs. Kelly."

"I'm not Missus any more," Marie Kelly said. "Where you been since, then? Your face looks familiar. I have seen you in the Ringer's before this." Sarcasm, all of it.

"Oh yes, darling, I'm a regular," Polly said. "I've been giving them the hand gallop with me hand full of warm candle-fat, see. They likes anything as gets them off. My Bill, he was always saying, never fuck a fucker, so I seztwim, father of five by then, who's a fucker if you're not a fucker? What you fink a fucker expects from a fucker like me if not to fuck them for fivepence? I asks you. I ends up with a nice Mister Cowdry of Ingleside, Rose Hill Road, in Wandsworth, but I steals various bits of clothing and makes my move. Thrawl Street, love. I'm back. That's what I am. And I am seriously thinking of having it stitched up. They can rub up against it, but they's not going to push away into it any more. I'll jam it up with sailcloth and stale buns. Only cows'll be allowed to moo at me muffin. Wear and tear, I call it. Men coming up, children coming down, it makes you cry out in your sleep for some crosswise traffic to turn all the scars into crosses. If you see what I mean, Mrs. Kelly."

"I'm not Missus any more I told you," Kelly said. "I thought I knew your face. Where *I*'ve been, you couldn't hear it rain for the swishing of the princes and all. Oh yes. I've seen the highest in the land. One of them took me off to Dieppe to be his fancy woman, but I was too demanding. He was a limp Leslie, him. But this prince, he was champion, he did it all night with this here servant girl—well, she served sweeties in a shop, and he didn't half swamp her with Mint Imperials, he filled her with a baby."

"In the Thames by now, I spose."

"No, off among the toffs. I'd been looking out for her till then. I wasn't good enough for the likes of them. But the worst was, they came and split them up, carted her off to a loonybin, and there she stays. It's enough to make you weep. A nice girl like that, took away from her little girl, and her stallion prince off in the army somewhere, putting his joyprong to the elephants. *India,* I'll be bound. Life hasn't been standing still since I saw you last. How are you, dearie? You know me, I'm up again, I've a bun in the oven. I made sure I was going to fall off the roof, three months ago, but, well, that was three months ago and the little bugger's growing."

"Jump down the stairs."

"I keep thinking about how they dragged them apart, him howling, her too thunderstruck to chirp. Take it from me, the next queen will be a confectioner's assistant. They was married, you know. Me a witness. And her a Catholic. Imagine."

Polly Nichols finished her rum, then asked Marie Kelly to buy her another. "I'll be off out soon, love, to get me dossing money. I'll see you right. I'll pay. Ta ever so. There was a child, then, that could be queen?"

"There was a child who could be queen."

"Well, ice my cake. I never heard of such. All I ever did was lift a few clothes from the workhouses and this Mister Cowdry, but I never thrumped with no princes. What prince?"

"Prince Eddy: Albert Victor Christian Edward, the son of his nibs the Prince of Wales."

"And all I ever did was pawn some clothes I'd nicked. Fyde known princes was offering baby juice, I'd have gone and stood in line for some. Once you have it, you never know what won't come of it. I was all right until my Bill, he says, you drunken slut, you have been *oaring*, I seen you, and I says he wouldn't know whoring if he sore it, and out I go, but eel give me five shillings a month, at least until he stops and the Parish of Lambeth summonses him to show cause, and he does, and they say, poor Billy Boy, you don't have to pay another penny for Polly with her pie full of maggots and common-or-garden tup-juice. From then on, Marie, nice name, a French touch, I am on my beam ends, in this or that workhouse, Edmonton, Holborn, bloody shitpiss Lambeth, I am having my insides banged out of me like raspberry jam just for doss money, see, they're none too particlar where they put it, slongaz it slides—did you say the Prince? A real prince with fancy embroidery and a crown? How did the likes of—" She coughed and began to laugh.

"Princes," Marie told her with haughty gravity, "have a way of graduating to me naturally. I'm a foamy trollop, and they can tell half a mile off. A few of *me* in the so-called royal family, and they'd have to build stronger beds and make bigger pyjamas. I'd have them sweating all night. Anyway, I know what to do now. Get a prince, that's what."

"I don't know, 'Rie," Polly Nichols said in her odd whimpering insistent whisper, "I wouldn't let the Lord God have me fiasked me for it. No more little strangers, God, if you don't mind. No more pearly pop-up for Polly, Polly's out of action. No princes and no almighties. I just want a little place to tend some roses, and a big slab of cheese to shave away at after midnight. I don't want any men, that I don't. And when I need, I'll twirl me twig."

"Princes have the wherewithal, darling," Marie told her.

"They even piddle in silver pots, and they have little gold-leaf hoods for their perfections to keep warm in until morning. I'd do it for free. I must not have had my head screwed on right when I had the chance. I wouldn't be supping rum with no Polly Nichols in no Ringer's if I had, I'd ha' been smacking my chops over the fat of the land. And I might yet. I want them to do right by that child, and I want a bit more than that as well."

"I has to go open me legs, dearie," Polly told her in a loud, experienced voice intended for all, "or I'm not going to sleep in a bed this night. How, though, do I manage not to spend it on booze, the demon, afore I get home again? Now tell me that. Without the rum I can't do it, but I can't get the rum without doing it. Maybe it's time for little boys."

"Little boys won't pay," Marie said, heavy and stern.

"But their daddies can watch," Polly quipped. "Gnite."

Perhaps it was the motion of the other woman going, the wind of purpose blowing a little sidelong puff against Marie: she had to go, clomping away to the lavatory, not for business but to be alone amid the mold and the dank lead pipes, the bubbling cistern and the stench of purge. Erect in the crude stall with its woodshed door, she imagined she had suddenly joined a famous regiment. Here she was, standing to attention as if commanded by some steep-voiced sergeant-major, or just driven by an inward hankering to be taut and prim. Perhaps, she thought, this was the military way of praying: you aimed your thoughts, your wants, clean past everything, not at God's face or the wounds of Jesus, but antiseptically into the sun, out of sight but at this very minute burning South America. She knew that much. She was bracing herself for the big effort; before getting above herself, she was doing penance in the shed that gave nobody dignity. Someone came in and banged at the door, only to hear Marie's thunderous plea: "Can't you tell? There's somebody *on*. Can't you hear the soul of a body breathing?" Away went the other, moaning "Oh, Marie," and she wondered who it was being so familiar. Now she stood right against the door, face, stomach, and thumbs touching the ragged planks, as if inhaling succor from the grain, as if—yes, she decided, being laid to rest while standing up. She was going to stand like this for ever.

To be Polly Nichols was one thing, but to be Marie Kelly was another; Marie did not need a scrap of broken mirror such as Polly carried around with her from one workhouse to another; she knew what sort of a figure she cut, with her almost bloated handsome features, all a bit large to start with and now afflicted with the mellow sheen of pregnancy. She had big brown eyes and a capacious, moistened mouth. Babes could be born through *my* mouth, she said, though let's hope not. I am a better-spoken woman than most, with a better head on my shoulders than most. I expect that bit more of life than they do. I have that extra bit of push. I can hold a smile longer, stare people down longer, go without speaking longer. I sometimes look like a reputable matron, that I do. One part of me can talk with the girls here, and what would life be without a ton of idle chatter among near-equals? But there are limits, and sometimes I like to have a solid think, not that it gets me anywhere, but it does keep the grey matter from rusting up. I do, don't I, have that more expensive look about me, not just an old put like Polly. I had a better bringing-up, I did, not that I asked for it, how could you ever *arsk* for it? No, it was just one of those little happinesses of fate that sometimes come a body's way, and then leave them with an indelible pride, if that's what I've got. I've got that, all right, even if, over the weeks, my nose and mouth and eyes are getting that little bit bigger, and there's a new whiteness shining off my eyelids.

About Annie now, I reckon we can do something, and about ourselves too. They must want to keep it quiet, keep it down, mustn't they? It's just the kind of bad news the royals don't want plastered all over London. They've a bad enough name as it is for whoring and swindling. Imagine, then, when folks hear how they've got it in for a poor Scotch confectionery assistant whose legs got widened by a prince with a moustache. I'll help her. I'll help myself as well. If I'm anybody. I'll eat all the hard-boiled eggs in all the pubs in Ireland, that I will. I'll show them a little something about loyalty and spunk. I haven't got a brother in the Scots Guards for nothing. Good old Henry. I slithered into it, I suppose, it's either that or life with Morgan-stone in the Ratcliff Highway or Joe Fleming in Bethnal Green.

Always have to be somewhere, with some poor old trump of a chap, a cracked cup in one fist and your doss money in the other, a sixpence with blood of your monthlies on it. I am thirty-five shillings behind with the rent and have but one way of earning it, even while sicking up in the street. Off to Aldgate and peddle your bum, my lass. What an outcome on a rainy night. I'd do better to let them boil me down for fat to put in soap. Lord, forgive a poor wench of the streets, once respectably married, now in the family way; just get me started again without having to hawk me thighs up and down Aldgate. For the few pence you get, the indignity's not worth it. Up you stand, my lord, with all your petticoats hoisted clear for action, see, the old one-two, bumpity-bump against your you-know-what. Like dogs at it in the street against some old brick wall, a shack, a rotten door, it makes no difference, you get a lap full of gruel and off you go to your next laying on of hands. My mercy, they never stop, but if you look an inch off-colour they want a bargain, a reduction, a lot more for less.

> "Once I was a nanny,
> Who kept the cleanest fanny,
> Sweet-smelling and oh so neat,
> Back there in Cleveland Street."

I sang. I'm better off with a violet plucked from the grave. I offer them a hair, fresh from the thatch of ages, telling them it's a violet from the grave, which it is, and they laugh, they know what it is and they clean their teeth with it, they slide it in between them and cock their noses for the smell of a ripe lady. Connoisseurs, these, they know what a con is in Dieppe. I haven't been all over the world for nothing. Ribbons. Yachts. Blue blazers with shiny gold buttons. And Marie Jeanette in a white silk dress. Now she wears a linsey frock again, red knit crossover, no hat or bonnet, black velvet body, dark dress. That's me. Drab as drab can be. I want something. I want something good. How do you write it? I want something good period. I want a period, by gum I want my period. Where would a comma go, then? Like that. Where would a comma go *comma* then? That's how they do it. When you want to slow up a bit, a comma, and for longer a full-blown period staining you all over your legs. I am going to lose it again. Here I go. Sick as a dog after chocolate. I wish I was in the Scots Guards and not a woman. Home to Miller's Court, my darling, hope against hope that a golden opportunity doesn't present itself en route because you dare not refuse, you dare not tell it to rub itself up against a nice old snail-slimy wall. You can't do that if you need the dibs. You have to have it. You have to spread and then pretend to die. All to soften that long radish of the lamplight.

On her way out of the Ringer's, she almost bumped into a gangling, severe-faced woman who spoke with a Scandinavian accent: Elizabeth Gustaafsdotter, which name she had buried like a dead silver fox when she married John Thomas Stride, who (she always claimed) had drowned in the *Princess Alice* with two of their nine children—the ship had been run down by a collier in September 1878. Marie Kelly never believed the story, nor the other one that Stride spread about: that she suffered from fits. Stride lived in Fashion Street with a waterside laborer named Michael Kidney, with whom she sometimes settled down to bouts of dedicated torpor, skivvying or darning to make ends meet, but she just as often took to the streets. "You still haff it," Stride said, which was her habitual way of putting a question.

"Oh, I don't know," Marie said, to infuriate; Stride liked clear-cut answers although she herself stayed safe behind the impromptu fabric of her yarns. "You never know."

"Please yourself," Stride snapped. "Tell somebody else who cares about you. Tell Polly, don't forget to tell Polly. Polly likes to hear about babies with French names."

Marie thrust forward and out, thinking how buxom she had become, no doubt on account of the baby, but wondering if beer could do it to you. The summer night was like a vault of silk, and she at once slowed her pace to inhale, drawn as always by pleasant weather into daydreams of unutterable splendor, but really dreams of other people's lives beyond her proper station, dreams of herself as one of the "fancy-women" of the Prince of Wales himself, backing him vehemently when he complained about how so-and-so attended a wedding in a black waistcoat, so-and-so went aboard the royal yacht in a Yacht Squadron mess jacket and a white tie, and somebody else wore his decorations in the wrong order. In this interior world Marie Kelly dressed special when visiting art galleries, as did her consort, who knew the answers to everything, once declaring, while she thrilled to his savvy, that it would be appropriate while in mourning to go to the races at Newmarket, because one wore a bowler, but not to the Derby because one would have to wear a top hat, and that simply would not do. She warmed to his easy codification of peccadilloes, not that she approved of his great big tiepin or his too-tight overcoats—he set the style for everyone else and they adored to look like him. After all, he was going to be the king; he was going to be crowned, so close behind him came Marie Kelly in that lazy, wafting, heavy-footed gait of hers, the very model of easy curving meat, offered to him all the time in his capacity as a *donnaiulo* (she knew some Italian too, especially words pertaining to erotomania and romance). Plying her trade in the street, as she usually had to, she dreamed her way through it, counterpointing the sordid or the rain-sodden with indoor escapades whose male figures sported soft felt hats brought home from Hamburg, shook hands with their elbow held stiffly against their ribs (a posture that the Prince had been driven to by rheumatism), and undid the bottom button of their waistcoats while sipping the Prince's "cocktail," made of whisky, maraschino, champagne, pineapple, lemon peel, powdered sugar, and angostura bitters.

"Now then, Wales," she would hear herself asking, "how's a bit of lower-class fanny strike you then? More muscle in it for what ails you, ducky."

He would puff himself out and forward, then rebuke her while eyeing her shape. "Not *here.*" At the races or on the yacht. Marie preferred the former as less giddy-making.

"Then where?"

He puffed cigar smoke all over her.

"They do say," she began, trying him with the sardonic, "that Lillies have a funny smell. Of death."

"Not one of my favorite puns, Marie-Jeanette."

"You'd rather watch a Lillie onstage at the Twickenham Town Hall, eh, Wales?" She would call him this after the fashion of La Goulue, the loudmouth star at the *Jardin de Paris,* who sometimes added *"tu paies le champagne!"* Now she asked him about Gladstone, the former Prime Minister, who not only preached purity to whores but used them for degrading purposes special to him, including mainly whipping, each bout of which he depicted in his diary with a tiny whip. "What does *he* do, Wales?" She heard the whish and the thwack.

"Well, first," he would say, entering into the spirit of a little conspiratorial smut together, "he sends the lady a bunch of narcissi and a twelve-pound tin of Russian tea, the strong stuff. Or he sometimes takes the flowers himself. When he arrives, he shows her the crucifix he never goes out without, and then rams it up her dress through all the layers of finery until he thinks he has done her enough injury to pay for the sordid do that follows. If we didn't have such realistic fellows at the country's helm, just think where we'd end up. None of your prudes for us. As I say, he gives her a thundering dunt *down there,* then withdraws it and kisses it clean. Now, he's the Prime Minister *as was;* Salisbury's quite different. Give me a Gladstone any day. Then he comments on the neatness of her waist and spans it with his hands, after which they get to work. He strips and she flogs, then they couple if he is of a mind to do so. Sometimes, though, he asks for a cowslip shower and she obliges at the crouch."

"Mister Gladstone?" Marie loved this scandalous part of their chronic conversation, wishing this was the minister to whom she had to write. No, even on the run, she'd try to go and see him, thrash him to a pulp, then keep him at her mercy with undreamed-of humiliations. "The *Pee Em?*"

"None other, my lass. You had best beware of Mister Gladstone and his whip."

"They do say he had Mrs. Langtry too."

"Mrs. Langtry volunteered, observing that he had the physique of a young Greek god and proportions befitting a virile baboon."

"Blimey," she said, "we breed some tophole rotters in this country. I'm glad I left Ireland behind me, honest I am. If to hell you have to go, travel in good company."

Such was the prelude to the first time she envisioned herself alongside two men of quality with whom she might have got on well, choosing to remain with them after the soup, the pullet, the mutton, and all those other dishes in which one bird was stuffed with something else that in its turn had been stuffed with yet another. She tried to get the order and proportions right: pheasant stuffed with snipe stuffed with truffles in which trouts' eyes had been embedded. Something like that. Anyway, after the ladies retire, Marie told herself, the whores get to work. She then adjourned with the Prince and Gladstone to the billiard room, where in the shadow of a screen depicting Salisbury and the poet Matthew Arnold engaged in erotic play with naked elves she would take the measure of their carnality, allowing them to test her with cues, chalk, and billard balls either on the hive-producing green baize or on a corner sofa. After the Prince had spilled his first, she let him rest while she gave Gladstone a good larruping. Then the three of them combined for the rest of the night, she telling the two of them they were in sterner company than ever before, Bertie telling her she must come hunting with him, naked in an ermine cape rubbed red with hot fox blood. "In the *battue*, er—"

"Pas de quoi, Wales," she whispered quick as a ferret, *"je comprends le français, j'ai passé quelques mois—"*

"We kill thousands of rabbits and birds, all driven toward us. I sometimes wish they were women, whom we would sample as best we could. Just think of it."

"A hunters' orgy," she sighed, rubbing table salt into the Prime Minister's welts. " 'Old still, Stoney boy, else you'll get a nice affection there." She was not only in her element; she *was* an element, purified and absolute: lust needing nothing but a mucous membrane to convert into a magic carpet. Portly, lascivious Bertie with the pointed beard slid a kipper into her while

Gladstone, after a few moments' indecision, set an ortolan alongside it, at which point she took their cigars from them and held them firm between her nether lips. " 'Old still," she said again, meaning something else. Or she cried "Watcher, cock!" in raucous, ribald greeting even as Gladstone, whose waist was only slightly bigger than the queen's, instructed her in how pain delivers joy—"a true experimental phenomenon," he told her, "of the human mind." Up he reared, taller than ever from injury, and she flogged him even harder for showing off.

"Yes, ducky," she told him, "like the poet says, now I am going to fart fire. You keep still now and stop your flinching. Who asked for it? Who *arsted* for it?"

"Why, *he* did," Bertie muttered, realizing he had just crossed over into spectator hell, where, if the spectacle failed to arouse it became abominable, and the woman Kelly swelled above them, all barnacles and greasy flanks, her cavities releasing sea-weed and her mouth heaving into view a viscous ectoplasm amid which ptarmigans, cakes, and trifles lost their shapely, tactful nature and became a hell-dame's droppings. Bertie all of a sudden yearned for his patient, stiff, and always-late wife, erect in her tight-curled wig, mauve boa, and shoes of white satin. Queen Kelly took them at their word and proved she could go far beyond them in sleek depravity, and then slink off home to a solitary bed like one who has given medical succour to those hurt in a street accident. Even after she had gone, though, or had been rudely told to trot her hams, they heard, each in his own way, Bertie aghast, Gladstone self-loathingly, the fierce and provoking cries with which she punctuated their undoing: "*Basta!* Queen of Hearts! Knickers! Black balls! John Bull! The vomit of Ireland! The scabs on the poor! Apricot tart! *Despunta!* Foggy gas. I'll take a motor brougham, lads!" Away she went into her wildest dream, ending it even as she began to believe in it. The sun that rose over her was down upon her before she knew it, and she wept at its cheek.

She never heard herself, having soothed her mind during her severest performances with an idyll, far from Irish, of orange blossom, Parma violets, shuntling golden Indian gauze and er-

mine trains delicately footprinted by dying wrens, all of which
fused into a high-blown aloofness she could not manage on the
streets or in the pubs; but she went on hearing Bertie and
Gladdy as they let out those guttural, towering, vainglorious
shouts of prowess, knowing (or dreaming) they had an incor-
ruptible audience at their mercy:

"See the monster."

"Ah, God, it gives, it yields."

"Oh that the Queen . . ."

"Wipe your mouth, madam."

"Whip me, Bertie."

"Whip yourself, Prime Minister."

"Why then, I'll whip you both," she at last said, having heard,
snapped loose from a dream within a dream, in which she was
performing the sinuous Moslem dance known as the *ghawazee*,
with a few minor variations of her own, all intended to provoke
a frenzy in her lords.

"Oh, such a mess," sighed Bertie.

"I know who'll mop it up, and what with."

"Ah, Africa."

"Oh, the Nile."

This was one side of Marie's voluptuous interior life. The
other, punitive in the extreme, yet still conducted with the
Prince in tow, involved an entire series of worse and worse
humiliations accepted instead of death. She kept imagining herself in the hands of some steel-featured Arabian Nights caliph,
really the Prince, who told her she had only a moment more of
life unless she agreed to eat an entire bowl of cow dung or cut
the throat of a proffered child. It was her way of entering into
the unthinkable, of approaching the metaphysical extreme of
the things she had to do daily because she was poor, ailing, and
rejected. If such things might be imagined, she felt, they might
be done. How much suffering could the human mind endure?
How much degradation was life worth? Such a question appealed to her because she often dwelled on the mine disaster
that had robbed her of her husband, and she could understand
why Stride liked to invent her poor husband's fate in the so-

called Great Thames Disaster. That she, Marie Kelly, did not live with the Prince, or any prince, in no way inhibited her from dreaming as if she did, supplanting the uneducated, graceful, generous Princess Alix, who would eventually work her way toward wearing the Koh-i-noor with the equally famous Cullinan diamonds and her Garter star on the wrong side because, she would say, it clashed with her other jewels. She imagined alternative lives for the royal couple, then thrust herself into the center of those lives, Princess Marie Jeanette of Dieppe, former consort of the famous painter Sickert, a woman at home in several languages, but most of all in the argot of the flesh.

They should hand the empire over to those who had no illusions at all and take it away from the dabblers, the clubland johnnies. She yearned for an aristocratic clientele who, while making perverted demands on her physique at its most private, would ply her with silks and stones, even creating for her some kind of title, to be relished in private, of course, but indelible as a tattoo: Lady Asterisk of Pimpernel Pier. How about that, with a purple sash to match? Inhaling the warm but far from fragrant air of a London July, she slowed her walk even further, trying to sense the tiny life within, the size of an oyster, perhaps, but felt nothing beyond the pressure of her body against her clothes. Her breasts swung forward uncontained, almost pulling her after them, such was their weight. A broth of a girl, she said, a well-glued trollop, going to waste in Aldgate because the Palace didn't want her, not knowing what was good for it. For a while, she had forgotten Annie Crook.

Munching up from a twist of newspaper a slice of fried cod the shape of an ax blade, she reassured herself with her favorite litany of self-esteem: You're an Old Testament girl, Marie Kelly, that you are. You'll get them yet. The fish was from the North Sea scalded in far-from-fresh lard, but she needed it, if only she could keep it down on top of the rum and the beer, an unpromising mixture. In another life she would be daintily picking at the cod with a silver fork especially crafted for fish, it would have slenderer tines and be lighter in the hand, would be notched and fish-shaped, with a lovely pattern embossed on the blade. Such refinements, she thought, then looked at the lines etched in her fish-handling hand, hardly visible except under direct lamplight, which she tried to get. As she did so, a tall mustachioed man carrying a bottle of champagne accosted her, asked her if he would be comfortable with her, and made an offer. Then he tried again.

"Comfortable or not, madam, I have to have *some*thing. The need comes, it does not go. It has been weeks, you see. Eau dew decide." It was Sickert's amplified solicitor, Peregrine de Explicit Ridgeway Ffoulkes Straws-Cuthbertson, bargaining *in extremis.* Her only answer, as if to embrace this long-awaited customer, was to vomit all over his long black overcoat, and even as she messed him up she wondered who would wear a November coat in July. As he recoiled, cursing, she handed him the fish leftover in ironic compensation, but he dashed it to the ground with his fist and swung away from her into the night, raving and befouled.

Here, anyone watching would have said, she went again, holding the gas lamp post with both hands as if to save herself from drowning, then letting go with one and beginning to work herself around it, executing some uncouth dance of celebration, though of what, with her mouth caked up and her head thudding? What? She was reliving a rowdy evening of not long ago when she and some of the others,—Stride and Nichols, Annie Chapman and Maria Harvey,—had welcomed a similarly warm night with beer and childhood songs, pretending to pick one another up, arrest one another for being drunk and disorderly, and becoming so drunk and disorderly during the arresting that people came outside to watch. The girls, one publican said, were having what they called a *frisk,* no harm meant, none done, least said soonest mended, and so forth. Sooner or later the police would warn them and take them into custody, but let them out again before midnight, when they had to make room for others more in need. Thus they would be free to ply their trade until dawn, getting enough doss money together to pay the rent by midmorning. They were an only slightly divided family, half a dozen or so among some twelve hundred prostitutes in Whitechapel, all of them women on the edge, making no kind of living but eking out a cobweb of an existence, undecided what to do next, if anything.

For a while, Nichols had lived in a house known as the White House, on Flower and Dean Street, where Elizabeth Stride, the Swede, had a room; but Stride had done some moving about, more than most, dossing also in Fashion Street, but mainly in Dorset Street, with Michael Kidney, which was also where Annie Chapman lived. Now Nichols lived mainly in Thrawl Street, only a couple of hundred yards from Dorset Street, where Marie Kelly also lived, in Miller's Court. When they did not run into one another at the Ringer's or The Frying Pan, they did so in the street, often while touting for business in the small hours, when they would briefly desert the men they had in tow and have a short, uproarious gossip, resuming in a better humor, the waiting clients having been eyed and ridiculed, nicknamed and anticipated (as to needs and performance). A loose clique of the loose, they had just about the same income and the same erratic relationship with one or two members of the opposite sex, whom they from time to time walked out on simply in order to get blind drunk in peace. In a sense these women, the Annie Chapmans and the Long Lizzes and the Polly Nicholses, were nobody's, rancid blooms who once had beauty and some hope, but now in the main bad livers, ruined kidneys, and little to show for it save an acute, intricate knowledge of men at their least subtle. Marie, the most ingenious and adventurous of them all, had once put on a pair of bloomers too big for her and rigged into her groin an old loaf scooped and lined with lard, affording accommodation for an average-sized penis. Thus equipped, the artifact having been carefully moored with string, she had gone out to seek a client and had successfully engineered him past his fourpence to a climax in a dark back street, even as he complained to her that she was carrying too much fat. He preferred his women more robust, tighter in the loins. "Sorry, darling," she told him, "one of these nights I do declare I'll be having my womb down between me ankles, and then what'll I do, walk bowlegged?" He had gone away in disgust, but Marie had saved some of the wear and tear on her anatomy, afterward handing the somewhat mashed-up loaf around in the Ringer's, to let the others see, sniff, and ritually squeeze. "Horn sandwich," she said, laughing, and Long Liz said she should have bit the offending member off, making it a real delicacy. Such were the high times they had together, and such the vulgar pranks they played, hardly more preposterous than the high jinks of the Prince of Wales or the lappets and veils, and headdresses of three white feathers, insisted on by his Mama at Windsor.

Chapter 16

Marie Kelly was a worldly twenty-four, at the right age for changing her mind so as to become this or that; with many deaths and degradations behind her, she still saw her life as something yet to come. The other women were older, not so much going off as gone; yet, oddly enough, they took their lead from her, perhaps because of her energy. They, who never thought of themselves as women of Whitechapel, seemed exactly that to her: a team, a class, a tribe. But, to Marie, the phrase "women of Whitechapel" (invented by Sickert) applied to many who did not live there but found themselves drawn there to fornicate, to dream, to sneer, to prate. Anybody having any connexion with Whitechapel lived in Whitechapel: that was her thought. By the same token she herself was also a resident of Buckingham Palace, having business there, and Cambridge, Windsor, and Dieppe.

"What are you saving yourself for?" Sickert had once asked her, intending no harm; she just seemed so young, so old, both at once.

"Until I turn into a bank," she answered. "Until a change so wonderful I'll know I won't need to change again. 'Nile sleep."

"After whoring," he said with a skeptical glint.

"Ah, me flower," she told him, "there's nanny, there's artist's model, there's chambermaid, there's cook and bottle-washer. Skivvying on your hands and knees is the worst, as I did when a young widow. Since I haven't no lands to speak of, no castles and estates, I make do with the muck in a flowerpot. Up to now I have no deer, nor fowl, nor rabbits, no grouse and no pheasants, no foxes to hunt. Butchernivverno."

"You want to be careful," he said, "you don't get lumped along with somebody else's foxes and pheasants."

"Beggar that," she scoffed. "I recall the No Trespassing signs nailed to the apple trees in Ireland, where the grass was greener, my love, and the speech more musical, and the sheep whiter and woollier. We just walked round them, the signs, I mean. They didn't apply to us. They were directed at human beings, see, and we, who were lower than low, didn't matter at all. Please come and trespass: that's what they meant to us, Walt, and 'twas a rare gamekeeper that fired his shotgun at us. We lived in God Almighty's armpit there. I wonder I left. One pretty slum with grass for another slum with toffs. That's the exchange I made, my dear, and look at me now. I look older than a duchess would at my age, don't I?"

Sickert framed her in a rectangle made from two thumbs and two forefingers, his right hand held palm outward. "Don't you ever," he hooted, "become a duchess, my lovely. Stay the wild flower you are. If you were small, and held under my chin like a buttercup, you'd make my skin shine yellow. *He likes butter.* They'd say that."

"I know what our Walt likes. He likes flesh. With his teeth into it. Preferably free. No, *Ail* never bee a duchess. No woman of Whitechapel ever will." He was only half listening. In his view, whoever was born and breathed had a right to a bit of land, as of weather and sea and sunshine, and he liked the down-and-out because in them he detected a forced purity, one they would never have had if their ancestors had had their wits about them. Much as, once, the land had been nobody's, so now the poor were nobody's too, but no one was moving in to plunder *them*—bar a few artists such as himself. Poor enough, yet not as poor as Marie Kelly, he saw poverty much as the ancient grass had been, growing rank and coarse, a dimension to be treasured with holy tenacity. What he hated was the rhetoric of money, the armor-coated assumption that men of power should talk to one another and to no one else; indeed, he and Marie Kelly, backed by the best-ambulant of London's poor, would have needed only a guillotine and some steps, a few tumbrils and some wool, to have a revolution of their own, to make the Thames run with blood. What sickened him, and Marie Kelly when she stood back from her business and really thought about it, was the way in which gentlemen with a few bob to spend might use women of the streets, women of the workhouse or the dosshouse, as their own semi-private dustbins or spittoons, and this because, of the two types, the female sex was the more mysterious vessel by far, therefore to be the more profaned, the more abused. It made sense to him that the superior mystery attracted the greater rage. People hated God more than they hated the queen, didn't they? A queen could be made, appointed, but a god could not, nor a buttercup, an ant, a glacier. No, *cunnus* was algebra or something incalculably worse, *penis* was arithmetic. A rising or standing prick, he had heard, had no conscience, whereas that other thing, all mucous petals and tiny red linked onions of futurity, capable of nine months' harboring and nurturing after five minutes of tupping, that was miraculous: to come up with so completely orchestrated a commitment after a splash from just about any indifferent johnny. Look at Annie, after Eddy. It was more miraculous than land or air or sea, it was the holiest thing he knew, but he wished its incessant profanation did not stalk his nights.

Women were on the streets only because men controlled the money. Were things the other way round, would women have men walking the streets, as *penistutes,* their lives on the line? He thought not, but he had no idea how to mend the world and its ways. Tempted to quote Lord Byron, something about sex's being to man a thing apart but a woman's whole existence, he held back; quotation was the coward's way out. The Annies and

the Maries had no future in the Dieppes of the world; a life had
to be made for them in Whitechapel, in places like Aldgate and
Leman streets, their "beat," not to mention Cleveland Street,
but he heartily wished he had not become their warden. Sickert
was almost willing to look upon tragedy, be moved, and then
go on living without too many painful afterthoughts, all of
which he would confide with well-bred equanimity to Ellen and
her set, then resume his contemplation of a color resonance in
something by Degas. Some folk were born victims. That was it.
No amount of conscience-stricken effort altered that, he was
sure.

All that was wrong with him was that he was not *whole-hearted,*
or great-hearted as it said in *The Odyssey:* he doubled back, he
feinted, he parried, he went about in disguises. In his rooms,
depending on what he had on hand, borrowed or stolen, he
dressed up as Napoleon, Degas, Whistler, Byron, Burns, and
many more; metamorphosis was his all. Had he been otherwise,
had he gone and rooted Annie and her child in Dieppe or its
environs without asking anybody's opinion, might not things be
better now than they were? Had he failed in a duty he had not
known, until recently, was his? What could he recoup? What
was it not too late to do even now, with Gull beginning to come
out of the darkness like an accredited bailiff?

After only a few nights of blather, as she got further and
further into her cups, Marie Kelly had infected her entire group
with her idyll, so that Polly Nichols now knew that Prince Eddy,
the famous shit-stabber from Cleveland Street, had raped a
shopgirl called Annie Crook, but she, Polly, was not sure who
had told her this: no doubt opinionated Long Liz, who never
believed anything but managed to get others to do her believing
for her. Long Liz, according to Annie Chapman, had said the girl
in question bore twins, one of whom was drowned in the
Thames by a death-team of a man and a woman. Marie Kelly
or Polly Nichols had told somebody that the surviving child, a
girl, had been hidden away in a padded cell on the Isle of Wight
while the mother, this Annie Crook, had been taken aboard a
steamer to Australia, there to start a new life, but not before, in

a London hospital, she had had her womb taken out just in case. That womb, according to Long Liz, now reposed in a jar in Buckingham Palace. Only two dozen rums later, Marie Kelly had been told by her friends that it was the girl who had drowned; the boy was now hidden away on the Isle of Man, and Prince Eddy had been ritually degraded by his regiment, who somehow had taken possession of the womb at a special dining-in night. Marie was the last person in the world to spurn an embellished story, especially one that she herself had started on its rounds not merely to watch its progress but to get herself some attention. It was like the larded loaf on the level of complex narrative. That the tale would travel, she had no doubt, and to the ears of people other than her boozing chums. The gist never left her, of course: the girl commoner who had fallen in love with a prince and married him, giving him (as the quaint expression had it) a female child who was to become queen of the realm. The kidnapping too found its way into the tangle of story, which also had Sickert (the painter gentleman) seized and transported to Australia, or Denmark, while Marie herself actually departed from her own fabrication, seized and removed first to the Isle of Wight and then to France, where she had disappeared, rumored to be living high on the hog in Paris, her allowance sent monthly direct from the royal coffer. All she had to do was to keep quiet, even in French (a language she was proficient at). It was as if, for her, there was safety in confusion: so long as the tale twisted upon itself, its basis was no threat, and lies could not be used against her, whereas the truth could. She had always known that. So, tempted by her sheer natural ebullience to adorn the facts, she adorned them out of prudence as well, co-opting Polly and Annie and Long Liz, and sometimes Maria Harvey and Catherine Eddowes, whose real name was Conway but called herself Kelly after the man she lived with.

In no time, a muddled account got itself multiplied by a quartet of willing talkers who regaled their friends with lurid tales of royal doings, from two twins drowned in a barrel of beer to a mother eviscerated and sent packing to the colonies while the prime malefactor, Eddy, malingered on Devil's Island by special arrangement with the French government. Only Marie Kelly survived (and some of the listeners in the pubs thought Marie was Annie or the other way round), and she was able, between one drink and the next, to watch herself becoming a figment in the seethe of gossip; now she understood how a voluble human might vanish behind a smoke screen of uncoordinated chatter—as good a place to be as any, she thought, once having started the ball rolling. There had been stories galore about the Prince, Eddy's father, and even about Eddy himself, but this was a new seam to mine. There were fascinating characters from their own set, to whom evil things were done relentlessly by those called toffs and royals.

Out in the night, stern forces-within-forces were gathering, just as apt to dishevel the truth as the tale-spinning of Marie Kelly. And, of course, as the tattle spread, it reached ears that found it more than a mere fairy tale of the down and out, but a living slander that, if it did not soon die a natural death, would die one of another kind.

Pleased as she was by the story's career, Marie kept a firm hand on the truth, the thing she was indignant about. Gift of the gab she had, but she also had the gift of remembering, and what had been done to Annie and Alice, even to Eddy so long as she thought of him as part of Annie-and-Eddy, made her blood boil. Was there not something bold and satisfying she could do about it, apart from starting half a dozen embarrassing rumours? She thought there was, but first of all she had to collect her wits and assemble what she knew of royal weak points. There was a way, she thought, and it would only work once—the first time; it would have to be done right, and all the links in the chain would have to be reliable. She talked her way through the rest of July and much of August, adapting freely until the Prince of Wales had become one of the Cleveland Street kidnappers and Annie Crook had been drowned in the Thames. But, night after night, sober or drunk, Marie did more than talk. She practiced her penmanship on the backs of old leaflets in her little room at Miller's Court or in the Ringer's, trying to strike the correct tone and arrive at the perfect phrase.

Clearly, one letter would not be enough, and each would have to reflect its intended recipient's nature and exact status.

When had she last written a letter, and to whom? Still less a begging letter. She knew she should have been writing to her six brothers and sisters, acquainting them with the trials of a London life, lying of course about the drudgery on her knees with the pearl-shaped lump of pumice or the square-cornered donkey-stone, but making the most of excursions to Dieppe with a toff who wore a white jacket and a carnation in his buttonhole. She was aiming, as she wrote, at the maximum of politeness; it was no use being rude, certainly not when speaking across chasms of ignorance and social indifference; you had to watch your p's and q's, and she wondered what *they* were. Surely her intended recipients would know: they were the ones who had invented such things, not so much for their own delight as to have something to humiliate inferiors with.

She had heard somewhere, no doubt in a less-uproarious pub than this one, that there was the elaborate way of addressing royalty, in which you recited all someone's titles to their face as if reading their pedigree to them before you began, and the simple way: you said "Sir" or "Mam," and that just about covered it. How did you best address people whose plate leavings other people collected and sold (chicken bones, for example, or cigar butts that had touched the sacred lips)? What could you say to people who had drawn up rules about a tickle in the throat (choke, by all means, but never cough), a sneeze (grind your teeth and, if need be, break a blood vessel, but never sneeze), and sudden bleeds (let them run, bite your lips hard)? She longed for etiquette, for the world in which it mattered and might be learned. The nearest to it she had ever come were the standard euphemisms of women on the game, as when they said to a prospective client "You will gain your ease, sir, in a trice, and then we shall rest you a while before going afresh." Or "I will be all right for what you want, just so long as you ask by touching where it is, sir."

Marie opted for straight "Sir" and "Mam," knowing that what mattered was her message, itself a thing so stirring that no reader of the letter would remember the salutation. Her first effort she addressed to Prince Eddy, whose capacity to read was limited, and she knew this:

It is not like the old days any more Eddy. When we laughed and made merry together in Cleveland Street. She is where she can not be happy, and your daughter Sir is being passed about from pillar to post. It behooves you we think to send her the necessary perhaps one hundred guineas to begin with. You can leave it with Mr. Sickert in Cleveland Street, who is your brother as you know. I am not so foolish as to think we could threaten you in this but it comes from the heart, the hearts that loved you in the past. I trust this finds you as it leaves me in health.

She had worried about "behooves"; was it *behoves* or *behooves*? She had no idea, and settled for what sounded most natural. She had never used the word before, but she was determined to use it regularly from now on, having mastered its contrary graces. When she read it to Polly and Dark Annie, they both thought that, for good measure, she should add a P.S. at the bottom saying they were all being threatened by the old Nichol gang that preyed on women of the evening, making them pay for protection they did not need. So, much prompted amid the pub's hubbub and tenaciously penning despite all the shoving she got, Marie extended her letter, but in her natural voice and idiom. She was tired:

Tho' I say it as shouldnt, there is a gang here in the Minories making menaces see and we have to pay them to protect us not that we need it. Should the child ever have to be here we would want a firm footing for her not a nanny that would be bashed about for non payment of her dues see. Polly and Dark Annie have put me up to this so it had better be a hundred and fifty guineas instead. Plse fgive spelling and such like, we are not Cambridge men, love, Marie Jeanette Kelly.

There was no need to rewrite it: she had a fair, large, looping hand, and it would probably have come out worse from being overlabored at. The letter would go to the brothel in Cleveland

Street, of course, and she liked the idea that all Prince Eddy had to do was walk a few doors down and hand over the money to Sickert, who, after all, was family. Blood was . . . well, whatever it was thicker than, she didn't believe in *that* stuff. Blood was blood and water was water. Wearied from her effort, she wished she did not have to write again, but Polly and Dark Annie egged her on, eager for novelty in the tight-cinched monotony of their underdeveloped lives. They homed to Marie's vigor and initiative like bees.

"Nah you gotta write dem uvvers," Polly said in her strongest cockney. "Weelelp."

"She don't need us," Dark Annie said. "Let's just watch. We might learn some*th*ing"

"Learn?" Polly swigged deep from her beer. "Yule never."

"Like how to talk right. It's not *uvvers* and it's not *somefing.*" Dark Annie set her beer down hard, in proof.

"I didn't say *somefing,* so there then."

"Shut up," Marie told them, "I am thinking what to say to his nibs. His Nibs being the Prime Minister. Mr. Salisbury, not Gladstone. He's a cleverdick, him, and you have to behave according. If I pretend he's somebody else, how about that? Somebody I already know, so it will come out natural-like. Myself, I favor the woman-badly-done-by sort of appeal, telling him, as if he didn't know all about it, what went on in Cleveland Street the day they lifted poor Annie and her Eddy."

"And then," Polly said deliriously, "the Queen."

"And then the Queen," Dark Annie said, rapt. "Erma Jestic."

"Then her," Marie said, aghast at the long vista of letters unrolling and then, delicate as some new-fledged linnet of spring, the first head to fall, smothered by linen but hailed with a cold, awed whisper by the mob.

Polly, for instance, was still married, and in her hinterland there were five children, the oldest of whom was twenty-one and living with his grandfather. Not having lived with her husband for three years, she had lodged with her father (a rowdy, quarrelsome time) and then faltered away into the dim round of workhouses, skivvying here and there for a few pence: Lambeth,

Wandsworth, and then the room in Thrawl Street or the one in Flower and Dean. Had she meant to go to the dogs? Probably not, any more than Dark Annie, apart from her husband for four years or more (he, a former coachman at Windsor, had provided Dark Annie with a lively fund of tales). She had taken up with a man named Siffey, or Sievey, who called himself that because he made sieves; but now he was dead, and her children had been scattered, the crippled boy having gone to a Cripples' Home and her daughter to some institution in France.

It was as if they, like Sickert, could not attune themselves to marriage, or even children, yet kept making feints at the condition, eager to be steady but without the mental consistency to sustain it. They were not so much lost souls, she thought, as lost wives, now espoused to liquor and whoring, living from day to day and hand to mouth, never knowing if they would have the price of a bed tomorrow night. It was a far from intoxicating freedom, Marie thought. It was a freedom to die uncared about, to sink into the mud and die namelessly, just for lack of a job, for lack of the desire to be a constant anything—a wife, a skivvy, a parasite, a mother, a grown-up daughter. Dark Annie, whose meek exterior harbored a violent temper, had even tried making ends meet by selling flowers and doing crochet work; she had nimble hands; but, like Polly, she had somehow connected episodic living with the quick-change moods brought on by alcohol. Yes, Marie decided: the drinking fitted the pattern they were already in, but it made the pattern firmer. That was it. They drank because they were erratic, and drink only made them more so. She was much prettier, oh yes, than Polly and Dark Annie and the others: less wear and tear; softer and moister skin (an *Irish* skin, too); an easier smile; fewer aches and pains. Sometimes, when she thought about her life and the kinds of women she mingled with, she drew her breath in sharply, almost as if having a pang, and tacitly exclaimed at the sheer involvement in life they had all achieved, mainly out of sexual aimlessness. But perhaps, in doing so much without, she and the other women had come up with a new kind of virtue. It was because they were poor that they denied themselves so much. You could never say that about people who became prime ministers. In such flashes of self-concern and self-recognition as these, she tended to lose the stable young woman at her core. It showed in her voice, didn't it? She had a strong but rather wet voice, as if she had a constant cold and was obliged to open her mouth to breathe, and doing so blurred all she said. She cleared her throat too often for anyone with confidence, but it was this voice—at least when it was not bawling or hooting, both of which she did well, with huge overbearing vigor—that made people feel sorry for her, recognize that within the brassy front and the meaty, flicking shoulders, all impatience and disdain, there was a small girl going wrong, a small Irish girl who had no more personality or happiness than that little hole in the bottom eyelid, near the nose, out of which tears welled only to drain back, and its name was—Runny Mede. Everyone had two. Without them you flooded your face or your eyes caked up from dryness. Just to see what would happen, she roared at Polly and Dark Annie, both of whom flinched and laughed. Now she used words: "Bottoms up, sluts of the Empire!" Again they laughed; but, when she used her other voice, the husky, congested, whispery-hurt one, they looked at her with sheepish seriousness, touched her, tapped her, gave her hugs. Ay, she told herself, the Marie Kelly pity machine is working full blast tonight. Why is it always night? When she had a cold, she sounded like someone speaking underwater and the whole world loved her, she sounded so red-raw intimate. Other women squeezed her even if they caught her cold.

She had waited too long; Polly and Dark Annie were squabbling already, shoving at each other behind Marie's back.

"Mek rheum," Polly snapped. "You're getting fat."

"Then drown in it," Dark Annie said in a loud, exaggerated voice. "Drown in me vat and choke on it."

"Better that," Polly yelled, "than be a one-hole woman like you, doing it all through the one place. You know what that makes of you, don't you, Miss Licking Dogdirt?"

The whole pub was laughing now. How had they managed to hear above the general uproar? Marie told herself that this was the tone of their lives. It was amazing such filth didn't erupt all the time, considering the miserable wages, the fleas amid which they slept, the lack of a future, the vileness of the food they ate. "Steady on," she told them, "there's thinking going on here. I've got my cap on, can't you see?" Polly and Dark Annie subsided like two abruptly contained panthers: verbally fierce, emotionally lame, they needed only never to have to focus on each other.

"Do the Queen while I'm here," Polly was saying. "Somebody's coming to collect me. *May keeoach aweights.*"

Dark Annie laughed her most lugubrious: "I wouldn't kleckt you, Polly, if you was the only woman left. Stones and stamps and fancy plates, oh yes, but you—no fear."

"Snatchrot," Polly began, "has been spreading like a black pudding all the way from the junction, Annie. The Black Plague all over again. And now sin yerskull. One of these days they'll have to come and cut your drain right out, full of dead rats and strangled puppies that it is. Mark my words. You'll see."

"Snotgarble to you, you mucky witch," said Dark Annie. "Let's let Marie here get on with her letters to the high and the mighty, those with"—her voice achieved threatening falsetto— "power of life and death over us all. Them as we are beholden to, may they rot in hell. Fie had my way, we'd scoop them out and fill them with sawdust. Then they'd be like the Phoss girls at the Victoria Match Factory—no jaws, no fingers, from all that dipping of the matchsticks in the phosphorus."

"Whatever," said Polly, "became of Little Alice Moss? The one that went around begging with her blind father—*'Buy a box of matches, sir, / Pray buy a box from me.'*"

"She's been done away with, I bet," Dark Annie said, "like nearly everybody else you ever heard about."

Marie was thinking about a man with a big bushy beard and many wealthy ancestors; she suddenly realized that Salisbury was a sexless figment, an abstraction whose power remained invisible, like the rays of the sun. It was hard to know what to say to him, but, if you couldn't tell the truth to the man who ran the entire country, whom could you tell? Be straightforward, she told herself: everything will be of interest to him. So, to the man whose main concern at the time was the partition of Africa, she addressed herself as follows, with Polly and Dark Annie watching her every word, murmuring and cooing as they realized what she was saying. It was like watching chicks hatch out on paper under Marie's labored hand:

Terrible things have been going on in your kingdom and I wonder if you know about them all. Polly and Dark Annie

She looked up. "Shall I leave you in?" Thrilled, they nodded and urged her to get on with the writing.

think you ought to be warned, and me too. I refer to April of this year when Prince Eddy and his Annie, his wife, were dragged into separate cabs from their living quarters in Cleveland Street and have not been seen since. Their crime if it was that was to have been lovers and to have produced a child a little girl now three years old. Perhaps you have a better idea of where she is than we do. She is not with her mother or father I can tell you. Dont you think something ought to be done? It is not a matter of etiqet is it. It is a matter of parents and children, you being a father and so on. Also there is the matter of money that Annie Crook needs for her child. You wouldn't want this blabbed all over London would you now, but if we can't get anywhere this way then perhaps we could start up a public subscription to get them started. Once people knew the facts they would dig into their pockets. Please answer Sir to Mr. Edmund Bellord of Perkins and Bellord or to Mr. Sickert painter of Cleveland Street. We are counting on you to do the right thing by Annie and Alice her child who is Lord Eddy's too.

The slip about Eddy's title came from sheer nervousness, as if inflating his rank (as she thought) might make her case stronger. Or did it? Perhaps a lord was lower than a prince. She scratched it out heavily and left Eddy untitled. Whether this would raise Lord Salisbury's blood pressure and cause him to do something rash with Africa, she had no idea; Africa had not entered her thoughts; nor had Salisbury's previous, casual interest in her whereabouts.

Yet she had not been snatched off the streets, out of the pubs, and July and half of August had gone by. It was high summer, a time in which people's attention wandered, even if you were Lord Salisbury. Everybody noticed the strange mixed mood she was in, her combination of righteous zeal and busybody presumption. Part of the whole endeavor was bravado, to be sure, and she knew it; bravado was part of everything she did, so it felt natural. Had she not been so heavy a drinker, she might have been more prudent, and the possible consequences might not have wobbled, as they did, in the margin of a euphoric rosy haze where pregnancy sapped worry and self-importance nibbled away at conscience. She was almost daring them to come and get her, but they could have got her long before this, so they didn't want her very much—which in a way minimized her role in the Eddy-Annie affair, as if she had not been the nanny, in London and Dieppe, selected out of all the women malingering in London.

"Well, will I do?" Polly stood up straight, shoulders back, all five feet two inches of her (Dark Annie was even shorter), like a soldier on parade, her boots actually those of a man, steel-tipped and with the uppers slit. As ever, Marie let herself be mesmerized by the seven big brass buttons on Polly's brown ulster: upon each, a female rode a horse and a man escorted her, his hand against the bridle. It seemed an Irish scene, both appetizing and dreamy, but Polly was too dark-complected to be Irish, Marie thought, as she nodded and said "A real bobby-dazzler tonight. Are you off?"

"Am I off, flower? I'm off like a piece of meat is off. Would I eat me if I was hungry? I would not. Yes, my dear, I'm off. As a matter of fact, I'm saving up for a new hat, a new hat for summer." Polly bustled away outside as if indeed she had someone to go to other than the casual clientele of the streets. Once there, she stood, sniffed the air, brushed off her front, buttoned up her coat even though the night was warm, and began to walk, as always, with gentle surrender in her gait. She was wishing she could write, like Marie, who had had all that schooling in France, or wherever it was, and she wished Dark Annie were not so sullen: too ready with her fists, but not ready enough with a kind word. It must be all the brooding she did on that crippled boy of hers. Why was Whitechapel so noisy, even at night? The answer, she knew, was that the slaughterhouses went on and on, with drays delivering the doomed and taking them away in pieces. The slaughterers bellowed, the animals made forlorn-sounding appeals, and the city was fed, or some of it—not hereabouts, she thought. It began to rain, only a summer shower, but Polly hunched herself up against winter, and drove on, willing someone to buy her.

A nice military band would pick her up, she thought, then giggled: well, *she* wouldn't mind, she'd get the new bonnet all right then, wouldn't she? But did whole bands go out on the game? Not after one Polly, it wouldn't be decent. She was wondering where the game would be by now if the girls, girls of middle age too, weren't so bloody good-humoured, taking it on the chin and in their tufted fannies, just so's the rest of the world didn't get too down in the mouth about things, like having to go out prowling along Whitechapel Road and Leman Street and Aldgate just to get a slice from a nice tart when they should have been having it at home from their stuck-up lady wives, all muslin and antimacassars, muffins and China tea. Well, she had seen a lot of buttered crumpet in her time, as well as a lot of Grenadier Guards standing upright in a snowstorm of talc and crepe rubber, and she wasn't going to lose heart now. But how she longed to do just that, in a fanatically genuine sense, feeling her heart slither down the length of her body and out of the larger of the two coal-holes, plop on to the pavement between her legs, with Marie Kelly and even Dark Annie crying out *Look, Polly's just lost heart, it's come out of her all bleeding and twisted up.* When that happened, she would expect them to lift her up and put her somewhere warm, and a stone hot-water bottle in the cavity where her heart used to be.

The thing Polly always tried to puzzle out was if she had had a life or not, or whether all of it was still to come. As she saw it, if you didn't know what life was like, as you did the taste of cauliflower or the smell of beer, you would never recognise it;

it could be in your mouth and up your nose until you were fifty, and you'd be none the wiser. Perhaps it would be better not to have anything different from what she'd had already: not tall enough, not thin enough, too much given to drink and stealing and pawning; not enough things to spread out on the top sheet of a freshly made bed and enjoy, just a piece of broken mirror, a long already gapped comb, and a pocket hankie in good repair but with stains on the folds from being carried about too much. She had spent most of her life heaving against a wall, trying to burst through it, depending how drunk she was, and then adoring it because it held her up, tracing the bricks one by one and the coarse mortar that held them together, like a mountaineer hanging to the rock face by sheer self-sedation. She knew what life was like as she felt, clawed, her way along the walls of Brick Lane on her way home from The Frying Pan, with not a customer in sight and the wind getting up. First a wall, then a bit of cold window, then more wall, and so on until the big wide gate, after which there was a wide drainpipe and a door, even if not in that order. She knew how to clutch her way past each, using her nails against the bricks and mortar, the tips of her fingers to guide her along the glass (you didn't want to tumble right in on top of somebody), and the full span of her hand arched for the drainpipe, always rather slimy and likely to give out a discordant creak as if the whole face of the building was coming down. As to doors, she knew the handle and sneck were at shoulder height; all she had to do was grab the handle and press the sneck down hard, then push; but the doors were always bolted, so she could hardly reach in and lay hold of a client and abscond with him up Brick Lane to a dark yard and a bit of paradise blighted. On her way to The Frying Pan she always anticipated how Brick Lane was going to be on the return journey, when she was the worse for drink, hoping that the police would run her in; but it was never early enough for that.

What did those ministering angels of policemen say? Did they say it to her or to Marie? Perhaps they said nothing and just hauled you in. They ran you in and out.

"Hullo, darling," they began (they never said hello, it was

too sissy). "We'll be hoicking you off for an hour or two now."

"I'd rather come with *you* than go to evven," she said earnestly. The earnest often run to italics.

"Blasphemy," they said. "We'll run you in for that too, if you like, Polly-Polly." They took her away for all the crimes in the world so that she could sit there behind bars and dream up new things to be hoicked away for. It never ended in there, in the warm, amber lamplight, the chirpy rustle of the coal fires, the big swoosh of shiny brass taps, the stern crackle of frying fat when the constables warmed up their suppers, turning the batter overnight from gold to bronze to black. It wasn't such a bad old place; and, even though she didn't have it in the sense of have a right to it, she had it to go to, on the strong arm of the law.

"Are you comfy, lass?" would come the heroic cry.

"Comfy as in a mother," she would answer, half weeping with contentment among undemanding men.

Without the police, what regularity did a life have? When you had, once again, gone too far, they rescued you from slobbering along a wall with loud sawing noises in your ears and put you into a curt and none-too-clean cell, there to come back to your senses. It was a seemly arrangement, almost like marriage; women on the game were, in a sense, married to the police, who pulled them in, put them out: in like a fury, out like a cat. Polly wished she were Marie, with all those years in front of her, not squandered and frittered away, but still to use, never mind how badly. Marie, at least, was always up to something new: selling things, arranging things, tootling off to France, knocking about with princes of the realm, posing for painters, writing important letters in which the Pollys of the world appeared, all right, but only as hangers-on, helpless as a poultice.

She walked back to The Frying Pan, looked at the same old faces, and walked right out. I'd rather be in the street, wetting myself, she thought.

Then she forced herself to go inside again, vowing to have

only one drink, preferably one bought by someone else who, seeing her, ignored the rings under her eyes, the perpetual sheen of sweat or grease on her face, the congealed grime under her fingernails, the dank look of her graying hair, the somewhat cross-eyed glare she wore when anxious, the way her breath smelled of gingerbread and porridge. Not much of a catch, she was nonetheless still game, and cheap as well. Somewhere else in London, she knew, other women were swishing about in light silks from India with peacocks unfurling their tails all over their bodies, while men in black and white suits cooled them with fans. Cooled who? Oh, the men in suits were not cooling the peacocks except inasmuch as the peacocks were printed into the silk. Those West Enders too were on the game, but they did it a different way. Polly wondered if, just once, she might pass muster in one of the big hotels, not even going so far as the bar, but hovering like a prize cut dressed in muslin, a brief vision of lechery in the lobby, seated or standing, willing to be burned at the stake like that French saint if only she could do it by standing in the warmth or, she adjusted for the season, where it did not rain, and if it did, it rained jewels and sweets. She would never get away with it. Why, the high-class women, like lionesses in silver paint, golden eyebrows, lips tinted green, would not even let her walk past their pitches. She longed to be one of them, knowing she could do the painting part, but it was the bearing she lacked; she did not know how to carry herself as top-drawer whore. Instead she slunk along, as she thought, at genital level, mouth panting open, willing to serve, like a long sausage skin waiting to be filled with mince. Fill and twist. Fill and twist. It was what lucky London lived upon.

Tonight, however, Polly clicked, and took her client into the yard behind the pub, where two other vaguely combined forms were already heaving amid the rubble and the uncurbed dandelions. She would sleep well tonight. She went into the act with almost jubilant relish, unable to communicate the fact that her joy was as unconnected to her partner as the moon to a barrel of tar. Marie hurried them along, but not Polly; and Long Liz insulted them throughout. Polly's way was to half persuade herself that this was the man of her dreams, and then suddenly recoil from the intimation of a half-bad dream. This man had his fingers in her ears, she had no idea why, and his teeth in her nose. In one motion, she swept her petticoats down, expelling him, shoved him from her, yelled "We don't bite here," and swept into The Frying Pan, money in hand. It was here she came to be alone, at least without Marie or Dark Annie, who favored the Ringer's. Yes, Polly thought, all we need around here is a pub called The Fire. You'd meet old friends there, bar none. They couldn't resist. Out of, into.

Did he finish? No, he did not. He would have to take his naughty little squirt home to his wife or his rocking horse, pink and pretty with wooden whiskered bum. She always wondered if, as she walked away, she were shedding droplets of syrup, if her thighs were befouled on the inside, as they often were. So first she always headed for the lavatory to clean herself down before drinking her bed-money and so condemning herself to a night's fruitless treadmill. Tonight, however, she had something to boast about. Dry-thighed, she pushed her way forward through the chanting throng, and ordered a rum to celebrate; she told about having written letters to those on high, all the way up to the Queen about— Well, would you believe it, a country girl who came to town and took up with a prince, a true charmer, by whom she had a child, a little royal baby who would one day be Queen too. One day, though, plainclothesmen came and took the prince away, the country girl in a different direction, never more to meet, and even now the child was at Windsor Castle, in a haunted cell, being fed on bread and water like Mary, Queen of Scots.

Those who heard her out said, oh, it's Polly at it again, but when she dropped the name Marie Kelly they all entered a state of vehement attention. Marie could not have done better if she, naked, had ridden a white horse through the streets. What a tittle-tattle London was.

Chapter 17

Marie Kelly was still having trouble with her letter to the Queen, and eager suggestions from Dark Annie and Long Liz weren't helping much. Tell her we are all women, they said, and that women know how to run things. Tell her all about what's been going on. Yes, Marie mused, there's lots to tell. Our attics are full of dead flamingos. The sewers of Buckingham Palace lead straight into the fried fish shops of the East End. All of our children are born with syphilis caught from the cocksmen of the Royal Family. Above all, tell her who the women are whose wardrobe consists of what they stand up in, and nothing else. Tell her about the simple, upset lives of Dark Annie and Liz Stride, who never know when the lightning is going to strike them, and who would take it in the mouth like sword-swallowers from the music halls. We are not slow to devour an opportunity. No, it was no use talking to the Queen as if she were a woman, or indeed a python, a huge tree, or a whale.

The problem was that Marie had no idea how much Victoria knew already. Assume she knows something, then.

Your Majesty: You perhaps know that a royal prince fell in love with a shopgirl and had a child by her. And then they were kidnapped in broad daylight to different places, and we think it should stop.

"Too brazen," Dark Annie said. "You got to be more politer. She's a Queen, she's the only queen, see."

"Liz?" Liz shook her head as if trying to dislodge something from her ear. "I think it'll do. You have to be blunt, elsewise they don't know what you want."

"Well," Marie mused, "maybe we should ask her for some money straight out. Give us the child to bring up and Bob's your uncle." They could go on kidnapping anybody, she supposed, until there was nowhere to put the kidnapped people. It was one way of making people circulate. So far, the only letter she really liked was that to Eddy, which had a defiant ring to it. That was because she had actually known him; he was not an abstraction, like Salisbury and his queen. What she was really saying to Victoria was that she, Marie, did not want to be next on the kidnap list.

"Funny word, kidnap," Dark Annie said.

"It was what they called it," Long Liz Stride declared learnedly, as she sometimes could, in her instructing-children tone, "when they stole children to go and work in the American plantations, a long time ago. They napped a kid. That was all. It's just another form of thievery, soon as you think about it, though there's some rather slow to do that."

Dark Annie's fist was up, wavering, but Long Liz was too tall and muscular for her. Nothing came of it, and Marie scribbled again after deleting the salutation. Now she became more enigmatic, scrawling

Once upon a time a certain prince got a shopgirl in the family way and you all know Alice what will happen to her so send her back with a few hundred pounds and we will see her to school no questions asked Mam. To our solicitors, please Mister Edmund Bellord Esq of Perkins and Bellord Cleveland St.

Your respectful subjects
Annie Chapman
Elizabeth Stride
Polly Nichols
Marie Kelly

"Polly can sign later," she said. "You all can."

"Better," Liz said. "At this rate, Mr. Bellord's going to have a lot of new business."

"*I'm* not signing," Dark Annie said, "you can put my name in, but I don't sign anything ever. It isn't safe."

"Scaredy-cat," Marie jeered. "You don't have the courage of your convictions. Some folks won't confess to being human, so you have to cut them open to see what they have inside them, and it's human all right. They always were. You have to kill them to make them prove anything worthwhile."

"I'm not one," Dark Annie said. "I'm just careful, that's all. Where I come from, your signature's like money."

"Where you come from, and don't you lift your fist to me," Marie snapped, "they sign with crosses and first they have to disinfect their feet with malt vinegar because they write with their feet, their feetses." At once she remembered the other Annie signing the birth certificate with her own little cross and she felt ashamed. What if a remark like that got back to Annie in the fullness of time? Queen Victoria was getting them all in a bad temper, beer and rum notwithstanding. Even the odd, heady good company of East Enders on a summer's night was no help: Marie's mood kept worsening. She was doing her letters in the wrong place, but she hated to be alone if she had to work, and she was trying to do the impossible, like a penguin trying to play cricket or a lady polar bear trying to have a human baby. She just knew it: policemen on horseback would soon be after them with lead-filled truncheons, leaning down from their saddles to cuff them with their helmets, which had spikes on the very top, so when they got you with the spike it stabbed into your face or your arm. Only to the poor would they do such things. They'll put paid to us, she thought, but I'm going to do it anyway, for Annie's sake, for Alice. If I don't, nobody will, and what have you got then? A zoo with no love in it, nobody to mourn your going.

Clearly, she was not going to be talking with the Queen. *Granted an audience.* And Lord Salisbury was hardly going to summon her to him to explain the finer points of her demand. Sickert, though, was bound to get into it sooner or later, and she had an uncanny feeling that Prince Eddy and she were going to have another conversation or two under a sooty bridge somewhere. For some reason, though, perhaps intuition raised to the level of flesh-crawling prophecy, she knew that she would not be talking to Annie Crook, the lost, the commandeered, the one most finally betrayed. Annie was gone under the hill, as they used to say in Ireland; her mortal lot had been taken from her and twisted, rammed into a hole in the wall somewhere to keep the wind out. She was caulking a boat. She was stray debris snagged on a cow's horn. She was a wad of wet paper stuck to the instep of a policeman's boot. She was the woman taken beyond herself and shoved out to sea with only a jar of marmalade for company. As for Alice, propped up somewhere posh in the corner of a long sofa, with her feet bare, her little dress pulled down to expose one flat nipple, and on her face a look of pudgy bitten-back resentment, she would end up being photographed a lot, never open to words with the likes of Marie Kelly, once a nanny, now a promising troublemaker. Face it, love, Marie told herself, you're doing it for you, for you as much as for them. You're good at this. You know how to get people on the raw. You won't always get cooperation, but you'll always get looked at. Is that all you want? She knew the answer, thinking now she would willingly settle for Dieppe, and a combination of roles: fancy-woman, model, friend, mistress, dab hand at perversion, housemaid, and nanny. It would be oceans better than Brick Lane on a Friday or Saturday night. Perhaps it would come to that after all, when Sickert realised what he could and could not have, but now he had a posh house in Hampstead, quite apart from his dives in the East End, and he would not want to be leaving it so soon, never mind how ugly his marriage had become. Marie was all ears, like some prodigious animal in an ancient fable. She wanted to dive upward through the social fabric, swing her exquisitely convex body into line with Victoria's throne and lower her naked, unGermanic parts onto the plush and then call Victoria's son, the Prince of Wales, in to her, telling him to forget his high-born trollops and come and get his first taste of Irish churn-made butter. That would show the womaniser in him what she was made of. Careful, Bertie, mop it with soft white bread, me durling. And when he went in to have his afternoon telling-off by the Queen his Mama she would smell the strange real-woman smell on him, thinking all of a sudden, *Boar? cow? greyhound?,* and want to give him a thrashing at once for having gone *too* far afield from that lovely porcelain Alix, tittering as Bertie and his mares got fat together and had to do it back-to-back, so to speak, which was not at all. Marie loved the thought of lascivious royalty, as if a crown were some kind of pelvis, albeit one highly jewelled and worked, but only if she could enter into the sensual fray somewhere, with any part of her body, just so long as it lay against some other part with divine right, for the sense it gave her that she could cuddle up with the absolute and bring it to a climax it did not need but nonetheless took. Left behind in Mrs. Morgan's tobacconist's and sweetshop on Cleveland Street, her bag of tricks and novelties would be gathering dust. She half yearned for it, though not for the chore of making sex pay; she cherished instead the sniggering that personified what went on in thousands of unhappy bedrooms and thousands of unreleased, thwarted souls. The realm of gratification, she thought (being its queen), had thrones of rubber, cones of catgut, crown jewels made of aching balls, slaves and syrups from Morocco, whips of best Andalusian leather, and photographs so gross they melted.

If only, with permission *à l'outrance,* she could have a couple of uninhibited hours with Bertie and his mother, Eddy and the Prime Minister, with a dog and a trained sheep for additional piquancy. How French they would all become, especially with her randy hamper open wide and its goodies on show. *Stop me and buy one,* she seemed to hear, perhaps a cry from an unfettered future. Or was the word *unfuttered*? The girl in the lewd photograph was herself, the one on the left as you ogled it, the one with what seemed to be the deepest cleft, the one closest to sprouting hair. Surely Lord Salisbury would moisten his lips while he peered at it and the Queen might be persuaded to undo him and feel him rise. Surely she had done such a thing with *somebody* at some time. And then . . .

It was to this impromptu Venusberg that Marie's mind turned whenever the letter-writing became too much for her and she wanted, instead, to stand in Brick Lane and scream fit to split the windows, all for Annie Crook. Letters were not violent

enough for how she felt: indignant, sickened, villainously defeated. Could she take a month and go screaming to all the
famous sites in London, wearing a big placard to protest the
Royal Kidnap? No; she might get away with it in Whitechapel
and Spitalfields, where the police patrolled in pairs, but nowhere
else; they would run her in and lose the key, and give her a good
thrashing for *lèse-majesté* into the bargain. Like a hyena made of
scum, she thought, that's what I'd be, none of your polite lady
protester. Perhaps, to make the case stronger, she should make
the whole thing a petition and then have it delivered, to the
Queen tied in pink ribbon from an old nightdress, to Salisbury
on a tin tray formerly used for cracked teacups, to Prince Eddy
rolled up tight and stuck into the backside of a dead rabbit.
Permit us to intimate, the covering letter would go. *Permit us to be
intimate.* Hundreds of signatures would carry the day. Perhaps
after that the constant dripping from Marie's nose into the back
of her throat would cease and she would never again have to
make those boglike sucking sounds as she strove to speak: the
Irish complaint, the comeover's quinsy. Everything would go
right then. It would not. All those drunken women would panic
at the first flash of a policeman's helmet; she needed a few who
would stand fast and represent the rest. And these she had, a
quartet of worldly souls as devoted to their Queen as to their
nightly tots of rum. Get on with it, Marie, she said, and she
decided to go home, inasmuch as Dorset Street and Miller's
Court were home, there in the kitchen on begged paper beneath
the whistling candelabra of flaming gas doing it right, doing it
copperplate perfect as if she were in school once the lodging-
house keeper, John M'Carthy (who kept a chandler's shop
nearby) had gone away again. *Gnite, old cock,* she said to him, and
she then told Julia Venturney and Mary Ann Cox that, yes, she
was making up for her lost education, writing things out at one
o'clock in the morning while her Joe, Joe Barnett, was upstairs
asleep in their four-shillings-a-week room, not waiting any longer for her to sing him to sleep with "Only a violet I plucked,"
which he loved in her steady contralto even though it disturbed
Mrs. Prater, who lived above them in number twenty.

"Letter paper," M'Carthy had said. "Paper what for?"

"Writing to my Queen, dear." Said with airy pride.

"Ho yus. I'll humour you, ye're a bonny lass."

And he had fetched, shown her, his writing kit, left some of it with her on the open-grained table. Her feet walked over by two cats, her mind soothed by a dripping tap, Marie addressed the great of the land and found them wanting. She reached impromptu into the depths of her mind for images and beings she had always looked away from, but with a grieving shrug, among them a big bird whose wings spanned twice the length of a human's arms outstretched. Perhaps it was an albatross of some kind, capable of staying away from land for up to five years. This bird cruised the oceans with massive leisureliness, taking no offense, seeking out no company, asking nothing beyond its involuntary lot, but aware of its vast wings making a shadow somewhere below it on the crinkled graphite of the seas. In its lifetime it covered the entire surface of the planet, certainly of the oceans, and in that way anointed them, or so she hoped: there was no sign, no print, but the oceans were the better for its having graced them with its passing. She watched herself reaching a hundred feet in no time at all, higher than the St. Andrew's Undershaft church or even the Royal Exchange; she would no longer deal with the minutiae, getting the signatures of women who could scarcely write (yet all better than Annie Crook, the dear departed), stirring the dormant conscience in a Prime Minister who played at paper houses. Oh to have the bird's big bill to peck Salisbury and the Royal Family with as she came swooping in over the land in the fifth year after twenty seasons out there of plumed, planing grandeur, her eyes attuned to the frozen ripple of the horizon, the heft of wind, the moisture load of the air. She would enfold them in her giant wings, ferry them out to sea, and let them drop, making room for Annie and Alice, for whom she would find some hospitable island clotted with honey and knobbly with apples. It was a dream likely to steal upon her more and more often, if not exactly sustaining her, at least granting her a crust of forbearance, like Sickert's painting or Sickert's scrimshaw marriage, like

moving from The Providence Row Refuge to the little tobacco
shop on Cleveland Street, swapping donkey-stone for the scale
that weighed out sweets, which surely was like ascending from
some kind of lower depth to an upper vantage; yet with hundreds of rungs above her in the ladder to self-sufficient, clean,
undeceitful sublimity, as if she knelt to pray in Limerick. She
felt as if she were praying before some storm, desiring calm sea
and prosperous voyage, almost as if she were heading out for
America, only when safe landed to be divested of the glorious
bird she had donned for the passage, and it walked behind her
ever after, a prisoner in paradise.

Twenty-four, she thought, was not that old, not too late to
change tack, but she wanted to start from before the beginning,
before the marriage, the explosion, the dole, even before she had
been a girl in that big, squalling family different from albatross
chicks only in that they did not squirt yellow poop behind them.
Marie, ogling the ghost of Marie Jeanette, at last reached the
point of signature, signing all three letters in her French mode
and vowing to follow up with similar letters to the Prince of
Wales, Princess Alexandra, the chief of police, the Home Secretary, the commandant of the Hussars, just about anybody who
might stir the soul of that sleeping lion, the nation, to bring
Annie and Alice out of rotting darkness, not to reunite them
with Eddy, not on your nellie, but to gift them with the holy
privilege of living within their own skins at their own speed. She
had read, last year, part of a novel just published, a weird thing
entitled *She,* about a beautiful and fabulous woman who lived
in Africa, a queen, a sibyl, a dulcet demon plagued with follow-
ers and gold, gold, gold. All right, then, she thought, all the
virtuous causes having been tended by the gigantic albatross
and the painfully decocted writings of her self-made name, she
could be a similar She, having outgrown sex altogether.

"And a shilling or two for the old me as well," she said,
unheard.

The big barren kitchen was deserted and chilly. Knocked-
over stools lay where they had ceased rolling. Benches no longer
sat parallel to the tables. No one pounded, swigged, troughed,

shouted or sagged. No toast, no steam, no reek of boiling greens. Even the gas pressure seemed lower than usual, the sound it made nothing like a referee's whistle, but more like the death rattle of an unloved puppy. She sighed, echoing the neuter hiss of the gas, and arranged the letters in front of her, marshaling them and giving them the nod. Oh they would do the trick all right, although it might be years before anything came of it. They four—Polly, Dark Annie, Long Liz, and she—might go down in history as reformers, four little nay-sayers in the vast callous onrush of lost women whose names nobody ever said, all of them in the uncaring Niagara of human history. *Lorn,* she thought, meaning without it. We are among the lorn: we are without life, life has left us behind its coach, first to run after it, then to walk, then to squat in the cart tracks and weep ourselves dry, just because we are women, whereas lorn with a candle between our legs we would not have qualified for the things done to women only. How does it go? Four shillings a week is forty-eight pence divided by seven days is nearly seven, they can't say I was slow with my sums, I'd have been a proper business woman I would. Well, seven divided by three men a night is two and something. What a price for letting a stranger push up your funnel for ten minutes, as if you were a rabbit hole wrapped round in woman.

She could not leave the letters alone now that, folded and sealed, they had a new decorum not of her making, having gone away from her into the realm of the dispatchable and receivable. All of a sudden, as the fire waned and the gas almost failed, making fresh shadows in which mice or leopards might be lurking, she began looking behind her, over to the far corner by the door where the walls were worn raw with all the bodies passing. In with fourpence, or out for lack of it.

Oh shite. She almost crossed herself. Someone had peeked in, a looming devastation of a form, but it was only M'Carthy wanting his pen and ink back, smiling at the letters on the corrugated kitchen table, making a motion with his hand to seize them and do the necessary with them. He caught sight of an address and lost the blood from his rotund face, but said nothing. Sometimes Marie was epic and grand.

"You *wouldn't,*" he finally told her.

"I did," she said, and thanked him fluently.

"Well, then."

"Never fear," she said, with a chilly smile.

"By gum no."

"We'll be seeing," she added, her teeth on edge.

"That we will."

They had only to wait, she told him.

"If you do."

"And I will, M'Carthy."

"Jesus, Mary, and Joseph."

"Them," she said, "too."

"I'll be taking these, then."

"Thank you kindly."

"If you ever need—"

"I'll ask," she whispered, softly as if pleading with herself never to do anything like this again, the strain and the bother like a lavatory flushed on yourself, the chain dangling over your face, brushing your eyelashes.

"You've only to ask, love."

Here came his free hand.

"No you don't, lover," she told him.

"Well, I only tried."

"You did that. I'm never free, M'Carthy."

"What with, love?"

"Any of it. No to landlords."

"Don't call me that," he said. "I'm a friend."

"With a bulge in his knickers. For shame, M'Carthy."

"Five minutes is all. On the table."

"Foo, you bugger, got it all worked out. Turned down the gas, pissed on the fire, sucked all the air out. I saw you coming, you big Irish lummock. They do say men of your caliber would be better off sticking it into a bog, all clay and rotting moss. Go for a walk instead."

"A feel, then."

Men were so relentless, but this might be worth a night's lodging, at least with Joe away.

"A fourpenny one, then."

"How about a week, me lovely flower."

"Quickly, then. Letters is tiring."

"Princes too, I'll be bound."

It was a huge oyster, cackling silently to itself in a salty tidal pool far from human habitation, even with her on the table spread-eagled, then reversed, her letters firmly held in her hand, her other rutching up her skirts as he gasped and heaved, getting his week's worth even as she prayed to Lord Salisbury to take her seriously, for the grace and favour the privileged were renowned for. When he let go, he was about at Wednesday, she reckoned, going by the way most clients lasted; she had gained half a week for nothing, not a bad way to end an evening of heavy writing to those in the golden chairs. M'Carthy scuttled away like a scribe, clasping his inkwell and his pen, while she straightened herself, ravished to be aiming upstairs instead of outside, knowing her week's work was done, having made five thousand bastards and many more out of loaves and fishes. A song framed itself on her lips, but it was a song of a bird, not of a used-up woman in Miller's Court. The vast pale albatross, surely a bird of the dawn, sang "Only a violet I plucked" as it soared away from the ironworks where her father had worked in Wales, from the colliery where some dearly beloved named Davis had blown to bits, from Morganstone the nonstop curser, from Fleming the hiccuping mason, from the Ratcliffe Highway, from Bethnal Green, from The Women's Refuge, and the building settled down as soon as it heard her contralto, which is to say it woke and turned more comfortably over in those narrow beds as if, as one corruptible soul, it heard a voice both burnished and delicate, something like its Muse, a voice with a sob in it, a loving salute much more than a mere gesture; rather it was a cry going home to God the short way, glad of one thing only: the voice that died left death behind along with life. Anyway, there she was, regaling them, serenading them at three in the morning with the dawn ready to leak down from a sky purged of rain, with M'Carthy's best pale milk ale leaking out of her as if she were a gutter, and her heart throbbing with gladness because her week's work was done and, as it felt to her, a lifetime's as well. Deep in her bed, empty of lover or friend, she took the huge bird in her arms, smoothed its monstrous wings down and back, and crooned it to sleep as it became smaller and smaller, its orange beak a little nib.

Chapter 18

'm off my arse at last, she whispered in a used-up tone. *Now I know what comfort was.* The way back was still marginally open, but she told herself she would be the bravest woman in the world if she slept on the decision and went ahead without changing her mind.

"Gnite, darling," she said, hugging herself, baby-talking (or was it something even earlier?), "iffle you back down now, Annie's ghost will come and live behind your ribs." Sleep wanted her, but something canny held her up there, erect as a Boadicea confronting the drab window that faced an interior with no heart at all, just an example of what mindless persistence with bricks and mortar and no taste could inflict upon the eye. Thank heaven it was night, she thought. These sounds are mine: a dog achieving ultimate quinsy; some drunken woman laughing with a throatful of phlegm that eventually boiled up and choked her off into a foundering gurgle; another woman beginning to scream, then cajoling or threatening, then screaming again, as if twin systems of vocal heroics were coming to birth at the same time, out of a swamp compressed into a bucket by the jealous God of wash houses and workhouses; and last, but most haunting, the summer wind, that whispered *Come on, Come on, the century is going to end, do something magnificent soon. Don't be nesh.* When Marie Kelly went to sleep, it was like someone going up a steep flight of steps in front of an old Roman building, as if sleep were an old god of a general, going up to him to plead her belly and her eyelids. *I went to sleep* was going to rank as vaster, more of a geographical sortie, than *I went to Zanzibar.*

She had addressed her Queen and her Queen's bonny man; her mouth full of cloud, her ears were full of scalding tar, her eyes had locked open amid a shower of powdered glass. Someone soon would come in and start her up again, no doubt the whimsically giving M'Carthy, whose hale tiddlers would—but never mind that, Lydies and Gennermen—the girl is dropping off, letters in her sweaty hand.

In that sleep she nuzzled and fussed her pillow like a puppy, seeking to hide under it and then withdrawing as its lightness seemed to hover above her the closer she got. Sleep was transitional, a stop on the way to another state whose impact on her eyes and mind would be that of a Cornish fog, no longer soothing but choking, as she learned the unsleeping nature of worry, its whirligig teeth, its nomadic unwearying zeal.

When Marie Kelly woke, she woke as Mary until she had spruced up her wits and become French: until now, when some little tender shoot of terror told her she was going to wake wanting to go home to Limerick, to sinks too low to lean at, to tables caked with mould, to chilblains and having to stand upside down to drain out your nose. Just like London, except in Ireland, and never mind what you did, you had a greater sense of hopelessness, you were readier for it all to fall through, the ticket to America to be worried to death by feuding dogs, then torn to shreds that floated away toward the sea on a sluggish brook. If I could only get away this once, she dreamed herself saying, I would never go away again, not even to Lunnon, not for a nearly nonstop drain of pale, not for tally-shops or skelingtons dug up, never having to be handy with me mauleys again, never having to clean out the water closets bare-handed, washing and mangling, having me buboes lanced. Praps, if I'd been unluckier, I'd have been one of those girls they skull-tapped by fifteen just to make them manageable.

As she drifted down, her vernacular came alive, a language understood but rarely spoken, suppressed by her impenitently Irish self, much as many women on the game suppressed all mention of wooden or bone devices that had come in before

Marie was born: *"inter Christianos non nominandum,"* as slumming clergymen liked to say to one another, often attributing such devices to Jews, otherwise known as crucifiers. Oh for a cozy bonnet shop, she sighed in the floppy hieroglyphs of imminent sleep. If I was a dodger, I'd cut it all right. Down with all painters and Christ-killers. You're allis being quodded for summut. I got to know every beak on the lot, none too perticaler, I. There was allis a chance, iffing you didn't behave too well, of ending up in Fleet Ditch in the aqueduct that spits you out into the Thames a long way off. Oh to drive through the Park in a pony phaeton, even if empty-bellied and scared to death you'll finish as a bag of bones under the floor to be dug up in 1900. My hands was so filthy you could have sown mustard-and-cress on them and had a good crop. It's a mortal shame. Praps not. I fought like a brick for my fried fish and bread-and-dripping even it did nearly kill me right off. I dessay blue ruin druv me to bad practices, and not since yesty morning either. I axes parding of all, I's hindustrious haint I? A bit cracky, a little screwy, parchmenty at me worst, dying to be diffrunt. In Paris I'd be Zulma, Modeste, or Fanny, none of your cheap Faux Cul or Belle-Cuisse, and I'd be seen in my equipage in the parks and have vouchers to the most exclusive high-society balls. I'd be Fanny de Kelly, hoity-toity, lewking dahn me nose. Proper la-di-da.

"It's nearly noon," Maria Harvey was telling her in the big wash of banana light from the poky window.

From under the ragged covers: "Oi had a big noight."

Maria withdrew, setting the mug of amber tea inside the door, leaving the door wide open for the blustery wind to search the room and make it pure. With eyes closed Marie stood and took the light on the chin, able in this tiny condign room to find anything by feel, Joe especially when he had been here. She could open and close the window while kissing him, with not a pause or a ripple in her pressure, and he would tell her, always, to leave the window alone, what could she want with changing a window in the middle of the center of the source of the intact heart—she never heard him out but made some such noise, unlearned, as *pshaw* or *huh-hush* and then bit him a little to provoke him while he attended to what felt to her the gaping wet wound below, too big for a baby and, as the old wives tales had it, outsized for the width of her mouth (the two were supposed to match, so that a lady with what the French called *cul de poule,* a tight compressed mouth like a fowl's asshole, had also a *con de poule*). And she wondered, in those blissful mental charges she used to have, if her snatch was sucking her mouth downward, depriving it of caliber. She had heard of one *grande cocotte,* unenvied, who in order to smile had been obliged to uncross her legs to take up some slack, and she had delighted in the suggestion of tight wiring. Either I'm a soup dish or a chamber pot, she thought: wrong proportions, but I'm twenty-four today, and tomorrow, and the day afer, they can't rob me of that. Days of a life, she had always thought, got shorter and shorter, even if you behaved yourself. You thought you were getting a full measure of time, like in the old Limerick days watching the milkman measure a gill at the door with a little bulge across the top of the can; but each day they docked you a second. She shrank from the arithmetic, but it was supposed to be, at a second a day, something like two days short over a lifetime, and then you leapt up refusing to go, shouting at the top of your voice the plans you'd made for the last two days. Did your voice also have a bottom, and, if so, was it split in two? Perhaps it was a minute a day, much graver, or even an hour a week. Well, today, she said, do everything, *ever'thing,* with truly Irish slowness. You did a week's work last night, dearie, on top of the letters. You did that. You did, in a pig's eye. How's your belly for spots today then? Time was God's and so she'd waste it. Today was a fine day for kneecap study, as she called it, or eye-trundling (behind the lids: up, down, left, right, then start again, until both eyes feel sluiced and dozy). If Joe wouldn't come back, she might have the room to herself, unless she sublet to Maria Harvey, in which case she might never need to work again. No, she would never have to work again only if she sublet the bed to several score a night, all the way up to the ceiling, where the webs blew.

Chapter 19

A kind of civic blasphemy," Salisbury was saying to Sir William Gull, who noticed how the other's tan made him look almost varnished. Salisbury had been to Dieppe, to the Chalet Cecil, and what he had found on his return had not pleased him. "It is not that I mind being addressed, but so egregiously. Who *are* these people? That was Her Majesty's question. Since you are the man of choice—I mean you have already had experience in this kind of thing, go and dissolve the noxious mixture, Sir William. Do us all a favour. Use your own judgement, as before, but make certain they *understand.* There is not a natural conduit from the lower orders to the Throne, certainly not on such matters as these. Put paid to them, sir. You know full well how to delegate. My own children, God forgive them, call me the 'The Goose.' I astound you? Good. It is a term of affection, but it sometimes startles me, as I pause behind a wainscot, to hear myself described thus, as if I have achieved little. But it is said within the tribe, you see, and is really a complex way of *not* saying something soppy. From outside the tribe, however, it would be a different matter indeed. How is young Stephen faring?"

Gull raised his hand, tilted it sideways to suggest a teetering in the young man's condition, allied with his own near-certainty that something, sooner or later, in one area of the body or another, might just be achieved—if everyone was patient. "Hovering," he said in his most intimate voice, usually reserved for patients.

"I thought so," Salisbury said, glowing. "Now, these drabs or whatever a civilized man might call them, are to understand that certain ways of behaving, of getting above themselves, will not do. I know they lack schooling in etiquette, but a little schooling in the cruder mechanics of decency would not go amiss. Be firm

without being a tryant to them. You know the type, sir. Bela-
bour them with responsibility and extort from them the promise
of the public schoolboy thrashed: 'I won't do it again, sir.' That
will be sufficient. Leave Her Majesty to me. She frets like an
ocean, but she calms wondrously fast. She does not like to be
presumed upon any more than I, or even Prince Eddy, who of
course has much to answer for. Get whatever help you need in
order to find them—this Sickert, and the coachman Netley.
They both know the area. Supererogatory preposterousness
makes me liverish, sir, as you know, and we do not want the
Prime Minister liverish. Do your best. Wash the postman's
hands. We have not had this conversation. You are on your
own, but you have Masons behind you."

For a moment, Gull felt as if another little stroke were cours-
ing through him, from the buzzing flutter in his lips and the urge
to puff air away from him to a sudden flow of heat from his neck
into his cheeks. Should it happen here, he would fall into Salisbury's arms. He almost wished for it to happen, to bring the
sanctimonious old blatherer up short, but he knew that what he
felt, for now at any rate, was excitement: he was being trusted
again, the chastising royal emissary, with behind him all the
righteous indignation of the best men in the land. *Town of salt:*
that was what Salisbury's name meant, but it would better have
been *grumus merdae,* a heap of excrement. They called him Goose
at home. Did he know what they called him in Guy's Hospital?
Whiskerfish. A poor name, but for him any name would do, he
who gave orders without imperatives, but seeded the waters, as
it were, chumming for prey. He wanted something done, but
propounded no directive; it would all be between Masonic sentiment and the doer's random initiative. It was as lowly a task
as he had yet been assigned, but he had it on his plate only so
that he might dislodge it to another doer, lower in station, who
would then report. He knew the ropes all right. He was, so to
speak, the chief executive officer of the country's conscience,
assigned a certain cancer for treatment, and he could think of
several measures, mild or harsh. He himself thought a big shout
from a policeman full of sausage and fartwater would work the

trick. These sluts backed down easily enough. A bribe or two would work the trick, or a thrashing followed by an antiseptic ducking in the Thames. The point might be made in a hundred ways. Oh for the ducking stool of old, the pillory, the stocks. But Salisbury wanted discretion, and he would have it, provided there was something congenial in the whole operation for Gull, not quite the man he was since last October, since which, although hale and lively, he had felt in merely intermittent health, as if a sick man, a man quite well, and a monster of health cohabited in him, righteously quarreling, making his jaws tremble and his tongue not quite screw itself round complex words. He loved an assignment, he always had, he was like the motto of the Royal Artillery, *Ubique,* meaning everywhere, or was it *Ich dien,* I serve? Unsure, he gave up on military Latin and stood inhaling the prosperous aroma of Fitzroy Square, exultant and enthralled. He was the conductor for whom the orchestra waited, but he was alone, and he began to unfurl his hands as if conducting, or just maneuvering loaves of air; he was a knight of old, thrilled to have so free a hand that he might infuse this undertaking with personal style, like an emanation from his soul. All he had to do was stroll a while, kick dogs away, and devise his plan.

His only complaint, unuttered of course, was that they had kept him from Eddy, whose skull his hands hungered for: the copycat tomcat who aped his father, old hornmeat Bertie. He toyed with the idea of impaling the young whoremaster on a long hot knitting needle shoved through the groin up into the throat and so into the brain. He would use heavy-gauge pincers. Perhaps the day would come, especially if his present assignment turned out to be no more than a trial run: he was still, by his Queen and her counsellors, he imagined, being tested for further service, to which there was no end; and he would belovedly give his life in her gorgeous cause, provided his own part got into the record, and a sash, an Order, followed him into his grave. With no more ado, he straightened up his heavy, muscular frame and went with long strides to where Sickert lived, there to set this final deference into motion. He knew exactly how to make Sickert, that dogsbody de luxe, fawn upon his knee, his boot.

As he strode, Gull reviewed his outlandish nature. Bridges, when he went beneath them, pressed down to make contact with his head and shoulders. Beds, when he slept in them, tried to roll themselves about him, enveloping him in cuddly mummery. Food flung itself in suicidal parabolas toward his mouth and dogs fell into line, in step, behind him, sensing his cordiality. Weather became inconsistent when he passed through it and clothes refused to be parted from his body when he tried to undress. He had an enormous sense of the protracted ceremonious occasion called his life, not that he came from the puffed-up, land-addled gentry, but he had been vouchsafed early on a vision in which greed and ringmaster power came together, making him some kind of a beadle-heir: one with the obdurate from-the-depths courage to turn the world upside down and shake it till it pleaded and squealed. Where this thought would have led him he had no idea, but he had caught up with the predictable Sickert, no longer in naval uniform, but in rather spry-looking brown tweed (surely a hot garb for an August day), walking with buoyant precision toward his studio. "Well met, Captain Sickert," he called. "Miss Kelly has surfaced at last. We need you now, and you are going to help, so long as you want the child intact. Shall we?"

Looking at Gull, Sickert saw, as many had before him, the heavy-featured face of a boy in love, as if having something to do had made the man radiant. How could someone have an expression that was at once overbearing, tender, youthful, beseeching, and prurient? Gull was like confetti, he decided: very different from the last time he saw him, a man of lightly sprinkled moods, some of which, however, were ponderous and devastating. What it took everyone who saw him some time to learn was that Gull had remained the aspirant, the boy tipped to do well; the moment he had something to strive for, some serious obligation to make love to, his face rejuvenated like the idealized one of a saint in a stained-glass window, far far indeed from the face of the successful physician, in whom surliness and acute attention put the watcher ill at ease. Gull was always worth watching, not least because the sea changes in his physiognomy were not of his own making nor his knowing; his face brimmed about in front of him, a coat of arms in flux, encouraging now this kind of person, now another kind, until just about everyone he encountered had been won over, to their sometimes infinite cost.

What had he said, this Norn of a doctor with the now-you-see-it-now-you-don't face? Had he actually meant to threaten the child, or was some ancient rhetoric in Gull having a spasm, was the semicivilized wielder of the skull-piercing knitting needle succumbing to figures of speech? Where, Sickert wondered, did the line draw itself? What was the age of the child you might justly threaten? Ten? Five? Three? It was he, Sickert, who had been threatened, of course; it would never reach the child, would it, this ravening governmental obsession with the happiness of the greatest number? Gull had mentioned Marie Kelly, almost a forgotten name in Sickert's Hampstead circle. To be accosted in broad daylight and at once be acquainted with the red-hot facts argued either that Gull was near the edge, ripe for toppling, or that he was maniacally sure of himself. Nobody overhearing him would credit what he had said. Nobody walked around London talking of such things without at least a hand raised before the mouth or a hot chestnut stuffed under the tongue to create mispronunciations hard to decipher. Sickert allowed the man to urge him along, bossing him by the elbows, giving him sidelong looks of lethal directness as if he were an erring child who had once upon a time dressed up as a naval captain and was now going to have the squalor of his ways thrashed out of him once they were safely behind a door that did not echo too much and there was a mat ready to soak up the blood and tears. Madmen were accosting people all over London these days, and Gull was just another, though of malevolent skill. Sickert sensed himself at a watershed in his life, and over it he would have to go into something worse than marriage, poverty, or failure, something more like leprosy or torture. The only thing was to humour the man and then turn him in to the police: wan dream, footling endeavour, inasmuch as Gull almost certainly had the backing of the entire constabulary from Sir Charles Warren, Commissioner of the Metropolitan Police, all the way down to the lowliest police cadet wetting his underwear at the thought of a walk through Seven Dials. In a fevered trance he let Gull propel him home into his studio and seat him as if he were some kind of invalid, Gull fixing him with those implacable dark eyes: the lord of brainpain himself.

"So," Gull began, "we are getting somewhere."

"Ah," Sickert said, out of breath and ideas.

"Letters," Gull said, and told him.

"Letters?" Sickert echoed. *"Foo.* Just letters."

"We need Miss Kelly, or was it Mrs.?" Gull went on, speaking like the most automatic of policemen, "to help us with our inquiries. She alone has the answers that, ah, certain exalted parties have to have. It won't take long, but we need someone well-versed in the East End. I am not exactly unacquainted with it myself, having toured the area with my friend James Hinton in the old days. His especial subject of study was the prostitutes of Whitechapel, when he worked as cashier in a woollen draper's there. I would walk over from Guy's, across London Bridge, and we would observe all manner of unfortunates. He always wanted to help them, like the lustful Gladstone, though I could not see why. I formed neither a taste for them nor a soft spot, but he was quite carried away with the whole idea. I think they drove him to despair. They were always too far gone. I edited his letters, you know, and wrote the introduction to his biography. What a waste of a wonderful man."

Sickert could hardly believe his ears. He was being treated to some literary ramble, the recollection of a friend, when all the time he had been expecting reiteration of the threat. All it had come to was a lingering affectionate look at James Hinton, of noble and exquisite memory—one of those who killed himself with caring. Then Gull steered sideways with a quick, though affable and off-hand allusion to Nichols, Chapman, and Stride, Marie Kelly's fellow-signers, taking care to say *colleagues* and *co-draughters* rather than accomplices, as if wholesomeness were his very pith and texture and, back in Guy's, there was no Pudding Club with Annie Crook at its festering heart, and no young Stephen, impaled like St. Sebastian, tucked away in an alcove of dirty sheets arrayed on a clotheshorse, snuffling and crying aloud as his very life dribbled away beneath him. All Sickert was required to do, Gull explained, was accompany him in the carriage amusingly named *Crusader,* Prince Eddy's old vehicle, yes, and even the same coachman, Netley. They would identify these women, and invite them into the carriage for a brief discussion, after which they would be let out, wiser but not even necessarily sadder for a mild telling-off. Sickert, if he would be so kind, would be the *cavalier servente* of this operation. What? Gull had the wrong word. Surely he meant *chevalier* of some kind, bowing low, addressing the drabs with quite spurious and almost cheeky graciousness. That was all. Gull would see to the rest. Sickert imagined them arriving at the doors of Guy's Hospital to drop off their human wares. Annie would soon have company. But what about Marie Kelly? He suddenly recalled that, among the women who had posed for him in Whitechapel, there was one, rather down at heel and frail, who because she lived with a man named Kelly, called herself Mary Ann Kelly, ignoring her real name of Catherine Eddowes. She had something of Marie Kelly's insolent bravado, but in a minor register, more of a chirpy sprightliness.

He saw her face, in his studious and thorough way, as the ideal and consummate manifestation of umber, that brown earth darker in color than ocher or sienna because of the iron oxides within it, greenish brown when raw, dark brown when burned: either way, perfect and permanent, shadow made syrup. If they got too close to Marie Kelly, he would try to fob them off with Catherine Eddowes, the other Kelly, the old one, almost thirty years older. It sounded preposterous, but try it he would have to if ahead of him there was this dismal chore of finding who was who. Nichols sounded familiar; Chapman and Stride he had only heard of, but surely others knew more, most probably Netley, who scoured all gutters, royal and otherwise in the hope of perpetual advancement. What Sickert was sure of, however, was that Eddowes had a sister somewhere in Thrawl Street while Catherine Eddowes lived in Flower and Dean. Let confusion reign.

Perhaps, Sickert thought, if they got to the others first, giving them a good scare in Guy's, they would never get to the real Kelly at all, and he could spirit her off to Dieppe. Again, in spite of himself and his high-toned aesthetic yearnings, he felt the craving of old for lower-class loins, for the way these women saw themselves as expendable and next to nothing, willing to be misused because truly they had only a faint relationship with this world, with happiness. He warmed to their meekness as he always had and yearned for more contact with their broken nails, their cheap-food aromas, their snuffles and their spit. Amazed that they had written letters of a blackmailing sort, though Gull was vague about this, Sickert told himself that Kelly had no doubt done the necessary like some articulate avenging angel on behalf of the unlettered Annie, and he loved her pluck. Where was she, then? He hoped they would not soon find out, and he wanted not to know because he wanted not to yield up that address under torture by fire and spike. Then he shook his head out of the old century it had just lingered in and resolved that, no matter what Gull told him, he would pretend to go along, all the while doing his best to thwart the search. It was the least he could do for Kelly.

True, she was more glamorous than Annie, but she still brought home to him the mother lode of the forlorn, from pinafores wet with washing-up water, and dried again on the body until newly wet, to those hankies soaked with the runoff from a cold, shoved home screwed up into the pocket of the pinafore and unearthed days later crisp and corrugated, as light as pith and utterly useless for wiping the nose with, yet as strangely endowed with character as a white rose starched and overlaid with caterpillars of the palest green. It had to be made wet again, either by being washed or just dampened, before it could be used. Some of these had lain in pinafore pockets, especially those used at the end of April's last cold, for several months, only to be unearthed as frozen flowers in September:

something hard and concentrated, with a bad and probably not-quite-dead germ at its core as in—Sickert smiled wanly— Blake's eternal rose. It was on these that the Pollies, the Maries, the Annies barked their tender noses all next winter, in the end wiping them on their bare arms, leaving parallel snailtracks of impetuous hygiene between wrist and elbow. These were the gestures of the life he cleaved to, believing that he painted frippery unless he delved and came up with moss and rot, bone powder and love manure.

Chapter 20

Partly under his tutelage, Marie Kelly, his Dieppe accomplice, who shopped daily like a bee, as if there were no tomorrow, had felt prompted to write letters to the thunderers of the land, an act so feckless and adorable that Sickert felt the tears begin to form as that lone Irish voice cried out among the spires and steeples for attention of some kind: a look at least as fond as a dog would get if it moaned. What exactly had she said? He could imagine the importunate froth she had whipped up, this bonny connoisseur of lust from Limerick, neither a slattern nor an unfortunate, but a woman of uncommon tenacity and semieducated verve. Why else had he painted her, slept with her, talked dirty with her, when he had the cream of London's artistic society to choose from? Now Gull wanted her for purposes even more devious than her own. Sickert wished he and she might bed together, one more time, and then remembered nuzzling among her limbs to taste the zone he was going to paint, so that somehow he might get the tang into the tint: vain hope, but the labor was one of love anyway, and Kelly had never complained. Lord alone knew what low company she had fallen in with, but he could imagine; and whoever they were they were not good enough for her. The best years of her life were already over; she did not know it, but she was slithering down the chute from fair-to-middling to perdition. Why, he should have married Marie Kelly instead of Ellen Cobham, which was like saying he should have plunged his face into soft, stale loam rather than tiptoe up to the greenhouse, but it was too late for that now. It was not Kelly but Gull with whom he had to deal, and Gull was explicit as a bludgeon.

For a moment he toyed with the idea of removing Gull from the scene altogether; with a brace of buyable toughs he could truss him up and lower him to his final reward in the Thames, weighted with stones. Yet was he physically up to such a feat, so murderous and final? One side of him wanted to do the heroic thing, with colors flying as a whole ovation from the gods egged him on; another side, that of Sickert the temporizer and social clamberer, said leave it alone, just coast along with it, and the whole thing would die down once Salisbury and the Queen had made their fuss. He tried to evaluate what Annie and Eddy had done against the letters of Marie Kelly, the former a kind of *lèse-majesté*, the latter a felony at least. If they lobotomized Annie, then what would they do to Marie, once they had her? He could see the day coming in spite of red herrings and wild-goose chases under the fraudulent auspices of Captain Sickert, R.N. Already Gull had a list of addresses for the women, but he was wise enough to know that his quarry lived in and around the pubs, walking the streets. "Seventy-four Brook Street, tonight," he said, as if addressing a coachman. "You will be there, sir, we do not want to have to come looking for you. The sooner we begin—well, you get the general idea. Bring your charm, your tact, Mr. Sickert."

Gull saw himself out, and Sickert saw how light on his feet he was for a heavily built man. Even without his trephine he could have crippled an entire generation of the well-to-do. There was something incongruous about a man so famous making house calls on so squalid a mission, but the word was that he had become eccentric. "Seventy-four Brook Street, tonight," he had said, "eleven-thirty." Had he said anything else? Sickert was remembering in layers, not in sequences:

"Seventy-four Brook Street, tonight,
eleven-thirty.
           We may be several hours."

As if different speakers had said these things, though not simultaneously, and things not addressed to him, but to the impressionable void behind him, into which the Netleys sank at night. Brook Street was Gull's home, and this gave Sickert a comfortable feel: they were starting in the West End, thank goodness, and it was to the West End that they would return, unless—he blanched and for a weapon grabbed a champagne bottle holding linseed oil—they were going to put paid to him tonight, truss him up and lower him into the river or take him straight to Guy's and lobotomize him before midnight chimed. He looked out furtively. Perhaps the advance guard was already in position, ready to fetch him if he did not walk out at eleven-twenty. The soul in him began to sag and dry up, as if all power of refusal had left him and he was merely a nosegay now, a guide, an interpreter, a finder of lost women.

As the third to Gull and Netley, as part of the most disagreeable trio in London, he felt degraded and failed, obliged to scuttle about in the darkness in the wake of events his own carelessness had caused. If he did not go, and they did not come for him, they would have their way with little Alice: was it as simple and grotesque as that? If he did not go, then they might come for him anyway and have their way with Alice Margaret. And if he went, they still might do her in. *They could please themselves:* that was the truth, and it was no good antagonizing them. Just perhaps, after their initial zeal had spent itself (the heady charge of being the Queen's executants at the Prime Minister's behest et cetera), he might be able to wheedle them into an act or two of kindness, as if he were suddenly to teach them a few words of Urdu and they would speak them, relishing the feel on the mouth of something exotic. One of these days, Alice would return from Windsor, or wherever she had been hidden away, and then he could take her to the greengrocer's off Cleveland Street, so long as he played his cards right.

Were the women going to Guy's? Tonight? All of them? What would he have to do? His trepidation was part curiosity now, for the criminal mind—Gull's, Netley's, his own, even—fascinated him every bit as much as the life of the lower depths. All he could do now, he thought, was go out for a chop and some ale; it was no use worrying about what the night would bring. For one reason or another he had to go and be alone in the *Crusader* with Gull, an experience for which he determined to carry a knife, as good a knife as he could find. Being more of a night owl than the doctor (he supposed), he would be the wider awake of the two, which would be an asset. Perhaps, one day, he would make a painting of this adventure, scurrilous as it was. It was not his usual form of a night on the town, and he could feel his nerves stretching out like small animals beneath his skin. It was his duty to find out what Gull intended; but, he fretted, whom to tell if the news was really bad? They were all in league at the top of the nation and would simply silence him. He shuffled through a heap of old papers on which he had written the names of the sitters who had pleased him most (scores of names in his tall and trenchant scrawl), but he could find no Stride, no Chapman, but a Nichols yes, and he wondered if this could be the one Gull had mentioned. Which, pray, was she among the scores of canvases leaning against the wall? She had dried back into the dimension of her peers after an hour or two of glorious individuality. If this was an augury, she would never be found: none of them perhaps.

If it were not an augury, though (and augury was not made of gold), the women of Whitechapel would have to look after themselves like foxes hunted. Were they that mobile? The woeful vision came to him of penniless whores trundling off to Australia uninvited, unmourned; and it struck him that London never wanted to give up its unwanted inasmuch as they furnished an uncouth backdrop for all the finery, the amazingly elaborate diphthongs that curled out of the mouths of the well-to-do, the cut glass and the titles and the sashes which, deployed against a backdrop of nothing or of other glass, titles, sashes, would lose their splendour. It was almost as if London had specially invented the category of the poor and then bred thousands to fill it. They came from far afield to be poor in London, because to be poor there was to be so with éclat. His thoughts were beginning to make him feel ill, in their turn, against the impending background of an evening's *Crusader* work in company he would never have chosen.

In a reckless mood he fished out his best finery, thinking that if he dressed in tails and a boiled shirt the night would turn out to be routine, nothing too severe. A tweed suit and no coat would have sufficed, but he was determined, as best he could, to exert some control over events to come, larding them with tone and decency: not quite the suavest dandy, but at least a toff on the town, even in Whitechapel. He could hardly think that Gull knew his way about the East End as much as he had boasted, so it would all depend on Netley, for he, Sickert, was going to obstruct the course of inquiry as much as he could, and surely, by sheer force of personality, he could interdict whatever process Gull got going in the *Crusader* before letting the woman off, whoever she was. They were going in search of women on a list, not exactly calling on them socially, but hoping to winkle them out of a crowd, whereas of course the hinge of the whole affair was Marie. If they found her first, and she might well have lost enough of her beefy bravado to be hiding, the whole affair would be over. One thing: she would stand out in a crowd, of course, being quite tall and eminently good-looking. If she were abroad, in the local sense, she would be a snip to spot. In a way he looked forward to finding her, committed even as he was to playing dumb and letting her pass by if he saw her.

She was brazen enough, however, to greet him even as he writhed and coiled in his effort not to notice her; her sense of safety went hand in hand with a certain public craving, not to mention an Irish fecklessness that took her from place to place as a walking tableau of female allure. She had whatever it was that made men lust, and she rejoiced in her power; though, if she rejoiced in it truly, should she not have been better off by now, what with her novelty sales on the side and her willingness to talk to men above her station? Why had she marked time when she might have propeled herself to at least horizontal fame? At moments such as this, Sickert longed to be an artist and nothing more: an arranger of only textures and surfaces, a savorer and a definer, disdaining to answer questions, but planking an artifact in front of yearners as if it were some extraordinary Roman courtesan of incalculable prowess, stretching and flexing with agonizing patience. No picture was static, he was convinced; the paint was always on the move, never mind how dry, or seemingly so. Atoms shifted and gases soared; the air was catalyst, and the humidity, and what looked like an autonomous work, to be hung or slashed, was much more of an extrusion from the atmosphere than it seemed; it was the soil rising up, the wind settling down, the puddle at the halt, air on parade.

The thing that bothered him this evening was his Englishness: was he English enough, as English as any Francophile could be? Somewhere lost within him there was his German-Danish blood, but of undominant tincture. The cricket, the ale, the loam, the verdure, the rain, the cuckoos and the sheep were all his. But there was always his Dieppe side to contend with, which sent him strutting for striped awnings, and umbrellaed tables on which he piled little dishes for the *garçon* to count. This was the side of him that wanted to be decadent, accursed, as far away from pipe-smoking wholesomeness as possible. It was not the surface of French life that he adored, but the *esprit:* the querulous infatuation with pure idea, by which he understood the idea that was all idea—the idea absolute. To the English such notions as these were sardonically concocted phantoms, put in the way to mislead bluff lovers of robins and larks. A graft like Marie Kelly, he had nothing in his mind's-eye view of himself that matched what she had once, with a sputtering giggle, announced to him about her breasts: the one on her left was Liberty, the other Equality. "For Fraternity," she said, "you have to fend for yourself. You have to go *looking.*" Perhaps he was too pompous, even too prim, to talk thus of his own body; he could learn from her how to plunge through the carnal to the degraded, from the obscene to the accursed. He always yearned to boost his share of dread.

If he forced his imagination below the lofty and the exalted, down through fog into the gutters and drains and docks and horse-droppings, it would rebound with something strange and undeniable in its teeth: unique salvage from the Sargasso of the slums. If God expected anything of Sickert's art, as he put it to himself when tipsy or just growing excited about an impatiens potted in his north-facing window, it was that he should force the least imposing of materials to yield up the most ravishing vision, not like Wordsworth ogling the daffodils (though Sickert respected his motive), but like Leonardo telling his painting students, as he indeed had, to study a splotch on a wall here, a crude excrescence there, until it began to seem to move, not because there was some goblin of life astir within it, oh no, but because, witnessed by that faculty of imagination, it could not hold still under the eyes' gaze. It was the old grain of sand idea all over again, except that, for Sickert, the grain was never enough, nor the splotch even. What he wanted was the clod, the tussock, the heap of mundane stuff destined, under his hands, to come to palpitant life, like a rainbow sprung fully formed from birdlime. So, then, as he always told himself, he believed in the gorgeous after all, and his passion for the drab, the hideous, was a mere preliminary, without which there could be no art at all, art being a matter of alchemy: you had to start with dross or the refulgent new epiphany would never happen.

He half-did an Affable Arthur, but stopped abruptly.

This was no night for dancing.

Where was Kelly, then?

What's become of Kelly?

Dieppe was calling him: Come home, cross the water.

Perhaps he could start a brothel over there, using these very women, a brothel-studio, a double act that sold Marie's novelties on the side, under an awning, with perhaps a little bookshop as its front.

Ready for dinner, although his stomach seemed to be gurgling overmuch, he took a big brandy and soda to calm the butterflies; it was as if he were preparing for an evening with Attila and Fagin, with all his bumptious old confidence gone to pot, replaced by an unnerving intuition that, when it came down to it, he would be the amateur par excellence, doomed to learn from ogres who, when they painted, painted in pain.

Chapter 21

Resplendent at Gull's door, he wondered whether or not to ring, and decided against it, choosing to watch for Netley in the black-varnished *Crusader* in which Eddy and Annie had toured what felt like centuries ago, romping and posing on and within huge veils of scented muslin. Some houses had carriage gates alongside them, and a coachhouse beyond. Well, Gull had the gates but no carriage, and, even if he had, they would be using the *Crusader* tonight, that bloated coffin on oiled springs, flanked by cozy lamps of mellow ocher light. It would come along the street, all the way to number seventy-four and here it came, advancing with almost reverential slowness (though why, Sickert was unsure), drably, quietly, with the dumpy figure of Netley muffled up against the night's warmth as if he paid weather no heed but lived in a climate of his own, unreachable and unswayable. He brought with him a permanent winter of brash depravity, from which Sickert, for the first time, felt the chill invading him, persuading him, if this thing had to be, to get it over and done with fast. How could he think thus? How could he begin to be willing to go along with it, turning his back on his coarse affinity with Marie Kelly who, from a punisher's or a murderer's point of view, made a habit of never being where she was supposed to be? Was he really on the verge of converting from sweet to sour, fractionally starting to choose the novelty of horror over the delights of love? What *had* he felt for Kelly? What did a man feel for his Kellys? Did he feel at all, at least above the belt?

As he stood there, after nodding curtly to Netley, who was uninclined to speak, Sickert had one of those wonderful bits of awareness that kept him sane: he was still in his twenties, he told himself (his late twenties to be sure) and much of his life was before him, full of wonders, triumphs, and masterpieces; he could ask no more, and the very idea was going to see him through tonight, just so long as he believed in himself. In a way, he was privileged, called to Royal Duty just before midnight, with one of the most famous physicians in the land. Part of him froze, though, at the image of Gull, who would have no idea how well equipped Sickert was against any attempt on his person, how much he had forethought any such preposterous chance: Gull cracking through sheer suspiciousness, Sickert cracking through overwrought nerves before the knife came at him in the gloom as the *Crusader* swayed its flanks. If so, he thought, it would be better to lunge at Gull as soon as the *Crusader*'s door closed, and slip away, leaving Netley to clean up after him. Netley would be used to such reversals. Slid down his stocking, point aimed toward his shoe, a long ornamental dagger (a painting prop) cooled his shin, just in case, although back in the studio, much to his surprise, he had discovered, in a nondescript old mahogany brown doctor's bag, used mainly for discarded paints, a metal case about eight inches long and two inches wide with, nestling melodiously against one another, three whetted surgical knives within: an heirloom, a curio, a piece of flotsam from Denmark or Germany, perhaps, unearthed from the basement of a cabin trunk, proof that there was once a doctor in the family, back in the old Schleswig-Holstein days at Flensberg. An odd, unkind smile crossed Sickert's face; he was thinking that the knife-case had seemed to come from the very name, from the Flens-part at least, as if concepts could generate things. He had no time to pursue the notion as Gull came quietly out, descending the steps without looking, he too dressed for February although it was August 30. Was there indeed a sudden cold that only Sickert could not feel? There was rain in the air, but nothing untoward beyond that. An umbrella would have sufficed.

Off they went to the East End without a word spoken. Gull hunched bulkily in his seat, perhaps humming under his breath; if he had brought anything with him—sketch, photograph, document for the women to sign—it was buried in the folds of his enormous dark overcoat, and Sickert sighed—he had been hoping for a glimpse of Lady Gull, or of the daughter: a skirl of girlish laughter to reassure him, a final peck from the adoring wife. There in the semidarkness he sat with the skull-puncturer, the vivisectionist, the *maître d'* of the Pudding Club, who threatened others into joining him on unholy missions in what would soon be the dead of night; except for the class of woman on whose track they were. Out of sheer nerves, Sickert was swinging his foot, quite into a rhythm, until Gull leaned toward him and tapped his knee with something hard and angular, in a silent *please,* and Sickert could think only: Out of all the painters in London, he has chosen me; out of all the doctors in London, he has been chosen to see to this. Lord knows what the night will bring. He was glad of the knife, though whether he could get it out fast enough he was uncertain; in the gloom he felt for it, making a slight crouch as if to adjust his sock, and there it was, like a cripple's brace.

Netley had already been at work since nine in the East End, touring and scanning, parking the *Crusader* and moving in and out of the pubs, asking discreet questions, then pretending to be drunk, doing an occasional reel, knowing his job, and certain that everything he did endeared him to the other end of society. Midnight, he personally thought, was too early to catch the women at their trade, but it was a good hour to catch those released from the local jail, among whom, surely, would be a couple of the women on their list. Whom they found first made no difference to him, but he wished with all the force of his distorted heart that his friends were with him to give him a hand: any one of the roughnecks the Palace used for its backstairs work. One pair of legs, he thought, but it's a tribute to me, really; I'm the best pair of legs in London, my second name, my middle name, is Please the Gentlemen: *Plysergennermun.* If to-night's women from the jail were the wrong ones, and his dog-ged inquiries had just about established that this was so (though the police made mistakes and some of the women used assumed names, especially those new to the game), it was going to be a long night, all the way into dawn unless they packed it in early. So: the police-station check, followed by a lot of fishing at random.

"Lord love a duck, Guvna," he had told Gull, "let it be only one a night, elsewise I'll be right jiggered what wib no sleep and blood on me 'ands. Wun's a chore, two's 'ard lybor, three's a crucifixion, and four—well, four's more than your bleedin' aver-age massacre."

"We'll see," Gull told him with glacial hauteur. Eel see, all right, Netley thought: *Ee allis sees.* I wouldn't doubt eel 'ave *me* wielding the knife afore he's done. And a shout'll go up: Is there a bleedin' doctor in the owse and the answer'll come: No, but weeve a coachman as likes to carve. Ho yuss. Ee don't so much cut the balls off the man as the man off the balls.

He sighed at this unsatisfactory work, wishing he could be safely tucked up in the Cleveland Street brothel with Prince Eddy or some other gentleman favorite—*they as have big stabbers,* he thought in the mental equivalent of a lascivious coo. But it is not to be. Slav to get on with it. Ice slav to go on with it until His Nibs is suited. Rot him. Soddim. What was it ee said? "Dear chap, apart from the finding and the driving, the occasional good heave, the disposal of the remains, and the cleaning down of the tumbril, there will be nothing for *you* to do. The lion's share is mine." Wot's a bloody tumbril then? A waggon from the French Revolution ee says. Why, they'd've chopped is knob off in seconds. Ee's one of them. Them others: the Nibses. Some Nibses is good, some not. I'd be-ed most of them meself wib a rusty saw. Better that than all this night work, putting blood in the bleeding gutters and not a penny in me 'and till lyter.

It'll rain or go dark before morning, he told himself, with all the weight and wisdom of the ages. Imagine the doctor wanting all that old muslin they used to picnic wib. Yards of it. Miles.

I know what he wants it for, but wild horses would never make me say, 'less they was tugging separate 'alves of me in different directions. I'd blab then.

Netley preferred princes to doctors any time. But this was the princes' own doctor, and fidgety Walt Sickert, the old mastermind, the snatch-ferret, out of his depth in high and mighty affairs of life and death. If only young Walt had left things alone, Netley thought; but he was too eager to get involved in a nice bit of slumming. They all were. Whatever they didn't have, they wanted it, as if it was the biggest diamond in the world. They wanted all the diseases they couldn't catch; they didn't want the ones they had. When he, John Charles Netley, got where he wanted to be, well-placed that is, he wouldn't be like them; he would remember what it had been like to be on the other side of the fence, or on the bottom side of the earth closet, where all the ashes fell to smell. The trouble with toffs, not that he would ever say, was that they didn't know when they were sitting pretty. They needed to drive a *Crusader* for a year or two, cleaning it and oiling it; they might think they wanted it, but they wouldn't know they didn't, really, until they had to do it. It was their way of doodling their thumbs, their well-manicured thumbs; and, in Cleveland Street, at number nineteen, they wanted a little whipping, pretending they wanted to be hurt, but they didn't know what hurt was. They wouldn't want *that*, not a real full-blast out-and-out flogging such as he had enjoyed when he was a boy, and the salt on the cuts afterward, some of it even in his eyes. Why didn't they all *come off it*, all this pretending? He, Netley, knew how to see to them, but he loathed them while doing it, especially those who liked to call themselves Masons, who did everything by numbers and silly little routines, doing people down, doing them in, just to show they had the power. How many of your poor were Masons? None. It might just be a good idea to imitate them a bit, he thought, even if you didn't feel the urge to do what they did; after all a bit of that power might rub off. If you behaved like a Mason, you might end up feeling like one. Uninvited, but one on the quiet.

All three of them were familiar with low life, but Gull not recently, not since his walks with Hinton in Whitechapel, so he was looking out with unsimulated curiosity and no small satisfaction, delighted to see life bringing so many so low after midnight: reeling about and vomiting, falling over and dragging themselves along on hands and knees, squabbling and wrestling one another, screaming and chasing, embracing and fondling. This was the life of the flesh.

It was like watching a disease: pullulating purulence. *"You look too,"* he told Sickert curtly, and Sickert asked himself silently *Who? For what?* Not a face looked familiar. And so the first hour passed. They paused to relieve their bladders, then set off again, cruising, patroling, going quite slowly, the real authority on who was who being Netley, who seemed to drive without even looking where he was going, such was his interest in the chore, his mind on the muslin, his heart set on Prince Eddy, whose body smelled of chrysanthemums, his memory on being thrashed. They were looking for a whisper, they were listening for a face, Gull with his flask of hot milk and his deftly wrapped sandwiches cut into bite-sized portions, two salmon, two crab, two roast beef, Sickert with his hip flask of cognac, Netley (out of sight) with his churn of cold fried fish, from which his gloved hands had an invisible sheen.

By two in the morning they had all begun to yawn and were on the point of giving up. One last tour, Gull sighed, and Netley cracked his whip, wishing himself erect in one of the sentry boxes outside Buckingham Palace, with a large quiet bloodhound sniffing at the thin aroma of tallow and vinegar that came from his groin. Only the night air as it cooled kept them awake. Sickert felt lulled by the *Crusader's* motion, and even Gull seemed to be rocking gently, not so much lulled as out cold. Ever since his stroke he had found sleep the easiest of chores; he slept too much, which was no doubt why sleep never refreshed him, or so he claimed.

Once again, Polly Nichols had staggered back to the doss house from The Frying Pan, all the way along Brick Lane, bumping into the walls, only to be turned away for not having the fourpence required. "My God," she screamed, "that's not much more than you get for stitching a dozen tennis aprons. No bovver. I'll be back. I'll soon have me doss money, look at me new bonnet, look at me jolly bonnet." It was black straw trimmed with velvet, rather somber and stately, though she spoke as if she thought it was a pleaser, likely to ensnare a bonnet-fancying gent along the road. She still wore the boots with uppers cut and steel clippits on the heels: men's boots that gave her a heavy, almost menacing walk, short as she was. On she reeled to the Whitechapel Road, wishing she had stayed at home, such as it was, instead of boasting "I've had me doss money three times today already, and gone and drunk the bleeder." Now, who had asked her, in the small hours, to call it a night? Ellen Holland, also of 18 Thrawl Street, who called after her "It's half-past two, darling, hear the clock?" That had been at the corner of Whitechapel Road and Osborn Street, where she had stood for a while, fingering one of the buttons on her brown ulster, trying to detect as if blind the figure of the female riding the horse and the restraining man at her side, a feel at another better form of life. She had almost fallen asleep standing up, then, out of habit, had begun to walk again, determined to gain her fourpence without walking much farther. It was better to be inside with Marie Kelly, writing another stupid letter, than rambling about here in the unpeopled night. Could she, perhaps, find Ellen Holland again, or Marie, and borrow fourpence, promise to be a good girl tomorrow and go and earn it? She actually took a step backward when Sickert addressed her out of the gloom:

"Good evening, my dear. This is no night for a lovely woman to be walking out alone. May I entice you to a little company?" Prodded by Gull, Sickert had stepped out, still aghast that Netley had at last recognized somebody; as the universe swirled about him, making him dizzy in spite of his sleepiness, he made a token bow and removed his hat, sweeping it low, then motioning in the same movement at the open door behind him. The horse coughed while Polly Nichols hesitated, still unwilling to put herself out for fourpence when perhaps she could borrow it, but enticed by the toff, the carriage, the vision of midmorning nicety, plus the thought that they would drop her off later and she would not have to go up Brick Lane again. "Well, madam, will you? These are dark days to be alone. May we offer you a lift to your destination, even if nothing else?" She was overcome by this surfeit of courtesy. And women did get murdered as they walked the nighttime streets, that Martha Tabram only a few weeks ago. "Ah, good," Sickert sighed, doing his job deftly, helping her up and into the company of Gull. Netley started the horse up and Gull at once, after she had settled her skirts on the thick muslin, offered a bunch of black grapes, a touch of even finer finesse.

If she had sat or posed for him, not to mention anything else, he did not remember her face; he chose them for their bodies anyway, and here in the gloom, poorer far than the broken light of the street, she was generic woman of the lower orders, declining the grapes until, once again, Sickert glossed the invitation, explaining how refreshing they could be on a steamy summer's night, but they were sorry, they had no wine. The absence of wine seemed to hearten her, for she at once accepted a grape, chewed it, took another, appeared to falter, then with befuddled regality began to slump sideways even as Gull reached forward to steady her, moved somewhat behind her, and wiped his palm across her throat with scarcely a sound, and then Sickert knew what had been done as Gull let out a short bark, heaved his enormous bulk upon her as if to rape, began to drag her clothing away from her stomach and thighs, his knife a clean flash as he got to work, his hands a pudgy flurry, not a sound from the woman other than that of air as he Sickert sat dumbstruck it had all been so fast. He was in a carriage rolling gently through the London streets while Sir William Withey Gull operated, as rarely, upon another human form, once known (he fumbled) as Mary Ann Nichols otherwise known as Polly. Had she recognized *him* in the gaslight and, soothed by that old memory even without remembering his name, entered? He would never know, nor would she. Here indeed was something to paint. Was that why Salisbury had chosen him? The one thing he did not remember at all was the ancient commandment against murder.

So shocked by what Gull had done, and by the speed with which he did it, Sickert felt as if nothing at all had happened and Polly Nichols were still in her initial phase of gratitude: a cockney tart being fussed over like a lady of quality entering a zone of safety, the first time in her life anyone had acted toward her with such amicable chivalry: Why, she had thought, I wouldn't dream of saying no, not when asked, not when they put it to me straight, I would always rather ride than walk, my bonny lad, little door swung open, big toff in black satin and fancy tie just waiting for me to get up there among them like I was the Queen of the May, and then, my goodness, another toff offering me some grapes although not a bottle between them, johnnies out on the town, their lady wives at home with their feet up reading big fat books, and I says to myself, no doubt they'll be wanting some favour or other with me skirts all hoicked up, a look or a feel, they have funny needs some of them, and who am I to say no, it wouldn't be one or even two of your fourpenny uprights, no fear, it would be top-drawer slap and tickle, my loves, it was the new straw bonnet as did it, fetched them over to me at once like a beacon at sea, and all they could think of was how can we get our plates of meat on that? If only I didn't feel so drowsy, so drowned and done, can't have been the wine, there was no wine, there was only me, the toffs, the grapes that did it, I am falling and nobody to hold me, right into the ship's wake all froth and a face in front of me, not the johnny at the door, the other one, not so kind, older, he has an arm around me for what I will never know, out of the frying pan, oh yes, and then some whispering, I am biting my tongue, I have to, it tickles.

Gull had severed the windpipe, the gullet, and the spinal cord, in one predatory flash, although having to start twice on the left in his motion from behind to the right, and then he had opened up the abdomen and made a couple of knife thrusts into her private parts out of spite or impatience, and Netley was already clattering away to Bucks Row in Whitechapel, where he and Sickert removed her from the *Crusader* and set her on her back in a yard crossing, with her clothes a little above her knees, right under the windows of a Mrs. Green, who was a light sleeper, and opposite the room a Mrs. Purkiss slept in, and she awake at the time. Of the three watchmen in the vicinity, none heard anything; nor did any of the policemen whose beats were nearby. The phantom carriage trotted up, disgorged, and moved off into the balmy night, past the slaughterhouses and their usual noise. It was a quarter to four when Police Constable Neil, whose face was to achieve fame in *The Illustrated Police News,* found the body, about threequarters of a mile from where she had last been seen.

Sickert felt his face blazing from shock, surprise, and indignation, but Gull, hunched up around the center of himself, looked no different and was not even breathing heavily. Lightning striking would have seemed slower. It was as if a snake had uncoiled, and Sickert had removed the body in a trance, knowing it did not belong on the blood-soaked muslin, knowing it should be in the open air of the night, knowing it was too late to intercede (there had been no space in time to intercede *in*). This was not quite the Gull of the Pudding Club, nor even of young Stephen's doctor, so-called; it was a man who had done all his thinking beforehand, for whom all that remained was to act with a knife hitherto unseen, hauled up from the scabbard of his being, wielded with professional flair in the gloom of the *Crusader,* as private a deed as anything done that night in London. At a tap from within, Netley paused long enough for Sickert to leave the cab and vomit, messing his toffed-up jacket in the process, after which he stumbled back in and stared at Gull, expecting—what? Explanation, apology, a bout of weeping? Nothing came from him, from the man who had converted medical care into medical bedlam, the certification of the insane into certification of the sane as insane, and then stretched his idea of mutilation to extend to disembowelment. Sickert had no idea what to do next, other than keep quiet. Here he was, blackmailed into being an accessory to murder in a moving carriage, and for some insensate reason not enough of him was protesting, the whole thing had become a matter of interest, as if an omnibus had run over a cat. The world went on, and, Sickert was amazed to discover, it was possible to go on thinking; it was possible to have thoughts quite unrelated to what had just happened there in Gull's private abattoir, no doubt with police approval, and never mind how vague Lord Salisbury had been. There went one unfortunate who would never again sign a letter to her Queen, the only remaining question being what Gull was going to do next. Was this the shock, after which there would only be tongue-lashings, or would the other letter-writing whores go the same way: graped and gutted, after being deceived with courtesy and fancy chivalry? How clever: one poor drab, Emma Smith, had been mutilated already, though not by Gull, who perhaps got an idea from it all the same, although he had not yet done what was done to Emma Smith—something, not a knife, rammed into her vagina with such force it had smashed the partition between front and back passages, and she had died of peritonitis. Imagine, then, Sickert thought, women walking the streets and waiting for the same thing to happen to them, and then Gull's carriage arriving with a well-spoken gent inviting the woman to safety. A stone lion had melted into life before her eyes and dragged her down, except—he was forgetting the grapes. She no doubt died with quite friendly thoughts of Gull, whose ravening made itself plain only after she lost consciousness: he was the other gentleman in the carriage, that was all, perhaps; the one whose flowery manners really had something behind them, not all gushy and smarmy like the dressed-up one. No, she could not have had time to compare, her credulous nature swamped by such overt hospitality, her body weary after a long hunt for fourpence, just to rent a room with. Real gentlemen, she must have thought, like to do it in carriages, while on the move, so why had she never thought of that? Why had nothing come down Whitechapel Road before? She must have been praising her luck, she the only woman on the prowl at that hour. She had clicked, as the saying went.

How, Sickert wondered, to get out of something this devilish. To Gull it was no doubt bread and butter, all in a day's work, but to Sickert it was an abomination, the trouble being that he found it, as he would, an interesting abomination, as if suddenly all his standards of behavior had washed into a sewer and he had become the young voyeur, not willing to admit to himself his interest in, his eagerness for, more of same; but flummoxed nonetheless by not feeling an outright loathing. Some tiny shred of him held back, no doubt the accursed one, as if he had never had a mother, or a family, or had never known the pangs of love, the average tug of everyday decency, the brushed and polished norms of homo sapiens. Some woman of the streets, with whom his connexion had been of the faintest, had been butchered in front of his eyes, and he was wondering how Marie Kelly would respond to the news, how she would make her getaway, and not how could he report Gull to the police; if he did, he and little Alice, twined together with wire, would go floating across to Dieppe on the next going-out of the tide. He would therefore have to evolve some way of living with what he knew, with no scream to guide him, not a whimper of protest from the woman to bring him bolt upright at night in a shuddering sweat that no sleep could blot. How do I, he wondered. Just when should I. If I could ever. He was a painter, an observer, not a professional man of conscience like James Hinton, the bleeding soul of Whitechapel. All he had done, he kept thinking, was to lift the body and dump it; no, he had inveigled the woman aboard, *that* was the culpable part, and he might have to pay dearly for it before he was thirty. When Gull fell, so would he, whereas Netley had no distance to fall, foul homunculus that he was.

With not a word said, he repeated to himself as if a spell might have been broken, *we did her in,* shrinking from that "we" with all his might, yet knowing it would not wash in court, if it ever came to that. Painting was a way of altering the visible world, and so was murder, but were these changes in any way alike? The artist was not a murderer, but the murderer was sometimes an artist—hadn't De Quincey written an essay even? He could not recall, but he was willing to concede that Gull, without a syllable uttered, took pride in having dispatched her painlessly, as it seemed. Had he never seen Gull in Guy's, shoving his rods in above the eyes, he might not have been able to assimilate so well what had happened this night (had he seen Gull stuff the severed heart into his pocket in front of the corpse's sister, he might have found tonight's work a matter of routine). He was mingling with people who treated human flesh as pigment, life and death as a canvas, the human spine as an easel, and he could not for the life of him look away from it with all of his being: with most of it, yes, but not with the peeping bit of him. Had God seen? Had God looked? If so, what had followed from that? No more than had followed from his, Sickert's, having looked and seen. Something unjustifiable was happening in the universe and there was nothing appointed to stop it. And what if she had refused? Would Netley have dragged her into the *Crusader* screaming? He and Gull were intent on having her, having gone to such lengths to get her, or any of her allies. It was Polly Nichols's bad luck, Sickert thought, without thinking of her name; if not tonight, then tonight week, sooner or later. The newspapers were going to go mad, but not yet; there would be a chance to sleep it off.

"I'm going to have to sleep it off," he told Gull, who said nothing for a while, then snapped "What have *you* done? Why, sir, you are no more than a lamp, a lamplighter. What you need to sleep off is a night's inertia. We will drop you off first, then Netley will see to the muslin. Sometimes his job is sheer boredom, but what can he expect? He lacks the mental qualifications to be a devil." He sat back and sighed, having wiped his knife and stowed it. My goodness, Sickert thought, here I was with a knife in my stocking even as he cut her up; what if, then, he had turned it on me, at my throat? I would never have been able to reach it in time. *Hide it higher up.* He knew then that he would be part of this grisly crew when it went out again, as it would have to until Gull, or somebody, was satisfied. Oh what a coach of darkness it had become, what a besmirched *Crusader* to go back among the gigs, landaus and landaulets, calashes and barouches and barouchets in Wanstead, where Netley rented it. Sickert's head swam with conveyances. He imagined Netley with the used muslin, then with huge swaths of fresh muslin, cleansing the interior of the *Crusader*, though surely not to anything like perfection: certain flecks and scales would remain there for ever, the last spoor of that poor woman, should there ever be searchers. Was it a worse fate than Annie Crook's? Had Gull been genial with Annie, letting her live, or had he dealt her an even crueller fate?

No one had ever spoken to *Sickert* with such workaday finality; all that was going on was shoptalk among gods. He worried about painful things he had never thought of before now: surely one foul deed need not breed successors, and a bungled atrocity was more forgiveable than one done right, wasn't it? There was no one to consult, not as there would have been if he had been a religious man. He was having to fast-improvise a morality among headhunters to whom the lopping-off of heads was almost a bloodthirsty curtsy. Growing up thus, as he was obliged to do now, was like stretching full length into a hitherto unknown region of pain. One touch into that region and there was no withdrawing hand or foot; long, matte strands of its own sticky substance, the devil's magma, came trailing after him, gray and cold. He was enwebbed.

Polly Nichols had not shrieked out, but in Sickert's head she made a steam whistle coming right from the disheveled mess of her underwear, the loose flaps of her body's front. He would hear that sound on his dying day, and on every day between then and now, once again as if she were a host of the downtrodden and poleaxed, her last interview with a man speaking lah-di-dah at her from a carriage. All had come down to a grape or two, a narrow natural focus that Sickert knew he would never be able to paint, or try to, without writhing, the more so because he had seen the grapes at work before, half admiring their allure and dispatch. What was it Gull had said? He partook (*his* verb, suggesting ancientry), *he partook* of grapes or currants to keep up his strength, and now Mister Sickert partook of murder, never mind how vicarious, and no amount of education was going to rid him of that taint, no amount of love or hatred or disease or apology was going to save him from the salt-rinsed flagellation his own mind was going to administer, making him cry even when aged, more than half dead, for transgressing, for going over so easily when he might have flung himself aside and out of the slowing *Crusader,* or attacked Gull with his ornamental dagger, asking Polly Nichols, *quick you're a heavy woman,* to put her weight on the berserk paraplegist with the surgical knife, impeding him just enough while Sickert gave him a young man's punch to the solar plexus, and then quitting the carriage after her whether Netley saw them or not, and running in sheer madness and dry-mouthed fright up any of the passages in the East End, anywhere to get away into.

If only I had, he said. Something had flowed from him, not strength but honourable ardour, down through the wheels into the defiled road, and there was no way of replacing it, no hope.

For his part, Gull felt that things had gone passing well: at least there was one voice stilled that he would not have to find room and board for, in the Pudding Club or some gathering like it. Odd, he mused, how remote these women were from him. He did not know them, nor they him. They were rabbits or hares, no more than that, and not as useful as the cadavers he made his career among. He felt like some Ancient of Days, hunched up there in his voluminous cloak on a windswept crag, then, as the moment came, striking without sentiment or favour while that idiot Sickert looked on in horror. He could expect little help from Sickert other than as a porter, an inviter, an identifier. Without the warm milk (though cool by the small hours of the morning) and sandwiches, he would have been hewing with an empty stomach, careless-handed and somewhat lightheaded, and he wondered when these drabs took a bath, how often; Polly Nichols had not smelled too well.

He could feel his body sliding away from him at moments of command, floating out of reach as if afflicted with levity, almost doodling with itself while he strained to make a vowel or a cut. Oh, he would get through his assignment, only he hoped that those who had assigned him, thus honouring him yet again, would realise how much it was costing him to lose his sleep and ply his trade in the dark, in a moving vehicle; though he enjoyed the cosiness, especially at first while the selected hussy was alive. Three to go, he reminded himself. Would Sickert stand the racket? Better that he should help than become a fifth body to take care of. Orders is orders, he smiled: here I sit in a mire of blood, thank goodness I took my coat off, a summer night, hardly a comfortable station for one of my standing, Sire, but we have to do as we are told, if only it did not take Netley so long to find the drabs who had the temerity and insolence to address themselves thus to their betters. Lady Gull will begin to fret if this goes on too often, her amazingly strong husband wandering about in the small hours in bizarre company. It has to be. All good Masons must rally to the defence of the realm. Or something like that.

A man not given to detailed plumbing of his motives (ambition was a tribute to God, he thought), Gull sometimes nonetheless caught himself brooding on the formal magic of female anatomy, reminding himself that women were partly slit open to begin with. What man worth his salt would not wish to complete the job with a razor or surgical knife and make a proper glory-hole of it? What he did was sculpting; and, although he bowed mentally toward the Masons, Salisbury and the Queen, he knew that something barbaric and heartless, even if only secondarily lascivious, tugged him on, almost as if he wanted to enter women headfirst in some comfort, not through a God-given aperture but through a gaping wound. Thus, in his jammiest dreams, he plunged upward to suffocation, ready, when he awoke, to cook up all manner of social and political reasons for what he did. Truly, he thought, I *am* a destroyer, and they have known this about me all along, acknowledging the swordsman in the healer, the savage in the savant. How many can there be like me? Every man in England has a touch of this gashing fancy. It is appropriate, just as, perhaps, all women harbour a desire to take a razor to the male member and make of it a trophy. Yet it is we who haunt the streets, whetted, lurking, every bit the boss.

I could use a hearty breakfast now, three eggs and six rashers, some kidneys and tomatoes, a few sausages of the thin, savory kind, and lots of freshly sliced bread caked with butter. But what can you do at four in the morning, splashed with blood? I could stop at the hospital refectory, but I would have to talk;

they wouldn't mind the blood, but I would mind the talk. So West Endward ho. He dry-washed his hands, flaking the blood away, then massaged his face with them, stirring his color up, and told the still trembling Sickert to hold himself in readiness. Netley would hunt, then report to Gull. And Gull would have Netley pick up Sickert for the next "operation."

Sickert saw: it was an operation on the body politic, nothing more and nothing less. The women were not women with parts, but they themselves were parts of the body politic, ailing and diseased, ripe for the knife.

Out he tumbled, his last vision of the interior being one of Gull wagging an admonishing red finger in the dawnlight with stained muslin turned burnt umber by the rising sun. Cleveland Street was a return to land after being marooned with madmen; but not once did he think of reporting the crime: to whom? You did not report the lungs of the body politic to its toes. Polly Nichols would not see that morning, but at least for a while she would be news, attended to for the first time in her life. Who had she been? What? And with whom? What, he wondered, would he have done had the woman in Whitechapel Road been Marie Kelly? He would have done something different, he was sure of that, and he could hear himself, as he leaned out of the carriage, the epitome of fashion, saying "Run, run, run." He doubted if Gull could have caught her. There was only Netley for that, and Netley was vicious. He drove and he fetched and he spotted. He would do anything. Sickert realized that the unspeakable thing holding the two of them together was not in the carriage at all, but out there on the high ivory hill of despotism. Without Netley, Gull would cease to function: he was a blade; that was all. Without Gull, would Netley go ahead in his own right, like a demented survivor subject to a special echolalia of the criminal classes? Kill at all costs? Well, then, why not simply walk away, or do the job with paralyzing inefficiency?

As Sickert, with increasingly emotive logic saw it, the other women would vanish once the news was out, or would they? He foresaw an awful drama in which they would get the final, complete point of Gull's bloody excursions only as they chewed the grapes. If *he* were one of them, he would know what was afoot the instant the news came out of Polly's murder. They would go underground, he supposed, just like that, but not to Spain or Australia. Like the milkman, they offered daily service, even to secure a bed for the night. He tried to unknow what he knew, just to put himself in place of Marie Kelly and her helpers, but he could not. He could not go backward, nimbling over the hurdles of effect and cause, effect and cause, until he was at the starting point again, outside his studio in tails and white tie, all spruced up for jollity.

Chapter 22

These women, Gull was thinking, lost still in a murderous aftermath, all have the same face: heavy cheeks and jowls, no slope from the chin to the ear, but solid and ponderous, index to stubbornness and force of character. Hardened, I would call it. *I have to get out, I am home.* Lord, what a night, too long and singularly short of joy. Away Netley drove, while Gull entered past the enormous engraving of a Highland steer dying in a mist and went upstairs as he was to his study, where he at once locked his knife-case away beside his Mason's manual, and poured himself a huge brandy and soda, forbidden but craved. His mind was trying to make sense of an image from childhood, when, on the River Lea or near it, he had watched a band of gypsies celebrating a birthday, and he had been amazed by the routine, automatic swirls of the dancers, in perfect time to the incessant music, yet somehow the dancers were planted, not part of the natural vivacity of the scene, there to represent vivacity, he had thought, rather than respond to it. That was presumably the role of these sluts in London: men went to them not for what they were, but for what they represented. Indeed, since he was not as ignorant of prostitutes as Netley and Sickert

might think, he knew that the phrase "M'Carthy's Rents" referred not to the actual rooms they rented but to themselves:
women for rent. Well, those who wanted them could have them;
he himself had not had a lecherous thought in years, but the
violence of sex was much more to him than a wan memory. The
main thing was to maintain decorum, about which not enough
people cared these days. The next woman, when they found her,
would have to be done more thoroughly than tonight's, who
had got off lightly, no more than minimally converted into a
demonstration piece, as in the post-mortem room. For all his
labors and footwork, Netley had produced only one, and she a
shadow luckily happened upon. The method was laborious, but
it was no good going about in broad gaslight to do something
of this kind: the women had to be brought into the cab, and that
was that. Once he got the hang of it, Sickert would be of use,
whereas Netley might go off the deep end, having all the instability of his class; but where else could one find a coachman so
corrupt, so buyable, so discreet, indeed calmly mouthless?

There he sat, by a coal fire whose end coincided with a tinkle
of coke, fondling a lobotomy needle, wondering how long he
had to live, how long he could count on his faculties. At times
his insides seemed to churn and fall, his vigor dispersed even as
he began to speak, and it was as if the pith had gone from him.
How much had he taken out of himself with his night's efforts?
Not much, perhaps; the knifework had been easy, the searching
had been worse, and the uncomfortable silence of the usually
loquacious Sickert worse still. He flipped from his jacket pocket
a small notebook, police style, in which he had written the
names of the women to be killed. He drew a small cross and a
wavy line. There they were, as if awaiting confirmation in
church:

> † ~~Nichols, Mary Ann~~
> Kelly, Mary J.
> Stride, Eliza
> Chapman, Annie

Hardly a large chore to a determined man. The blood on his hands, badge of his orthodox calling, troubled him not at all; but that on his overcoat would have to be mopped out tonight. He stood at a big-bellied jug and poured water from it into a floral basin, dabbing at his coat, then moving swiftly to his desk to retrieve a tin of tobacco, with a plug of which he rubbed the stains, making them brown. Next time, he thought, be careful, not so eager: take a smock. Have Sickert dress you before the woman enters—no, that will unnerve her; so do it in a trice as she bites the first grape, or wait for her to fall, and then do it. He could not bear to waste a minute, he wanted always to keep moving upward socially or medically, his heart on some kind of treadmill invented by his barge-owner father to test young William, and young William, duly tested, wanted to go on being tested with things that made others bilious. William Withey Gull wanted to achieve basalt sophistication in the face of things so horrid they annihilated the power of the mind to quail. Oh fig, he would say to himself, *oh fig,* the essence of sophistication is never to be surprised by anything, never to give the new its full flagrant reputation, never to be *taken by* something. Even the stroke, stunning as it had been, had fast become part of his collection, another symptom recorded for use, no longer his, part of the Gull medical history, but stuck out there among the daffodils and the celandines and the roses as another natural phenomenon: a horse chestnut that fell on the toe of someone's shoe while they were out walking. He had willed away its personal import by the sheer strength of his perfected or honed aversion: having for so long practiced on the suffering of others, training himself not to heed it lest it detract from the pure blue flower of knowledge pressed dry between the halves of his brain, he was qualified to bypass his own suffering too, his being put out, incommoded, *knocked* (as the villagers used to say in Essex) *off his buttie* by a clot or a hemorrhage or an embolism. Well: he had walked away from it, stung in his hubris, of course, and told by the temporary halt of his stride that he was slowly becoming human, likely, sooner or later, to be one of those convicts who, condemned to death, awaited hanging and were said to be Detained During Her Majesty's Pleasure (DDHMP, they actually said), *deedeeaitchempee:* waiting for something else. He was waiting, he knew, without having that railway waiting-room feeling, for some sense of further subtraction, as with young Stephen, whom he was going to allow out soon, back humbled to his college at Cambridge if he so chose, or to some Clerkship of the Assizes on the South Wales circuit, as his father had suggested, not wishing to see such a misogynistic barrister go to waste. Will he, Gull wondered, relapse before I kick the bucket? It would have been better to have had him with me in the *Crusader,* rather than the taciturn, surly Sickert, who clearly had no taste for altruistic butchery. Or even young "Collar and Cuffs," he wondered, using Prince Eddy's nickname; after all, Eddy already had the pox, contracted in the West Indies in '79, so the paresis would begin to show up in fifteen years, about 1894; until then he would be a presentable henchman.

To work, then. For a week or so, while the public impact of the murder began to develop, Netley would watch for the remaining women and establish their patterns of movement. The women would relax, perhaps; it was no good going after them straight away, and the same would be true after the second woman was murdered. Always allow an interval both dramatic and therapeutic, he told himself. The uncaught victim always thinks the one before her was the last, meaning It is all over, I need not worry. We shall see.

He decided to bring Sickert into the killing more, if only the man would budge; he seemed interested, though shy of it.

Chapter 23

When Charles Cross, carman, walked to work he called it walking for the Lord, inasmuch as he was neither awake nor asleep, but wafting workward without quite feeling he was anyone at all, and certainly nobody with any desire to be up and about at 3:45 in the morning, when London's fogs were at their dankest and the warmth of summer was hours away from renewing itself. I belong to the brigade of the unwanted, he told himself: all that wants me is work, and the rats. There are those who—and then there are the others. I wouldn't be surprised if, one of these mornings, some of those bodysnatchers didn't grab me as I walked to work. He shambled, he lurched, he trundled, and all these motions got him there, quite sober, but he felt seasick, which was to say landsick, fit only for a more horizontal posture, asleep until noon. He was aiming at a gas lamp at the street's far end, on one side of him a warehouse wall, on the other some terrace houses: a familiar, almost soothing scene at that hour of the morning. Anything unusual was bound to stand out, and it did; in a gateway that led to some stables, he saw a bulky bundle and crossed over to investigate, half grateful for something to train his eyes on, to make his brain assess. Polly Nichols was lying on her back with one hand almost in contact with the stable gate and the other raised to her brand-new bonnet. Her skirt was up high, almost to her waist, provocative he thought, wondering if she had been raped and beaten senseless. He stood up, oddly dizzy, and looked for the attacker, who had perhaps just fled. Cross wondered if, in his stupor, he had seen some man materialise from the bundle on the ground and melt away into the gloom; to think it was almost to believe it, but he thought, no, if I had, I'd have a sharper recollection than I have. I disturbed nobody, but she still feels warm; her legs do. I heard no steps. It's quiet now: no slaughtermen raising Cain. I heard no wheels. Is she alive? "Hoy," he said to the footsteps behind him, approaching fast, "come and look at this here woman, will you?"

John Paul, market porter, had already stepped off the sidewalk into the road to avoid him, but now he paused, reluctant to become involved: perhaps this man had just attacked whoever was lying there and was putting a good face on it by pretending to have found her. "Give me a hand to get her up," Cross said. "No fear," Paul said, "she's just had one too many, that's all. If I start lifting drunkards, I'll never get to work."

"Let's get her on her feet, anyway," Cross said, getting impatient at the waste of his time too. Instead, Paul knelt down and felt at Polly's face and hands, both cold as glass, and he was just going to say "She's dead, I think," when he felt a vibration in the ground, wandering and slow, but tangible: wonderful in that it seemed a sign of life where he'd thought there was none, but deplorable in that he had just been allowing all kinds of gloomy thoughts to rise and now he was attending a drunkard after all. Going off in different directions to find a policeman, neither had any memory of blood, but it was there all right, seeping out onto the stone from between Polly Nichol's legs beneath her hauled-up skirt, which was blotting it up. Constable Neil had been in the vicinity only moments before, and on his return he shone his bull's-eye lamp into the gateway and murmured the one word "Murder." In stages and sections they began to see her severed throat, her open eyes, her arms, still warm, and felt shocked, not so much because yet another dead woman had appeared in the streets of London as because sooner or later this sight would come to just about everybody, like a curse, a death-tax, a challenge to wholesomeness and charity: you had to learn to care, even when murder turned into an everyday occurrence caused, so the rumours went, by butchers, slaughterers, day-labourers, foreign workers, Jews, Latvians, Americans, Polish barbers, Russian doctors, and sundry firemen and tea trade clerks.

Soon after this, several policemen shone their lamps on the body as a Dr. Llewellyn made a perfunctory examination watched by some slaughtermen on their way home; they had been hosing down, tidying up, getting things ready for another full day, and it was odd to leave the one scene only to find butchery of a different kind going on in another. When they lifted the body up to the ambulance, which was like an elon-gated perambulator, as the word suggests, they saw how much blood her clothing had soaked up, but not of course the blood that went into the muslin in the *Crusader*. Her legs were still warm, Llewellyn said; she had not been dead for more than half an hour. Off they wheeled the body to the mortuary adjoining a nearby workhouse as a bucket of water was thrown over the patch of blood on the ground. Instead of taking Polly Nichols into the mortuary, those wheeling her left her in the yard to await the attentions of two paupers, inmates of the workhouse, who were having breakfast and did not want to miss it for someone dead. When they began to undress her, it was clear that one of them was having a fit, or the beginnings of one, convulsing with Polly's red-brown ulster in hand, then the brown linsey frock and the woolen stockings with black ribs. They erratically exposed her in front of Inspector Helston, who began to see the full extent of Gull's work: the jagged hole in the abdomen and various other bruisings, and sent for Dr. Llewellyn to come back and do a more thorough post-mortem. He was soon theorizing about a left-handed person's having done these fearful things, and with a knife having a blade seven or eight inches long—perhaps a cork-cutter such as shoemakers might use. Polly's possessions added up to one broken mirror, a white pocket handkerchief, and a comb. Stenciled on the bands of her two flannel petticoats the inspector found Lambeth Workhouse's laundry mark, but not even the workhouse's matron could identify Polly Nichols, and soon there was a procession of women coming to view the corpse until someone at last said it was Mary Anne Nichols of 18 Thrawl Street, Spitalfields. The mirror-piece was coated with what looked like dried beer; the hankie had been used, and there was a blood clot on it, perhaps from a bleeding nose before she entered the *Crusader;* the comb had several teeth gone and deep scurf at its roots.

No one could understand why the murder had been silent. Three watchmen in the area had heard nothing, any more than Emma Green, of New Cottage, and Walter Purkis, of Eagle Wharf, and William Louis, watchman at Messrs. Brown and Eagle wharf nearby. Those groping for facts heard that Dr. Llewellyn had said the mutilations had been done before her throat was cut, but here was Emma Green saying "Light as a feather I sleep," with Mrs. Purkiss saying "I was wide awake at the time you say, and we are right opposite, aren't we?" Those who sketched for a living arrived and hovered over the body with fat white pads and soft pencils, making the most of Polly's Chinese eyelids and narrow forehead, big sharp-cut nostrils and blood-soaked hair, her shoulders of a young girl.

Outside the mortuary a death-hungry crowd watched and

muttered, aching to see them do something even if it was only to wheel away the empty body-shell with its two big wheels, its four-stave rest affixed just past the wheelbarrow-type handles, and its raised bonnet at the far end, the whole enclosed in tarpaulin on ribs. Every now and then a few policemen would come outside and make as if to wheel it away, only to back off while others approached it from the side to keep it from wobbling. When they did move it, their reverence befitting a body within, the sound it made was creaky and frail, the tiniest gravel made it falter, and many a one looking at the high bonnet, over where the head and shoulders would be, wondered at so large an allowance of air for lungs so still: a homage to what had once worked, perhaps, a pious hope for all others. Those who had got in to see Polly noted that someone had used the comb on her hair and placed a pillow on her chest as if to balance the one behind her head, which kept the gash to the minimum. She lay in a crude wooden coffin, at outrageous peace, like someone bound sooner or later to float away, perhaps to the East London and District Railway station, perhaps downriver in a ship burial, her lisp forever silenced, her bonnet wasted.

Gradually the horror, but only as a horror among horrors, unfolded from the prosaic reports of Constables Neil, Mizen, and Thain, Inspectors Spratling and Helston. These made their way into the deft copperplate of Frederick George Abberline, the inspector in charge of the investigation, a man who always hungered for more knowledge and punctuated with buoyant casualness. *The Penny Illustrated Paper and Illustrated Times* depicted Polly Nichols on her back with her long coat all the way down to her ankles, misspelling both her name (like Gull) and that of Constable Neil, and asserting that robbery could not have been the motive: Polly was so poor. Three murders, the paper said, had now taken place within two hundred yards of one another (the other two victims being Emma Elizabeth Smith and Martha Tabram, whom the paper called "Turner"). Anyone pondering the matter might have concluded that it mattered little what women so poor were called, or so dead, so ruined; phantoms from a class, they graced the twilight briefly and then sank into the sludge of London, from which no one ever rose. Which was humbler, which was crueler: to be called by your right name all your life, only to be misremembered after death, or, after death to have a new name all at once as if another you had died? Tabram was dead, but Turner had what was called a new lease on life. Reading the press's continual misstatements, Abberline sighed, and tried to stop thinking such thoughts: Tabram was dead and would never be a Turner. Women of a certain class were being murdered almost daily, and he wondered, in his sedate but worldly way, if death, in the lives and world picture of prostitutes, might not amount to some kind of consummation. Not that they were "born for death," but that, tweaking and fanning the extremism of men with undeniable hunger for miscellaneous sex, they invited violence as women with headaches to plead, pains in the pelvis, dark secrets of adulterous satiety, did not. No, he thought, all women were the same; none would go to the game if they had enough money. They certainly would not walk the streets, with not even a bed to return to if they didn't click, and all their worldly goods in their pockets— poor Nichols's comb, hankie, and broken mirror sat in his mind and chafed it. He envisioned himself making tennis aprons at threepence per dozen so as not to have to resort to the streets, and felt glad to have pen and paper. The police, he thought, always have to resort to the streets; we are the *other* streetwalkers nobody ever mentions. In his handwriting, "31st inst." had given way to "31st ult.," as August yielded to September. He took a deep breath and wrote again:

We have been unable to find any person who saw her alive after Holland left her. The distance from Osborn Street to Bucks Row would be about half a mile. Inquiries were made in every conceivable quarter with a view to trace the murderer but not the slightest clue can at present be obtained.

It seemed hopeless, like interrogating the weather.

During the week that followed, Marie Kelly and her cronies lived on, worked on, in a state of drunken anesthesia, weeping for Polly, afraid for themselves, yet obliged to walk and perform. For more liquor, they had to find more clients, and having to cope with more clients drove them even more to drink on top of the drink that blurred their raging grief for Polly Nichols. Marie had always known that they ran a risk: the streets were dangerous, had never been safe, but now she looked over her shoulder during the sexual act, lest someone come and get her even *in flagrante,* and never mind the client, whose throat might get cut too. No, it was always women who got killed, she thought: what was that old German expression—kitchen, *Kinder,* and coupling? No, that was wrong, and the truth was kitchen, coupling, and killing. Women were born to be killed, weren't they? Because they were soft and sloppy, wide open and open-hearted? Something like that. Men hated women because women had babies and they killed them either because men didn't like babies or they wanted to have them themselves, and not by proxy. Well, she thought, I'm a prime bloody target now, I'm even sicking up my beer from the presence in me tum of a little M'Carthy, I'll be bound. From the first. He doesn't believe it, but Marie knows. "What do *you* say, Liz?"

Stride shrugged, then seemed to bark. "It goes with the job, don't it like? Bun in the oven, razor at your throat. Poor Polly, she never had no chance."

"Poor Polly. She'll never budge again."

"God save her," said Stride, in a gush of emotion.

"Well, He didn't, then, did He? God," Marie said with her mouth exactly at the rim of her glass, "had His prick in His fist when that happened, didn't He."

"Hush, Marie," Stride said. "Drink up."

"Could have been us," Marie said slushily, "easily could have been you or me."

" 'Cause of the letters?"

"Nah, some rejected husband roaming the streets, itching to get his bloody own back. Any woman'd have done, flower."

"Well, bugger *him* then."

"I'll bet," Marie said with her Cleveland Street twisted smile, "somebody already did. These gentlemen like it all ways, like old Eddy."

"Stabbers," Stride said. "Thy're stabbers all."

"At least that," Marie said. "Any little touch down there will do for most of them. It's like it was all connected up for trouble. They're like steam whistles, you know. Any old sod of a move that relieves the pressure, so's they can have a good squirt, darling, and they want nothing more to do with you. I wouldn't be surprised, that I wouldn't, if whoever did Polly in was letting off steam, like, and then when he'd done it he was all right, he sort of wished he hadn't let himself go like that. I wouldn't be at all surprised. Imagine, he cut her up, he cut right into her innards. Now what kind of a man does that? Well, he could hardly do it to his wife, could he now? She'd object. What did he expect to find inside?"

"Treasure Island," Dark Annie said, half of her face purple and swollen from some gruesome battering.

"You've been boxing again," Marie said.

"Liza Cooper, that bitch. I feel like a sick cat that's eaten nails. Always having trouble wiv that bitch, all about a bit of soap. Imagine: *a bit of soap.* I hope somebody gets her too. Give me a knife and I'd cut her belly open myself. And I'd fill it with carbolic soap, that I would."

"We," Marie told her, "was just thinking about poor old Polly. I'd like to remember her like she was, not as she is."

"Polly was always asking for it, *arsting* for it," Stride grumbled. "Too much swagger, you see."

"Ah, bollocks," Marie said, heatedly, "who'll have you if not your own? Stop carping. When it comes down to the wind-up" (she rhymed with *hind* not *sinned*) "you've only got your own to turn to, to put you six feet under. I'd never have called her a bloomer, no fear, but she wasn't so bad. Not as off-putting as a horny cobbler, but a little impudent strap of a woman, like. They do say she had family, but all that came out of her titties was pondwater."

"Don't you speak ill of the dead," Dark Annie said. "You'll pay for always for that. She was all chopped up."

"Who, me flower," Marie answered, somehow turning grief into aggression, "gave you that grand coke in the chops? Have you been quarrelling again?"

"You don't listen. I *said.*"

"Oh, I mustn't miss a word of Mistress Annie Chapman when she's at home?" Marie supped deep from her glass. "I'll have you know, I've better wood to cleave than listen to you. Poor Polly's a goner, and here we are pissing ourselves for lack of something to say that's right and decent. Poor soul."

"Bugger off," said Annie Chapman, hardly able to move her lips. "Just you go buggering off, you stupid put."

"That's right," Marie said, quick and derisive, "you go calling your betters names. I'd expect no less."

"Put the wood," Stride said wearily, "in the hole, both of you. All you can do is drink. One of these days I'll be off to Liverpool, and then some other places."

"Your coach awaits, moddom." Marie curtsied.

"First clahss," Dark Annie said, mimicking the la-di-dah.

"We'll come and wipe yer arse," Marie said. "Just walk on us, flower, we're only doormats. Scum of the earth. *Liverpool?* You don't even know where it is."

"Up yonder," Stride said, pointing north to Stockholm.

"She's right," Dark Annie said.

"Up my arse," Marie said, pointing northwest. "That's more like it."

"You *would* know," Stride said at her most ironic.

"Would, darling? I *know.* I'll bet you a mouthful of spunk I'm right. Scouse is half-Irish anyway."

"Keep your mouthfuls to yourself," Dark Annie said.

"Yes," Stride said feebly. "Don't spit at me."

"Rubbidge," Marie said to them both. "You're both so full of rubbidge, an' all. Drink up, it's time to go to work. Our train's in. Our bus has come. The waiters are waiting. The pricks is swishing on Whitechapel Road."

"And don't come back," Stride said, "wiv your froat cut."

Marie was dreaming of Ireland as she went out, of the way people talked, as if talking were enough, if you were really good at it, and it would feed and clothe you, she knew not how, but it had always seemed that way, if you could only capture in one sentence all the intonations of grief and joy that contended in one cry of a seagull, the cry harsh and unappeased, like a vocal scissors, a bereavement in midair looking for somebody to land on in the wind-up.

It was strange: all the time, like a properly brought-up Irish girl, she listened for the voice of God, Who did not always have His prick in His fist, but all she ever heard were the voices of the women of Whitechapel, going more and more to booze to quell their pain or obscure time, and mispronouncing more and more the words that life depended on, as when Stride, bubbling on from cup to cup, began with *ask* and moved to *arst,* these to be followed with ten minutes of hearty bibbing by *arstle* and *arstarkle*—"What are you really arstarkling me this time?" she would say, eventually descending to something like "Wodge yew reedid arstarklid misdime?" Only Marie, attuned to Irish brogue, could fathom Stride's inebriated Old Baltic. Similarly, Dark Annie (whose lips too often had bruises embedded deep and would not move as she intended them) would go from *wiv* to *wib* and, finally, *web,* at which point her meaning dwindled into the darkness. Do I sound as daft as them, Marie wondered? Do I sound as if I have been licking shadows? The awful truth was that anyone listening heard the drink-flubbed speeches of women waiting to have their throats cut, not that they always remembered, it took a recent murder to pique their fear, and then they walked with smaller steps, their knees close together, and, even in late summer, their collars tugged high about their necks. And now the season had begun again.

Chapter 24

Many things haunted Annie Chapman, Marie Kelly's favorite tippling friend at the Ringer's, from that crippled son lodged in a Cripples' Home and that daughter sent like an unreturnable parcel to the institution in France whose name she could not recall. Her husband was dead, her children had gone, and even Siffey, the sievemaker with whom she had lived on and off for two years, liked her less now that the ten shillings weekly no longer came from her husband in Windsor; there were no pensions for coachmen's widows. I have failed myself, she said, I have let down the side; I don't have to go on the game, I really do not; I'd be better off selling flowers or crochuring (her word for crochet work). She felt as if an enormous chunk of her being had swung away during the night, borne off by some grape-green wave from out of the depths, as heedless of her potential as a woman and mother as of her talents in other ways. She felt devastatingly incomplete, obliged to choose between her emotions and drunkenness; she had signed Marie's letters because she felt it somehow extended her to do so, made her more important, got her out of herself, not so much noticed by others (though a Queen, a Prime Minister, a Prince were initially involved) as awakened to herself. What had Amelia Farmer said to her on Monday? "You're pushing yourself, Annie, you are taking too much on." That had been because Dark Annie had the black eye from Liza Cooper and a painful, bruised chest. What had it been about? The soap, yes, the soap for The Pensioner to wash with, so he could be clean for yet another of his infrequent weekends with Dark Annie, and she had forgotten to return it, not as big as it previously was and therefore an object of less consequence, and had slung that halfpenny to Liza telling her to go and buy some fresh. That had been all. After a hard night at the Ringer's, they had both staggered back to the dosshouse, muttering and jeering until there, in the mildewed kitchen, Liza, a sturdy and truculent woman she had known for fifteen years, slapped Dark Annie's face, saying "You reckon yourself lucky, you stuck-up slut, that that's all. You open your trap again and I'll really let you have it. So be said. Don't you come to me any more for soap and don't you toss your bloody ha'pennies at me, you toss 'em at some-body else." Dark Annie was still reeling, her eyes full of tears; it had been less a slap than a thump. She struck back with all the vigor and weight of her short stout bulk, but Liza Cooper outmatched her, kicking her and hammering both fists into Dark

Annie's breasts and eyes. She just hit and hit and Dark Annie only now and then hit back.

That had been Monday night, and Dark Annie was even worse on Tuesday, aching all over, half of her face like rancid meat, dark and glossy as a bluebottle's back and belly. She and Amelia Cooper ran into each other by Spitalfields church. Dark Annie could barely stand. "I think I'll go and do the casual ward for a couple of days," she said thickly. "I'll let *them* look after me, if they will. I'm badly off. I feel proper peaky. I shouldn't have taken her on, not me. I've had nothing today except a cup of tea. No, that was yesterday. All I can see is him, The Pensioner, scrubbing at his armpits and his groin as if he was some kind of furniture, see. Lathering up like a skivvy. I told him he didn't have to get *that* clean, not for me, but he said as how it was a rare event, and I was going to get what was coming to me, whatever that was, from him or Liza Cooper." Her thick, prominent nose was still swollen. "It even hurts me when I piddle," she said. "I'm a right mess, aren't I?" Amelia Cooper pressed tuppence on her for a cup of tea and cautioned her not to drink any alcohol.

"What's the good giving way?" Dark Annie said, mopping her brow as if for blood. "A body has to pull herself together, or she won't last." By Friday she looked no better, but was telling Amelia Farmer that she had to get out and earn some money or she'd have no lodgings to come home to. But who, Amelia was thinking, would want to go with her, she looked so used-up and ruined, like a patient between hospitals, on the way from first aid to the last rite. "Don't you like to go off to Stratford on Fridays, duck? Isn't Friday your Stratford visiting day?" But Annie was too sick to do anything, she said, everything she did was painful; she felt jiggered, ready for the butcher's clamming house; but she finally made her way to 35 Dorset Street, where she had lived for the past four months but not the past week. At about seven she approached Timothy Donovan, the lodging-house deputy, and asked if she might go into the kitchen, where she stayed until almost two in the morning, napping and sighing, dreaming of her son in the Cripples'

Home in Stratford, all the rounded lines of her bulbous face pushed beyond their usual perimeters, as if someone had inflated her to make her undesirable. Dozing, she willed herself asleep until Donovan awakened her. At Crossinghams, as the lodging house was called, there was a tradition of never letting anyone sleep for too long in the kitchen; Donovan forbade it, and, as he none too gently put it, a woman should be out in the streets earning her rent anyway, not idling away her time, like Dark Annie, with a belly full of booze and potatoes.

"I have to have it, my beauty," he said, prodding her. "First I sent for it, now I've come myself. See how important you are. Now then, Annie, you've had half a night already."

"Good for it, I really am," she stammered from sleep, through bruised lips. "Trust me, that's a good fellow." When he refused, she dragged herself to her feet and left, hiccuping loudly all the way.

What had she said to him? He tried to recollect. "For the love of pity, Tim, I've been in the infirmary. Just you look at me. Did you ever see worse? Trust me for the doss. This is me night for a drink, truth told, and I'll be doing without that as it is." But she was half drunk already, and he wondered how she had paid for it, not knowing that, even in her wretched condition, she had worked part of the evening serving drinks at a pub in Spitalfields market. What had she said last? "Don't you go letting my bed, my lad, I'll be back. You'll see. And with the necessary." True, her bed was still vacant, though not strictly hers. Off she had gone in the direction of Brushfield Street, walking straight and quite erect, from the rear not unlike Queen Victoria herself, he thought, but neither of them any good at fisticuffs; he dreaded the day that Eliza Cooper would come and quarrel with him about a bed or anything else. Better that Eliza Cooper, the Eliza Coopers, should come and do his job for him, police the Crossinghams, and then he could sleep more, eat more, take his pleasures as he found them, under the sheet or at the bar. She'll never click, Annie won't, he thought, not looking like that, and she'll be back, and then my job will get troublesome, and I might just give in, mightn't I? She has not much more life than a bunch of old dandelions put on a midden to rot, and she not even fifty,

I'll be bound. Why is the world full of these women, who never stay put, never earn enough, never keep their kids, never use their own names? Who are they?

He had some view of their joint fate, but no clear notion of how many of them dropped dead in desolate and nettle-infested yards, or gave up the ghost in the infirmaries, or walked into the river, from the silt to the sludge to the quicksand mud while dreaming of a sometime family sundered as a lightning-struck tree, their eyes gone by fifty, their innards blistered by gin and fried food, their feet walked raw then horny, their looks poxed away, their minds abacuses of cut-rate favours, their names no longer their own but degrading synecdoches like Long Liz and Dark Annie or would-be honorifics like Siffey from Sievey from Sieve. In their thousands in the city, in their hundreds in Whitechapel, they added up to the armature of life gone to waste, fragrant trumpets of fertility debased into holsters for the penis, and of course raw meat for those who, nameless and uncontainable, hung around with knives and razors, clubs and thuggee cords, acids and pitchforks, bayonets and steel-tipped boots, to do them in and bring them down, not the Gulls but the impromptu madmen of London with not a Masonic thought in their heads, nor any heed for the complementary abstract hypothesis, indeed a twit for twat, of impromptu mad *women* lurking to disembowel their fair share of men. They were never there: there were the done-to and the doers, that was all, and the traffic in death and mayhem went only one way. The higher these women rose, the deeper they sank in when back on earth.

Chapter 25

I f Queen Victoria was not one of the women of Whitechapel, as of course she wasn't, then why was she fretting about them, as she had *not* about all the other women murdered, some five hundred in 1887 alone? Why was she fixing on Polly Nichols, as if hers were the only salient murder in living history? Why did she exact from Lord Salisbury a promise to do something about it? She exacted it from him because both he and she knew the other names on the list, the names from the letter, and they knew that Polly, whatever her ranking had been in the light militia team of Kelly, Stride, Chapman, and Nichols, had become irrevocably the first. There were others to follow, but perhaps they had not expected William Withey Gull to be so thoroughgoing a ghoul. Chided he may have been, but he went on with his duty undeterred, making the headlines, having annulled Annie Crook and slaughtered Polly Nichols. In fact, he waited one week and then, after Netley had scoured the pubs and the streets asking and listening until he knew that one of the women signers was walking around with a black eye and a badly swollen nose, set things in motion again, sending Netley to Sickert's studio in Cleveland Street, where he left a message tucked in the door, saying it would be Friday night, midnight, into the small hours. When Sickert arrived and found it, un-signed, his knees went soft and he sat there in the little entrance, quaking and nauseated, knowing that he could not bear to see it happen again, it was beyond the pale, it was not human. So shaken was he that he at last convinced himself that the next woman, especially if it was going to be Kelly, was going to get a severe talking-to, that was all: no grapes, no knife, no quick gallop to some unlit court or obscure passageway, but a *ticking-off*, a *dressing-down*, a *real wigging*, as if administered by a headmaster in full cry with cane in hand, and Thomas Arnold or his son Matthew in mind. Oh, please let it be just that, he sighed. If only she had never written those letters, if only the others had not signed. He had always known that Marie Kelly was going to do something flagrant; properly handled, she would have made almost as humble a social debut as Lillie Langtry herself, who went nowhere until invited to a certain soirée at which she was so clearly the most beautiful woman present, unjeweled (she had nothing to wear), and in the simplest of dark dresses with the plainest hairdo; but Millais saw her and at once asked to paint her. She was made.

Marie Kelly's debut was likely to be different, conducting her not to the stage but to—he almost said the scaffold, but withdrew from the noun and said *mat*, yes, she was going to be on the mat, that was all. Gull was going to read the riot act; any more bloodletting would be redundant. Surely the point was plain.

Heeding the echo of his own thoughts, Sickert decided that this time he would dress down, by which he did not mean reprimand, of course, but try to look less tailored—in a tweed suit and a soft velour hat tugged hard over his face. He was with them, not of them, and were it not for Alice Margaret and Gull's patent mental instability he would not be going along at all. Yes, he told himself, we are going to address them all tonight, give them a good joint telling-off and send them about their business with a warning. Polly Nichols had been that warning, of course; now he understood. She had been made an example of, one such as the others could not fail to comprehend: the next time they meddled, by word of mouth or letter, then the ax would fall. It was as clear as day. It was logical, it was almost seemly, from a certain point of view: Eddy's, Salisbury's, the Queen's. They did not want the dregs of London rising to meet them. All of a sudden, he saw Gull's problem, explained to him by Lord Salisbury, which was to make any one act of murder stand out in the context of murderous London. Sickert did not know that Gull had been studying the Masonic manual of ritual murder, excited as a child with an undreamed-of bauble. He was less interested in Freemasonry's having bloomed from a craftsmen's guild into a secret society than in Jah-Bul-On, the god of the Masons, formed from Jahweh, Osiris, and Baal, in the service of which bizarre trinity Entered Apprentices risked death and mutilation should they break the rules. In Masonry, Gull knew, one ascended toward the thirty-third degree, past the rank of Master Mason and Royal Arch Mason, after which a Mason was obliged to help senior Masons in evading the law, never mind how heinous the crime. Sir Charles Warren, Commissioner of the Metropolitan Police, had already passed the Royal Arch, having also managed as a mere lieutenant-colonel in the army to acquire honors and titles usually kept back for generals. Masons in political power ran countries for their own pleasure and convenience, cutting lordly figures in public but flaunting themselves at Masonic gatherings with elaborate, hubristic names such as Grand Inspector Inquisitor Commander, Sublime Custos of the Royal Secret, and Right Resurrected Prince of Jerusalem. Eddy's father, the Prince of Wales, had been Most Worshipful Grand Master of England since 1875, a title that fused both kinds of titles: the Masonic and the royal, as if Gull had transformed his own title, Physician in Ordinary to Her Majesty the Queen, into something bloodcurdling and grandiose. Who cared so long as the title evoked Masonic slicing of the throat from left to right (only part of the Entered Apprentice's penalty for blabbing Masonica to the world at large), the correct placing of intestines on the shoulder of the victim, the removal of triangular flaps of skin, as of eyes, ears, and nose, and the penetration into someone's head of the drill called the Lewis? Gull saw Solomon's Temple gleaming in the firmament, the Ark of the Masons, and thanked his stars for so surgical a polity, in whose furtherance he might slice and bow, bow and slice, helping his Queen against the rabble. Victoria did not know it, but she too belonged to the Masons—to all those men, from the Prince of Wales to Warren and Sir Robert Anderson, only just appointed head of the Criminal Investigation Department.

Gull was dreaming of regalia he would one day swagger about in, based perhaps on—what was it?—an honorary doctorate from the University of Istanbul: nothing fancy, just a plain saffron satin cape with a heavy gold chain at the throat, and a hat of black velvet. Add to this, he thought, a hood of intricately crafted peacock feathers and boots of silver silk and a mask of amassed gold leaf with prongs into the nostrils, and all would be well; he would look his station. He would win his seniors' hearts. He would merely extend his arms, bow meagrely, and gain acute and sustained attention.

There were ways of catching even the public's eye, and Gull intended to be the master of them for as long as he needed to; he had a free hand and an inveterate calmness when in the presence of unfrocked human flesh. A heart in his pocket was no more strange than a cut throat in front of his face. He had learned to look with stilled awe, with imperturbable receptivity, as upon himself in the act of having a mild stroke, he his own specimen, he his own symptom. There were times when he was almost nobody, which was not to say that he was become just a blade; rather, he became a charge of electricity, a facsimile of the deity who, even when he was prayed to, looked upon human pain with no remorse, little agitation, and no interest, all in all preferring to contemplate the doom of fish or birds. This was the same unholy calm that Gull had felt on receiving his first fountain pen, and, within it, the long rubber teat that sucked up ink and leaked it useably to the split in the gold nib. With this pen he had vowed to fulfill his mother, who had bought it for him. He knew how good he was going to be, and how rich, and the intervening struggle did not occupy his mind at all. At sixteen he had all the assurance of the consummate achiever, thinking only that the inevitable took too long. So, in a way, he was never pleased; he just inhaled a little more as the right things happened to him, and then moved up a rung.

Sickert knew, of course, that if anyone could find Marie Kelly, he could, and she the other two; but why bother when they must be as aware of things as he? He had to play both Judas goat and savior, and the gulf between was too much to bear. Was an Alice Margaret worth a Kelly? If he ever had to choose between the two, and perhaps he did, which one would it be? It would have to be the child, to whom he responded in uncanny ways, feeling as sorry for her as he had for himself, captivated by her incommoded innocence, her paradoxical ancestry, her uncouth pawnship. Were such choices bearable? He would never find out if his pipe dream of the three women's being dressed down (and no more) came true and the coach rattled merrily away to Brook Street while the women grumbled and slouched their way back to the East End, pausing to argue among themselves about the stupidity of letters to high places, about getting involved in the affairs of others, about the time wasted on aftermaths. And Kelly would tell Long Liz what Polly had told Dark Annie just before—or Long Liz would tell Kelly what Polly had said to Dark Annie just after—or Dark Annie would tell Kelly—he wasn't going to work the patterns out, but he knew what their free-ranging *bavardage* was like as their level of intoxication rose and bloomed. The horror would melt into prattle, that was all, and the headlines of the past few days would vanish into their incessant mouths. It was really true that Polly Nichols had been killed and mutilated, but nothing had happened for a week. Nothing else had happened, and they were beginning to believe that Polly had just been unlucky: a buyable street violet crying in formulaic cockney: "Who'll buy me blooming lavender, my loves, sixteen branches for a penny?" Many had, he supposed. Vegetable-sellers still stood on their orange boxes, magazine-sellers were still busy at Ludgate Circus, Levesons still warranted and kept in good repair for two years their "Landaulette" and "Parisien" perambulators, and even the blow of death might be softened with an official-looking hearse that had pleated black drapes all over it and, at each upper corner, a black-swathed effigy, a venerable anonymous bust, filched from the Elgin marbles. London swallowed its horrors daily and made them anew, knowing it could always toss them back with enough gin, enough of a head-fling. Polly would survive only if they made up a rhyme about her in the East End and children played jump-rope to it.

As for Gull, he knew what had to be done. If all the killers in London had each been making a point, those points had merged, and anything supposed to stand out had to do so by virtue of its exceptional style. The doing could be no one else's, and all his fellow-Masons would know it. I am on high, he told himself, addressing those even higher up. London is ours.

Chapter 26

One way of accounting for Dark Annie Chapman's last hours would be to say that Gull, Netley, and Sickert found her at 5:30 in the morning, after many tedious searches throughout the East End, and occupied themselves with her for half an hour. Never had Sickert seen so many dark alleyways or, in the gaslight, so many blanched ruined faces attached to bodies that would not straighten or even move forward. Not even during his own nocturnal rambles had he seen such wastage of the human frame; London slept while these waifs and demons capered about in the half-light, raving or gesturing, wrestling one another or trying to advance on hands and knees, vomiting or coughing with feral vigor. He had not known there was that much liquor available, though he did know that the parade of the lost began soon after eleven o'clock, which was when the dossing houses re-let their unoccupied beds: turnover time it was called, having however nothing to do with apples. The exodus from the dosshouses took place about the time the police stations released the drunks, giving them a chance to earn their living, if they were women and not too far gone (what was the point of taking them to court the next day and imposing upon them a fine they could not pay?). So the bedless and the fourpenceless trudged through the streets at the same time with no chance of getting drunk unless they clicked, and those who were sobering up had to join them. Actually, those in jail received better care than those in a fourpenny bed, as, out of some not altogether regimented altruism, the constables and the jailer looked in on their charges, whereas the M'Carthys and the Donovans who ran the Crossinghams had a business interest only, intent on warehousing the poor. Those who went to jail, however briefly, entered into an almost religious system whose formulas and rituals remained intact and even evinced a mysterious tenderness for the down and out. As Sickert knew, the clients came from other areas of London and were rarely drunk; the street flotsam was mainly female. Few of these women would ever be accosted by the venerable William Ewart Gladstone, and taken home with him to be propagandized over scones and tea, or cakes and hot chocolate—whether he was then Prime Minister or not. The error of their way was what Gladstone propounded to his select few whores, with minimal effect, though he did convert several to a different, more exquisite diet designed, perhaps, at least in his own mind, to sap the voracity of the flesh or stiffen the moral fiber of fallen women. What shook Sickert was the untamed flow of the wretched, seen not, as was usual with him, from ground level, but from something in motion, so that those slouching or loitering in the streets seemed to be marking time or even walking backward, caught in one of death's mighty rallentandos.

Through the streets they toured, prisoners of the *Crusader,* and even more so when Netley swung down and went off on foot to look. It was then that Sickert heard the sounds of Gull's mastication as he downed sandwiches and milk, buns and coffee, even a few grapes—my God, Sickert thought, *hoped,* all he has to do is eat one of the wrong grapes and this whole expedition goes for naught. I wish, I wish. But Gull, who never spoke, in the dim light retained an expression of ponderous acuity, made no mistake and seemed to have endless funds of patience and an enormous bladder, never once having to leave the *Crusader.* He must, Sickert thought, be sitting in such a way that the liquids do not percolate to his bladder but remain trapped above the belt like mountain lakes. If this thing were worth doing at all, it might be better to start at dawn, or an hour before it; Sickert found himself amazed to be thinking so prosaic a thought when their purpose was so foul. Or, once again his hopeful side flashed through, the chosen woman—with black eye and bruised nose, as yet wholly invisible—was just going to be yelled at and then discharged from the audience, so to speak. Alas, back came an urgent Netley, who spat a few words at them as he remounted: *"Go'a,"* said with a glottal stop, intending that he had seen Dark Annie wincing along somewhere and would quickly get them to her.

At first she refused, glaring at them in fatigue, impatient with everybody and eager to go nowhere, a being wholly unstarched, yearning for bed and food. Nobody had made any offer for her services, she had no money, no drink, no food, and hardly even her legs; her entire body still ached from the drunken brawl with Liza Cooper, and she was thinking of going back to the casualty ward, just to get herself into a chair. It was that or going to lie down in one of the overgrown yards between the blocks of terrace houses. Once again Sickert had to officiate, this time beginning with more of an argument: "You look weary, my dear, and none too well," hating himself for doing it. "We are all weary tonight, it has been a long journey for us. May we drop you at your convenience?" He was careful to keep the idiom of the patronizing toff out of his address; treat her as a lady, don't say "dearie" or "darling," even when she answered.

"Nah," Annie Chapman said, "I'll walk it, Keptin."

"Honestly, madam, it will be no trouble."

"You not *arfter* anyfink are you?"

"Only some beauty sleep, madam. Please." He smiled his most ornate smile, knowing that she did not know how this dialogue had gone, only a week ago, with Polly Nichols. He felt sour and despicable, doing it again, but the vision of a dismembered child seized his mind. He offered a hand, a big warm hand, and that did it. In she came, to Gull's gross apology for the lack of wine, a little sitting there among them on the heaped-up muslin, then a grape, her first food this day, even as Gull babbled on about how grapes, currants, and raisins sustained him; he was a children's doctor, he said, affiliated with Dr. Barnardo's Home for Working and Destitute Lads, as if he knew about her crippled son. She made no sound other than a sigh, three-quarters unconscious before she even bit the grape, and Gull was at her throat in seconds, mild-mannered but swift as a gorilla, and it all began, the clothes went upward, the knife spun and floated, Gull reached into her and twizzled, then removed some organ and slid it into his pocket all wet. After that, Gull told Sickert to help him to remove Dark Annie's rings, which took some forcing, and Sickert looked at her hands only, imagining himself far away, not doing this at all, but his eyes craved the sight, the butchered belly in the tiny charnel house, the shambles in the gloaming—for art, for love, for *what?*

"Dark Annie Chapman," Gull whispered as he took a rest, "sometimes known as Siffey. Friend of Mistress Kelly and Mistress Stride. If only there were time to do another. But look, it will soon be light."

Sickert knew he had not seen it happen, or his head would have exploded. All he could hear, apart from the creaking of the *Crusader* and the sound of the horse's hooves, were the last little interjections of both Polly and Dark Annie as they succumbed without quite realizing how grievous it was going to be: Polly Nichols's frail, waning, almost comfy murmur of "Gorblimy, gents" and Dark Annie Chapman's pure, scalded sigh—"I'm goin'." Somewhere on Hanbury Street, he and Netley lowered her gently to the ground, off her coming an odd aroma of suet and glycerine. She had last been seen going from Dorset Street across Crispin Street to Brushfield Street and she was now only as far away from the dosshouse as she would have been at the other end of Brushfield Street. She had gone nowhere all night, in fact retracing her steps in the same vicinity as if ground walked over again and again were somehow less taxing. Netley had seen her leaning against a wall as the brewer's clock chimed the half-hour of 5:30; a dark man in a deerstalker hat was walking away from her, calling back to her "yes" even as she answered "No, no" without waiting for him to finish. In fact, the *Crusader* had dropped her off where Netley had seen her, as if to be tidy, but in a state of shocking disarray: hands raised with palms upward, legs drawn up with feet on the ground and knees aimed outward, on her back, some of her intestines set on the right shoulder. Netley had made this final arrangement while Sickert, heaving, had positioned her rings at her feet along with some pennies and two brand-new farthings that Gull had supplied, muttering something about brass's being the sacred metal of Masons. Round her throat Netley had wound a scarf before they lifted her out and down, Gull having attacked the spine with such ferocity that her head was almost free. This was the very scarf she had been wearing when she clambered in to join them, her heart faintly uplifted by their show of chivalry.

Again Sickert had blood on him when he entered his studio, shaking and aghast; again he washed it away as best he could, marveling at how fast it changed hue, wondering if she had been found yet and if he had dropped anything at the site. Surely Netley was wrong to visit the same spot twice, as something dropped on the second occasion would matter, whereas something dropped elsewhere, *anywhere else,* would not matter at all. Why the return to the point of origin? Was something luring him on? Afterward, Gull had sat still with an almost juvenile smile, his hand on whatever it was he had slid into his pocket, as if it were some prodigious exhibit to startle the examiners at Guy's, whose requirements he had long since met and had indeed, in his own right, stiffened for subsequent generations of candidates. A souvenir, then? Sickert shrank from thinking further: he was not going to get away with this, he knew. Best confess. Give himself up now.

But to whom? There was no way of shedding the burden, not if he believed in the malefic power of Gull, no keener demonstration of which he could imagine than what had just gone on in the *Crusader*. Once again *he* had not been the victim; indeed, about Gull today there had been something Saturday-afternoonish and bumbling, almost as if he had been on his way back from a rather soothing cricket match in which not much had happened save a whole series of decorous stalemates. For all the ferocity of his attack, the man had been oddly mellow. Sickert told himself he would not go again, but he knew he would have to. Why, Netley himself might do him an injury; his role was far from limited to cruising the streets on foot, and the pubs, the entries, the yards. He too, like Gull, had delusions of being demonic, and they were not delusions altogether, as Sickert was going to find out.

They had dumped Dark Annie less than half a mile from Bucks Row, behind a lodging house that sheltered seventeen souls, five in the attic. On the ground floor was a cat's-meat shop, and on the first floor Mrs. Davis's packing-case business. There was a yard in the rear and, alongside, a passageway that led to the stairs; tarts took their pick-ups to both the yard and the passageway (which had an unlocked door at either end). Dark Annie had gone back to the squalor she came from. Her feet pointed at a small woodshed, her trunk was parallel to the fence, and her head was half a foot short of the bottom step. John Davis, who found her at about six o'clock, had been unable to sleep between three and five, but had then dropped off for half an hour, as was almost usual with him. He had moved in with his mother only a couple of weeks ago and he could not adjust to the racket of the carts outside. He heard the church clock tolling six as he inspected the yard door, which tarts often left ajar after using the premises, opened it and saw Dark Annie's remains at the bottom of the steps, abandoned-looking on tufts of grass and flagstones. For a moment he tried to go back to sleep, blurred there with his pants belt in his hand, and then he saw several men from the local case-maker's shop, called to them and said to come and look at what was in the yard. They came over, but hung back short of the steps exclaiming and whispering as a crowd began to form and screams began to fill the nearby streets. Finally someone ran to find a constable, and a workman, after taking some brandy from his flask, found a tarpaulin to arrange over the body. They had seen her face already, though, bloody like her upreaching hands, and the long black coat shoved high over the bloodstained stockings. Her left arm was on her left breast, set there by Netley on Gull's instruction, giving her a sedate, composed appearance Gull had not intended; but what unsettled them all most was her having been cut wide open, eviscerated, and then, as it were, put on display.

Inspector Chandler had to tussle his way through the milling mob when he arrived to take charge. He cleared the passageway of onlookers and awaited the divisional surgeon in the yard, which emptied. He had the tarpaulin removed and some sacking put in its place, sensing that a sack was somehow more human, whereas a tarpaulin was for a machine or a fixture. Dr. George Bagster certified Dark Annie as dead and had her removed to the mortuary in the same wheeled shell that Polly Nichols had occupied only a week ago. Searching began, its yield a comb in a paper sheath, together with a piece of muslin from Gull's supply, cut away during his tantrum with the knife. These they added to the rings and coins. Then they found part of an envelope bearing the seal of the Sussex regiment on one side and, on the other, the letter M; the postmark said "London, 28 Aug., 1888." In a twist of paper there were two pills from the casual ward, for pain; Dark Annie had slipped them into the little fold of the envelope's corner for safe keeping. Without coming into play they had stood intact between her and Gull's knife. Had

Sickert seen all this he would have retched again, knowing as he did, and the raucous mob did not, that Dark Annie had been the second in a special series. Murder was happening and, in its ramshackle and psychotic way, it was going to happen again, as if Gull controlled the whole world, beyond the power of any queen or prime minister to stop him. He was doing it for Masons who had finessed his way to the highest medical position in the land; he was paying his debts with a sword and a series of sleepless nights. No one was looking for a pudgy doctor of enormous repute, not yet. The offender was a Jew or a Slav, it was said, swarthy with a narrow mustache, shabby-genteel evening clothes, and a rattling, jingling black bag. Various women had been accosted by this man, who then made an appointment with them for a drink or something more intimate, at The Queen's Head in Flower and Dean Street, say, or at the Ringer's. Suave, well-spoken Lotharios came to mind as women began to take chances in the streets. "What's in your bag, sir?" some would say, and remember the answer for as long as they lived: "Something that ladies don't like." Several had seen Dark Annie and her killer haggling in the street, then going through a gate or a doorway together, his arm about her shoulder, where her innards were soon to repose, and this same murderer was supposed to have scrawled on the yard wall "Five; fifteen more and then I give myself up." To some other woman he was supposed to have said "You are beginning to smell a rat. Foxes hunt geese, but they don't always find 'em." In fact, the man some of them had seen had been the indefatigable and ubiquitous Netley, short and full of rattle, viewing the clientele in the pubs and the talent in the street, looking for Kelly mainly, but with an eye to Polly Nichols, Dark Annie Chapman, and Long Liz Stride, also gently asking questions: "Who's that fine strapping wench by the bar, then?" Moved by the variable grandeur of the whores, he had sometimes made Gull and Sickert wait while he took his pleasure with one or two of them in these very streets, to ease his nerves, he told himself. His chore was both tedious and exacting, out in the air and always, after it all, he had to canter home and clean up the mess, stripping the *Crusader* of spent and scarlet muslin, mopping and sluicing, and then restoring everything to a fine unmitigated polish. Short, muscular, and vibrant, he haunted the byways of the East End as if he were the killer himself, and increasingly gave himself a chill by giving others the chills, pretending to be what he was not but grimacing mightily in hell's penumbra and so gaining rewards not compassed in money. If only, he wished, the other two would join him as he strolled the neighbourhood, each knowing who he was and who the other two were, which would give them total power over the entire population, knowing as they did which types of knives Gull was using, how Long Liz's tongue was going to protrude from her swollen face by dawn, and how she would be dressed and trimmed.

The perfect bloodthirsty hypocrite, he actually paused to help epileptic street women (though they sometimes bit his hand) and to tousle the hair of filthy cockney children; he gave to beggars, he shepherded the blind and the maimed, and he bought people drinks as he imbibed information; in another century he would have been the perfect totalitarian policeman, German or Russian, sent prowling in a raincoat. Curiously enough, in all his wanderings, he saw no other murderer and heard nobody saying "No" behind a fence or a wall (after which there came the sound of a body falling: he never heard this either). He never came face to face with a single one of the victims, although he often enough ogled them, watched them drinking or vomiting, wiping their faces or walking away with someone picked up at the bar. He could, he thought, have paid for and possessed either Polly Nichols or Dark Annie Chapman, and the sight of him on high with his whip and his barracks-room smile, with his swollen member not far beneath it, might have incited them even more than Sickert's debonair diphthongs to enter the *Crusader*. No need, he decided: after all, they might have said *Enough of you for one night, Johnnie-Boy;* they would have thought we wanted them in the *Crusader* only for pleasure, not serious business, and not got in. So, no. If, like Gull, he suffered from the *idée fixe,* the idea was usually not very good, whereas Gull, for all his depravity, had a lofty mind.

For the next few days the tenants of 29 Hanbury Street did a roaring trade, for pence allowing sensation-seekers to look from their windows at the scene of the crime (or at least the scene of the body's deposition). Some more zealous than most pointed out dubious bloodstains, none larger than a sixpence, some as small as a housefly. One woman had seen Dark Annie serve at a pub in Spitalfields market only half an hour before her throat was cut. The talk was that the killer had taken the pelvic organs with one sweep of his knife, that there was a growing market for such organs as were missing, and that the amount of innards culled was what would go comfortably into a breakfast cup. John Richardson, who when he was in the market came and checked the padlock on his mother's cellar flaps, she a widow living at 29 Hanbury Street, had sat down and cut a piece of leather from his boot to ease his foot; had he done this an hour later, sitting on the top step, his boots would just about have been on Dark Annie's head. It was not there, he said, at a quarter to five in the morning. A leather apron had been found, which sent the police after John Pizer, a bootmaker who not only wore a deerstalker hat, but had several old hats in his possession (ladies'), and five long sharp knives as well. The going price for a uterus was twenty pounds. In the end, Pizer sued the newspapers that had libeled him; his alibis were sound, but not his short-lived fame.

Chapter 27

Up to now, Marie Kelly thought she had a fairly full idea of human emotions: she had felt most of them, some of them too often, one or two like a piece of iridescent heart-stopping feldspar that made her cry with joy just because God, in His superb and awful matinees, had ended up creating it: such her notion of love, of marriage, even of agonizing bereavement. Had life not been wonderful, would the grief have been so vast? When she saw her husband being blown apart in the mine, in the zone of fire and dead-end dust, she knew that something good had trembled for the last time. It was given to women, she thought with stagey self-assurance, to become expert grievers, to let their eyes pour with hot acid and then go out to the site and, piece by piece, reassemble the beloved with squeeze and spit, doing upon the restored hulk a tender pat-a-cake that said it would take Evan Davis the collier back in whatever shape, just so long as he never went burrowing again into the bowels of the earth: his leg where his arm should be, his head swiveled through one hundred and eighty degrees so that he faced backward at table and had to be fed according. That. She had trained on such things, almost as if knowing the murders of Polly Nichols and now Dark Annie Chapman were to come, wrapping her heart in nettles and thistles and thorns. Polly dead she had almost learned to accept: those who walk the streets die in the streets, and not at moments of their own choosing. But with Dark Annie gone, so brutally rearranged in full view of everyone, Marie began to wonder, not about the letters but about chance and hell, luck and the demonic, deciding that a woman had no chance, not unless she went about with a friend or two, preferably with a pointed umbrella. The trouble was that even the most experienced tart could not tell a murderer from a client; every time she cosied up, her neck was at risk, her hopes were lined up like blind mice for lascivious slicing, after which everybody was so wise: yes, well, I'd do Minories and Middlesex streets, and Old Montague and Brushfield, but I wouldn't venture near Bucks Row and Brady Street, Hanbury and Lamb. Every girl had to draw out in her mind the map of her solicitings. That was bad enough: being drawn to money, you were sucked along to death as well. Worse, there would soon be nobody to talk to, not even about murder; she had been close enough to Polly, in an abstract, civil fashion, without ever getting curseword close, as she had been to Dark Annie, but they all got sloshed together and somehow, without explicitly talking about it, pooled their hand-to-mouth joys, whether or not only one out of the three of them, or the four, had a bed for the night or money for fried fish and some warmed-up spuds. Together, they had managed, thriving on a good cry as a joint act, a series of indiscriminate hugs almost sisterly in their tender blindness, sometimes drinking from the same last glass of beer before going their separate ways into the night, hoping to click before their feet went numb, and the one who was on her period never told the client, unable in the dark or the flickering gaslight to tell blood from other forms of wet. Many a night they had stood seeping the blood that made them mothers, almost as if they straddled London with a tender dew, one foot planked firm and arrogant, full of swank, in The Poultry near the Mansion House, the other in Commercial Street not far from the Jews Free Schools. A big splits.

It was awful to have so little, but also to need so little, as if they had been born with desires shrunken, so that a new hat was like an ovation from within, as with Polly Nichols, and a bit of an envelope bearing the seal of the Sussex regiment and the scrawled initial of somebody who had cared enough to write, crude and cuneiform, *yew are sumthing speshal, M.*, was a sample from the Field of the Cloth of Gold, a drab's Agincourt. On things so little, so transitory, they doted as archbishops did on their robes and emblems, the essence of these women's lives being portability: they bore with them all they had and they sometimes gave to one another the discarded hat, the spare pill from the casual ward. Marie knew all this, being the most analytical of the group, but she had now reached a point, to be talked of intimately only with Long Liz Stride, at which she had to walk abroad and devil take the hindmost, or get off to Dieppe, to begin with, then bury herself deep in Paris for a year. Just to avert bad luck.

She had accosted the Queen, the P.M., even Eddy, as if *they* were indeed whores of the grandest caliber, high-priced, whose worldly goods not even a regiment of hussars could move, not even the finest steamships that plied the ocean. But to go to Dieppe, certainly with Long Liz, would be to turn her back on Alice Margaret, for whom she had in her blundering imperious common way done so much, as she thought. The only way was to go and ask Sickert what she should do.

Neither Polly nor Dark Annie would have a funeral, that she knew; the good-byes had been said before they began. Every night was a good-bye, every M'Carthy and Donovan a mercantile pox to bargain with, every drink a skid on the way to more drunkenness, every client a reminder of those poor, sad, ineffectual best beaux: William Nichols, now living in the Old Kent Road, his wife a wreath made of air and stolen clothing; Joe Chapman, the Windsor coachman who had sent Dark Annie ten shillings a week until death cut it off, as anger had made William Nichols cut off his five. Dirty-nailed, naïve, short-legged, aimless but provident men, they had hovered in their ladies' orbits and then given up hope of weaning them from thrump and booze, except for the drowned, *if* drowned, John Thomas Stride, and all those children lost like new-shelled peas, and then Evan Davis, collier, gassed if not dismembered first. And never mind the Siffeys or Sieveys, the Morganstones, the Flemings, the bed-warmers, those who held their women's hands in dreamtime, who came and went and made scenes and slammed them in the chops for the merest transgressions.

The truth, Marie Kelly told her ailing brain, was that women were mainly alone and best off alone and, in the wind-up, when facing the Almighty with not even ten shillings to grease His palm, best off alone then too. Oh God send us mercy, she thought: I do declare they are coming after us with all our rubbidge.

Oddly enough, as loud-mouth philanthropists began to rave about the easy profits from prostitution and landlording and the reformers began to inveigh against lawless, poisonous sexual intercourse, things quietened down again, from the eighth of September to the ninth, then from the ninth to the tenth, and thence to the twentieth, twenty-first, twenty-second, twenty-third, and it was as if some war had come to an end and the women of Whitechapel began to say: They took the sacrifice, the offering of blood was made, the dread landlords of the night have decided to let us off again if only we will talk clean and watch us ps and qs. The women still looked behind them, venturing into the shadows to sell the only thing they had that humans wanted, while those most authentically indignant formed what they called a Vigilance Committee, something no doubt destined to remain awake forever, scanning both dawn and dusk for men with razors, apes with bayonets: *our police force is inadequate to discover the author or authors . . . we the undersigned . . . intend offering a substantial reward to anyone, citizens or otherwise . . .* One Samuel Montague, M.P., offered five hundred pounds for the murderer. Marie Kelly and Long Liz Stride began to quieten down, but not with the sang-froid they had achieved after Polly's death. Now their minds were scarred. They were together, the only two; they more than many others had in common something that tore them in half and reassembled them gimpy and slack. Their throats were sore.

"We'll never be the same, us two," said Long Liz, hugging Marie's hand at the Ringer's; they knew nowhere else to go. All places reminded them of the dead.

"Stick together, love," Marie said thickly. "If anything would drive you to drink, this would. If we had a hundred pounds between us, we'd be better off in France."

"Stripe me," Long Liz sighed, mouth full of pork pie, "the only way to get the money would be to claim the reward."

"Then we'd better wake up our ideas," Marie said, her mind on Polly's new hat, Dark Annie's black eye, both of which had blown away from her, no longer subjects for tenderness, but final, definitive, stark, what the world was really like with its clothes off.

"Do you think," Long Liz was asking, "there's really somebody out there just waiting for the likes of us?"

"There's always somebody out there waiting," Marie told her. "Waiting's not getting, though, is it? If he goes according to average"—she paused—"he gets one every ten days. Work the odds out for yourself, darlin'. He can't be having us all, can he now, whoever the blighter is."

"But he *is* waiting," Long Liz persisted, "waiting his chance, his turn. Somebody's bound to catch it."

"Well, never fear," Marie said at her most stoically jocular.

"Never dare, never win. What if us women was to walk the streets with carving knives in us petticoats? I mean, not to get *him,* but to shove them into just about any men around, to whip up the same sort of scare. I do declare I wish we'd started it, and now the men'd be running from us like partridges, instead of the other way round. Sod them. Damn them. Look at us. Who are we? Do you honestly think women like us are worth waiting around for? *We're not worth killing,* Liz. We're not even, half the time, worth a fourpenny pokey. In God's mouth, it's a sin that we're not, that it is. He should have made us better. If I were not the sex I am, and I had a pair of ripe good ballocks, would I go after the likes of me? No, I'd be after the likes of Lillie Langtry, just like Prince Bertie. They say he sleeps with his dicky-bird in his hand, just in case. Now you stop thinking about Polly and Annie. Their time had come, I spose. Think about all the survivors there are, think about how little we're worth killing, flower. Then you'll feel better. I'm going to cry my eyes till the day I die, but I'm not going to bury myself just yet. It's a cruel world, God love it, and you haven't to weaken, no matter what they threaten you with. No matter what"—she broke into an odd brogue compact of cockney and inebriated Irish, talking like some stock personage off the stage—"they tretten you wid. Buck up, Liz, there's animals in the sea worse than men, and we can't even swim, can we now?" Then she remembered the so-called Great Thames Disaster and the five hundred drowned, among them the carpenter John Thomas Stride and two of his nine children. True or not, the sad story had irresistible poignancy now. "Sorry, lass," Marie whispered, patting Long Liz on the shoulder. "Me tongue ran away with me. I'll tame it yet."

Then she told Liz that she would go and ask Sickert what he thought about the murders; if there was an easy and cheap way to Dieppe, he would be able to find it. If she had had the faintest idea what his role had been so far in Gull's atrocious outings, she might have gone to the police; but she would have gone only halfway, wondering who the police really were and if they sometimes for a Saturday-night lark carved up women. She lived in a muddled world in which some facts were absolute, requiring no trimmings or modifications, and some were malleable, subject to weather, whim, and desire. In the end she found herself unable to add things together: the likely and the impossible; the acceptable and the unspeakable; the humdrum and the lofty. So she thought she was both in danger and out of danger; desirable and no oil painting; a leader and a born pawn. Since Polly's death she had developed a new sense—that the ground was opening up in front of her and one look down, of precipitous breath-held untrustingness, and she would whistle away out of sight, not for something done, but *because*.

Perhaps this was why, now she had realized the mythic element in all courage, she tried to live recklessly, inviting the bristling bear in the darkness to hug her to death even as she howled the one word Whitechapel never heeded: Murder. In attracting the killer to her, she somehow weakened him, wanned him, and why not? If only enough of them could thus weaken or wan him before he struck again, though he might never, they could perhaps turn the tables. Her mind's eye filled with an infernal vision of a human being spurting purple ink like an octopus as he crouched there in rough shag cape and velour hat of charcoal black, cowering and whinnying as three or four burly trollops carved him up and passed out the pieces to the waiting horde. *That's what you call showing them.* All that happened next, though, in Marie's mind, was that Polly and Annie came humbly toiling through the darkness telling her to drop it, to get on with her work, it wasn't a woman's way, it wasn't worth getting topped for. For all she knew, they had all trafficked with this man already, and he was a purely spoken gent with lots of books at home and a lovely confidential way of talking, like a doctor or one of the gentler commissionaires at the big hotels, never moving the girls on but, as it were, sipping them as they hovered, his mouth where his eyes were, his braided uniform dazzling in the sun, his hands big collops of worn-shiny gladness. Any man, Marie held, might want to do a girl in, any old time; it was in the nature of the male, half of their charm reposing as it did on throwing their weight about and being irritable. Get past that in any man, she held further, and you were dealing with soft wet bread.

She was almost ready to claim that some good was bound to come out of the killings; that was the way nature balanced things up, harsher than Satan for the Pollys and the Annies, born in eternal ruction and gone down to sewage.

"You dreaming agyne," Long Liz said. "You got that treacly look."

"Well, booger it," Marie said, "I'm dreamin' horrors. Would you like some of them? A little tasty sample? No you would not. I was thinkin' of how girls get older but go on thinkin' of themselves as girls and before you can say Jack Robinson, London's full of old youngsters squabblin' over the next coffin, the next unmarked grave. They'll be havin' no decent burial, those two. The doctors'll be havin' a fine old time with the remains." Some fates just did not square with a world in which the saying *Bob's your uncle* stood for a norm of impromptu optimism and the saying *How's your father?* was another norm, of civil procedure over the bread and butter, the boiled leeks, the fried eggs on fried bread. What you said when you wuz good.

Sickert in Hampstead was a man in the county of reprieve, living on borrowed time, meaning the hangman could come and have his way with you, say in the middle of breakfast with a sausage in your mouth embedded in a mouthful of mash; the noose would force it out of you into the all-encompassing black hood. When Ellen finally decided to move her possessions, she would end the lease, or whatever respectable thing remained to be done, hardly important to him who owned little unconnected with painting. Some of the books were hers, but most of them his; he would have to come and collect them up, once it had been settled that the two of them would not be getting back together. In an odd way, because such a move was always for the having, or had been when they last met, he did not take it seriously; had she refused to contemplate it, though, he would have been insisting on it daily.

Perverse Sickert, he said to himself, you're living a different life now: you have crossed over into the terrain of the forbidden, the grievous, the damned, and all these well-bred privileges are as so many snowdrops to you. Having seen what you have seen, and become an accomplice simply from not having run away and be damned to the child held hostage, you have condemned yourself to mark time with bloody footsteps. No longer a man among men, you are the monster among the teacups. You have *fallen*, do you know that? How far, and where to, are matters not for you to judge, and you should quake that one of these days you might indeed be judged, then turned out into the Kalahari of the heart, waterless and blinded, doomed to wander while pleading for an unattainable forgiveness. Should the news ever come out, that you have Gulled and Netleyed yourself to fiendish perdition, your work will have the unmistakable aroma of madness, and collectors will amass it for its gossip quality: *These were the very hands,* for by then no one will care who used the knife on whom, it will all have merged into one dismal bloodletting in a city that should instead have turned its back on profit.

At that moment, among the shriveled flowers and the faint ticking of kettles and pans as the air in the deserted house cooled and tightened up, squeezing the metal, he knew that he would have somehow to incorporate his sense of history or doom into his work, not overtly painting it, not converting atrocity into a daub, but insinuating something: his reluctance, the true facts, the background to the hideous deeds already dominating the minds of Londoners. Was there a way of saying that he, culpable, was guiltless? Or that, helplessly enmeshed, he had fought to save his intrinsic decency? Special pleading, he wanly noted. Those who had served had served. Besides, it was not over. This was merely a lull as his unthinkable allies refreshed themselves, took even deeper breath for the final act or acts. Why did not the very furniture leap from his touch? Why did not the rugs on the floors shuffle away from his feet, his loathsome step? There was no one here to point at him, but there would soon be millions, unless, of course, thanks to Gull's insane ingenuities, the truth never

came out and he, Sickert, was obliged to live out his days
wondering if it would not have been better to be pilloried for
his part, to have it out in the open, letting the cognoscenti and
the rabble watch him tear his own eyes out in Trafalgar
Square, donating the profits from the sales of his lugubrious
and scandalous works to the Providence Row Women's Refuge. Of course he wanted it both ways, being suborned to
watch and yet having the rest of his life, unimpeded as an
Alpine freshet, to regret everything in. So far, so good. He
winced. So far, utterly unspeakable; how could there be a sequel? How could Gull go on, with his last few thousand gasps
defaming the very notion of evil itself? The flayed carcasses of
Polly Nichols and Dark Annie Chapman roamed through his
head and did not go away, but hovered there in the half-light
of the *Crusader*'s interior: a smile like a facial curtsy; a whispering sound from the butcher's block as pressed pork lapsed into
slices; almost a gurgle, oh definitely, as he and Netley heaved
the bodies, one, two, into a grave dayspring so apocalyptic
that Londoners would forget to eat, even to cry. They would
dog him wherever he went until he lay down and ended it all
with a razor in the bath, Roman style, or from a high belfry,
say that of St. Jude's, Whitechapel, murmuring I was not good
enough to have lived, I gave all my self-perpetuations to the
devil, I helped turn London into a sinner's drain.

He had seen the phenomenon before, of course; indeed he
had discoursed upon it at one or two assemblies of painters,
calling up the ghost of Leonardo, who said that *splotches moved* if
you looked at them long enough. He looked again at Ellen's
favorite chair, already abstract as a collapsed ceiling in its
dustsheet, and yet it moved as he peered at its back; he was
still the indignant swain angry with her for being too diffident,
for respecting his feelings *too* much. Yet that was her nature:
cool, a little nurse-like, tolerant as a sky. All she could not
abide was his not needing her enough, or his needing a sewer
to match her unicorn quality. Again the back of the chair
budged, wavered sideways, and he was sure his day had come,

that whatever darkness held sway in the universe had come to get him and he would not have to go off into the night with Gull again. In almost capricious relief he stood up slowly, recognizing in the movement the same thing he had watched in self-righteous crowds who got to their feet to stand in awe of themselves.

Could this be Ellen, here to sign and seal? To end things with a clandestine visit to the scene of her guiltless downfall? If only the chair would not waver thus, implying that he was a wavering man; this was his bed, made, and he should come and roll in it. At this point, as Sickert floundered between hallucination and caustic nostalgia, he wanted to paint the scene: the chiaroscuro with the furniture on the move, as in that story of de Maupassant; but his sense of smell made him float, drenching him with patchouli, woolly patchouli as he liked to call it, no pleasant perfume of summer flowers but a searching musk, was that it? Cheap, perhaps, and overpowering him, it rose from the chair as if someone had sat naked in it for years and each time that person or any other sat there the aroma rose from the cushion, compressed into pungency. Stench of whose ghost, then? He stared, shivering with fright, wishing for something brown and yellow to arise from the chair and waft him away into the Hampstead twilight, but this time a commanding effigy came upward from the chair, slyly almost, uncoiling: an overweight anaconda, he thought, personifying lord alone knew what viciousness in himself. He backed away, trying to exhale only, but his heart was bouncing, ready to escape and leave him confronting the lurid form, oddly plump for a snake and more evocative of something from the music hall. Instead, however, even as without looking he tiptoed to the French windows, half wondering if he needed to use his knife, he heard the voice he might have been hoping to hear, if voice there had to be, one that was Irish done in caramel, not quite whispering in the dank stuffiness of that room, nor murmuring either, but gently booming what it had so evidently rehearsed:

"Now then, Walt, it's only *me.*"

Chapter 28

He was sure it was a voice, perhaps human even, but his deviant mind had taken him away to a prison where he and Gull and Netley had to suffer the long drop after being condemned, the only unusual facet of the proceeding being that Gull, as one created baronet of the realm, was entitled to be hanged on a rope of silk. Sickert could not figure out why such irrelevant thoughts came to mind. No, not irrelevant after all: the shape writhing in the armchair, the voice curling out toward him, were those of a witness no doubt, ready to swear. He did not want to think. "Only me" was the phrase of a person self-belittled lifelong, or belittled by others. Dying, they said it's *only me* going. Starving or choking, it was only ever me. This was a woman's voice, though, not altogether familiar, not Ellen's, and then he knew, but the voice was saying something else:

"Gave you quite a turn, didn't I, Walt? Out of sight, out of mind." Marie Kelly, to be sure, rising not from the dead but from a chronic absence. His mind worked again and he saw the link between the two: the twirling form of Gull, neck snapped, was also the form of Marie Kelly rising from the armchair like something out of the Indian rope trick, a spiral without gravity.

Was he going to need the knife? Did she have a pistol? He suddenly saw that, for bizarre reasons of her own, she might want to start wiping out the murderers, he being the easy one. But she knew nothing of Gull, knew nothing of his own part in this, though more than enough, he guessed, about Netley. He was still wondering what to say to her, both levity and lechery being out of the question, when his mouth and throat combined to say "Marie Kelly. It's been a long time."

She was not getting right to the point. "I've come to have a look at how His Nibs lives as a married man. Our Walter and his Missus. Not bad for a painter, is it now? Where is she, then, Mrs. Hoity-Toity when she's at home? I bet she's walked out on you, old Walt, because you didn't keep your trouser buttons tight."

He had never needed to answer Kelly when she talked this way, her voice adjusted for the maximum of near-falsetto onslaught, a whine with an accusation running through it like a vein. He could smell rushes and muddy sea roses, he thought, and he quite distantly wondered how she had made her way across London, certainly not to chatter idly, but to pin him down, to make him say something culpable and definite. He told himself to let her begin; that was what Gull would do, wasn't it? She might end by attacking him, in which event he could end up doing Gull's work for him (get the *Crusader* out there fast, Netley to help him heave the body). He was hardly in the mood for an erotic bout with her, not that, in his previous ones, he had ever intended it; she had led him on with earthy finesse to the point at which his organs took over. This time, in the gloom of the empty house with none of the clocks ticking, it was an appointment of another kind, outrageously unstated.

"You've come a long way, Marie."

"Well, old cock, at least I haven't had me froat cut on the way, no thanks to you, I spose. A girl never knows when she isn't going to be going home after a hard day's walking, does she? Alice Margaret, now, where is she at these days?"

He thought he knew, but they could have moved her; she might be anywhere. Nobody was going to tell him until they needed her off their hands. "Oh, Windsor, I suppose," he said in a shrunken, oddly denatured voice, ashamed of what it said before it spoke.

"And you'll take care, in the end."

"As God is my witness."

"You read the papers?"

"Do I read the papers?"

"Polly Nichols and Dark Annie Chapman. *You* know."

"Of course I've heard. It *is* Whitechapel, after all."

"They're on to us, Walt."

"Who is us?"

"All of us—Polly and Annie, you and me, Prince Eddy. They're going to wipe us out, and then there'll be no scandal left. Last of all to go will be Alice Margaret. They've got her mother already, haven't they? I was wondering what you thought about going to Dieppe, and never coming home. If only we could get the child, we could set off. And Annie too. How can we get Annie back to send her abroad?"

Her vision of Dieppe appealed to him. It was oddly thrilling to be in this big, vacant house with the mature and sensual, rather massively built Marie Kelly, exchanging treasonous whispers, as if she knew all he knew and had done all he had seen. Annie seemed too far away to care about, somehow, and Alice Margaret unreal; the only valid things were the two deaths and the unfinished career of the madman on four wheels, the royal Gull, ravenous to do Salisbury's mild bidding in the most savage terms. Never would he tell her, beyond a few vague warnings. She asked for the fare to France and he offered to give it to her, though not tonight; he would scratch around, sell some paintings, and do it that way. She seemed to believe him, asking how soon, and he demurred, saying four or five days, knowing that if he really cared he would have said let's go and get it now, I'll pack a bag and we'll be out of London before dawn. Whatever has to be done has to be done in a blithering hurry, Kelly my girl. Why then, like some petrified man unearthed from the bowels of a cave, did he not move? Could it be that he really looked forward to what Gull would do with her and he wanted to watch? He thought about the hovel she lived in, that made even his run-down studio seem a palace, and wished he lived in a world more just, more obliging, more maternal. There she stood, almost opposite him, but still only a silhouette, as he to her, each waiting for the other to cease fencing and deliver the straight truth.

"Have you heard?" she said mysteriously.

"Heard?" he said, unresponding.

"Do you *know?*"

"Nobody tells me anything," he said in a petulant lunge.

"They just shove me around. Don't you remember, I'm just a poor bloody painter rubbing his sous together."

"Ay, but you know people, Walt. What's going on, for the sake of Jesus? If they're trying to get my attention, they've succeeded. I'm boozing now whenever I can get the price of it."

"You might as well, Marie," he said, speaking from far away where none of this mattered. "I do myself. I've done all I can do. I shouldn't have done any of it. Look at the trouble I've caused—Annie and Alice Margaret." Then he said it, like someone having a purge. "You've been doing some letter-writing, I hear."

"How did you hear that?"

"A dicky-bird told me."

"Fat lot of good that'll do you when they catch up with you, Walto boy. Mark my words, they'll leave nobody alone. We'll all get it in the neck sooner or later."

"Talk, just talk," he said, shuffling the rug into soft ribs. "I think you'll be all right, honest," he lied. "If there's anything I can do, I'll do it. Dieppe wouldn't be so bad."

"Well, flower," she said with caustic ebullience, "money doesn't grow on trees or up arseholes, does it now? Are you going to pay me in bananas or what?"

"I'll see," he said, wondering what his true motives were: having gone this far, he wanted to be rid of it all, perhaps even to the extent of being rid of her and Alice Margaret, and then making a proper gentleman's attempt to patch up his sundered marriage. The side of him not conscience-stricken wanted to go back to Cleveland Street and start painting, just flush this mess away and say its hosannas later. Was a man responsible for all he did? When a man had been a sentient onlooker, and no more, how much did he owe to whom? Telling himself that Marie Kelly could not read his mind, he caressed the dagger in his sock (his first movement in several minutes) and looked and looked for the penumbra of horror that should be surrounding her: the imminence of slaughter, the ghastly halo of Gull's grape-induced coma, the destroyed smile on her face when he, Sickert, stepped down from the *Crusader*, raised his deerstalker hat and invited her aboard as if he genuinely meant to save her feet and, indeed in these parlous times, her neck. Such a fate I usher you to, he thought, almost reveling in the role he would not have to play; he could revel in it, could he not, when he would never have to play it? He would certainly never go so far as to identify her; they were like brother and sister under the aegis of fornication, were they not? Was that what she had come here to find out? Could he be Mr. Facing Bothways, who both knew her and could go willfully blind? Neither made a move, not even for one of their perfunctory hugs; it was as if each would infect the other. If they stayed apart, nobody could trace them back to where they had come from. Indeed, she might have been followed. Where was it written that Sickert would always go out with Netley and Gull on their nocturnal sorties? What would be easier than to polish them both off somewhere between Hampstead Heath and Whitechapel? Sickert knew now that the full armature of so-called human motives was crammed with flecks of the random, most of all for those who flew by night and achieved the unexpected by simple dint of not thinking too hard about what they were doing. He was a traitor to someone, that was certain, but he wasn't quite sure to whom.

He had to figure out how much he owed; making a small gesture did not, he told himself, obligate you all the way. Handing a coin to a pauper did not make you a citizen of the country of misery, did it? Some artists, he reasoned right there while Marie Kelly did her pillar of salt before him in that house reeking of furniture polish and whitewash, were not morally committed to their daubs. He who saw in the spat-up phlegm of the music-hall songbird the germ of a new color was not morally obligated to her lungs. He was going to spend the remainder of the year pondering, this provided Gull did not ax him first.

"You know, Marie," he at last said, "if I can gather my wits together, I think I know where the tea is, and we can boil the kettle. I've a right to be here, daft as it sounds." Her laughter put his teeth on edge, so he went hunting for wine, brandy, Scotch, a bottle of any kind, and they finally sat opposite each other on dust-sheeted armchairs, drinking gin, not reminiscing about the old days, a fair number of which they had shared in what he thought of as more auspicious times. She had little to say, seeming content with a moment in which she could eye him and remain alive, in which no one was on her trail, no one was sidling through Whitechapel with a photograph, asking for her. Here she was in a vault, a tomb, in a house already marked for frozen debility, neither favoring her nor harming her, whereas he was monarch of all he surveyed. They were two people whose passions had a rancid side, whose prettiest delectations of the spirit had a flavor of rot. Each saw this in the other, but they had hardly confronted it orchestrally, made the most of it. Now, she thought, they would never have the chance, since he was as doomed as she; though the horror of what had happened to Polly and Dark Annie appeared to have passed him by as some typhoons do mandarins.

"Feeling better?" he said wanly.

No answer told him; she was beyond it, almost beyond feeling, and, beyond that, beyond caring. She was ready for affable anesthesia, so he hugged her, inhaling that South Seas scent of her, and she hugged him back in the full conviction that they were victims together, two viles adding up to a convenient niceness. Properly meshed, they could have worked wonders together, she thought, of flesh and canvas, of exotic fame and classless grandeur. It was too late now, she knew, although her nostalgic soul craved for Dieppe, though a Dieppe overlaid with Limerick lambs and the brash rhetoric of Irish pubs. Once you got to Dieppe, you could have everything, couldn't you? All nations eventually fetched up there, for fun or something graver, like the Prime Minister, Lord Salisbury, who, she'd heard, kept a chalet. Dieppe was a paradise to which you invited yourself. Both she and Sickert made the overtures to something sexual, but neither cared to go ahead, preferring to purr together in this dismal suburban box far from shops and trains, and he suddenly thought: If she stays here, she might be safe. Imagine the *Crusader* clattering up here. Gull would never dare; he functions only in Whitechapel. But Gull was off his head, now and then anyway, and the indefatigable Netley, the spy, snoop, and voyeur, would sooner or later get the right idea, and another corpse would appear, this time in an area with tone and tweed. How, Sickert wondered, did you use a house without using it? How did you walk the rind of the planet without actually treading on it? It was like asking how you lived a life without ever doing things infamous and then, on top of that, doing things even worse. One wrong step was all it took, and down the gradient you went screaming, lapsed from being what your headmaster called A Boy of Ability Who Does Not Concentrate or Work Hard to a slobbering demon, a mother-defiler, and a wife-strangler. Sickert had begun to believe in the criminal aspect of his nature, waiting for it to come at him in the dead central core of sulfuric darkness and get him doing things he knew nothing about, squandering his gifts on gorgeous perniciousness.

Marie Kelly was shouting, not so much from gin as from a fit of newborn irritability, and he could not fathom to whom she was calling, at least not until from the shadows there came another form, even bigger and taller than Marie, making his racing blood cool for a moment. "Long Liz," Marie said. "View met? Walt Sickert, darling, he's me only mate." Long Liz had been the surreptitious witness of all that had been said, and now she slunk out of the darkness behind the big captain's desk to come and have gin with them.

"No, I don't think we've met," he said, slow-motion. "Then now we have," Long Liz said. "This lovely place is going to waste. Wives, I reckon, is great wasters of nice howjedo's, at least in my book. Folks doesn't know when they is best off. Me, I lost two children in the Great Thames Disaster, two of my nine, and John Thomas too." In the dim light, Marie was shaking her head, tapping it with her forefinger to announce that Long Liz was off again, off her rocker. It was quite like old times. "This house is like a boat, isn't it?"

"Have you two been here before?" Sickert asked sternly.

"This is our first, duck," Marie said jovially, flinging both hands outward as if to encompass the setting or make the fact flower beyond its normal range. "No, never."

"Home sweet home," Sickert said tipsily.

"She did a flit on him," Marie whispered.

"They often do." Stride like a denuded chorus.

"And then," Marie chimed in. It was like pub talk.

"You see, we know," Stride informed him.

"And then," Marie said, "he realised how well off he had been with a couple of chippies in the worst part of London, thrumping like a Turk in Cleveland Street and no quetchtions arsked, no quarter given, none arsked. I bet you was harder, and pointier, my darling, there than you was ever here, for all the cushions and the fire irons. I do declare I can see better now me lamps is lit." How her Irish cockney slipped and fell.

"Oh, I don't know," Sickert responded tipsily, "even bad marriages have their moments, and good times with tarts have bad ones too. The straight and narrow isn't all crown of thorns, ladies, and the primrose path can be a stinking bore."

"Heark at him," Marie said. "Mr. Knowitall."

"If you ask me, and you won't," Long Liz said, "men is lucky to have us waiting around for them. Where'd they be without us to give their nastiness full play? I've seen them come and go, and I've only learned one thing: even when they like it they don't like it, they don't like liking it, they would always rather go on to do something else than do it again. An apple a day, just to keep them from getting a headache. Many a woman I know can think of nothing else for days, even when they're doing it, but not your men: men like to dump it and clear off. It's like this froat-cutting caper that's presently going on: same thing. They can only cut it once. They can only do you in once, and they only want to *do* you once, too."

If she only knew, Sickert thought, how Gull goes at it not once, but twice, then again, slicing after poisoning, then cutting them open to be sure of something, almost like an archaeologist of the flesh. He never seems to tire of it, though he tires of waiting to get on with it. He was never a surgeon, more a physician, so perhaps he'd always wanted to cut bodies up and apart and all they'd ever let him do was peer and prescribe. That must explain his passion for what's beneath, as if he was the head of some Secret Service wanting to know what's really going on in, oh, Italy. Let's cut it open and see. These women are guessing, cheering themselves up by thinking they understand his motives. Why, he is like some ancient loyal retainer, Lear's Kent, I imagine, saying whatever he says at the end—my master calls me, I must not say no—wanting to go out in a blaze of fidelity: nothing too crude or too awful to do for his master. He wants to be the ash on his garden, the offal on his midden.

Now the two women were almost weeping, perhaps because he was ignoring them, and then they cheered up, achieving a simultaneous hectic, giddy laugh, but Sickert held on to his thought, vaguely resentful that he had to spend his time chattering with whores in the precinct of his desolation, the house he could not abide to face alone.

Then why had he come here in the first place? For something to do? No, he had merely gone walking, the light likely to last until past ten and enticing him out, along, into the flurry and shuffle of people taking the air in spite of the new disemboweler in the streets, almost as if daring him to pollute so beautiful a late afternoon and early evening with his ghoulish bloodlust. Had it been winter, Sickert thought, he could have taken Marie and Long Liz to a music hall to cheer them up with a song by little Dot Hetherington, all tinsel and toot. That was what they needed: a tune, a trot, a chorus. It was too late now for any music hall, though they were having one of their own, impromptu, in here, their clothes undone, their faces almost invisible, their throats raw from the gin. Little expecting anything, he asked Marie Kelly for a tune, and she responded at once, almost like a choirboy trapped high up in King's College Chapel, achieving on this evening a series of notes so pure he felt a tear begin; she hymned the place she had come from, a boy soprano wanting a new life out of the blue, and no more hand-me-down lovers:

> Only a violet
> I plucked
> From my Mother's Grave
> When a boy, when a bo-oy.

How poignant, he thought, to a man obliged, against his will and decency, to look on at the toil of murderers. She is serenading one of the destroyers, passive as he might be, singing for both dead women, giving them callow good-bye. He tried to sing along but desisted, having neither the voice (as an actor might have) nor the occasion. What he wanted was not a song but bellowed grief and outrage. He tried one, but succeeded only in halting the singer in mid-"Mother," so that she sang "From my Mo—," acceptable in the circumstances yet disruptive of the mood, whose maintenance required not a syllable wrong, no splits, and no caesuras. It was as if she, or he, had drawn a white line across the night sky so as to delineate something, east from west, say, or high from low, only to end up bisecting a miracle, which meant that all of a sudden only the line showed.

"That's enough," he shouted across the yard separating him from Marie Kelly, "but thanks for the tune. Come and cuddle instead, I have a fierce desire to be held and made a fuss of." They wasted no time, enfolding him like marauding eiderdowns, tweaking his loins to no effect but managing to arrange themselves in such a way that, willy-nilly, even as he talked he tongued and laved them without taking much interest in his accomplishment or their pleasure, and quite unaware that both women were naked on the rug with him, almost as if posing for him to paint them, for which of course he would have been obliged to retreat to a safe and dry distance. On the three of them toiled, soggy with drink but managing a sedate lasciviousness: exactly what his mood required as he licked anonymous mounds of samite flesh, vaguely his for the hour, as the tenor of their lives prescribed, but this was free or for the price of the gin, and he wondered if, deep down, this was all he ever needed, either a roll on the rug or a woman-sized udder, never, he said, never to be slashed wide open, oh never that. Surely, if there could be a reason for doing what Gull did, it was the defenselessness of flesh, its openness to wounding. Left to their own devices, however, flesh and skin made a superb job of staying together, rarely coming apart. Balloon and air, they were lovers, especially in such buxom wenches as Marie Kelly, bigger than he remembered her, whereas Stride, though sturdy, was narrower and suggested muscle to spare. When his hand felt Stride, he recoiled a little, knowing she could blast him with one poke of her arm, whereas he fell swooning into Kelly's pillows, half inclined to suffocate and have Stride tug him out like a violet from his mother's grave.

They were having such a boozy, undemanding, fleshly evening that they never felt hungry, never wanted to be anywhere different, or with anyone else. Slowly their talk became fouler, their motions more overt; the women's wriggles were more deliberate, more spasmodic, while his own motions were dreamlike and soft, not what they needed. Next thing, feeling *de trop,* he found the women pleasuring each other with sighs of unsimulated gusto, none of which stirred him, but he smiled at their pleasure and wondered what Ellen would say or do if she were to walk through the door. He felt like a scribe at the mating of satiny mastodons; he tested the heaves and wobbles of those flanks and collops, marveling at the sleek rigor of female anatomy, wishing (briefly) to change sex so that he might partake of this, better far than tramping around London's meanest streets for sordid inspiration. The sounds he could never paint, and this disturbed him as their mutual relish had an exquisite, tidal timing, but he knew in what hues he would brush their pallor, their heavings, their moods quick-changing from languor to frenzy. It was a disrobing of the milkmaids on a floor of cream, in a cleft of carnal air trapped between the furniture and the ceiling, pungent and dank. Flesh and skin were fluid, coppery or brassy to the taste, and naturally conducive to meditations on, drawings of, the fox's brush, the rhinoceros's pleats, the flamingo's rose-fleecy breadbasket. All of it was one, even though the two immediate samples for his consumption happened to be two fallen women; they had not fallen in his estimation but had soared voluptuously in the dismal light, teaching him about the sallow colors of ecstasy, sallow because there was never enough light anywhere, not in Victoria's England, by jiminy. In Dieppe, yes, as in the Midi, the Riviera. He knew he would have to paint Marie and Long Liz sometime, without actually seeing them at it, but having slaked their frenzy with his soul.

For most of his short life he had been able to press from day to day without interrogating himself too keenly about his ultimate motives. Sickert knew where he was going: to the pinnacle of the art world by thirty-five, say, and as he sometimes told people about himself, he would do almost anything to get ahead. Yet to speak thus was to traffic in such banalities as fame, whereas the meatier, the nastier, question had to do with the one thing he wanted his art to achieve, and he was beginning to recognize that it amounted to full visual deployment of the lives that had no hope, in whatever segment of society; so his ambit included despair and boredom, the squalid and the sordid, the down-at-heel and the tarnished, the trite and the verdigrised. He had become almost a past master of the done-for, hoping always to find it and finding it so often that he sometimes wondered if his zeal had brought it into being in an otherwise or hitherto palatable situation. Does imagination, he wondered, actually transmogrify?

One day, he told himself, he would drown in all his browns: all those sauces, soups, and glues his mind had lingered on, in a coprophile's tizzy. Some had called his view of life mournful, dreary, lackluster, but he simply felt that the flags and pennants and superb ribboned awnings of life were a bonus sent to taunt, as if music were a fluke from the cough or painting some by-product of conjunctivities or literature the offshoot of the fingernail scratching at a scab. If then he thought thus, why should the doings of Gull distress him so much? The man, like Sickert, wanted to reach undreamed-of extremes. Only a deity, Sickert thought, could endure the massive contradictions of the double nature he envisioned, both enchanted and revulsed by the clashes in his creation. In his moderate way he had careened off the human map, far behind Gull of course, but trying all the same to strike the very nadir. Had he, he wondered, sported with Polly Nichols and Dark Annie Chapman, the late lamented, as he had tonight with Long Liz and Marie Kelly, would he now be feeling the authentic throb of terminal shame, or would he, never mind how secretly, be revelling in having tasted a sensuality so close to oblivion? The *frisson* in the imminent cadaver? Was that what he wanted above all?

Now, having shifted their doings to another register, they stood and began to hum and warble, then to sing "Only a violet," singing not to one another but to themselves, relievedly and perhaps shamefacedly announcing that they were still alive, still kicking. Where had Marie's song come from? he wondered. Why did she sing no other? Her untutored voice had done its share of screaming and berating, but when she sang this lyric she achieved an odd, aloof decorum that Long Liz could not match, nor shambling Sickert with his unreliable baritone. They were serenading the house without meaning to, no doubt thanking it and taming the echoes. Now they sang one after the other the same phrase, "Only a violet," again and again, he with raucous gusto, Marie Kelly with temperate reverence, Long Liz Stride with nasal incisiveness. It had become their theme song, something to haunt them during events to come, but only Sickert knew this, wondering as always if the next encounter in the *Crusader* was going to be a mere scolding or something more dreadful—and with whom? He could not believe that he was looking at potential victims, functioning as some kind of witch-doctor, willing the future to go this or that way. Clearly, he was as close to Kelly, in his disheveled way, as he had ever been to Ellen Cobham: on a level that found them together opening their legs in front of each other, airing their genitals, and generally having a candid scratch or two, after which they came abruptly and wordlessly together. Could a man do all this with a woman destined for execution within the next few weeks? How could he endure it, romping with her thus, and with Long Liz less expertly, only as a prelude to seeing them both in tatters? As a category, the appropriate no longer grew on its old stem, bore its habitual flowers, but lunged out at him, a conger eel with conical teeth for petals. He was one of the select party of executioners, his role minor, but he would nonetheless be a witness, an accomplice, and then what would he think about himself? Who would forgive him? Did the mind seal itself off like an envelope so that one could get on with the chores of daily living? His head would not explode, but he would never be able to whistle "Only a violet" again. Marie's song would drop into the vat of the dismembered along with her remains, and be forever accursed, yet only for him. He felt catastrophically alone just now; after tonight, either woman would respond to him that little bit more warmly, anticipating a good time of whatever kind. They would come to him at a wave, a gesture, already guessing what he had in mind, and before they saw otherwise they would have become part of Gull's abominable empire of the flesh, already dead and gone in the first few seconds of grape poisoning, hardly distinguishable from their living selves, but irrevocably switched from one dimension to another by a fleck of poison, and then transformed by *force majeure* with the knife. How he was able to think about such matters, even in hypothesis, he had no idea, deciding he must have somehow schooled his mind: after the first horror, the second was fractionally milder, wasn't it?, so by the time he reached his hundredth (his Old Hundred, he thought, like the hymn), he would be hungry for even more violent stimulants. Nothing by then would stir him, he would have become murder's leading sophisticate, destined to paint violent crimes with the same sang-froid as he painted boats, flowers, and bottles of wine. Perhaps society needed someone such, whose bloody hands did not appall him, to foster life's unspeakable side. It sounded grave and taxing, this new career, but he was not sure he would live to pursue it; he was likelier to have his neck officially broken for having been an accessory. No, Gull said the police would give them no trouble: amid the carnal uproar of London, a few more murders hardly figured. It all depended, he knew, on what Gull did next; the furor was already dying down, and even the most imaginative of streetwalkers had gone back to the game, looking behind them less than before, less than last week, as if the avengers had drunk their fill and life could go on being comfortably wretched.

"Time to go, girls," he said, intending nothing immediate. It was all he could think of to say, but, attuned to orders or instructions, Kelly and Stride at once began to dress, having been dismissed. Their mercantile selves took over from their impulsive ones.

"I," Marie said, "feel just like one of them Maoris in New Zealand."

"Why?" Stride asked. "What's Myries when they're at home? What's Myrie about us, dear?"

"Oh, I don't know," Marie said with lazy confidence, "I just heard about them, see, and I said my life's like theirs. They just bugger about all over the place, coming and going when they want to. Don't you feel like that?"

"You're much more tied down to business," Sickert said, meaning to go on and say more but suddenly drained of ideas and emotion as he recognized that it was these two Gull would be after. Imagine, if Gull had only known that they could be found together in the same place, he would have been here at the gallop, grapes in his hand. He wanted none of the other women in London, accepted no substitutes. Sickert was treading on coals too hot to bear. Indignation thinned his voice and took the resonance out of it. Could he perhaps, in a hurry, sell this house not his and so finance an escape to France? What Marie, Stride, and he needed was a boat, a yacht, a schooner, so that no *Crusader* could creep up on them out of the night. He felt Gull's knife score his own skin and rip through his entrails: Walter Sickert, victim number three, painter and frequenter of whores. No wonder, then; he was asking for it. All his days he had complained to himself that life rarely expressed itself in a conspicuous melody but was almost always a mess of incomplete and forgettable themes no one could ever decipher; it was not a symphony, he used to say, it was a cacophony of cancelled afterthoughts, a maelstrom of botched quotations, the whole thing unworthy of a God who surely, if any entity could, had a clear and organized mind. Why was God not like Brahms? It was no use posing such questions, but this shabby discontent had always dogged him. Life seemed to him to have filled up like a dustbin; it had certainly not been shaped from above by a genius pounding out sublime chords during the hours of darkness.

"Look at 'im," Stride said in her broadest, stagiest cockney, " 'e's lawst in fawt, just you watch 'im fink."

Sickert stared at them from some New Zealand of the mind, almost unable to recall who they were and what they were doing in the house of his marriage.

"Darling Liz," Marie replied, "don't you let him bother you. He's a thinker all right, and he's not all fun, are you, my flower? But he's better than some of the johnnies I get between my legs. At least he'll laugh with you."

He, Sickert thought balefully, is soon going to be laughing on the other side of his face; the work of oblivion goes ahead, grinding his conscience down into chalky atoms, soon to blow away while the dedicated painter reduces all hues to a drainage green, like an angry child who rubs all the colors together until nothing remains recognizable. He was thinking of Dark Annie disemboweled, of the sheer visual turmoil that came to birth before his eyes in the *Crusader*. If all the forms of life were melting down, surely what they melted into should be something just as holy as the forms: the molten wax of waxworks, crammed with possibility and hope and shape, magnificently latent; but he did not have that feeling at all, he was adrift in a world of destruction and decomposition, an artist in a shambles, and he could not understand how someone such as he, a connoisseur of life's mutterings and sulks, its puddles and distempers, should be feeling so little awe before the image of the human flayed. His indignation depended, he saw, on the holiness of the human effigy, as on that of rabbit, elm, or thrush. Shape, he saw, was the thing God-given, and not flesh, not offal, not blood. He loved the dry.

Having made a perfunctory attempt to tidy up, the three of them walked outside, still tipsy, and chatted loudly until he decided to go back into town with them, reversing his usual way home. Now it would be Hampstead to Primrose Hill to Islington to Canning Town, and so on. He moved between them, and arm around each, cutting back the usual stride of his long legs, and pondering the irony that, because he was escorting them, they were safer than they would have been, except that he was who he was. What on earth would he do if a carriage rattled up behind them and someone, doing *his* role, leaned out and offered grapes? Was Gull making Netley drive him around London without telling Sickert? It was doubtful; the team was small enough when it was three. Long Liz and Marie had no idea what he had been doing, as unable to smell the blood on him as to pick up the horrific images in his head. People were amazingly apart, he thought. Nothing was more private than a brain. "How you getting on, Walt?" He wasn't sure which one of them had asked, but he answered, facing forward: "Nothing extra, love," and kept going, his head aching, his eyes full of nettles, and what seemed the beginning of a summer cold in his throat, clogged with iron filings. He kept trying to clear his voice, but it remained fogged and costive. He had always felt safe in the streets of London, and now, the third in Gull's trio, he felt even safer, although that was surely an illusion: just because he was among the doers rather than the done-to gave him a degree of safety only from Gull and Netley, and that itself was far from being a sure thing—one of these nights they might strip *him* on the piled-up muslin instead and dump him in some East End yard, whether he had a knife on him or not. A shotgun would have been more useful. Should he show Marie and Long Liz his knife, slide it imposingly from out of his sock, and so enliven their walk with a touch of bravado? No, why on earth? It must have been the drink thinking. All he had to do was navigate, a toff roaming home with two tarts across the face of the vast hecatomb of fear and levity that London was. What he was doing was not far from what he had always liked to do, but tonight he was not going off with Bessie Bellwood to her rooms in Gower Street, there to dive into tripe and onions and rough-tongued talk. He was going back to Cleveland Street, either with Marie and Long Liz or not, with nothing in mind more than a good sleep, although these nights he never slept well. The *Crusader* pounded through his dreams and Gull's firmly upholstered face loomed from windows, balconies, kennels, and oil paintings, his mouth so stuffed with grapes that they protruded, making a proboscis. What Walter Sickert needed was something to keep his imagination sweet, although Long Liz Stride's wide, pliable mouth, the horizontal epitome of tolerance, turned to him now and then, elongated by a smile, made him cheer up when he looked left, as did the big scented polar bear of a woman called Marie Kelly on his right. They advanced as an unsplittable phalanx, spinning unattached pedestrians this way and that, never quite colliding with anyone but presenting even from afar as a weapon bearing down, all three of them in step more or less and *aimed* at a distant point. So it seemed to passersby, who gave them knowing grins and patronizing nods. That was what too much money got you: double pox, but for double the pleasure. They saw a tall, gangling fair-mustached rake with a sardonic mouth, flanked by one middle-aged tart and one young one, unlikely to be his sisters or even his maidservants, all three the worse for wear with skittish laughs and occasional bursts of uncoordinated humming. They did a slovenly march, inhaling one another, and sometimes, for show, deliberately veered to the side and walked straight at a building or a wall, halting in giggles at the last moment, then veering off the other way into the street. "Whoops," Long Liz Stride would cry on these occasions to Marie Kelly's pungently whispered "Jesus." Sickert kept his peace, happy to have histrionic women on either side of him almost as if he were on the stage again and they three were doing an impromptu music-hall number, hardly a caricature of his Affable Arthur (long in abeyance), but the walk of rhythmic good nature, the well-timed strut of cockney resilience. They had a willing audience, a long perpetually unfolding carpet of stone flags on which to perform, and a superb velvet evening for a backcloth.

Now and then Sickert felt an intense euphoria, marching forward like this, as if the three of them were on the prow of a vessel aiming westward to discover America. He, Stride, and Kelly were the new Londoners, clicking their heels to a novel cadence, perhaps even a foretaste of the twentieth century. Breasting the wave, he thought, chucking the past behind us, and all murderers, all mutilators, all careless guardians. As they went, gasping, they exchanged sloppy kisses, much to the

amusement of those watching, and Sickert felt quite at home
between Stride's emphatic, heavy features (those of a head
nurse *manqué* except for her debonair, flexible mouth) and
Kelly's voluptuous bloat, set off by her small, almost rosebud
mouth and her delicately sculptured petite ears. If death was
waiting round the corner for them, then they would pound
toward it with elated arrogance, daring it to come to them,
treating them as one body, their aromas fused: Sickert's own
that of phosphorus, from matches, and Scottish heather; Kelly's
patchouli as ever; Stride's some kind of spiced seafish long harbored in a rolled-up pinafore. They were walking off the human
map, he thought, three of the most endangered people in London, putting a brave front on things. So far as he could tell, no
Slerch and Senna were coming after them; no Slerch and Senna
could have kept up this pace. It was a lovely night for fisticuffs,
he thought; a few quick slashes with his knife and they would
be free in any case. Could they run? He thought so, asking the
women to try it, so they now advanced in a badly managed
sprint, broke ranks briefly and ran their separate ways, Sickert
easily going ahead. After this, gasping and perspiring, they settled back into a sedate step, and he at once thought of Dieppe,
how he had strolled there with Marie Kelly and Alice Margaret
and Annie Crook, cock of the walk, the impressionist *en famille.*
Still, London would have to do. Embraced, as now, by two of
those beyond the pale, he felt at home, restored gently to earth,
his spry intellectuality leavened and curbed. If only what
cheered them cheered him: Gull's inactivity for two and a half
weeks. Sickert knew what was to come, in all likelihood, and it
was going to come for them, not for close neighbors or intimate
friends, but for *them,* and he was almost certainly going to have
to be one of the ghoulish trio. Go to Dieppe, he said to them,
until at least Christmas. "We'll get the money somehow. We'll
borrow it." They laughed, appalled by his ignorance of whoring,
thinking he meant them to go out and earn their fares. "Lord,"
Stride gasped, "even with the whole of London tupping us, me
boy, we'd never get enough." But it was more than that: something he had never quite understood in spite of his long sojourns

with prostitutes, some irony that made them sitting ducks. He called it inertia, but they had no word for it, instead thinking of it as staying put while shifting from bed to bed, dosshouse to dosshouse, man to man, in the vocation and the neighborhood, expecting a sudden call from God, or rescue, or reprieve. They wanted to be near their friends too, even where those of them now dead had plied *their* trade. "If I were rich," he said.

"But you're not," Kelly snapped, breathing hard. "Be said."

"I will." He began a ripe sulk.

"You won't," Kelly told him.

"Don't you know," Stride asked. "Can't you tell?"

"Tell what?" Sickert said. "Tell if I'm rich?"

"Painters never have any money," Marie Kelly said snippily.

"Well, Whistler does, then." He wished he'd kept quiet.

"Who's Whistler," Stride said, "when he's at home?"

"Daft name," Kelly sighed, at the end of her tether, "let's rest." They did, holding one another erect, in Islington, where he grew up. Look at this looming lofty hill, he told them, taking them to Milner Square through the menacing dark tunnel from Upper Street, and they shivered, said it was like a gaol in the treed square, but he was chattering on about how sometimes the muffin man's bell clinked with that of the hurdy-gurdy, counterpointing the dismal, blockish feel of the place.

On they went, southward, and he showed them his own Duncan Terrace, elatedly telling them to notice how the streets looked like battlements best seen against a sky of silver and charcoal, and they *ooh*ed, as he wanted them to, and then he pointed out Colebrook Row, where Charles Lamb had lived. *Who was he,* they said in unison. So he led them away, not bothering to answer, down Noel Street, steering southeast, having ignored The Angel and the rebuilt Grand Theatre and they pushed on half-breathless until they had to rest, facing inward as if not wishing to be recognized, heaving their hearts up into one another's faces while the evening and the crowd flowed round them unaware of the fear, the pride, the recklessness that made them temporary mates who warmed their hands on death as if it were some amiable fire, all propinquity and Xmas cheer.

"You like to get away," said Long Liz, gasping, "from there," and Marie thought about how, at table during high tea, her mother had sunk a teaspoon into the just-mashed pot and touched it lightly to the backs of her children's hands to make them good. Whoever got it first felt a snake bite.

They might have boarded an omnibus, such as the *Favorite*, but they liked the idea of marching on Whitechapel at dawn. In his head they would always be running now, either from something or someone. How many assassins would there be in the crowd they were passing through? Five hundred perhaps, each of whom in the course of a year would put paid to one woman as if he were eating a lump of exotic fruit. How many potential murderers had they brushed past this very night? Not doctors skulking in hansom cabs, but nature's gentlemen unredeemed, born to the knife, the club, the broken bottle? How many of those they three had brushed against had had the faintest idea that he was one of the evil three who had already done in the Nichols woman and Dark Annie Chapman? No, he smiled, I had a woman on either arm, so I brushed against nobody at all, my vicarious lethal nature touched no one, and how lucky for them. I am not a bad man, only a man wandered too far away from the discipline he understands and needs. I should have abstained from altruism, which got me into this pickle in the first place, converting me into the reluctant inviter, the dapper enticer, an effete role to be sure. I need to break out of this before it's too late, but all I can hope for is that Gull has done, is going to let them off, these very two, with not even a chin-wagging. He has wearied of the carnage, the muslin, the *Crusader,* and gone back to the vile delights of the Pudding Club.

He could see himself taking them both off to Bath, on the theory that no woman was ever likely to be disemboweled while taking the waters or playing slap and tickle in a vat of healthful mud, or indeed taking tea with a cucumber sandwich in the enormous atrium while cripples flowed past in wheelchairs like multiple siblings. He would never do it, though, perhaps because he still did not believe that Gull would slouch back into action, having made his point and slaked his thirst. Sickert trusted to an incalculable providence in which he did not quite believe, much as, when drawing before painting, he drew a grid of squares on his canvas so as to get the perspectives right.

When he was workmanlike, providence came out on his side, but he knew himself only too well, much more interested in the uncoordinated buttocks of a nude woman walking away from him, with that faint fume of hair showing in the join, than in making proper allowances for depth and scale. He well knew he was an opportunist of a painter, which rather suggested he was a man of action, a virtuoso of the spontaneous; but his imagination was not his body—it could go into all kinds of perilous places and come home unscathed, indeed manured and enriched beyond his calculation, whereas his body hung back, not from fear or diffidence even, but simply to be the thing, the entity, that did not go forward. For sheer contrast, while the mind advanced, some other part of him had to hold back. In a sense, it was his mind that entered the *Crusader* and imbibed the ghoulish deeds therein, enticing the Polly Nicholses and the Dark Annie Chapmans, whereas his body, seeming present, held itself in abeyance, out of almost theological austerity, declining to touch, trying not to smell, willing itself never to flinch: to be present at its own absence while the transcriptional whirligig of the mind went on noting and tabulating, taking down the evidence, but no more fleshly, no more substantial, than a spider's web arranged across the right angle of a trapeze flying over the floor of a circus.

It had indeed been said of Sickert that his most forward quality was his aloofness, that at his most dangerous he was a man turned abacus, capable, as he himself knew, of observing frightful things without taking up any stance toward them, refusing to give to baleful phenomena the reputation, the epithets, they merited. This meant that, for much of the time in which he watched Gull, or thought about him, Gull was not sadistic, ghoulish, brutal, but merely the man who shoved in this needle, went for the throat with that knife, rummaged deep in a dead woman's belly for some visceral prize not long dreamed of but taken almost as a matter of course. Sickert had always assumed that his nominal callousness was part and parcel of an artist's makeup, a sine qua non of the kit. Cold and scrupulous watcher that he was, he nonetheless could go off at the wrong angle, finding sudden grief in the smiling faces of cockney urchins or almost intolerable joy in certain funerals. His responses were mixed up, and this had bothered Ellen, whereas it struck Marie Kelly and even Long Liz, who still did not know him very well, as the funniness of an arty gentleman, akin to the oddity of those who purchased smeared underwear for much more than it was worth or paid to be whipped, scalded, touched with hot lead. The prostitute's approximately tolerant response to the world about her was exactly the kind of appraisal he needed: seen by Kelly or Stride in their rough and ready way, he was normal; appraised by the decent folk of the world, he was an inherent monster of passive appetite, as likely to go berserk as to bend his face to a ferocious smell.

More hospitable than most men and even most artists to what came next, he might wake up one morning with his mouth full of ordure and, before having the obligatory retch, calm his mind and nerves so as to savor in full the incongruity, the fatuity, the wild-card aspect of it. Extremes he associated with excellence and moderation with mediocrity. Gull could not have had a more attuned observer to watch the transit that had led the eccentric doctor from the punitive crudity of the Pudding Club to the barbarism of the *Crusader,* onward to whatever Gull was to do next, having like a toy been overwound.

"Glum chops does move no mops," said Stride. "Not here, love, don't you see? This here is Flower and Dean Street, where truth told I have lived off and on, but cause of my Mike, Mister Kidney, I've been elsewhere, Flower Street sometimes, darlin', but most often at thirty-five Dorset Street, where I can't bear to go again. Who would? It's where poor old Dark Annie Chapman used to live. Dossing there would be like going into a grave, wouldn't it now?" Heavens, Sickert thought, they're all on top of one another.

"You come with me, flower, to Miller's Court. First, though, let's have a drink at the Ringer's." Sickert fished out enough

coins to pay for their rum and their doss, wondering why painters had to be altruists to the world at large, and then took his
leave. "You walk straight, now, luv," Marie Kelly called after
him, after smooching him hard. "I'm walking on air, girls," he
shouted back. "I'll save one for you, duckie," Stride shouted. "It
was grand."

He strolled away, wondering if anyone in London loved
walking as much as he did, noting how the jingle in his pocket
had lost its bright and varied tune. It would be easy, he thought,
to restart his ailing marriage for financial reasons; after all, it was
for those reasons he had entered into it. Should he send a telegram to Ellen, down in Midhurst? No, he would wait until the
coast was clear, and all Gulls gone. What would happen if he
asked Gull himself for money, playing the starving artist? The
man would no doubt offer grapes of one kind or another. How
could he sell half a dozen canvases, all at once, so as to have a
nest egg? Aiming for Cleveland Street, he yearned for a chop
and potato, but fought the urge down, bought an apple instead
and so arrived at his studio in a somewhat appeased state, only
to find a note from Gull under the door, smeared from Netley's
hand, telling him when to be ready: midnight, three days hence.
He felt his heart stop as if smacked and then resume untidily.

Chapter 29

Having spilled rum on gin, both Stride and Kelly had
become roaring affable, but not to Michael Kidney who,
after a long day laboring at the docks in a pall of smoke,
had stopped by the Ringer's for a pint, but also in hope
of seeing Long Liz, who only the day before had left him, as she
often did. "My mind's all Dark Annie," she had told him. "I'm
off." "Go and live in a bucket if you want," he said. "You'll be
back sure as houses is houses."

"Look who it is, flower," Marie Kelly said.

"I'm not going," Long Liz shouted. "No fear. That house has a curse on it."

"Then don't," Marie said. "There's always me. Half the time I never know who else's been in the bloody room most of the night. Come in, I tell them, it's a shop. You're welcome to my shop any time."

"Well," said Michael Kidney, "look who's here."

"You snap your braces, Mister Kidney, and bugger off." Kelly defended with zeal. *"We'* ve just had some drinks with a proper gentleman, see. A real champion. French-like."

"Ten a penny, proper gennerman," Kidney said. "Please yourselves. Home, horse."

"Now," said Kelly, "wasn't Mister Sickert a bobby-dazzler? You should have seen him lording it about in France with me."

"I no doubt should," Stride said wanly. "But I didn't."

Life, she was thinking, isn't a bad old bugger so long as you are willing to do your bit. Having to turn out into the streets at midnight and after isn't so rotten if you only remember what it is like to do it in winter. This is warm for September. She was alone, willing to remain so, although she knew she had to earn something this night or she would have to go back to Michael Kidney, something she was not yet ready to do. That little jaunt over to Hampstead with Marie, to meet Sickly, had been a peck of fun; if only life was more like that every day instead of one in fifty. She was quite willing to walk all night, hoisting her tall back high and stepping out in almost military fashion: out for a walk, as the saying went, she felt inexplicably pleased with herself, what with the streets having quietened down again and streetwalking gone back to almost normal. In her pocket, making a faint rattle in a small tin that once held cigars, some pawn tickets kept her company, a link to things she did not have to carry around with her, neither the biscuit barrel nor the last, a weird cast-iron thing like a letter L but with a half L sticking out on one side so that the whole thing would sit on the floor without wobbling when Michael hammered the nails in; if not Michael, then the drowned husband of the moment. She felt lighter for having pawned such things. Perhaps that was why she had bought a little twist of cachous to sweeten her breath while walking. Some clients liked to kiss and some complained when she stank of fish or just ordinary bad breath, and she often told them: "A girl can't go gargling her life away unless she has something to gargle with, my man. You supply the necessary and the worst I'll stink you up with is rum or gin. You can't blame a woman for breathing, can you now, or for being a bit snotty at the best of times." Few clients argued with Long Liz, who had a knack of drawing herself up to her full height and butting them with her bosom in the region of the heartspoon, unless the man was truly tall. She was beefy too, one of her favorite tricks being to lean forward during the act, shoving the client off balance, so much so that some of them had fallen backward cursing and fumbling at their loins. "A bad case of uptipped cock," she would sometimes say, or "John Thomas taking a little nap again." They found her a pushy, demanding, almost haughty tart, a woman of too much energy and spirit for the role she pursued, and her face had that settled, experienced look as if she had seen everything several times over; her standard expression was one of sedate worldliness tinctured with smile. She suited herself and, being Scandinavian, thought herself tough enough to go without two meals in a row, knowing she could live off her body fat, even her muscle, if she had to.

Tonight, perhaps in happy memory of the night out with Sickly in Hampstead, she was sporting flowers, red and white carnations, one of each, against the moldy fur collar of her black coat. Even in summer she always went out in her overcoat; it was the best way of carrying it and she sometimes thought how women of the night dressed as if there were no seasons but only one. Kelly had given her the flowers, telling her to watch out for the late-summer wind, but Long Liz knew that it was the permanent wind of London, neither warm nor cold, neither dusty nor wet, the exclusive property of streetwalkers, those clotheshorse nomads of the ghetto bounded by Hanbury Street to the north, Commercial Road to the south, hemmed in by Commercial Street to the west and the London Hospital to the east. To them a wind was always blustery just as brussels sprouts were always rather searching (a good laxative, that is) and a spoonful of arrowroot was good for the runs. In some ways she, who had often turned her hand to something better than whoring, enjoyed the reduced quality of her life, of a life on the game, not being responsible for too much, knowing only one kind of human being (the woman of loose morals, so-called), and therefore responding like a saint in an ecstasy to such transient delights as carnations, cachous, her own bottle of gin, a chunk of hotel soap, a secondhand bonnet poshed up to look like new. Somehow, she suspected, being on the game made her more appreciative, but she wanted her flesh to be as young and ripe as Marie Kelly's, and she took to blaming the London breeze for drying her out before her time: "Always a wind, a *blustery* wind, in my attic," she said in summary, "and here I am going about with all my windows closed." The time of swooning adorations was over, fifteen years over, but she kept intact some piece of her heart for what, in her cups, she stylishly called "hand-me-down pleasances," never quite sure what she meant, but indicating a modicum of joy in coal-black circumstances. Perhaps because she was tall and could see over the heads of others to a greener prospect up the road, she remained buoyant and boisterous, not yet humbled by her calling to the point of the mouth's being insucked, the mind shut off, the eyes tightened to a querulous squint. Her big, abrupt gaze made men quail, but they got used to it and came for more, and, when she took the time to talk with them, she regaled them with her vision of herself as a wasted woman who could have been a nurse, run a café, or a dosshouse even. They agreed, and tipped her almost as much as they tipped Marie Kelly for her roaming forefinger.

Going up Commercial Road with a swing in her gait (it was early), Long Liz became aware of a horse-drawn vehicle behind her, keeping pace with her until she halted, looked to her right and saw, of all faces, Sickert's, looming from the window, half-smiling to indicate hello, then coughing hard, the nasal voice of one with a full-blown cold saying to her, as the *Crusader* slowed down, something conventional, by no means a request or an invitation; indeed, he seemed to be saying, deep in his clogged throat, "Sorry we can't give you a lift this rainy night, we're full up, flower. It's an invention of the devil, to be sure. You freeze in winter, you smother in summer. It loosens your teeth and ruins your hat. Give my love to Miss Kelly." Netley, who had spotted Stride and warned Sickert they were overtaking her, heard none of this and paid no attention, as if his work were done. Sickert settled back into into his seat and gestured annoyance to Gull, who had not heard either. It was as if nothing bad would ever happen again. Now Stride resumed her drunken waltz up Commercial Road, swiveling her hips from the pride of having been greeted by Sickly of the other night from his carriage. Things were looking up in spite of the wet.

"Tell Netley," Gull said at last, unrolling something he had been warming in his lap. "He knows what to do." He did, stopping in a back street and motioning to Sickert to come and help him, but Sickert hung back while Netley forged ahead eager to reach Long Liz before the night swallowed her up. It was hard to miss her, though, her shambling lollop like no one else's, her head held high as if ready for the knife. Then she saw him, saying to herself Here he comes, not Sickly, the other one, he must have been taken short, he wanted it fierce, they often do, they would put it into their mothers, it must be like when you have to go and piddle something cruel and nothing else will do, you have to go. He saw me and I took his fancy even if I am not on the first flush, nice breath and all mingled with the scent of carnations, I'm a walking nosegay, I am a streetwalking nosegay. Here he comes, with his horn at the ready, I'll be bound, the money in his hand. Well, he will not be putting it up a duck tonight. Yes, dear, can I do anything for you? Say it, Liz. My, what a noise.

At this point Israel Schwartz was turning into Berner Street from Commercial Road. As he was passing the enormous wooden gates at the entrance to Berner Street he paused, catching sight of a man and a woman by the little wicket gate cut into one of the main gates, their voices drowned by singing. The man was tugging at the woman to get her into the street, but she was putting up a considerable fight and seemed to have physical bulk; she was not playing hard to get, it was more than a token fight, he said, the woman was getting angry. At this point the man managed to spin the woman around and threw her down in one simple, contemptuous movement, at which she screamed three times. Now Israel Schwartz became aware of another man standing lighting his pipe on the other side of the street, apparently unconcerned by the scene enacted in front of him. Now the man who had felled the woman looked up, saw Schwartz and shouted "Lipski," the usual term of opprobrium for an unknown Jew ever since a Jew of that name had been hanged the year before. The screams had not been as loud as the shout, Schwartz decided as he moved away, anxious not to be involved; but the second man began to follow him, so he ran off toward the arches of the London, Tilbury, and Southend Railway, and at some point the pursuer gave up. He kept wondering if the shortness of the attacker had made the other man appear so tall, or vice versa. Two young men, he thought, the shorter one dark, the other fair, both with moustaches. It was about a quarter of one in the morning, and within moments Netley and Sickert were back in the *Crusader* on their way to an appointment with the person Gull called "the Kelly woman," due to be released, Netley said, from the Bishopsgate Police Station soon after midnight, drunk or not. They raced away from the loud International Workers' Educational Club at 40 Berner Street, into whose yard Netley had shoved Stride's body after cutting her throat in full view of Walter Sickert, who now kept waiting for pain to strike home to him as if he were human and had really been on the rug in Hampstead with this same woman only two days ago. Death, he thought, could not be inflicted so trivially, like the clincher to an argument; it just could not be so impromptu, so casual, something you could watch while enjoying a good pipe. He was smoking because someone had told him that the warm air from a pipe's stem soothed the sore throat that went with a cold. "Or makes it worse," had been Sickert's response. He tried it nonetheless, destined to become a cough on legs even on this night of nights. He had expected Long Liz to get up and go waltzing away in her highhanded fashion, but she did not move and he did not cross the road to look at her. Now he knew what Netley was made of, though about Walter Sickert less and less. How could he have stood and watched, half knowing what was to come? How could he have followed Netley as he accosted Stride? Why had he not intervened, doing the obstructive equivalent of the deceit he had practiced while talking to her from the *Crusader*? If he found murder so repugnant, why had he on one occasion done his best to forestall any such thing and then, on another, gone along meekly to the slaughter to smoke his pipe? Had Stride, Marie's good friend, counted for nothing? Was he under such a potent threat that he had not dared to lift a finger? Back in the *Crusader* with Gull, he thought he had mounted the wrong conveyance because, by the gaslight as they passed successive lamps, he saw Gull now attired in a bright yellow or even white set of fisherman's oilskins, from rubber boots to a sou'wester with its brim folded back. Gull was dressed for work.

"Finally," Gull was saying to himself, but Sickert was too busy wondering if Netley had been obliged to throw Long Liz Stride to the ground because she was too tall for him to cut her throat standing. Why had he, Sickert, gone after the Jew whom Netley had reviled as Lipski? What had been that splash of red and white in the decrescendo of Stride's falling down? Had Netley mutilated her? No, he had hardly had time, he had rushed away. Sickert's fingers found in his jacket pocket a piece of chalk he had been experimenting with, to lighten certain shades, to draw on rough dark paper with. Was it billiards chalk? No, he knew it wasn't, it was white, round, short, snapped in two.

If he had a brain, it was not functioning. Something appalling had happened, and the wind still blew, the East End still smelled bad, the noise of the slaughterers' drays had gone on, his own blood had continued to flow, contained, conserved, whereas Long Liz Stride's had flowed out on to the flagstones, he had seen the beginning of that. Now here was Gull dressed for mayhem to be committed upon the body of Marie Kelly, with whom he had also disported himself in the Hampstead house, on the rug, and walked home across London with. He should never have let them out of his sight. This very second, they should all three have been in Dieppe; indeed, two days ago, prolonging their cock-a-hoop walk to the coast, the Channel, and somewhere safe. Gull's task was almost done.

He knew now that a man might engage in unspeakable things and still survive, retain his grasp of the cursive line or colloquial French. It was not the same, though, as if he had been hunting for deer or boar; after even that, something in him would be broken, would it not? Irreparably spoiled at the same time as he recognized the need for such violence. Hunting in the mean streets of London was something quite different: it had to come to an end. Even Gull wanted it to come to an end, he wanted to round things off this very night, which was why the *Crusader* was going at speed to the right police station, the right street, in which Marie Kelly would appear after being discharged. It was as if she had commanded a cab to meet her after some weighty appointment to take her to a fashionable hotel, The Metropole or The Fleece. He could see, now, why men joined the Masons, wanted to join them, for if you went beyond the law you needed to belong to some cadre that made a fetish of going beyond it, of being always above it, of being the law above the law. It was savagely lonely otherwise, he could see that. Already he was in a trance, being carried along by the superior will of others, as unable to refuse as to think. It could never be happening: the object of this harum-scarum chase through London was to get to the music hall on time; that was how civilized people lived, people who did not go disembowelling in stark holy righteousness. As well to develop a passion for toasted snow as to try and hold on to his old, decent self. Why am I here? Sickert wondered. I am here simply because of Alice Margaret and the threat to me. It is a choice between death and complicity. Why, they may even kill me off later on, once their loathsome foray is over; after all, I might blab, I might tell it all in my old age and become a nine-day wonder. If I were they, I would remove Sickert along with the rest, I surely would, and they have the stomach to do it.

It had been an uproarious night at the International Working Men's Educational Club; semidisciplined debate about the issues of the time (poverty and republicanism) had given way to shouting and that to dancing and singing, all of it some nuisance to the cigarette makers and sweatshop tailors who lived in the terraced cottages opposite. Into their windows poured a big avalanche of light from the club, and it was toward this that the club's steward, Louis Diemschutz (a name that made folk suspicious, he said: a Communist Jew agitator, perhaps?), drove his pony and barrow, shaking his head at the things his wife allowed. She ran the club both night and day while Louis worked as a costermonger, infiltrating his cheap costume jewelry into the better-off suburbs of London. She burned in gas, he grumbled, what he made with his barrow, but how could he be in both places at once? His pony balked at something and pulled left, causing him to tug hard on the reins, and then it shied again, so Louis poked at the obstruction with his whip, knowing he would have to get down and shift it, but reluctant to do everything in one motion. He struck a match, but it was still windy and the match blew out. He had seen enough, though, to recognize a female body, drunk or dead, right in his path, so he halted, rushed into the club, came out with a lighted candle from his stock and several club members whose levity struck him as possibly inappropriate, depending on what they found. Of course they found Long Liz Stride, dead and wet in a pool of blood, and still warm. It was only 1:00 A.M. The next few hours saw the thorough search of all houses and rooms in the vicinity and the inspection of hands for blood, including the indignant merrymakers from the club. No one knew who she was, but they knew what she had been, and their hysterical cries were mainly for themselves, not for those it had already happened to. How many more like himself, Louis Diemschutz wondered, would be finding murdered women in the small hours of the morning, and wondering why they came from Europe to London, supposedly a haven of safety. Sooner or later, he mused, everything gets found, although not solved. You could so easily have your throat cut in the back alleys, for reasons the police would never discover, and you would not be long remembered, not even by the Socialist Working Men's Educational Clubs of the World, but if you were a member of *nothing* you were nobody at all, were you? Safety in numbers had something to commend it, he decided, and the bigger the number the better. Would his pony have walked over the woman? He doubted it, but it might have walked right past without shying, in which case he might have gone to bed in the usual way, and left the dead woman lying there all night. He did not like the element of chance in this, haunted as he was by the thought that the world of the future, in which workingmen read books for a purpose and not just to better their minds, would have to be based on corpses, the yield of all revolution. Surely this woman's murder had not been political, just an act of revenge and unbridled sexuality, yet she did not look interfered with, poor big slop of a baggage in her musty black, one of the thousands who haunted him, who could and should have been doing useful work instead of trading their vulvas for pennies.

At this time, the fourth victim of Gull and Netley (and of Sickert too) was telling the jailer, George Hutt, at Bishopsgate Police Station that she would go straight home to Spitalfields and sleep off the remainder of her hangover. "I'll get a damned fine hiding when I land there too," she told him. It was too late to go and sleep it off at her sister's place in Thrawl Street and she was still feeling a bit wobbly.

"Or with your brother," George Hutt said in his friendly yet austere fashion. "At least you has folks arsking after you. That's more than many do, mark my words."

"Brother?" she said. "I haven't got a brother, so who?"

"Wanting to know when you was due out, arsking right as rain for Mrs. Mary Ann Kelly. Sounded right to me."

"Well, then," she said, "I have a friend. It wasn't my gentleman friend Mr. Kelly, I'm sure. My husband, I mean. He never does things like that."

"Thousands wouldn't, dear," he said. "You can go whenever you want." He signed her out and expressed the hopeless wish not to see her again in the state she arrived in. She was a perky, garrulous little bird of a woman. Yes, he thought, Chirpy is the name for her. Ever a little quip like a touch of birdseed. She proved it by twitting him as she went out, still reeling slightly. "I've the Queen's garden party later on today," she chortled, "rain or no rain, wind or no wind. I'd better be off."

"You had," he rumbled, "Her Majesty likes her tarts on time, she does that. Good morning, m'am." Out she went and was carelessly identified by weary Netley, the only woman coming out, from his high perch. One tap of his whip on the superstructure of the *Crusader* and they were off, snailpace, to pick her up out of the windblown rain. When Sickert, his face trembling in every part, peeked out, he could not have been happier even if he had been praying for such an outcome. In fact the woman in the street was Catherine Eddowes, who, as she had intimated to her jailer, lived with a man named John Kelly and therefore passed herself off as Mary Ann Kelly, less often as Mary Jane. She lived only fifty yards from Marie Kelly, but did not know her and had certainly not signed the letters. Now she saw Sickert leaning out, his face quite composed, inviting her in from the rain. Well, she thought, I am not much of a sight tonight, this morning, but I don't get many takers, I'm more than a bit past it, if they have the spirit to want me then they can. Even if it was only a ride, it would be better than walking home in the rain at the mercy of cutthroats, whoever they were. These were toffs, doing what toffs ought to do a damn sight more often. Of course she would. She mounted, sat, smiled, and took the grapes, only slightly put out by the sight of a toff opposite her in yellow oilskins—for the rain of course—who handed her the grapes, patting her on the knee, while the other man kept saying *Oh have another, please have another.* Then Gull was upon her with pent-up savagery, less a Mason, Sickert thought, than a barbarian, making the blood fly far from the muslin, as if he hated this total stranger, this frail body, with all his heart. She was the last one, the cause of all the trouble, and he fell upon her like a yellow thunderbolt, cutting away her nose as if it had antagonized him for years, even as her linnetlike mind saw some resemblance between being invited into a carriage by toffs and, long ago, in some twisted parody of a high-class evening out, going all dolled-up with her parents to Uncle Reginald's for high tea, but not really for that: the deep purpose of their visit had been to hear Uncle Reg belch after eating and say "Manners," which made those near him flinch right out of their chairs. An evening out, but of an unusual kind: that had been virtually her last thought as she took the grapes and bit home, nodding indulgently at the flavor, the kindness of the fisherman fellow, the good manners of the tall young one. She felt stunted and bedraggled, this Eddowes-Kelly otherwise known as Conway, a Welsh name she had always thought, aged fifty looking sixty, therefore astounded to be accosted when she had virtually given up on the game, not from desire but because she was no longer physically appropriate, not even within the generous limits tolerated by the East End. She gave a chuckle, a gurgle, a long serrated sigh and she was gone from life, much too easily, as if all she needed was a slight tap and she was over the edge, Gull and his knife whittling her down as she fell, killing her three times over for being Kelly.

I am watching, Sickert told himself, I cannot be watching this. I have a knife in my stocking, I can kill him for doing it; but he did not, not even as the lobe of Eddowes's right ear fell and dangled, the knife hit the face and the lower eyelids, then the throat. He closed his eyes against what happened to the pathetic, shrunken body, instructing himself that this would have been Marie Kelly but for luck and Sickert. When Gull found out he had butchered the wrong woman he would be furious, and the hunt for Kelly would begin all over again. The dreadful thing was that Sickert had now developed a sense of series; a vile tradition had begun to form; experience had ordered itself into a pattern such as he would never have dreamed of, and it might extend itself, with ease, to little Alice Margaret or himself. When he opened his eyes again he could see that Eddowes, whose name he did not even know, was open from the breasts to the groin, and Gull was tussling with something inside, yet without moving his shoulders or back. The hands and wrists were doing it, and his crouch was almost that of someone hunched in prayerful reverence. He wanted to leap out and cry to all of London that murder was going on, right among them, sealed away in a little moving abattoir, but he could not move. His vocal cords had gone dead, his eyes were aswill with some caustic untearlike fluid, and his body was frozen into an intimidated cramp. All he could think of were some pages from a pamphlet Gull had given him to acquaint him with the ways of Masons, but he remembered the details incoherently, such as the word *Juwe*, which had nothing to do with Jews but recalled a salient killing by three famous apprentice Masons. Arches and lodges and squares and mitres and lambskin aprons moved about in his mind, yet to no point; he wanted to remember nothing, especially the rank stench of decomposition that filled the *Crusader*'s interior as Gull began to finish up, slashing quick triangular flaps of flesh from the face of the once perky little woman stranded beneath him. All this time, Netley had kept the horse trotting about Aldgate and Whitechapel Road. Anyone peering in would have seen only the bunched-up form of Gull in yellow and the anguished, blanched face of Walter Sickert, new convert to horror although, as he had begun to suspect, not hitherto against it. In their travels, they actually passed the real Marie Kelly several times as, finally certain that the streets had become safe again, she plied her trade, standing still, then moving ten yards along, cursing the rain showers, wondering how Long Liz was faring tonight, happily recalling their night out and in together up in Hampstead with Sickly, as Stride called him, and resolving never to write letters to people above her station. She had to earn her doss, but with all her heart she wished she were Marie Jeanette, earning it in France, with Camembert and that lovely French bread to go home to, and some wine, the real stuff, to wash it down, and almost any toff to see her through the night: Sickert, Eddy, or even Bertie the Prince of Wales, a man with an unfailing eye for a pretty woman. Saint mercy, she thought, you're not thinking like a woman who's knocked up, Marie girl. You have the divil of a time keeping anything down, don't you now? Is there going to be solid months of *that*, then, or does it leave you be after a while, once you're punished enough for what you did? In God's mouth, it's a penance, what you pay for in the wind-up. She changed from one pitch to another, but business was slow. Without in the least dreaming, she did think she saw the same carriage go past her and come back, then go past her again as if touting but not quite able to decide on her or somebody else: one of those Mary-Anne John Thomases, she thought, who want the thrill without any of the infection, without the bad breath and the need to speak or pay. That was it. Next time it came past her, if it did, she would bang on the door with a bottle plucked from the dozens in the gutter, against some of which its wheels had jingled merrily when going by. And she would shout in at the window, "Get it out and polish it, old cock. Make your bloody mind up, there's hundreds waiting as can't hold on any longer. Do you have a taste to thrump or don't you?" She had been outdoors for hours, within the space of only one of which Long Liz and Catherine Eddowes-Kelly-Conway had gone to their Maker undone, trapped for ever with an unambitious thought in mind, gone for ever from their beloved sisters, only one of whom, Stride's, as the newspapers said, had had a vision of Long Liz at the moment of the murder, leaning over her bed in walking-out clothes, telling her not to worry. How theatrical. What odds would anyone have given that the drab carriage patroling the streets had within it a furnace of sorts, a mad doctor and a dithering painter? If there was hope for London, it was not at the hands of such men as these: Netley asking where to drop the packet, as he said; Gull, being devoutly Masonic tonight as this final one was Kelly, the brains behind it all, and telling Netley "Mitre Square, of course, where else?" Then he could rest, go back to his Pudding Club, release young Stephen into the world again (or had he done that already?). The fatigue of doing two in less than an hour had blunted and sapped him, but he was glad about the oilskins, initially his wife's idea against the rain, especially as he pressed the heaps of muslin on the seat, marveling at his luck that Stride had been dealt with outside; otherwise the *Crusader* would have been as-will with blood when Kelly entered, and she would have balked, oh she would have yelped a mouthful at the sight of that. These sluts had no composure, not even at the sight of the operating table; the only way was to accept things in the same way as a doctor did, looking at them from outside. Now Netley could take the oilskins and clean them for himself or burn them, it made no difference to Gull, who would never need them again, not once they had disposed of the packet in Mitre Square, a place drenched in Masonic references, not least since it was the site of another murder, that of the woman praying in the Priory in the sixteenth century, slaughtered by a mad monk who then killed himself. She had been killed in a holy place, just like Hiram in Solomon's Temple. He wanted the violent connection as well as the Masonic one: Hiram's Lodge had met there, and at the Mitre Tavern the Union Lodge and the Lodge of Joppa met, and the Lodge of Judah in Mitre Street only a *stride* away. He liked that, grateful for the adventitious labors of the sweated brain. His very own lodge, The Royal Alpha, when it did not meet in the West End, met either in Leadenhall Street or at the Mitre Tavern. It was hint enough: there was not a Mason who would not know that he had paid his debts, had been obediently grateful in the twilight of his august career. Read it, Salisbury, he thought, as a parvenu's payment, or his praise. Netley had stopped the *Crusader* and now, as Gull had instructed him to do, was scanning the neighborhood for policemen. Fortunately for Gull, the rain had begun again, and the wind was gusting, so the usually busy square was more or less empty. It was one-thirty. Out Sickert clambered, retching, holding on to the piece of chalk in his pocket as if it linked him to a better world. Netley got down, went inside the *Crusader* and hoisted the remains toward the door, where Sickert, in a frenzy, took hold of Eddowes's legs. Out she came now, broken at two places, and down she went, left there with her insides slapped against her right shoulder. A small square of her bloodstained apron fluttered down beside her while Sickert, out of his mind and frantic to do almost anything, wandered a few streets away and scrawled there on a stairway wall a jumble of the first things that came to mind: a contorted and obtuse transcription of mad dogs trapped in a stairwell. Thinking at roughly the same time of Lipski, Lipskis,

Jews, and Judas, he wrote "The Juwes are," then halted, aware of the garbled spelling, only to resume clumsily with "The men That," as his brain cast around for some definitive emphasis, even as Netley told him to get a bloody move on. "Will not," he added, in one last push with the chalk, "be Blamed for nothing." What a mess. It would confuse the police anyway, set out as a poem: a sign that he had been there, disagreeing even while grateful that this other woman, not Kelly, had come along at the right time. Gull was bound to hear about his mistake, by which time Sickert wanted to be gone at least as far as France. The wind blew the bloodstained bit of cloth away from the body toward the wall he had written on in the passage of Wentworth Dwellings, Goulston Street. Eddowes, who had dreaded arriving home to the mercies of John Kelly, had received a hiding she did not deserve.

It was evening before Long Liz was identified as a woman almost always taken in for being drunk; she also was subject to fits, which gave her a certain novelty in the police station. She kept walking out on him, Michael Kidney said. They were forever rowing and he hadn't seen her since Tuesday. Gradually the list of her possessions began to join with that of what was found inside her and what had been done to her: cachous wrapped in a twist of tissue paper; food partly digested, cheese and potatoes and flour; a deep cut in her throat matching the line of her silk check scarf and some gradually healing sores. There were big bruises on her shoulders where Netley had forced her to the ground, and under her collarbones too. The little pocket in her underskirt had contained a small lead pencil, a broken fragment of comb, an intact pocket comb, a tin spoon, the key to a padlock, some buttons and a hook for fastening them. Slowly they came forward, those who had seen, or claimed to have: a laborer from an indigo warehouse, who had seen her with a man who said to her at some point "You would say anything but your prayers," which reinforced the moral interpretation of the murders; James Brown, a boxmaker who had gone out for some supper at a quarter to one and had heard Stride saying "Not tonight, some other night" to a man in a long dark coat that reached his heels; the first man, however, had worn a deerstalker's hat, whereas the second was wearing the round hat of a sailor. Israel Schwartz, who had not been allowed to testify at the inquest, had nonetheless reached and inflamed several wild imaginations through the popular press. Netley emerged as twenty-eight years old, five feet eight inches in height, dark-complected, tiny dark mustache, black cutaway, hard felt hat, collar and tie, "respectable appearance" as *The Police Gazette* said, with a parcel wrapped in newspaper. Or he was thirty, five feet five, fair-complected with a small brown mustache, chubby face, wide shoulders, with dark jacket and trousers, a black cap with a peak. He had already vanished into the night atop the *Crusader,* a man in both reality and myth so generic that he could be found almost anywhere, which meant that most of male London had killed Stride and her carnations.

Later that day a drunken Michael Kidney reeled into the Leman Street police station and informed the detectives there that if he were a constable, and the killing had happened on his beat, he would have shot himself straight off. Sickert had felt much the same and truly wanted himself no longer alive, not in the state of mind he was in. The events of the night should have swallowed him up too, so that he would not have had to go back to civilized life as he had known it, and never mind Marie Kelly's fabulous luck: her survival only meant that she would be taken care of later on unless he, Sickert, could come up with a rescue of some kind. He had already spent most of the money sent by Alix for the eventual upkeep of little Alice Margaret, though he had promised himself to repay it. If they will only wait until I am famous, he said, but Gull would finish things off at a demon's speed once he realized his error. What on earth was he going to tell Gull? It was so dark he didn't notice it wasn't the woman he had known intimately? Where, he wondered, would they find *him* after Gull and Netley had done their work? Sorry, Doctor, I was not thinking: there was a certain resemblance—no use, because Eddowes was a sparrow, Kelly a tall fat plumed nonpareil of the pavements. Better make a clean breast of it then and say, yes, I was trying to save Kelly. Then Gull would say, Very well, Mr. Sickert, your part in the next murder will be salient. Here is what I want you to do.

In fact Gull, still unaware of the mistake made at Mitre Square, was digesting a fatty breakfast in his upstairs study, on his knee a map of London's East End, on which he had drawn bold lines with his fountain pen, the first running from Bucks Row in the northeast to Hanbury Street in the northwest: Nichols to Chapman; the second running from Buck's Row slightly southwest to Berner Street, where Netley had killed and left Stride; the third running westward from Stride to Mitre Square. The figure he came up with pleased him enormously, incomplete as it looked; off the map it soared, pleasing the Mason in him with more than a momentary neatness. Then he drew the fourth line, to make a parallelogram, and one diagonal, plus the numbers.

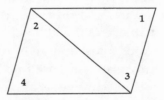

God was in His heaven. All was right. Gull had created a Masonic emblem: two triangles, akin to those cut crudely in Eddowes's face, and he was purring, having gone to some trouble to decide where each corpse was to be placed, taking into account the whereabouts of the first sighting, the pick-up, and the exigencies of the night, such as tonight's. What he did not yet know was that Eddowes did not count, and that the holy plenitude of Mitre Square had gone to waste, but he would recover and notice how the left-hand line, linking Chapman to Eddowes, cut straight through Dorset Street, where Marie Kelly lived when she was at home, so the line would go forging on, but solid rather than phantasmal and unstated. Either way, he would have the twin triangles that represented the altar top of what they called the Holy Royal Arch. On the mantelshelf, marooned in preservative glycerine, sat Eddowes's left kidney, next to Dark Annie Chapman's uterus, to him as heraldic as the parallelogram of two triangles. They would go either to the Pudding Club, as part of an experiment in which women fed on women (*were* fed on women, he corrected himself) or to some other destination for the sake of dramatic effect. His mind inclined him toward the latter, for the kidney at any rate (cooking *that* was so obvious), whereas the uterus would be more appropriate for the sludge served up at Guy's. Already he had the glimmering of a plan, the fruit of his having been obliged to work his toes hard after the stroke last autumn: wriggling them, using them to pick up fallen things in the bathroom and the bedroom, all because the nerves had weakened. A natural extension of this was to take pen in foot, as it were, and write on butcher's wrapping paper on the floor, all smoothed out so as not to disrupt the pen's flow (greaseproof paper would not have worked, although he liked its rough fascia). He was already proficient, though making the letters outsize, holding the paper still with one foot close to where the other foot was writing. Little did he know how Sickert too had convulsed into writing, although of a rather different sort—giveaway, monitory—whereas what Gull wrote was mainly, so far, the names of diseases and chemicals. Now he drew his two triangles, or rather the open figure that implied them, for exercise's sake writing in Bucks Row, Hanbury Street, Berner Street, and Mitre Square rather than the names of the women deposited there; all an attuned observer had to do was connect up the sites and, to a Mason at any rate, the pattern, the sublimity of the doings, would become plain. He had been obliged to insist rather heavily that Netley do as he was told: he just could not go dropping the women off at random, Gull had told him, as the whole thing, the whole operation, was planned, and if it did not come out neat there would be trouble. Finally, Gull thought, he had done something exact: when his hand wavered or his eye clouded, this would still abide, cut cleanly into the amorphous miscellany of life in this world. World in which Eddowes, found in a drunken stupor on the pavement in Aldgate at 8:30 P.M. on

Saturday night, then propped by a constable against some
shutters, only to sag sideways and somewhat forward, and finally loaded into a cell by two constables to sober up, ended
singing quite cheerfully and finally left the Bishopsgate Station at about half-past midnight, chirping "Gnite, old cock,"
walking away homeward toward Spitalgate. William Gull had
reversed her path, taking her in the opposite direction toward
Mitre Square, though, once in the cab, she had seemed to care
little where she was going, she was so exhausted and compli-
ant. A total stranger—no, they were all total strangers to him,
thank goodness—a woman wholly irrelevant had wandered
into the heart of his grand design and had not even disrupted
it, as he would discover, once his rage was spent.

Chapter 30

Sickert was brooding too, but had no Lady Susan, no obse-
quious wife, to tend him, with a nail file removing flecks
of blood from beneath his fingernails, and no questions
asked; Gull was a physician after all, and had done many
a post-mortem. What bothered Sickert, and made him go to the
door several times to check peculiar noises (he never knew who
might be lurking there, knife or razor poised), was the way
Netley, who had known Marie Kelly, although not as intimately
as he had wished, had "identified" her when "she" came out of
the Bishopsgate Police Station: facing her, more or less, though
the gaslight was feeble. Eddowes-Conway-Kelly had been a
smaller woman than Marie Kelly was, altogether more slightly
built, quicker of step, more of a chirrup. Not only that: Netley
was a vicious zealot, proud of making no mistakes, and he
would no more have confused Marie Kelly with Eddowes than
he would Eddy with the Prince of Wales. What Gull and Sickert
did not know, however, was that Netley, overcome by his mur-

dering of Stride, had been drinking hard ever since, which added
even more alcohol to the skinful he had begun the evening with.
Two a night, with him doing at least half the work, was too
much for even Netley, and he had seen Eddowes through a
painful haze, remarking her as the woman who came out next,
the one and only, and so Eddowes was doomed though invisible
and Kelly was saved, though only Gull knew for how long.

London went into an unprecedented convulsion as soon as the
news of the double murder came out, although it was nothing
loud. The ghastly word circulated in a whisper as the police
printed and passed out leaflets and pamphlets to accompany
house-to-house searches. The Thames police quizzed sailors
about Asiatics, visited all local butchers, inquired into the presence or the moving-on of Greek Gypsies, and even looked into
the case of some so-called cowboys who were part of the American Exhibition. Terrified that Sickert's word "Juwes" would
antagonize a mainly Jewish district, the police erased the whole
message without first photographing it, when it would have
sufficed to cover up the one apparently offensive word; but they
did transcribe it, trying to mimic the handwriting originally
there, which was odd when the original would have been a
better copy of itself. Infatuated with redundancy, the police
then photographed the transcription. Sir Charles Warren, the
high-ranking Mason who had become Commissioner of Police,
claimed he read the one word as "Jews" and that was that. He
was only waiting his appointed moment: as soon as Gull had
finished his grim quest, or was certain of its completion, Warren
could step down, having effectively done what he was supposed
to do: impede the investigation and keep the police files more
or less empty. Aware of the night's events, he assumed that Gull
had written on the wall to boast and proclaim the Masonic role
in the murders: too close to the bone for Warren, who believed
that, while Masons might run the country and *should*, with lethal
cryptic power infecting and infesting the benign machinery that
kept the poor in place, they should not hang their washing out
to dry. He was there to keep them reticent while applauding
their red deeds in private. After all, he was the man who in 1887

had crammed Trafalgar Square with six hundred Life Guards armed with muskets tipped with bayonets, in the end killing one of the poor and injuring some hundred and fifty people. There was no need to be discreet about things like that; in a sense, these Guards were the poor's own soldiers, and it was better to be bayoneted by your own than by somebody else's; it was more open, more British, he thought, whereas things Masonic, never mind how much they affected the Guards and the quelling of mobs armed with pokers, were deathly secret. Four thousand police had added pith to the Guards stationed around the square, and the riot had been stopped. It had been an open, military victory over the unemployed, with their cudgels and red flags, egged on by Radicals and all kinds of Socialists, including George Bernard Shaw and the poet William Morris. If the rabble wanted a decent living wage, or even jobs at all, they would get a lesson in decorum instead. They did, but an unfed rabble rumbles and waits.

Salisbury, plump and mothy as he might seem, knew which men to put into which slots, and when to get them out of the way or out of the country even. If Gull was to be given a free hand as a wolf ravening down on the fold in which the spellbound or oblivious whores waited for whatever was going to happen next, he would have to be protected from himself, at least until he had done his job. A man as self-willed as Gull would brook no guidance once his way of doing things had established itself, but he might be shielded from uninitiated and innocent constables, spies in the house of Guy's or indeed Fitzroy Square. It was a matter of muffling a tiger without discouraging him. Who else would have killed these women for the Masons? Who but Gull would have committed such devilish knife work, showing off incognito, except to those who knew?

Gull was having an idiosyncratic orgy of his own design on behalf of his Queen, Lord Salisbury, and Jah-Bul-On, the god of Freemasons; but it took his pseudo-proletarian letter to galvanize London from frantic torpor to vocal panic. Written in red ink, it had gone into the mouth of the Post Office two days before the murders of Stride and Eddowes, mailed in the area known as London E.C., for East Central. His overture, Gull called it. He followed up on the 30th of September with a postcard bearing, like the letter, the identical signature: Jack the Ripper. How he had chortled as his right foot inscribed the letter's to-be-famous words, sweet and appalling meat for newspapers to reproduce, beginning "Dear Boss" and ending "Yours truly Jack the Ripper," with, in between, his arrogant caricature of a whore-hater:

I keep on hearing the police have caught me but they won't fix me just yet. I have laughed when they look so clever and talk about being on the right track. That joke about Leather Apron gave me real fits. I am down on whores and I shant quit ripping them till I do get buckled. Grand work the last job was. I gave the Lady no time to squeal. How can they catch me now. I love my work and want to start again. You will soon hear of me with my funny little games. I saved some of the proper red stuff in a ginger beer bottle over the last job to write with but it went thick like glue and I can't use it. Red ink is fit enough ha ha. The next job I do I shall clip the lady's ears off and send to the police officers just for jolly wouldn't you. Keep this letter back till I do a bit more work, then give it out straight My knife is nice and sharp I want to get to work right away if I get a chance. Good luck.

Yours truly
Jack the Ripper

Dont mind me giving me trade name.

wasn't good enough to post this before I got all the red ink off my hands curse it No luck yet. They say I'm a doctor now—ha ha

Yes, Gull thought, pondering the English of what he had sent to "The Boss" at Central News Office London City, the prose

befits a River Lea bargeman, but I'd have been better having
Netley write it, getting some of his saliva on it for show. He
liked the letter's lumpish uncouthness, its mistiming of tenses,
its misrepresentation of his views on whores (for whom he liked
to think he had the most intense sympathy, ever since his walks
through Whitechapel with Hinton), its erratic punctuation, its
pharisaical mixture of imperatives and prophecies, most of all
the postscript rotated leftward through ninety degrees, giving
the whole epistle an unbalanced, broken-legged look, all that
was missing being a *bah* or two (but *bah*s seemed to him rather
middle class whereas *ha ha*s were self-consciously proletarian).
Was this how Netley would have done the thing if asked?
Would he have been cruder, nastier? The "trade name" was a
stroke of genius, he thought. The whole of London, but especially the East End, had been wandering around in a trance for
which there was no name, no cause, and now all of a sudden the
menace had a name to be reviled by; it was as if Brazil had never
been called anything at all, or Greenland, or Madagascar, always
there in its amorphous complexity but incapable of being referred to. Well, now they had the Ripper to whisper about and
scare the children off to bed with; it was the most potent-
sounding, most awful name in London, the one that gave the
shakes to queen, prime minister, and chief of police all at once.
To do things right, he should really have gone back and rebutch-
ered Nichols and Chapman under his newly revealed name,
since it was only in retrospect that people would regard them as
his own work, inimitable and copyright. To rub it in, he sent the
postcard that began "I was not codding," using the same leaning
golf flag of an I. Even his fake handwriting was becoming con-
sistent, something he had told himself to watch. For a while he
thought about the timing of the murders, as he had recently
thought about the locations of each slaughter and the placing of
the bodies afterward. He wondered if, having found Stride in a
place that spoiled the parallelogram of two triangles, he would
have passed her by. Now he had to decide what to do with the
rest of his life, with his Pudding Club patients both male and
female. More research was what he wanted, and more post-

mortem work, but he dreaded the waning of his powers, the loss of his physical grasp. Strokes always recurred. And you had little chance of dying of something else in the meantime unless you lived a completely reckless life. Was he living recklessly or not? He had no idea.

When the newspapers told him he had murdered the wrong Kelly, not a *Marie* at all, he wanted to get his hands on Sickert and Marie Kelly in the same evening, but he had orders to leave Sickert alone: use him by all means, as a local expert, but do him no harm. Sickert, as Salisbury knew, was Alix's property, Eddy's pretend brother, and indirectly a man in whom the Prince of Wales might take an interest. Gull raged in vain, always liking to clean up after himself, but only too well aware how, sooner or later, everyone gave himself away through little involuntary things, like men leaving a public toilet and giving themselves quick reassuring pats and taps in the area of the trouser buttons, just to be sure it wasn't still dangling out, or dangling canary yellow, or still dribbling, while all the world looked on in a fit of censorious hilarity. Poor Eddowes's death impressed him not at all: she had died that monarchy might thrive and indeed had held on to life with so poor a grip she deserved to be severed from all she hated and all she loved. The only thing that soothed him after killing the wrong woman were the extravagant figures of speech used by those who found her. P.C. 881 Watkins had shone his bull's-eye lamp into the nooks and crannies of Mitre Square and had found something that melted his eyes: she had been ripped up, he said, like a "pig in a market," her entrails "flung in a heap about her neck." All he had to raise the alarm was a rattle, but a watchman who had been sweeping the steps had a whistle to blow. Gull doted on such particulars, eager always to see himself as others did, and especially their view of his handiwork. *The Police Gazette*'s description of Sickert he thought quite fair ("age 30, height 5 feet 7 inches, or 8 inches"— *Sickert growing,* he thought—complexion fair, moustache fair, medium build; dress: pepper and salt colour loose jacket, grey cloth cap with peak of same material, reddish neckerchief tied in knot; appearance of a sailor." Why did Sickert wear that damned red scarf? To draw attention to himself, or to draw attention to it only? In which case, why not show it once, then, and thus mislead Warren's halfwits? Most of all he delighted in his opportunity to read Dr. Brown's post-mortem statement, graced as it was with almost chromatic details in which, for Gull, Eddowes came to life again:

(1) the carotid artery had a pin-hole opening

(2) The cut commenced opposite the ensiform cartilage

(3) being gristle they could not tell how the knife made the cut (Gull, the gold medallist, smirked at their English)

(4) Attached to the navel was 2½ in. of the lower part of the rectus musela of the left side of the abdomen

(5) There was a stab of about an inch in the left groin, penetrating the skin in superficial fashion (Sickert's cut, he sighed, the only one the bastard would try).

"You'll never have the chance again," Gull had said in the *Crusader*. "She's five times dead already."

"It wouldn't be as if I had anything to do with—killing her."

"Just a touch," Gull said. "Like this."

"Oh, I see," Sickert said. "Not much. No more than this." It had been as if a dentist were guiding his hand, enlisting his cooperation. It had been no more horrific, he found, than touching a poached egg with a fork, but he had never seen a knife this sharp. He would never grow to relish, as Gull did, the sketch of the corpse done by F.W. Forster at the Mortuary on Sunday morning, September 30, at 3:45, filling the jagged incision (a hand wide) with delicate crosshatching that halfway down became little roundels and nozzles, like exposed penises peeping end-on from within the gash. Worse (but exciting to Gull for its irrelevance), a hand seemed to have come from behind and clutched upward from underneath the groin, to support the loose and flapping skin of the cut. Forster had drawn Eddowes with her arms rigid, almost as if flexing to lift invisible weights. Later on, Eddowes was stitched up from neck to loins, made quite presentable in fact for the photographer except for the zigzag seam running down her front. Sickert's cut was quite invisible. Thanks to his sway at Guy's, Gull was able to lay his hands on all manner of medical evidence in the case: the spoor of his knife, as it were, fastidiously tracked by cameras, artists, and police doctors. They were his only audience apart from Sickert and Netley, and he recalled how Eddowes, so light and frail, had risen with his knife at certain points, almost coming back to life and rising toward him to exact revenge.

Out in the other world, as Gull had begun to call London, Warren had negotiated with a breeder in Scarborough for two champion bloodhounds called Barnaby and Burgho, with whom he said he was going to track down the person they now pin-pointed as Jack the Ripper. On Monday October 8, in Regent's Park at seven in the morning, on a surface bearing heavy frost, the two trainee dogs chased an appropriately scented policeman after he had taken a fifteen-minute start. On two occasions Warren himself, gasping and giggling, became the prey, unable to run at his fastest because he laughed so much. The dogs ran well, both night and day, but Warren was never able to commit himself to using them formally; he kept testing them on various stretches of open land at Tooting and Hemel Hempstead. Soon enough, the dogs were sent back to Yorkshire. Warren lost heart, at least as far as charades with dogs went, and the public clamored increasingly for his removal from office. Warren, they said, was a doodler and a fraud.

It was not long before women of the streets were joshing one another with "I do declare the Ripper will be coming for me next" or "He'll be getting you next, dearie, with your innards on your shoulder." *The Illustrated Police News* depicted the various stages of what sometimes seemed a composite murder, using such pregnant captions as "The Murderer's Chosen Spot," "Last Leavetaking of the Victim," "A Strange Man Tried to Induce Girls to Go Up an Entry with Him," "Awful Scene Witnessed by the Doctor," to "The Murderer Escaping from the Window," "The Strange Story Told of a Man with a Black Bag," and "Lured to the Slaughter." And, much more stylish than any letter written by Marie Kelly, there went to the Queen a petition signed by a horde of educated suburban matrons, beginning:

"To our Most Gracious Sovereign Lady Queen Victoria" and continuing

Madam—We, the women of East London, feel horror at the dreadful sins that have been committed in our midst and grief because of the shame that has fallen on our neighbourhood.

By the facts which have come out in the inquests, we have learnt much of the lives of our sisters who have lost a firm hold on goodness and who are living sad and degraded lives.

While each woman of us will do all she can to make men feel with horror the sins of impurity which cause such wicked lives to be led, we would also beg that your Majesty will call on your servants in authority and bid them put the law which already exists in motion to close bad houses within whose walls such wickedness is done and men and women ruined in body and soul.

We are, Madam, your loyal and humble servants.

Marie Kelly called the petition "a long soft lump of snot-gobbling grovelling," still able in the midst of grief and inexpressible horror to fight back verbally, to give better than she would ever get, although thinking these days like a woman enclosed in steam, denuded of her bosom friends, and given by herself not much hope, not with Polly and Dark Annie and Long Liz gone, and that other one, not even one of her gang. "Only a violet I plucked" was the song she still sang, but she rarely finished it, at least in the first few weeks of October, although with each day gone by she began to think of herself as the only survivor since it was at long last over, quite unaware of Gull not far away, smiling at his anonymous reception, at the fuss and froth, he having by then sent out his famous foot-written letter from hell, addressed "From Hell," to George Lusk, head of the Whitechapel Vigilance Committee:

Mr Lusk
Sir I send you half the Kidne I took from one woman prasarved it for you tother piece I fried and ate it was very nice I may send you the bloodly knif that took it out if you only wate a whil longer
        signed Catch me when you can Mishter Lusk

Writing this, Gull had made more up-and-down strokes, and longer ones, than he intended to, but controlling his right foot (or his left) was not easy, and he sensed there was too much pent-up, coiled energy in the lines than he should have allowed to show. Not only that: no illiterate would write *knif* rather than *nife* or *whil* rather than *wile*, or would know how to spell *piece*. He should have waited before sending it and made a better job of it, calculating his performance more. But he was always in haste, even to make a mistake. The whole of London was fluttering with letters, and Gull smirked to think that Marie Kelly was a better prose writer than his bogus Ripper. Next he had to send a blank postcard to Netley with, surreptitiously written near the address, the date when he was to renew the search for Kelly.

Something was lumbering about inside him. His emotions had become solid physical entities and were circling like dogs preparatory to lying down. Perhaps he was changing his mind about things, perhaps even about Catherine Eddowes, who had not been Kelly, perhaps even about Walter Sickert who, in his shamefacedly honorable way, had tried to save Kelly by passing off Eddowes. By reading his newspapers with more than his usual diligence, Gull had begun to learn a great deal about his recent victims, and now he was catching up on Eddowes, who used to go hop-picking with John Kelly, partly to have a holiday away from London and partly to make some money. *So this was the life he had destroyed;* it always amazed him how much life, how much sheer ongoingness, there was in the unlikeliest of people. Eddowes and Kelly would walk back to town, a feat which impressed Gull, and they had done this every year as long as they had known each other, getting back this year on Thursday the 27th of September. Ah, he breathed knowingly, she had no idea she had only two complete days to live. Walked home to London on Thursday to be killed early on Sunday morning. Netley had discovered she was expected back on Thursday. Had she stayed down there picking hops, she would have been alive in October. Forty-three years old. Many had died at that very age, Gull thought: every age was eligible. So: Catherine Eddowes and John Kelly, he mused; he read on, paraphrasing with impassive geniality, almost thinking of his victims as his friends. Eddowes and Kelly had nothing between them but a pair of old boots and an old flannel shirt, so they popped them both for three shillings, with which to buy food. Their first night back in the city they spent at the casual ward in Shoe Lane and by Friday Kelly had managed to earn sixpence, which he said would buy them some sausage and mash, bubble and squeak, but Eddowes talked him into putting fourpence of it toward a night's doss, and the remaining twopence would buy them some bread, on which they would have to make do until she clicked, perhaps on Saturday night. She had only a few hours to live, she need not have worried. Gull had begun to feel intimate with Eddowes now, coming from the far periphery of her life and creeping toward the center, there to put her lights out without her suspecting anything, drunk as she was. Before he killed her, however, with the remaining twopence, which had taken on an invulnerable permanent air, she went to the casual ward at Mile End. When she woke that morning, her Kelly was waiting for her, angry she'd spent up, had bought no bread, and she must have wondered then (Gull thought) if they were going to spend the rest of their lives wandering about on the surface of Earth, scrambling here and there for menial things to do.

"Whatcher," she always said and he always answered "Good morning, Catherine." He was formal though grimy.

"Bugger today," she told him. "We're right strapped. Maybe Annie will lend us sixpence or something, to get us started." Annie, the newspaper said, was her daughter, and here came all their dirty linen into the open, Gull thought, because of my knife and the letter-writing of Marie Kelly. It's a scandal. In the event, she did not get far, having collapsed not so much from drunkenness as from lack of food, and of course the little liquor that she drank had a violent effect. Down she had gone, to be raised up by one sedulous constable and put in her cell by two. That was 8:30 on Saturday evening. She had only hours to get through, Gull thought, and by then we had already topped Stride. At the time he had not noticed the Michaelmas daisies and gold lily pattern of her dress, which he had unceremoniously rammed up to her chest, or her threadbare linsey skirt like Nichols's, or the dark-green alpaca petticoat that no one thought noteworthy until she was dead and mutilated, and then, all of a sudden, every detail was a volume of human interest. Pedantry, Gull thought, look how they harp on her mucky chemise, the brown ribbed knee-stockings patched with white cotton, and the men's laced boots (again rather like Nichols). Did I know while dismembering her, he asked, that her black cloth jacket had a fake fur collar and three big tin buttons, or that her black straw bonnet was prinked with black beads and bits of green or black velvet? Nothing of the kind, old Gull. These women, having nowhere to hang their clothes, wear them all whenever they go out, like a shop going for a stroll.

Now he read the table of her worldly goods, relieved it had not been himself who was dismembered—the list would have gone on for ever, to be capped with his favorite biblical text: "What doth the Lord require of thee, but to do justly, and to love mercy, and to walk humbly with thy God?" He had even seen it recently, on the wall of the Working Lads' Institute in Whitechapel; it sat in his pocket, written in copperplate on a piece of card, and he was going to have it reared above his body when he was buried. Poor Catherine Eddowes, the unprofiting hop-picker who should have gone to Bermondsey and cried on her daughter's shoulder, had borne with her wherever she went not only her clothes but all her goods, just like Nichols, Chapman, and Stride: nothing to die for, nothing to write home to mother about, nothing to defend with one's life:

 1 white hankie with red border
 1 matchbox holding cotton, 1 blunt table knife
   with white bone handle
 2 short-stemmed clay pipes
 1 red cigarette case with white-metal ornament
 1 printed handbill from a music hall
 5 pieces of toilet soap
 1 tin box containing tea and sugar

    1 half of one pair of spectacles (one eye piece
       attached to the bridge)
    1 three-cornered checked hankie
    1 ball of worsted
    1 red mitten with the word Gazelle on the label.

Much more than Polly or Dark Annie had had, or Long Liz, almost making Catherine Eddowes seem a woman of property not to be taken down lightly. Gull wished he could simplify his own life to such an extent, achieving some kind of chamber music of penury, or not having furniture in his rooms lest he affront the purity of space. He wanted to possess things, he a worldly Mason, only a shred more than he did not; he wanted to bear his mind, and his devotions, aloft like thuribles and orbs. Clearly, this Eddowes woman blew her nose as often as she smoked but washed much more often than she did either: commendable, he decided, and even a good argument for restoring her life to her if she would agree to cease reading with one eye. Now he saw why she devoured the grapes he had offered her in the *Crusader:* the little chit had been starving, and for company as well as food. No wonder she went out like a light; she had, as it were, been struck by lightning. Had he known she was not the Kelly he needed, he might have been gentler with her nose, uterus, and kidney. But he remembered having been provoked by the Stride woman's refusal to enter the *Crusader* and his having to leave her to Netley. He yearned to hear those who in the streets and pubs said to another "The Ripper he has struck again" or "The Ripper has been at work again this night." They had no idea where he would strike next, but Sickert knew, of course, and Sickert was going to have to do the honours good and proper: blunt and definite, and made to watch, to yelp. Perhaps there truly was such a thing as destiny, Gull thought, meaning a destiny both symmetrical and shapely: the richest doctor in London, perhaps in the whole of the British Isles, was putting paid to some of the poorest drabs in Christendom. There was poetry in that collision of opposites. He had often thought, as he aged, that his head would thin out and his skull resemble something like the head of the pit viper, but bigger of course, and he would become a literary rather than a medical figure; advancing with increasing skill to a profusion of books as his mind raged forward on several fronts, squirting and spraying ideas almost too numerous to count. He would achieve uncanny poise, leaving longer and longer gaps between books of apparently unsurpassable mastery, at least until the next one came along, so that over his last decade or two his output would seem a chain of steppingstones, each work a colossal *constatation,* as the French would say, proffering the final word on everything yet with Olympian coolness. No fuss. No argy-bargy. But something as specific and deliberate, overlapping nothing of his own or anyone else's, as Bach's *English Suite Number Six:* clear-cut, swathed in uncontaminating radiance.

Chapter 31

He could not, of course, look forward to publishing his Ripper letters, almost forty of them having gone off by now, some horrific, some Gothic, some uncouth and crass, some taunting and overbearing. Hundreds of others in London were writing them, so he thought the real Ripper might as well do his bit. The whole of London kept siphoning off its accumulated blood lust and ghoulishness, getting the dangerous black stuff into the open where it belonged, spewing out the fear-filth and class hatred of many decades, making all murders and mutilations come from the same life-loathing demon, just for the sake of convenience, focus, and drama. It mattered little who the Ripper was; London needed him, just as it needed its queen and its river, its docks and its music halls. The Ripper, verbally at any rate, had a thousand imitators, all of whom wanted to curdle the blood of the impressionable, none of whom would have believed the truth that the Ripper, *tout court* as Sickert liked to say, was a quiet city doctor, a Mason, doing duty for his queen, who had been *noxiously affronted,* sir. The Ripper was a man whose wife set his slippers by the fender, tried to make him eat less butter on his breakfast toast, and used to keep the lamp lit when they made love. Susan Gull: paragon, as he liked to say. When his neck was stiff, she rubbed it, and when he had a shaving rash she popped the little white heads with her mildly pointed fingernails. If this was the ghoul infesting London, then perhaps the city should have more ghouls, more Gulls, and then five thousand women of East London would find something *really* unthinkable to write to their queen about; their petition had revolted him, and he called it mealy-mouthed, slobbering, and gauche. And what had the Queen's response been? He had almost forgotten, but it had been Germanic: "The madams do go on, don't they, they do seem to care about sin."

Now Gull had to cook up something to make Sickert behave himself, and after a while the notion came. It would require some little work, but Gull had never shirked work, when either ascending the social ladder or shaking it from the top down. Truth told, Sickert should do the next job, under appalling duress, so that they could all see what kind of man he was, but he would probably faint at the vital moment. Yet there were ways of enforcing his obedience. He would release Annie Crook from the Pudding Club, reunite her with her daughter, then hand the daughter over to Sickert, saying Unless.

Gull saw himself, not without humor, as the gigantic purged spider at the center of an entire social web in which people he did not know, and had never heard of, did his indirect bidding or went out of their way to anticipate needs he had never expressed, not as his own. Doctor George Baxter Phillips, for example, had performed superbly at the inquest on Dark Annie Chapman at the Working Lads' Institute in Whitechapel Road early in September, saying "I think I had better not go into further detail of these mutilations which can only be painful to the feelings of the jury and the public." How often, in English public life, the suckers of a silver spoon had managed to bury the facts in the interest of some squeamish, squirming, exquisite archetypal Englishman. It was as if, Gull decided, truth were some auxiliary branch of the diplomatic service, which depended on hypocrisy and prided itself on letting the people never know anything until it was too late. The Coroner had driven hard at Phillips, who then said, on the second day, "I still think it a very great pity to make this evidence public. These details are fit only for yourself, sir, and the jury." The truth was that the Masons had handed the word down and Phillips had heard it.

Gull, now, was more of a physician than he was a Mason, and an egoist more than he was either. It disappointed him when the atrociousness of his doings got suppressed, not that he would feel the thrill of his name in print, but he would enjoy a *frisson* when he read what he had done and then joined to the name of Ripper now on everybody's lips. He was the anonymous, almost enviable cynosure, and he was beginning to feel the killer's passion to make himself known in the simple interests of culpable glory. Who was the noble killer who, to while away the time before his execution by the silken rope, had written his autobiography, telling the full truth, only to be pardoned and let off, racing away from the jail in such ebullient joy that he left his autobiography behind and so had to be apprehended again and verily hanged without benefit of time in which to revise his written works? Well, Gull would never tell, he thought, and his confessions would have to take the form of uproarious, offensive letters to the public ear transmitted via the police and the newspapers in a pseudoilliterate dialect, like this:

Old boss you was rite it was the left kidny i was goin to hoperate agin close to your ospitle just as i was going to dror mi nife along of er bloomin throte them cusses of coppers spoilt the game but i guess i wil be on the job soon and will send you another bit of innerds

From this mishmash of stage cockney and an educated man's faltering pretense, Gull got his joys, yet always berating himself when he saw the result in print, and blaming not so much his foot as his unquenchable education, making him write "going" instead of "goin" and "guess" instead of "gess." What he needed, he established with a grim smile, was the help of the Annie Crooks of this world, the true illiterates to whom words were so much earthenware, soft before the oven. Perhaps he could somehow delegate his writing chores to the stunted, blunt women in the Pudding Club, the trouble being that they did not know enough words to get themselves a chamberpot and were now so far along the course of diurnal devastation that they could not be harnessed.

The entire reading public agreed that he, the Ripper, was an educated man, but what good was that? His wife thought so, too, unaware of his nightly doings. When he had written, in postscript to the above letter, "O have you seen the devle with his mikerscope and scalpul a-lookin at a kidney with a slide cocked up," he was giving the game away, no more, no less, and he was spelling far too well; so why not lard into these uncouth macaronics some even more contrasted elements, such as "diurnal devastation," slap it next door to the "devle with his mikerscope"? Why not? Why not let his imagination soar, with eventual sly allusions, in a year or two, to the River Lea, barges, Guy's Hospital, the Pudding Club, grapes, the *Crusader,* Netley, Sickert, the yellow oilskins, the parallelogram drawn across the East End, and heaven knew what else, succumbing to the age-old desire to fascinate and torment one's readers with clues, playing on their desire to savor pertinent consecutives? What a tour de force that would be, especially if his book, or the book of his life, could end exactly with his death, so that in one installment they would both have him and not have him, *that old dog of a doctor,* taking us in like that all along, and he such an outstanding cit-i-zen, pal of the Queen and the P.M. and the like, slicing intestines up for the Masons. There was serious work to be done yet, before he retired from extraordinary service, from Her Majesty's Secret Service. There would be more bloodletting, rectitude, honor, and some forays into verse, always dismissed by the Press as the botching of imitators and buffoons. Not so:

Four and whore rhyme aright,
So do three and me,
I'll set the town alight
Ere there are two.
Two little whores, shivering with fright,
Seek a cosy doorway in the middle of the night.
Jack's knife flashes, then there's but one,
And the last one's the ripest for Jack's idea of fun.

There was also this, as yet unsent, but nearer the bone:

One little whore left, with a nice soft belly,
A crafty whore with the name of Kelly
Who with malice aforethought and obscenities unseen
Writes begging and threatening letters to her Queen.
Well, Kelly will soon be changing her stripes
When the Doctor slips his hand into her tripes.
In her pocket just a thimble and a comb,
In the nice clean Ripper's pocket her shiny womb.

A woman on the Isle of Wight claimed the Ripper was an ape from a wild beast show; she had been reading Poe's "The Murders in the Rue Morgue." A forty-six-year-old widow opined that the Ripper "respects and protects respectable females," and Gull allowed that she might have italicized her fourth word without incongruity. He became accustomed to reading that his privy member had been infected, that he was using the body parts from his victims as poultices to suck the syphilis virus from it—an old Chinese and Malay remedy, as he knew without being an old China hand. Or he was a demented Buddhist, or someone from India practicing *thuggee,* or an old soldier driven crazy by sunstroke, using a poison-tipped weapon (Gull nodded appreciatively). One correspondent said he knew the Ripper was two men, named Pat Murphy and Jim Slaney, and he could tell the police where to find them: a dream had told him. Gull had seen this letter, and another one from a certain Josiah E. Boys, formerly a private with the King's Own Scottish Border-ers, warning the City Police Commissioner about a message written on the wall of a water closet in Guildhall: "I am Jack the Ripper and Intend to do another murder at Adelphi Arches, at 2 A.M. I will send the ears to Colonel Frazer." When Gull received a message from Lord Salisbury by special runner to come and view the Epidemics/Pandemics file at his earliest convenience, he went, and not a word did they exchange about his ongoing quest of blood; he read the cuttings and letters as a medical man interested in the welfare of the city's population, and soon gathered that the Ripper, whoever he really was, must be a madman, Turkish or American, in some intimate way mutilated, suffering from delirium tremens, either a hair fetishist or a transvestite Jewish slaughterer, either a maniac Socialist or a gloating lord, either the halfwit who used to moan during services in St. Paul's Cathedral or the star of a stage production called *Dr. Jekyll and Mr. Hyde.* Or he was William Onion, a lunatic whose nose had been smashed by a thrown pepperbox. Or Dick Whittington the Second, or a team of Germans who skinned people and used their skins as disguises affixed to themselves with American glue. Ladies of high station had written in, offering themselves for martyrdom. The vaults of the old Jewish cemetery should be watched, he read, and the sewers of London searched. All men wearing black turbans should be taken into custody. Dummies with springloaded arms should be strewn around the city to entrap the Ripper. Women police should wear special velvet-muffled collars with steel points embedded therein and discharge corrosive fluids at his face from glass syringes. Detectives should be imported from Russia and France and Germany. Anyone bearing what seemed to be a chloroform-drenched hankie should be arrested, as should anyone hanging about to blow his nose near to other people. Whitehall should be cleared of all but one hundred pairs of dectectives and prostitutes (Gull liked this program for exact venery). The newspapers should print warnings about a medically oriented psychopath and women should carry with them a piece of paper generously daubed with birdlime, which they would clap against the Ripper's back. Or alarm wires should be fastened to the pavements' curbs and alarm buttons placed every thirty feet. This was a suggestion from a Yorkshireman emigrated to Cleveland, Ohio. Whores should carry revolvers, bells, and whips, as well as jars of whitewash. "Or," said Salisbury, eyeing his prize physician, with amiable yet distant interest, "we might advertise for an authority on paraplegia who has recently suffered a mild stroke."

"The direct method," Gull said with exaggerated insouciance. "It might work very well, sir."

"Temptat clausa," Salisbury responded, quoting Tacitus, knowing that Tacitus often used the present tense for the past when he wished to be especially vivid in a context of pastness, and that the (neuter plural) noun stood for all manner of closed, secured, hidden, camouflaged things and people, ideas and beasts, to be opened up. "I rejoice," Salisbury went on, "to think that a liberal, moderately inventive translation—but above all a responsive one—would go something like: He tried with all pertinent force, though not unsubtly, to open up or otherwise lay bare all the things or places that had been sealed or closed, from envelopes to sewn-up women, like those African and Arab johnnies—ah, that's enough."

"Quite," Gull said resonantly. "Thank God for a lucid mind in the engine room. I mean the seat of power, and love."

Going off at a tangent that seemed to please him, Salisbury said, "Busy Ripper, these days. *Quisquis.*"

"Tiring."

"But not permanent, the appointment, Sir William."

"Loyalty is permanent, Prime Minister. Some of us do not come into office, go out of it, then return. Some of us will always be here."

"Just so, Gull." They had glanced off each other with mellifluous courtesy, Gull deferring to the man who had vouchsafed him a further look at the bulging Epi/Pan file, Salisbury doing his best to maintain a cool but attentive hauteur during the exchange, realizing that he now had on his hands that most dangerous of men, the uncelebrated celebrity whose anonymous fame would soon wash all the common sense out of him.

"When, then, Sir William?"

"Early November, sir. Mr. Sickert got something wrong, but he will perform well in future. His own future will depend on that."

"Ah, Sickert," Salisbury breathed, filtering exhalation through his fingers, "a gifted one."

"An instructable horse, sir."

"Bully. Then, we are done."

"Not quite, Prime Minister," Gull said, as one savant to another, opening out his map with the parallelogram drawn thereon and divided into two triangles.

"A noble, moving figure," Salisbury said, stirred more by the man's naked pride. "I see."

"The argument from design," Gull said. "I could abide no other."

"There will be something in this for you," Salisbury said vaguely. "I can command it. Do finish, though. It is already dying down. We can soon be wholesome as doves."

Chapter 32

Gull had always known he would be famous for medical feats. Now, however, he seemed to have been remade into an alloy of the sternest depravity, credited for things he had never done, would not dream of doing. At different times, parts of him felt feathery, granitic, viscous, as if he had no control over himself; and he no longer had even the *illusion* that he was in control of his body chemistry. He was being tugged this way and that by myth and history, by dreams and rumors, by the newspapers and the Prime Minister (who had begun referring to "Her Madge"—was that an access of intimacy or was it, like a working-class locution he had heard recently, just a way of saying things more easily? Eton and

Harrow, those twinned perfections of grooming, became "eaten and arrer"). What an age, Gull thought, to realise I know little about the world, when all along I'd thought I knew it all: I who go slashing throats and cutting into bellies am a sociological naïf; I who lobotomize the unfortunate, or the fortunate, depending on your point of view, I really need a St. Bernard dog from the Swiss Alps to see me through. Imagine the killer, the Ripper, going out to catch a Kelly, but needing a big brawny kind dog with a barrel of brandy under his chin to get me to the scene of the intended atrocity. Perhaps, before going further, I should make a clean breast of the whole affair to the newspapers and have them standing by to watch the last murder. They'd stop it, of course, so just give them enough clues to get them there too late. The corpse, ladies and gentlemen, will be deposited on a line connecting Mitre Square and Hanbury Street.

I am really dangerous, yet only to women. So it will always be men done up as women who come to get me, or well-muscled androgynes. To them I say: you are alive in a time you will never forget, because none of you will survive to remember it. And the little tyrants of gentility must hate having a Ripper on the premises, yet never deflowering (are there virgins yet in London?) nor even sexually molesting his chosen women. Imagine a loin-stabber who shows not the slightest lustful interest in his victims, but piles up their insides on their shoulders like so many sheets of newspaper on dead fish. I am much odder than they thought I was. Satan is a family man, with his favourite cup, eggcup, and toast rack; a familiar place at table, always facing the sun; and, upstairs, a trousers press, a tie press, and a box of pearl-studded tiepins. An ordinary gent with special powers. I wear the hankie in my dress pocket plucked into a high enough frill, or point, to blot my mouth on it at dinner or in assemblies: a deft bit of bending, so fast they think they haven't seen it.

He was showing Sickert an extraordinary sight that brought tears to Sickert's eyes. In the Pudding Club—which in Gull's mind merited initial capitals only when he thought of it as an institution rather than as a process—Annie Crook, with two

black eyes and a look of explosive despair, was standing alongside her three-year-old daughter, imported for the event from
her palatial isolation at Windsor, restored to a natural mother
who, while hugging her hard, seemed not to know what to do
next and so began to dither sideways, raising her hands at imaginary objects in her way: in a word, mumming and miming,
which is two words, and gaping, which makes three. Yet there
were no words in Sickert's brain for the appalling devastation
of her personality, the shipwrecked blank of her face. It was as
if someone hamfisted had washed the motherliness and humanity clean out of her. This, he knew, was no casualty ward such
as the already dead women had gone to when the going was too
rough; here, in Guy's, lobemaster Gull created a zone in which
making casualties was the prime purpose; the place was some
kind of counternursery, a cancellation ward with, in it, relics on
legs, relics on haunches, relics supine or prone: women who, if
they were going to go anywhere, were going to the morgue.
Some of them, he knew, had been well-spoken, not illiterates
like Annie Crook, but aunts and mothers with pretensions.
Brought to Gull for diagnosis (usually nothing more than a little
impertinent eccentricity), they tended to remain with him because, in the family's cries of concern, he detected also the
beginning of the paradoxical human huff that said: we hate
death, so we hate the dying; we hate illness, so we hate the ill;
and would like to be rid of them because they make the dogs
and the cats nervous, the tradesmen skittish, the postman reluctant, and so forth. Gently he peeled them away from their
families like stamps from unmailed envelopes until they floated
free, before eventually sinking on the dusty meniscus of water
that once was warm. He staged a font in reverse, so to speak,
rebaptizing them with two holes through the bone above the
eyes, converting them to the religion of Gull, who felt stronger
in the world, more fulfilled, altogether more of a savant, if he
had some castoffs to experiment with or merely to observe as
they slithered down the glacis from sanity and dignity to what
he had reserved for them lower down: a pig's trough of slop and
potato peelings, populated with stale loaves cut in half, wormy

beets and rotten fruit, as if he were stewing up and leaving to ferment some devil's cocktail to be sampled with eyes closed and breath held. Red-letter days in there came about when the daily broth included bits of dead dog or severed uterus, all ground up in a mincing machine, or on other very special days an Eddowes half-kidney. If it was an experiment, it was a shaggy one; if it was merely a device with which to humiliate his charges, it was an utterly successful one. No one recovered and no one complained: they thought the world outside was just the same.

So here was Sickert watching Alice Margaret already dipping her finger into the mess and taste-testing it, as a child might, while her poleaxed mother stood by in a shuddering trance, vaguely aware that something was wrong but able to rectify it only with a strange barking sound that Sickert had heard at the zoo. Annie, it was clear, was going under, having been there since April, already in the condition the Throne wanted her in: just able to recognize, if not her child, at least some bond between them, as if Annie were a gorilla and Alice Margaret a rhesus monkey. Annie recognized the simian bond while Alice Margaret, with an almost indifferent simper after all those nannies at Windsor and the Princess Alix, looked through her as someone not sufficiently her own or anybody else's. Perhaps, in ten years, if she lasted that long, she might escape to live out her time in a kennel with a clay pipe and a blind dog, a blind seeing-eye dog, a blinded seeing-eye dog, a seeing-eye dog blinded by Gull with his dissecting knife, a dead blinded seeing-eye dog like those East End children rolled dead under the table but ignored until the smell became too much.

"Now," Gull was saying, "we are not monsters: you may take the child to your greengrocer friend—Mr. Henry Fletcher. The powers have looked into him and approved. You may take her this very minute, if you wish. The mother is to be transferred to a superior ward. But the child is yours. We shall require one more service from you, sir, in early November, I trust. If you oblige, all will be well. If not, both you and the child will probably make a new acquaintance: the river. Tied together, I should imagine, with your throats very loose. If you see. Take the offer, sir." It was as if the man had swallowed a big fat moth that had left its dust around his mouth. What *was* that stuff? Snuff, Sickert thought. What did Emile Zola say? Each day you have to eat the toad of disgust. So here was his toad, mud-ripe and wart-rough. To get away from there he seized the child's hand as if it were the handle on a moving train and hastened out, coughing and almost vomiting. His final image of Annie Crook was of a face mushroom pale and worked by profound twitches at which she plucked with both hands, seeking to find and strip away the tiny animals that made her face hurt, gnawing on her, nibbling and tweaking. Alice Margaret said not a word, and heard nothing either. Gull had already signed papers that would send Annie Crook to the St. Pancras Workhouse.

Good, good, good, Gull decided: we are getting them all to ground. We shall know where to find them. Lightning had vanished into the earth, although his science told him that lightning also rebounded to the heavens at colossal speed. The eye could not track it any more than the bumbling police with their black-and-tan, big-headed bloodhounds could scent his rottenness: Jack the Ripper, one of the most famous names in English history, to be remembered and celebrated when nobody could tell one Henry from another all the way up to Henry the Eighth. Trust me, Mam, Gull whispered to his Queen. A Mason has to do things with a sense of structure: he has to observe certain requirements; but he gets the job done, whoever the rabble might be who have to be stopped. Mister Sickert looked green about the gills today. No gift for being a father—I can tell that, having brought up a son and a daughter myself. He would be better off in France: something twiddly about him, isn't there? When he took the knife and pushed with it, he handled it like a palette knife. Perhaps, if I fitted him out with his own set of oilskins, he would plunge in like the rest of us; but the next package, Mistress Kelly, the real one, happens to be an old chum of his. Not that anything would stop him if he were suitably threatened, as he has been. I just want his contribution, not as an accessory, but as a principal.

Weary of brooding about Sickert, he longed back to 1842, the year in which he became a Mason, and was hired to teach Materia Medica at Guy's Hospital. The year after, he had taken over as Resident Superintendent the little asylum for insane women that was now the Pudding Club. He had always preferred his life when it seemed to swell gently along as if it had read Aristotle. Now, however, it heaved and lunged, changing vastly and not always for the better. He felt confused. Was he obliged, he wondered, always to have a clear head about what happened? Could he not remain in two minds, or even three, and get away with it? Was clearheadedness such a virtue? Did he always know what he thought? No: only that he had been thinking hard and had emerged from it in a dither, too tired to care, too steeped in blood ever to be his own self again. His *old* self. That was it. But was he really that different now? Might it not be that, even with blood on your hands, you could remain essentially the man you had always been?

It never occurred to Gull that London might have responded even less well than it had to the Ripper murders if, say, some Jacqueline the Ripper had made a fetish of throatcutting and mutilating one cabinet minister after another, with *their* innards and eyeballs being sent around London sliced up, accompanied by heavy-handed, boisterous letters in comic English. It was because the whores were, or seemed, expendable that the rest of London (other than the East End) found the Ripper such an intriguing fellow, even an object of much merriment; it was as if he were spending his mordant energies upon offal. Indeed, some had argued that Polly Nichols, Dark Annie Chapman, Long Liz Stride, and Catherine Eddowes Conway Kelly had achieved a degree of fame otherwise unthinkable for them, and would perhaps all have been happy to have been martyred, could they have been aware of the legend that would surround them for ever, quite emancipating them from the enclaves of class and status in which the five thousand who had petitioned the Queen were doomed to malinger until the Reaper scythed them off. Gull had heard such opinions floated in Guy's itself as he pottered about, pretending to usefulness, getting blood on his hands to counter the mildew in his brain. He could not see any career for him beyond Marie Kelly, and he wondered if Kelly and Sickert between them might turn the tables on him and Netley and toss them into the Thames.

Gull did not know that Annie Crook still had some idea of a place to go. Not the workhouse to which she was being sent in a horse-drawn ambulance, but somewhere bright and smooth that she remembered from her childhood: her mother, Sarah, had spread a big old white sheet over the frame of a clothes horse reared up to make a roof, so Annie and her sister had a tent to crawl into during the summer, except that sometimes when they were too lively the clothes-horse fell flat upon them, they squealed, and resumed playing. Nothing went back up faster than that old sheet. Warm with flowers, furry as old green bread, dangerous to be in because you might roll over on some tiny robin's eggs laid by an improvident bird in the first sweeping flamboyance of the year. Annie believed that, if she held to this vision or intuition, she would go there and nowhere else, never mind what Slerch and Senna thought about her destination in the borough of St. Pancras. Who had St. Pancras been? What had they burned *him* for? Or had he got off scot-free? She knew nothing of the Ripper or of the fate of Marie Kelly's friends (and Eddowes), but she had an uneasy feeling as they tugged her away from the room in which her child had come back to her, even though she'd recognized Alice Margaret as someone seen underwater: a very small shrunken old woman becoming younger by the second until she became the girl last seen—when? Had it been years ago? She no longer knew, accurately, what a year was, though she had spent half of one in the Pudding Club in chronic, sleepwalking delirium bad enough to get her rated as sullen by the few women there with any judgment left. She had assumed at some point they would all be taken out and hanged in a courtyard; that at least would bring a breath of air, a glimpse of sunlight. Her head was functioning, but only enough for modicums. She had forgotten Eddy, but not Sickert or Alice Margaret, although her recognition of people had an injured, dawdling quality she rather enjoyed; it was almost like watching a flower grow, or a pregnant mare swell. Something came of it sooner or later if you had enough tea to drink, if you chewed enough raisin buns or pikelets; you had to fill up with starchy things because in the hot weather they wouldn't give you heat lumps as meat did, and there was a so-called food, Parrishes' perhaps, a sweet red liquid that was supposed to cool the overheated blood and smoothe out hives until they were flush with the surface of your skin. When a nettle stung her, she had always rubbed the blister with one of the dock leaves that usually grew nearby; and taking the red medicine reminded her of that.

Sickert, of course, was determined to get her out of the workhouse, but he knew he had some phalanx of the government against him, and not just the murderous Gull. If only he had money of his own instead of a wife with too much of it, to whom he did not speak. Could he, he wondered, muster a brigade of painters to rescue Annie, break in and bring her out, taking her all the way to France? He knew he could now take the taciturn Alice wherever he wanted, and in a way this was a bad thing; it gave him the sense that he was accomplishing something worthwhile and need not do much more. The temptation was to leave Annie be and devote himself to her daughter, who even now, as he gathered up things she might need, was poking through the stacked-up canvases in his Cleveland Street studio, humming at some, making a fierce whooping noise at others (presumably those she did not like). Words to her were alien, she who carried the gene of deafness from Alix via Prince Eddy. She made a silent, stark, uninterrogable presence for Sickert to walk by, nothing like the cooing little imp she had been in Dieppe. His head was pounding from all the strain and the hoping on top of the horrors he had witnessed, and he wondered if there were anything heroic in what he was doing. Was worry heroic or just a kind of mental marmalade? Alice pouted, but her pout had now developed an almost wry distortion, no doubt from watching the bewhiskered mouths of the nannies at Windsor, where she had grown accustomed to the sunken garden's sides: they checked her headlong runs and saved her ball. Her hair looked greasier, he thought, her cheeks much fatter (she must have been eating well for the first time), and her arms pudgier.

Handing a sovereign to Henry Fletcher and the little bundle of clothes, toys, and small saleable paintings he had collected against Alice's reappearance, Sickert promised to come by each day, but what he saw in Fletcher's face frightened him. Fletcher was a lover of precision easily flustered; his eyes watered and his wrists quaked. His wife was lame, but addicted to children, of whom she no longer had any; she was a born looker-after, but Sickert wondered what she would make of a child who not only could not hear but had just, once again, been sundered from her mother. To Alice, the greengrocer's shop would be another Windsor, minus the sunken garden and the great big bed and the long lady who let Alice feel the tympany in her Danish throat.

"She have the run of all the old toys," Fletcher was telling him. "Saved every one we did, for the sentiment, see."

Had he said sediment? Sickert's head was abuzz with pain; he would have to go away and paint, to settle his interior down. Then he might be able to think clearly.

"She's in good care," he said redundantly.

"The best, sir."

"If you need anything—"

"We'll say, but we don't, up to press."

"Then I'll be off," he said, with labored slowness.

"And we'll be here."

"Yes."

"The mother—how long—"

"Not much hope, Mr. Fletcher. She's been going home for some while, going down, if you follow me."

Mrs. Fletcher, in from the shop, cooed and somehow made her body rounder and more winsome before offering the hug that Alice rebuffed. *"She*'ll settle, sir."

"I wish *I* could," Sickert said, and left them to it, realizing that Gull had tightened the vise about him, pushing hard against his face the face of what would happen if he failed to deliver Marie Kelly up to them.

Chapter 33

After the double murder, Netley himself began to feel he had broken through to a new status in life: beyond the law, of course, but so exquisitely attuned to what the Masons wanted that he no longer had to wait for orders, from Gull or anyone else. Once told, forever zealous: that was Netley, who in his sleep kept hearing Gull hand down the commands of kill, capture, wound, maim. If Netley had known the word he would have seen himself as an energumen, possessed by a devil. He did know that something thick and dreadful united them when they three took the *Crusader* out in the small hours among the milling tarts and their clients, where the gaslight was weakest, the soot stickiest, the damp most invasive. Ideally, he thought, they would do their murdering in Dockland, next to uninterrupted expanses of oily unrefreshed water, with rats promenading around them for company, ready to lick up the spill. No doubt of it, Netley could be fanned on; ever willing, he could be energized by events, and the double murder now kept him in a state of constant murderousness like a human elevated to godhead and dangling over the entire human race, his fangs unretracted—or so he saw himself, as a fee-fi-fo-fum person, to be feared even when asleep.

Yet it was the furor rather than the actual murders that made him steam; he too wanted some of the panic to lap all the way to his doorstep, and he wanted the sense of adding to it while it was developing, even if what he did got swallowed by the huge swamp of horror. Hadn't Gull instructed him to use his own judgement about Alice Margaret, who had been nestled in Windsor Castle among the tombs of all the little princes who had died? Off he went to prospect and peer, knowing where she was, and reckoning it would only be a matter of time before she came out, was ushered out, for fresh air, a commodity in which the working classes believed devoutly, the Fletchers every bit as much as the Netleys. Only two days after the murders of Stride and Eddowes, he spotted Alice Margaret in Fleet Street at four in the afternoon, crossing opposite Anderton's Hotel with someone who looked like an oldish nanny. He literally ran over her with one of the wheels, ostensibly by accident, so much so that he himself took her, nanny in tow, to St. Bartholomew's Hospital, where she was examined without delay and pronounced in severe danger. She was not expected to live, certainly not by Netley, who by then was far away, having as it were delivered and decamped. In offering to transport the injured child, he kept ahead of the police, badly overcome by the hiccups, such had the excitement been. Now he knew how anonymous the *Crusader* could be: a man might kidnap the Queen and get away unidentified into the surge of the streets, nameless and faceless even in the moment of fame.

When Sickert, whose mind had been strangely occupied with Netley since he did in Stride, heard about Alice Margaret, a lancing cold moved through him, yet he could not quite decipher what had happened. Alice Margaret was going to recover, thank goodness, although badly scarred. Had Netley (it must have been Netley, mustn't it?) calculated the impact that precisely, so as to create a warning? If he had killed her, one of coercion's means would have gone. So why was Netley so abandoned, or so premature? Could any semiilliterate coachman work out the exact degree of damage he wanted and then inflict it, to the nearest eighth of an inch? No, it must have been Netley, now a full-fledged murderer rather than a fetcher and a carrier, going off half-cocked, infatuated with horrific gesture rather than attentive to Gull's exact orders. Why would they kill off the only hold they had over him, Sickert wondered, and all the time this question revolved in his mind, sapping him and torturing him, as if there were some piece of the puzzle—an obvious and garish one, to be sure—he had missed. In the end he decided that Gull and Netley had taken a dangerous chance, no doubt buoyed up by the plural atrocity of the other night. Either that or Netley had gone off his rocker, at a loss for something to do, someone to kill, someone to mortify. Sickert began to cease to worry about it. Alice Margaret, a hostage to fortune, was alive, but she might have been dead. Some things, Sickert berated himself, were quite beyond his ability to put right. After all, he was not responsible for everything in the firmament. What was it that someone had said to him one day, apropos of some painting, neither his nor Sickert's? "It just about made me sick." Sickert had retorted, "Did you analyse the vomit?" Now he knew that there were some things you just did not analyse at all, because the details were beyond you. They made you feel worse.

He gave up. Had Netley been intending to frighten Sickert into service he had grossly overdone it, alerting him to a possibility of reprieve that would cost the child her life. He already knew when Gull would go forth to soil the night and the early morning again. It would be any day now, but always with a one-day warning to get ready. Sickert had begun to lose himself in crazed speculations, stunned by Netley, numbed by Gull, exercised beyond grief by the distress of the Fletchers, who felt somehow to blame. Now Sickert knew he would have to do as Gull said.

Surely they would not ask *him* to kill Kelly, his sister in the trade. Was that what Gull was working up to? If they handed him the knife and the oilskins he would kill Gull on the spot, he was sure of that, and then Netley could gallop off with the remains as he and Kelly slipped away. All his remedies and escapes came right out of Shakespeare, he thought; the actor in him was leading the tactician by the nose. Come off it, Walt Sickert, he told himself: you'll never win that way. Do something excruciatingly definite. The bolder the better. Don't think about it. Do it. Or they will be at the door with the *Crusader*, itching to get started on the last woman. He had better go and look for Marie Kelly, disguise her as Netley and rent a carriage, persuade Gull into it with some tale about the *Crusader*'s having broken down, and gag him and tie him up. Could a Sickert wrestle a Gull to death? He had the height if not the weight. But which of them would be niftier with the knife? Never mind: Sickert would have the so-called element of surprise, overrated and calling for nerve.

Now Sickert knew he was approaching the end of his life; premonition stalked him like a perfume, and he asked himself why some people come into this world for only twenty-eight years. Could they not be told beforehand that they would have to live fifty-six in only half that number? He also wondered how many of Gull's notes to him, delivered to the house in Hampstead, had made their way to Ellen before reaching him, and, if so, what she had made of them, no doubt construing them as billets-doux. *Evidence,* he sighed. But if Marie Kelly and the late-lamented Long Liz had been breaking into the house, they themselves might have intercepted Gull's imperious notes, perhaps without realizing who they were from and what they were about. One way of writing to Marie Kelly, he suddenly saw, was to address himself to his own house; she would do the rest. He hoped heartily that she had other refuges to run to, better ones than a house that Gull no doubt already knew about. Netley would have been scouring London for weeks, accumulating information, quizzing the locals, eavesdropping and following. It was the man's nature as well as his chronic calling. Why had Gull waited so long? Had he had a change of heart and decided to let Marie Kelly live? In the weeks since the deaths of Stride and Eddowes, Kelly could have been gone to Calcutta; it was only a matter of money.

Marie Kelly might have made a run for it, but her common-law husband Joseph Barnett had insisted on her staying put, where she could be looked after, and John M'Carthy, the lodging-house manager, by whom she was pregnant, insisted that she go back on the game to earn some of the money she owed him. " 'Few don't, my lady." M'Carthy had told her, "I'm going to move Maria Harvey in with you and Joe Barnett out."

"Joe Barnett won't stand for the likes of that, or that," she yelled. "He won't stand for either, so put that in your chandler's pipe and puff it rotten."

"Mrs. Harvey moves in," he said stern as a parson, "and Mr. Barnett moves out. Or he pays for another room. I has to get things horganized."

In the event, when told, Joe Barnett shouted "Well I'll go to Trent," meaning not that he would travel north but that he couldn't believe it. He shoved Marie Kelly all the way across the twelve-foot-square room with one blow and she reciprocated, causing him to slip and ram his beer mug right through the window, cutting his arm. "Now, look at that," he cursed, "look what you've made me do."

"Don't fight women out of your class," she told him, bitter with frustration. "I'm heavy, see."

"No, you're not, Marie, you're a bloody dumbbell."

"You'll have to go."

"I'll be well shut of you. I'm off to Bishopsgate. Send any telegrams after me, even if they're from the Queen." In fact he did nothing, not on this particular evening, the 30th of October, and they two and Maria Harvey, another prostitute, spent an uncomfy night together, in the course of which Joe began to paw Maria, who hefted him a blow in the belly, which woke Marie, who was in the bed (Joe in the chair, Maria on the floor), who then slapped him hard with a left-right motion of her right hand. There had never been room for two, and now there were three. In six months' time there would be four. "Maria can go to New Court soon," Marie said, but Joe had had enough by now. "Maria can go to the devil," he muttered. "I'm off to civilized folks. Mark my words, you two'll have your hands on each other soon as the door closes. You make sure to stuff some rags in that bloody window. M'Carthy will be months before he has it mended."

He still cares, she thought, otherwise he wouldn't have said that about the window. He'll soon be back once Maria's mizzled off. If only I didn't drink, I'd save, wouldn't I? I would. But then, I know how the rest of the world lives, never mind the other half. It isn't a case of seeing-if, I've *seen.* I live at number thirteen, that's me, and if Maria wants to stay, then she can. We'll go to the dogs together and tie their tails in a knot. Jesus, he doesn't even like me to sing my fav'rite song, and he goes on taking no notice. Indeed, she had explained to him that Polly, Dark Annie, and Long Liz had all been chums of hers, and it was an easy guess as to who'd be next, but he had told her to stop imagining things; secretly, though, he had decided to move out of the way for a while, lest he himself encounter the Ripper when he was after Marie, or be falsely accused of doing her in. As soon as he had gone, she felt an overpowering sense of relief, like a rain-shower from Ireland, and she construed it as euphoria, a sign from heaven that all would be well, and all manner of things would be well. God wouldn't let her feel so nice if things weren't at least going right. In the wind-up, she said, I'll be all right, right as an oyster. All very well for him to say it isn't decent to go on the game in my condition, but work's work and brass is brass. Some of us haven't any choice, not with the M'Carthys of the world on our tracks, their hands in our knickers.

Joseph Barnett, however, could not make up his mind. Sworn to stay away while she went on the game, or had the Harvey woman living in, he decided to risk being associated with her still and came back daily—from the 31st of October for a whole week, either to give her a few coppers from what he'd made at the markets, lifting boxes of vegetables, or, as on Thursday the 9th of November, just to tell her he was sorry, but he had nothing to give her.

He's not such a bad old rump, Marie thought, he must love me a lot to come every day like this. He'll be back. She looked with possessive affection at the little narrow court in which number 13 had its own entrance; she even doted on the drain-pipe and the grating, the broken window, the tiny arch through which one had to approach her door. If only Long Liz or Dark Annie had been here to savour this moment; but she must not think like that. If they had been here, they would have put their heads together at the table in number thirteen

and concocted a letter to the Queen that would have made the
one by the five thousand women of Whitechapel look like a
dog's breakfast. All of London, she thought dizzily, was like a
snowstorm of letters even though it was only November, a
month she liked for its smouldering grieving quality, its dank
silences, its mahogany hues. I have known a powerful lot of
the dead, she thought, but I don't go to funerals. And I don't
read those dreadful papers that come out with bad drawings of
the faces of the dead in them, full of lies and daftness. She
sang a little, extra loud so that Mrs. Prater in 20 above her
would hear her and be vexed. "Only a violet I plucked from
my Mother's Grave," she sang with a sostenuto trill, extending
the vowel in "grave" for as long as she could, "when a boy."
"Whayn ay boo-ooyyyy." She knew the rest of the song but never
sang it, holding that nobody in their right mind needed all of
a song, only the part of it that broke your heart, and in singing
it again and again you both healed and fortified yourself. She
had seen "plucked" written as "pluckt," but she didn't like
elisions, she wanted the full value of the suffix in case you
wanted to sing it what she called long-legged: *pluck-èd,* in other
words two syllables, whereas you should never make a silly of
yourself by singing grave as gravy. Oh no. The real sillies were
those policemen who couldn't make their minds up whether to
buy the two bloodhounds, Burgho and Barnaby, although the
tale of Burgho's having been taken back to Yorkshire to compete in a dog show, and Barnaby's having been taken to sniff
out a burglary from a shop, had given all of London some
needed light relief. Secretly, Marie Kelly hoped someone, the
Ripper or someone else, would poison both dogs; she found it
crude to have bloodhounds nosing around in the drab little
corners in which her friends had been found dead. I'm the
only one they haven't got so far, she thought; are they saving
up their best to get me good and proper? Or is it over? Has the
Ripper quit? I'm damned if I'm going to trot off to Ireland just
to flatter the likes of him. I'll toss me petticoats up high and
gas him to death, that I will. He'll see.

Chapter 34

Bravado, she already knew without couching it in such terms, was an art form, requiring an icicle in the neck, a net in the stomach to curb the butterflies. Deep breaths were an asset, too, and á little splash of cold water on each wrist before you got started. It helped to fix your eyes on a far point that never moved, as if you were balancing—as if you were a balancing act. Men doing it felt their nipples turn inside out, but women usually kept their nipples facing the world outside, not so nesh as men. Was it true that if you were near your last day the ground felt rickety when you walked on it? If you were for it, she'd heard, the air around seemed sort of lacy, like some kind of foam, all kinds of dogs came after you, not bloodhounds only, and your food rode up and down inside you, never able to settle, so never digested, so not nourishing you right, and you felt weak and gassy.

Well, she did, but surely that was the baby, for the sake of whom she would soon have to retire or a little stranger'd end up sucking on something much thicker than Mama Kelly's nipple, and redder, harder, less nourishing. Lord love me, she thought, I'm nothing if not a walking temptation.

No doubt about it, she was blaming herself, she was trying to drown the baby in gin or rum, and she had forgotten that other baby, Annie Crook's, at Windsor Castle, her playground a big sunken garden that you could have filled with water and made into your own private lake, her last room the Prison Room above the Norman Tower, not a child's room at all but a turret, a chamber with too many sides, from the outside shaped like something designed not to roll around in a giant's hand. Nothing the child threw upward ever reached the ceiling, it was so high, and the walls were lined with precarious bookcases, never touched because the removal of just one book might have brought the oak frame and the remaining books tumbling on the inmate. It was a room in which to immolate a child, a young prince, an unwanted lover; one twist of the key sealed them in a frigid hexagon, and the child's hands and feet were blue each day when she woke. The mice were the real occupants, at night forming a muscular carpet on which no one dared to tread, and the child in the dark felt her breath heavy and cold in her chest as she lay there on her back, knowing at so tender an age that she had been brought here only to play and freeze. It would not have been difficult to forget her up there. Everywhere there were little places for little bodies as if sundered small lives were the mortar that held the place together, half-ruin that it was. From the Prison Room she would go, sheathed in a windowless cradle, and the imagination sustaining her would let her slither away into history like a corpse in a canvas bag ushered down among the waves. But they had let her go, Marie remembered in her alcoholic stupor, she had gone from that awful Prison Room to the corner greengrocer's in one go.

The child was going to be all right, Sickert had promised it, whereas she herself, uncouth and broody, had begun to go finally downhill, not least because nothing had happened to her. More had happened to Alice Margaret. It was almost intolerable how the lovely Marie Kelly had been spared the things that had happened to the others, made to wait and wonder, then to go around blatantly asking for it, then almost to lose interest and tell herself, in a fit of loquacious whimsy, she was no longer an interesting woman at all, even to Jack the Ripper, whose eyes were hot coals, whose hands were steel claws, whose teeth were hedgehog spines, whose breath was river gas—she could think these dreadful things up, but she couldn't make them go any further, she couldn't make them *do* anything. Somewhere in London, she said, to get things started, there is a man who cuts throats in two main movements; his mother must have taught him how. This man had already removed from the world the dear and departed Polly, Dark Annie, Long Liz and that other, and perhaps scores more. Had the other three just had bad luck, bad luck of unspeakable caliber, since they were three among something like sixty, working on the assumption that a woman was murdered daily in the East End somewhere? She could almost believe it as she looked at London from the wobbly stance of the drunk: that, in all this teeming metropolis, there was now not a single Ripper with her on his list, not for the next month or six. Could she sniff him as he advanced or see the ghastly green marsh-gas light coming off him, like a smoke with verdigris in it, his clothes made out of old black lettuce, his hair alive with maggots, his veins and arteries on the outside for simple lack of sheathing? He was there, certainly, but his interest had taken him elsewhere, to strangling cattle on the cross-Channel boats, perhaps, or lurking for the next comer in the Prison Room at Windsor. She was alive and kicking, she told herself, raw as one of those people in Australia with the woolly black hair and the scrubbed-white teeth: *a-borry-jynes,* she whispered, one of them *aborryjynes,* not in the trees but walking on the desert with all the kangaroos for company. She was as much at sea as that, but she was safe; she had made her nerves wait it out, as safe in Aldgate or Leman Street as she would have been crouched in a bookshop in Essex Street, Strand: Seeley & Co., late of 54 Fleet Street, but why had she remembered? That street had bollards in it, around which you might dodge any Ripper who came after you, even in the dead of night, or the pink of the small hours, and then you could dart into Seeley's and persuade them to stock your latest little provocative book for gennermen.

Those had been the days, when she was in a different trade, hawking other meats. Somehow, now, she felt herself aging, a slow and unhygienic glue in her joints, all from the baby of course, and who would pay for her then, either as a whore or a mother? The length of most gentlemen's responsibilities was about three minutes if you were lucky; that was about as long as they liked to be involved with you on an intimate basis. Where was she going to go, before her dying day, so that she could set up on the mantelpiece, like so many conquests or angels' hands, the visiting cards, no, the invitations, that poured in, to tea or scones, to cream cakes and lemonade? She was thinking of Mr. Gladstone, Prime Minister before Lord Salisbury, and wrongly supposing that the latter was the charming, pompous man who took the whores home with him, all on the up and up of course, so as to reform them over pecks of light refreshment. How she longed to be accosted by Lord Salisbury of the bird's-nest beard, ushered in through the front door in Fitzroy Square not far from Cleveland Street, and made to see the error of her ways, so much so that, when the Ripper arrived later on for dinner, slobbering to get at her throat, the good lord would calm the monster and feed him lamb chops. Then the P.M. would keep her on, not as a skivvy or a *fille de joie,* but as an a-borry-jyne, someone so remote from his own way of life that he had to keep her on the premises as a zoo of one, as if she were a parrot brilliant at recitative and he had so much heard that plaintive Irish lyric, *Only a violet I plucked from my Mother's grave when a boy,* that even in the House of Commons he would burst forth with it in the middle of a serious speech and end up dabbing his eyes for the sake of all mothers and old Ireland hopelessly lost.

Like that.

She was only trying things out.

There were no invitations on her mantel. There was no mantel. Even Little Alice's Prison Room had had a mantel, where the invitation cards could acquire a touch of ancient, royal soot. Only in hell, where the Ripper wrote from, would she have invitations, and she would tuck them all up underneath her hell-skirts, her inferno petticoats, even among, if it was the wrong time of the month, the storming mess of her jam-rags. That was where invitations belonged, to see if they would wither or falter in an oven as hot as that. Let the Ripper come, she babbled inside her head, I'll choke him with a sodden clout, I'll gag him with slithery blood. That's the only thing he deserves. I wonder who he is, a gentleman, I wouldn't doubt: your ordinary rough workingman'd be slaughtering duchesses by now, to be sure, cutting them up for the pearls within, or just to see if their digestions worked the same as other folks's. Lordy me, I'll die if I don't sober up.

Here I go, he doesn't care: billycock hat, face like curds and whey, moustache like a ginger ferret, a lot like Sickert but too short, not him at all, and he beareth, nay he porteth, in his pudgy hand a one-quart can of beer as if it held all the rivers of Ireland. In and out in a jiffy, sir, I'll have ye squirting before you can say Limerick. Mrs. Cox is coming in behind us, no client; Marie gets them all, they can't do without her, she's a pillow of the community. "Gnite, Mary." "Gnite, flower. I'm going to have me song farst."

The man with the can of beer let the door slam and, when Mrs. Cox had gone, Sickert tiptoed up and yanked the key from its hole. For the first time he had seen how Marie Kelly conducted herself with a client, how she clicked.

He was hoping to lock her in or out, Gull having decided that, in view of last time's mix-up, he wanted to have his "interview" with her in the privacy of her own lodgings. Sickert himself wasn't quite sure what to do, but he could tell that Gull would not be fooled this time; indeed, it looked as if all three of them would be calling on her, so it would be plausible that, seeing two familiar faces, she might conclude that Gull's was that of a friend, at least the acquaintance of friends. She was a famous friend of the dead women. She was one of the most attractive women on the game. She was beginning to forget things that had happened and grieved her; the onrush of life past her and around her was so violent and thick that she longed for some abrupt exemption, tapping her way into zones of being she had not the means to describe, but she knew she wanted to sneak into a fold and hide there encrypted, hoping that nothing much would happen for the next ten years.

She almost sighed, having browbeaten herself into not responding, yet here was another customer, the worse for drink, and all he needed was a cuddle and a cackle, a bit of slap and tickle, and he would not even remember what he had had or not had. He wanted his jollies, so she fussed him up a bit, tousled him, tickled him, rippled her fingers through his pubic hair, and sent him packing with a quite firm slap on his rear end, calling after him "Now, Bertie, don't you go telling your mother about it." He was gone, Sickert saw him go, and then heard Marie doing her song all over again as London settled down into early autumn, a cool and a wet one, too. What had happened to those golden, light-swamped days when death and cold seemed to have fallen out of the reckoning, and bands of children, unable to sleep, roamed the lanes and back alleys chanting songs about buttercups and daisies? Had that ever happened or was he too dreaming, dreaming in private parallel with Marie Kelly, whose time had almost come? He could sense all the clocks in Creation creaking around to when she would have to deal with Gull, Netley, and himself, half-convinced that they would come to invite her to some gamy party: a more sordid aftermath to the raucous evening at Sickert's house in Hampstead with Long Liz Stride. According to Netley, who had been doing his usual job of lurking in the vicinity, Gull had himself been to take a look at Marie's Miller's Court and and remarked the broken window as if it were some impediment to his plan. The only thing Sickert could think of now, when it was too late to dodge or feint, was to make her agony as short as possible, getting her in a jolly mood to begin with and then bringing down the curtain so fast she did not have chance to switch to a mood quite different.

In the room above Marie Kelly's, Mrs. Prater yawned one of those yawns that commit the mouth to uncoordinated sounds resembling an actual word, unrepeatable and not attractive, and usually ending in a waning wheeze. She was fed up, having been out in the wind-driven rain for four hours without clicking once. Not removing her clothes, she lay on the bed and went straight to sleep, cursing the young tart in the room beneath, who seemed to find takers even though she was always heaving up the contents of her tummy, right there in the road like a rusty old pump. Having failed to dream up something with which to soothe herself to sleep she concentrated on thoughts of the first tot of rum she would have tomorrow, soon after dawn, at the Ten Bells pub when it opened for the trade with the porters who worked the market. Something to burn her awake, that was what she wanted, like a benign scald against the lingering damps of a November night.

Much more at peace than her neighbor, Marie Kelly took in a series of deep breaths, knowing it calmed her to do so. Life wasn't a bad old bugger when it left you alone, whatever that meant. It wasn't just that she wanted peace and quiet, which were worth having; she wanted there to be peace in the world above and beyond her, a general calming-down amid which a shabby man with a billycock hat and a taupe moustache didn't bother you, whether he was drunk or not. Otherwise she'd pack up everything, give all her things away (it'd take two seconds, she thought), and jump in the river. All you did then was just breathe water until you didn't breathe any more.

Her experienced eye moistened somewhat as she thought of infants being born this very day whose destiny to walk the streets was already firm, and whose pretty little hairless private places had on them a label that read "For Public Consumption" or, worse, "Public Convenience," in between a rat and a manure heap, on top of a grating, next to a leaky drainpipe, with their fish and chips pouring up out of them at regular intervals on a tide of lukewarm beer, on a rainy night in the East End, and the chances of having their throats cut high. If you had a mind, she thought, as the key stuck in the lock and she failed to hear, being so engrossed; if you had a mind, then you sort of thought your way through life, bending your needs to fit what wouldn't change. Wasn't that called education? Wasn't that really why the Prince Eddys of the world went to Cambridge University? She tried to imagine an Eddy with a mind, but she could not, and the door began to quiver, then move. Lying on her bed, she thanked her lucky stars for its being a bed and her own, not half Maria Harvey's or Joe Barnett's. Had she really, in the course of the evening and the early morning, asked George Hutchinson in the street for sixpence? Had she no shame? Had she really been outside the Britannia talking to a man, she hatless, in velvet bodice, dark blue shirt, and a maroon shawl? What had Hutchinson said to her question? "I can't, dearie. I've spent all my money going down to Romford and back."

Had she again said "Hutchinson, me flower, *will* you lend me sixpence? I'm good for it, you know"? And what else had happened in Thrawl Street? Had some well-dressed client actually addressed her, when she was miles away, shocking her and making her laugh her Limerick cackle? "Madam, you look as if you would be warm and juicy where it counts"—just what you'd expect of a gent in gaiters and an astrakhan coat and wearing a heavy gold chain on his waistcoat, a horsehoe pin on his black tie. Lord, she thought, a fancy one. They haggled, she recalled, and she told him there were certain services she did not entertain, although these were readily available elsewhere down the road. "Then you'll settle for meat and two veg," she had said, and they had both burst out laughing as if it were the best joke in the world. "You will be all right then, for what I have told you, flower," she had said, hadn't she, and he had tugged his hat over his eyes, abruptly ceased laughing, and walked alongside her with his right hand on her shoulder, sort of proprietorial. Had she really ever said, "All right, my dear, come along now. You will be comfortable, I promise." Had he then kissed her and, on being told she had lost her hankie, given her his, a bright red one smelling of camphor and snuff? The trouble these days was that she had let things slide so much that what had happened a month ago had the immediacy of today, and vice versa. Her life had so little in it that she made the most of things, spreading them out like a child with toys on a rug. One day soon, Marie knew, she was going to retire. Marie Kelly was going to look after herself for once, rather as if having decided she could understand only so much, and that amount was much smaller than she had expected it to be, as if life were a handful of eiderdown which, when released, expanded to the size of a football.

So she would be cutting her losses, reconciled to living out her days in genial befuddlement, a condition almost like happiness except that it lacked the element of personal endeavor and attachment. Flat on her back in the overture to a dream, she had seen nothing of the door's gradual opening, but she had attributed the draught from it to the broken window; indeed, she and Joe had got into the habit of putting a hand through the hole in the glass and opening the door by slipping back the bolt from inside, risking a scratched wrist, even when they had the key: it had seemed somehow more intimate, less formal, and it was one way of accommodating the broken window into their joint life, making use of the mishap. It was much what other people did, preferring to come and go by climbing bodily through the windows on the ground floor, as if a house were not a house but an outhouse, or what, higher up the social scale, people did who had both a front door and a back door, always using the latter as the former and not using the former at all, but keeping it triple locked and lagged with bits of carpeting, even plugging the keyhole and swathing the inside in thick curtains as if there were poisonous gas in the aspidistra. All this, she considered, was a sign of originality: not doing what you were supposed to do, and, sleepy as she was without being able to keep her toes from wriggling, she noticed how often she identified originality with defiance. In her book, it was enough to be defiant.

By now she had heard Sickert inhaling his eucalyptus-drenched hankie, but she was profoundly relaxed, after none too good a day, and she was accustomed to hearing coughs and snites, sniffles and the gargling-up of phlegm, from all over the court: such noises-off went with the climate, and half the time she thought the noises came from her own unquiet stomach anyway. She started to sing, got only the first three words out, and sat forward fast as someone turned up the gaslight and she saw three men facing her: Netley in his usual dark tunic and riding breeches, Gull in his yellow oilskin, and Sickert attired this time in a voluminous painting smock, on his head a red handkerchief tied in knots at the corners. Then she started to laugh, a sound full of gusto and self-disdain:

"Got an appointment, have I? Three at once? A trio of right toffs, two of them familiar. Who might you be, then, sir, when you're at home? Did you catch any today? I'll bet you've been fishing in some funny rivers in your day."

"My name," Gull told her with severe formality, "is never known."

"It's true," Sickert said. "He's anonymous."

"I thought that," she said, "was only when you thrumped

yourself, my flowers. I'm not that ready, lord knows, and it's been a long and thankless day, but who's first then? Have you worked out your marching orders, gentlemen? I'm glad to see *you* again, I must say," she said to Sickert. "I never did like to think of us as strangers."

"We'll never be strangers now," he said in a choked-sounding, knowledgeable voice that made her shiver and look at the other two: all of a sudden she felt alone, afflicted with a helplessness and a paralysis that these three, she suspected, were not going to help her with, as if she were the last woman in the world and they wanted the planet to themselves, for whatever rotten purpose.

"Well," she said, "call me a dirty name. I'm not dressed to receive gentlemen, I'm not fit to be seen. Turn that light down a bit, lovey." This to Gull, who incredibly did as he was told, willing to play along in the penultimate farce provided he was able to finish it in his own fashion: no nonsense with grapes this time, none of Sickert's monkey business, no rushing the job to race off into the night after some other tart being let out of the station because she had sobered up. No, this was going to be Vesalius in full blush, he promised himself, done on by far the youngest of the sluts named. It was rather a shame, he thought, but he didn't want Netley and Sickert taking sexual advantage of her at the last; he wanted all the things of death to go with death, no deflections.

How the mind chatters, she was thinking, even when you're bone-tired, as if it was something you wound up, or it was a sort of gy-ro-scope, spinning its colours for no good reason, unless God Almighty liked to hear the sounds of all the minds humming even when they weren't thinking anything particular. Nice of Walt Sickert to bring his friends, the driver who ferried Eddy to and fro; a nasty bit of work, she thought, but he reminded her of the good old days when they were all together in Cleveland Street. That other one, he seemed too far gone to be on the game with anybody, but you never knew: there was many a salty flame in an old dog, especially if they took their time in the build-up to the wind-up. I have seen some of the old ones, she thought, get the horn that won't go down, as if they'd got a crick in their back and transferred it to their Jamesy-boy. Hers was a Jennie. And they don't want it, she said to herself; you can always tell when they've come for it, they fidget about and look you up and down slyly, they giggle a lot and breathe hard in your face like naughty schoolboys. So the question now is, what do they want at this hour? Are they doodle-alley or is it a social call? No doubt they want to make a special arrangement and Walt has put them up to it to be nice. It then occurred to her, briefly, that one of these men might be Jack the Ripper, unknown to the other two perhaps, but here to see what she was like, what kind of neck she had for the razor. *Nah,* she said, they wouldn't go to all that trouble, they could get me outside right as rain. Leastways, that's what the bugger's been doing with the others. It's not an indoor affair, it's outside, like a football match, and the wind's in your hair as you're going down for the count. "Well, gents," she said, "what shall it be? Double tossoff with a suck in the middle? Who shall be which? I must say, this isn't the hour, I was half dropped off, and I've done three today already. Do you want to line up then? Best prices in the East End." She saw the oldest man seem to flicker in his oilskins as if spinning his cock, and she thought: He'd better hoick them up or we'll never be able to find it. No, he was making a move to go behind her and she thought, Oh the dirty bugger, in front of these other two. What do they call it, some of them? *Urning.* Imagine that. All's well. Out with your thrumpers, then, ladies, she thought: "Are you ready, gentlemen?" With both hands ready, cupped and wet with spit, she crouched obligingly for Gull the oilskin-yellow sodomite to lift his cape and get into range, whiling away the seconds in between (at least, she thought, my trap is free for song), she began again the song that said it for her, in London, Ireland, or Dieppe: "Only a violet I plucked," and then began again, but ended up breathing hard and nasally into the words themselves: *Ownlee ay vy-eau-late Oi par-looked-t.* It was a lovely trill and Sickert stood openly weeping while Netley looked ahead, stern squat obelisk that he was, knowing he was going to have to help with the cleaning up.

There was muslin, but not on the floor. Gull took her by the hair from behind, left-handed, and in a flash she looked right, saw the knife coming at her like a flying comb, was able to scream the one word "Murder" before there came that mothwing of a traveling caress, not so much a pain as an overconfident contact started once, then again in not quite the same place. How fast she felt drained as she went down, wondering who was that creature all in yellow behind her, who held her, spurting, like a good old friend holding a friend in the act of throwing up. She faded into a brown crash that fogged her eyes.

Finally he let her body sink in its heaviness to the wood, even as Netley stripped the bed, then knelt to hoist Marie Kelly to her final reward as a letter-writer, back there on it, where she only moments ago had almost fallen asleep. Mrs. Prater, in 20, above, woke with a kitten walking on her neck, but she was sure she had heard a muffled, incomplete-sounding cry of one word, surely "Murder" or "Mother," she was unsure which, either from down in the court or from one of the houses. She listened hard for more, but she could hear nothing at all in the pre-dawn's crystalline vacancy. If she got up for every shout she'd be a jack-in-the-box for sure, and it was most often the liquor screaming anyway, it was rarely anything from the heart. But Sara Lewis, a cruising laundress of 24 Great Pearl Street, come to visit her friend Mrs. Keyler in Miller's Court at half-past two in the morning, had been dozing in Mrs. Keyler's favorite chair when she thought she heard someone say, quite loudly, a word which finished in an unfinished scream: enough of a hint, one would have thought, that something was amiss close by. Yet women of Mrs. Prater's and Mrs. Lewis's caliber had learned to stand fast. And, with the Ripper still on the loose, though losing fame, the bed, the chair, were more desirable by far than being a target in the street. No fear, they both told themselves, having heard the Ripper's fifth go down to inglorious defeat while, in the hollow aftermath, Gull made Netley turn up the gas and start a fire in the grate with some women's clothes (Maria Harvey's, actually) left folded on the chair. Yes, said Sickert, gagging, mesmerized, remade in stone: one white petticoat, one crepe bonnet with satin strings; a red hankie; a black overcoat, a small shirt, and two big shirts, men's no doubt, and grimy. He fed them to the flames, adding a hat and a rolled-up skirt, then lit the candle for Marie Kelly, his bosom friend and helpmeet, gone roaring up to her Irish reward, and he wondered with nauseated interest if her last thoughts, before Gull slit her carotid artery, had been of any cheer, perhaps of only slightly resentful bawdiness. Somewhere in that stench there still roamed the smell of pineapple or fresh oranges which emerged from her when she was aroused, as during the last time up in Hampstead. And some clinical, shameless part of him wondered if in any way the extreme shock of murder had, for however little a time, excited her. It was in the air, but losing fast.

Oh God, thought Sickert, to have been here and gone through it and still feel so warm even as that ghoul plies his knife and whole sections of her keep coming away lofted, steaming, intimate, only recently *mine.* Because he had eaten nothing all day, he was able to respond with dry heaves only, whereas Netley was chortling gently and nodding at Gull's ferocious delving. Onto the night table went her breasts, followed by her kidneys, as if some avid god were watching, being propitiated, and the flesh from her thighs, her ample thighs, and her legs. A neutral watcher would have said this woman had enraged the man to the point of insanity; surely it was jealousy and hate that drove him to such a conniption fit of butchery, but they would have been wrong. He was cutting for his fellow Masons and his Queen, though more for them than for her. He was flaying her dead, with the bedclothes rolled all the way down, her own slip where she had left it on a chair, and her body still in her chemise, rent as it was. Then Netley hacked away at the face, and the neutral observer would have been right this time, especially when he chopped the nose clean off and then began to skin the forehead, giving Marie Kelly the appearance of an ancient ape. After all, she had resisted his advances back in the good old days, and Netley never forgot, never mind who had hired him, never mind what his unholy commission was; he had a berserk sense of neatness, and only a profound sense of grudge kept his future symmetrical and whole. He wanted to pay them all off, Sickert and Eddy too, if he got the chance, and even Gull for paying him so ill. All his rewards would be on earth, he knew; nobody drank blood in the afterlife.

Now that the mess on the bed looked less and less like Marie Kelly, Sickert began to calm down; he had only dreamed that she existed and that he had disported himself on the rug in Hampstead with her and Long Liz Stride. How many meat-eaters mourned the cow? Gull might have been operating, slaving hard to save a life, with grandiose puffs and squeezed-up little curses as things went wrong. Sickert marvelled at the man's persistence, his utter lack of shame or guilt, his chubby bent form devoted to an act of bloodletting bound to have historic fame. He was like a god whose creature had gone wrong and he was wrecking it, but Marie Kelly had been a sly beauty, a buxom triumph wasted on the streets, ideally a nanny and a voluptuous companion, tanning herself gently on expensive balconies, putting a tidy sum away each year, having many but owning none, heartening many but loving none, save a child here and there. God grant that he leave her eyes alone, Sickert thought distractedly, even as the hobgoblin doctor only two feet away took one of her hands, in an almost friendly gesture as if to guide her to a seat in an omnibus, and rammed it deep into the remains of her stomach and Netley, in one fling, set the bloodstained muslin on top of the dwindling blaze in the fireplace. This was God's studio in reverse, he thought: an art of botch, a nest for the poet-peasant with a passion for insides. And after this it would never happen again, it would be monstrously over.

Now, trying to be human again, Sickert blew his congested nose: a human sound, but Gull was still flashing his blade, up and down, in and out, sometimes across, and now the remnants were losing their geography, their names. Does he need to go on like this? Sickert wondered, watching the liver go between her feet like some mucous tuffet. Somewhere in all that on the bed there's a three-month baby. So now he has killed six, did he but know. I cannot smell.

Next, helped by Netley, Gull removed his oilskin, revealing himself in full dinner attire, ready at something like a quarter to six in the morning to go out to eat although clearly too fatigued, and perhaps a little dizzy; he actually sat on the chair that bore Marie Kelly's daytime clothes. Netley rolled up the oilskins and made a huge blaze with them, from which they had to retreat, feeling as close to one another in that tiny room twelve feet square as they ever had in the *Crusader.* Were they going to toss prize portions of Marie Kelly into the fire? Sickert wondered now, fondling the key in his pocket, wishing he could unlock the past and stop it all from happening. At least there had not been screams, accusations, the looks that broke the heart, that ruined the rest of life. Gull, who never smoked, lit a cigar and choked on it, handing it to Netley, who inhaled it mightily with imitative aplomb. There was nothing left to do. Sickert doffed his painting smock and hurled it in a ball at the spitting blaze, all of a sudden hoping that the room would catch fire and burn up all the sorry stuff left behind them. He locked the door, the better to contain the devilish aura of what they had done, and marched away in step with the other two, some fifty yards to where they had left the *Crusader,* and he half-expected to find the horse butchered too, but it was contentedly supping from a trough. London was good to horses. All along, Netley's horse had dragged the heavy *Crusader* behind it, alone when there should have been a pair, or even four. Imagine the high and mighty killing whores on the cheap, Sickert thought; we lumbered when we could have sped. Poor horse, nameless even to Netley, its caustic Muse.

It was almost light and the streets were coming to haphazard life with prostitutes such as Elizabeth Prater from up above, who had scuttled out at five for her first tot at the Ten Bells, unaware of the charnel house beneath her. She would never sleep well again, mainly for fear of what was coming up the stairs. Had she seen the respectable pair, escorted by their surly-looking coachman, she would have seen them as two all-night johnnies at last going home to bacon and eggs, and her soul would have felt for the coachman obliged to wait up all hours for two such paragons of quality. Sickert himself was wondering what they meant to do with him; now was not the time to do it, but within the *Crusader* anything might happen, though Gull was exhausted from his travail.

"That," Sickert told Gull, "was the most appalling thing I have ever seen." He was talking to dispel tension, not because he wanted to converse with Gull.

"Join the medical profession," the doctor told him with a rancid laugh, "and see the body. You get used to it. You end up rather craving it. If you want keen sensations, my boy, come to Guy's." Then he laughed, inhaling.

"I did." Sickert slapped his knee.

"And?"

"Do you expect to get away with it?"

"Do you?" Now Gull pointed a chubby finger.

"Oh no." Sickert wanted to kill him there and then.

"Oh yes. Accessory they call it, but they've no hope of doing anything about it. Commissioner Warren resigned yesterday, by the way. Told no one. Just went. Good timing, I call it. Perhaps he will come to Guy's, a volunteer. Or go to Switzerland—many of them do, they like the neatness and all the explanations. Good country for the police type."

"So you do expect to go scot-free."

"I am guaranteed it." He had burned his cutting gloves.

"By whom?" Sickert already believed him.

"By power. By the powers." How sedate he had become.

"I did not know there were such powers."

"To them this is a bagatelle," Gull told him, with two hands that came slowly together and cached something tiny.

Sickert would always keep that key, and what he had locked with it would always be shut: the appalling presence of Marie Kelly in her pomp was to be a sight for nobody; the room was to become like those rooms in which ghosts had manifested themselves, ever after chilling the invader from the waist down. In a word, she was entombed, and he regarded her as such. For a while this even came to be, because the door was locked, and the only man who could order it broken down was Warren, who had just resigned. At a quarter to eleven, though, the lodging-house keeper, John M'Carthy, sent Thomas Bowyer, his factotum to Marie Kelly for the rent in arrears, the thirty-five shillings that she owed him: eight days' rent, the familiar albatross around her intact neck. After Bowyer's knock got no answer, he went to the window and shoved his hand through the hole after pushing the rags in. Now he was able to flick the muslin curtain aside, a muslin curtain at whatever level of poverty being de rigueur for blurring what went on within: Marie herself had spent many an hour twitching the curtain and adjusting it, making it the perfect interior baffle. When it did not hang just right, it irritated her into a hundred abortive rearrangements, each one precluding the effective manipulation of the next. Muslin curtains were never right: they were there to be fiddled with permanently.

By pushing aside the curtain, Thomas Bowyer managed to glimpse the shambles within, hardly able to credit seeing something such in a *room*. The very first thing he saw was what seemed a couple of weekend joints lying on the table that sat in front of the bed. Well, it was Lord Mayor's Day, and there was no harm in buying in advance, but Marie Kelly did not belong to the class that bought joints of meat. Next he saw her body, shapeless enough to be a liquid almost, and the big patch of drying blood on the floor. So he staggered away and told M'Carthy, who did not believe him and asked him to repeat it: "Good God, do you *mean* that, Harry?" he said, always calling Tom a Harry. "You wouldn't be joshing me now, would you?" Come and see, Bowyer told him, and, while M'Carthy, whose baby lay dead in the center of the mess on the bed, stood and grew dizzy, Bowyer went for the police. An inspector called Beck sent a telegram to his divisional superintendent and Inspector Abberline, the main "Ripper" man, showed up, at once commanding Miller's Court to be closed off. "Bloodhounds," he said. "We need Burgho and Barnaby," and at once wired the missing Warren, requesting them. Nothing happened. Nobody came, but medical students, intent on their Lord Mayor's Day frolic ran through the streets, jostling policemen and dislodging their precarious helmets. Later on, *The Star* was to observe that, if the Ripper had been looking for attention, seeking to impose an event of his own upon a city festivity, he had succeeded. He stole the thunder of Sir James Whitehead, the Mayor, and disrupted the procession: newsboys pounded through the streets with placards and special editions, crying "Murder—Horrible Murder!" as administrative London, with half of its police force in indefinite abeyance, tried to assume a mien of gravity and well-bred amenity. The Ripper, proclaimed *The Star*, "got his sensation. While the well-stuffed calves of the City footmen were being paraded for the laughter of London, his victim was lying cold in a foul, dimly-lit court in Whitechapel." She lay there until 1:30 P.M., when Superintendent Arnold decided to wait no longer for word from Warren and had one window removed. When he looked in, he saw it all, the throat and the torn abdomen, the almost amputated left arm, the forehead, the thighs, the pile of flesh on the table, including the nose and breasts. At last a photographer arrived, and talked of a method by which the retinas too might be photographed. The method came from a Jules Verne story and could be attempted with the eye unseated and lit from behind by incandescent lamp for three photographs: first, of the pupils illuminated; second, of the nerves stimulated by an electric charge (with the eye illuminated as before), and, third, with the eye not lit up but the nerves again stimulated. In this way, it was supposed, those who had died violently named their killer from beyond the grave since their retinas' last images were of him. No one tried this; it amounted to no more than the famous bloodhounds; but, it was true, Gull had left Marie Kelly's lovely eyes intact, mainly for dramatic effect. He had wanted her to be staring from the top of her own remains, and she was. The only photographs taken were of the entire body. M'Carthy then, finally, smashed open the door with a pickax. Who had locked it, and why, they had no idea, but Abberline pointed out that the murderer had not done it; the key had been missing for some time, as Sickert himself knew. Marie Kelly's removed clothes were still in a neat pile on a chair. There was no knife, no sign of any struggle, and there were warm ashes in the grate, where intense heat had actually burned off the handle and spout of a tin kettle. What on earth, Abberline asked himself, had the Ripper burned beyond some women's clothes, some odd bits of which remained? There was no bellows at hand and no fuel with which to augment a light-giving blaze.

As Sickert ambled through the crowds in the greasy streets, he wondered why he was going to Miller's Court, but then decided it was more logical, if he were innocent, to be among the sightseers than not. Hushed outrage was all he heard; not a syllable about the august majesty of the Lord Mayor, whose event this was supposed to be. Dorset Street was aswarm with people when the news broke that the body was being brought forth. Police lines broke and scores of amateur ghouls got their first sight of the grimy, badly scratched shell as it came out, topped with a bit of sacking. Onlookers pulled off their caps and shed more than a few tears as Marie Kelly made her last public appearance and rolled away to Shoreditch mortuary. Now the police, grateful for something to do, boarded up the window and padlocked the door, leaving one of their number on guard outside, though there was nothing to steal. Away went the ashes, to be picked through with an archaeologist's care. Fake Rippers, at some risk, walked the streets, as Sickert saw, pulling fiendish faces and asking gullible sightseers what they had heard about the latest murder, then walking away saying "I know, I know." Any man carrying a doctor's bag was immediately arrested, although let go once he provided an address. Not to be outdone, Sickert actually told one woman "I did it," and had to run from a howling mob she gathered around her. Puzzled by his own reckless behavior, he wondered why he was so offended by the false Rippers. He felt a certain vicarious right to pretend to be Gull. And then he wondered, if he was not going to tell, who would ever know? Never mind, Sickert kept telling himself as he wandered about among the Lord Mayor's crowds, it is over. It is never going to happen again. I can walk the streets with ease.

No more Netley, no more *Crusader*. No more Gull. He could

concentrate on Annie Crook and the bruised Alice Margaret, neither of them under the filthy grey sheet that now covered Marie Kelly, who, said *The Pall Mall Gazette,* looked like "one of those horrible wax anatomical specimens." That he was a criminal accessory refused to sink into his being, as if such a phrase were a slur beyond tolerance. He had had no choice in the matter and he had instigated nothing beyond soliciting the women who wound up in the *Crusader.* Much as the Coroner had abbreviated the inquest, no doubt in accordance with some order from on high, "from the powers" as Gull would say, he abbreviated his own part, as they wheeled the remains of Marie Kelly away, his bedmate and accomplice. It was as if those five women had been swilled into the sewers of London, where the Queen did not follow to make sure, and they would end up among the trawlers, even in Scandinavia where Rippers floated their enemies out to sea with a kipper tied to their heads for gulls and skuas to impale. When would Kelly's buxom image go away?

Chapter 35

The only thing remaining to Sickert, he knew, was to paint. All he needed was sufficient distance from events, not to be clear of them altogether but removed enough to tame his head. He could hardly paint in a manner obvious and direct, but he had always had a knack for implication, for cryptic allusion, and in that lay his hope. He could bury how he felt, and what the truth was, in crimps and folds of allusion nonetheless detectable by a kindred soul willing to make a little effort of extrapolation, or guess himself/herself blind. Before Warren resigned, he had had someone draft a catch-all pardon that ran in the papers as follows:

MURDER—PARDON. Whereas on November 8 or 9 in Miller's Court, Dorset Street, Spitalfields,

Mary Jane Kelly was murdered by some person
or persons unknown, the Secretary of State will
advise the grant of Her Majesty's pardon to any
accomplice not being a person who contrived or
actually committed the murder who shall give
such information and evidence as shall lead to
the discovery and conviction of the person or
persons who committed the murder.

Had this been Gull's way of getting Sickert off the hook? Yet
how could he unhook himself without incriminating Gull? Did
that mean he should denounce Netley instead? After all, Netley
had killed Long Liz Stride; why not the others too? No, Sickert
thought, this is a way of getting me to come forward, and then
Gull and his high-up Masons will entrap me. The whole of
London would have me to focus upon, whether guilty or not.
How many times in law has someone come forward in response
to just such a document only to be hanged for a minor transgres-
sion? *I* know all about figure and ground, juxtaposed colours.
What is the difference between the case where Person A comes
forward and admits his accomplicity while denouncing Person
B, of whom no one has heard anything at all, and the case in
which Person A says nothing at all and just waits for B to be
caught? Once caught, B will say anything, but the law's eye will
be on him, not on A.

Specious or not, this reasoning was enough to convince him
to lie low, waiting it out, sticking to his art, and being incredibly
tactful in his choice of models. Had he had enough of Whitechapel and Spitalfields, the Minories and Dorset Street? Did he
suffer from headsman's itch, driven to tell, even if telling cost
him his life? Some people could not resist the temptation to see
what people would say once the truth was out. Would Gull
succumb to that? No, all he would do was have his Lady help
him nightly set his aching feet in a bowl of hot water laced with
salts.

Sickert had already caught himself in two minds: wanting to
lard his work with hints about the atrocities, which was the

painter's version of headsman's itch, and wanting to savor the secret, even if it meant that Gull and Netley would go free. The sensationalist in him battled the moral man and won. For posterity, he thought, *everything;* for the present, not very much except for the utterly astounding deductive mind. An artist owed it to himself to pursue and peruse extremes of human conduct, shuffling over the line now and then if he had to. It did not necessarily lead him to criminality, any more than Byron's attending executions with opera glasses had, but it could, and if it did the artist had to be strong enough to resist the urge to tell: and thus be less than an artist. He knew he was not going to respond to Warren's still valid open offer of a pardon, never mind how much it seemed aimed right at him. Gull was a devious bird and Netley was a working-class dervish.

Doctor Gull, Sickert whispered, how do I get rid of this cold? Have you a cure? I hold my breath a full minute. I pinch my nose. I get drunk and go to bed. Instead he inhaled turpentine, which helped a little, suddenly aware that he need not worry. Police methods of detection were hardly sophisticated, consisting in the main of legwork and circumstantial evidence; London was already a roaring circus of informers and liars, fantasists and attention-hunters, and clearly the police were not working at full power. They had been advised to hold off.

Not far away, at 74 Brook Street, for Gull, having had his head stroked by his wife until he began to snore, all the agitations of a week ago had again dulled themselves into the curative affrays of sleep. His last thought before drifting away had been that Sickert, whom he had worried about, had come through quite well, neither wailing nor fainting, but doing his part, seeing that hussy off. He had been right to send Netley after the Crook woman's child. *That* had convinced the painter to do his duty.

"Take your own time," he had told Netley after the murder of Marie Kelly, "but do something again about the brat of Windsor, not this year certainly, but perhaps next summer when everything has quietened down. And Annie Crook. We at the old firm want a clean sweep." Netley would find it hard to wait for his bag of sovereigns, for one murder more, and then another; but he felt part of the tribe, the old-boy network, commissioned and confided in by the go-betweens of prime ministers and queens, the coachman of princes and executioners. He rather fancied himself roaming the streets, again in the *Crusader,* in a yellow oilskin, soliciting throats to cut. After Long Liz Stride, he would find it easy; he had found it easy then, in fact, and he wondered why he had been so good at it, not in Gull's heroic class of course, but quick and accurate. He had seen the results of Gull's frenzied knife work, and in the case of Kelly he had seen the doctor *in flagrante* with mouth in the semiprofessional pucker to which Netley aspired, indeed rehearsing it while driving. Gull was relieved; Netley was thrilled; and Sickert felt he had passed a sublimely difficult entrance examination to a superior college at which the Man in the Iron Mask was Principal. Now, he felt, he was one of a hard new breed whose work would have a unique core.

His brain was far from steady, but he knew his future as a painter was secure because he had lifted the jaws of death wide, put his head in between them and looked around at stalagmites and stalactites, none of them aimed at him. If you did that, you somehow deposed death, forestalled it, were able to paint it as if you had lived through your own death. It was a case of metamorphosis through empathy, best done (he shuddered) with those nearest and dearest to you, but almost as good with the Kelly gang. He had learned much about his old *nostalgie de la boue,* a mild hankering when compared to his new *nostalgie de la mort,* not just a French thing, but as viable and popular in Bali as in Paris. He felt older from his ordeal, yet somehow less frightened. Having gone this far in his convulsive thinking after the event, he had the first of those sudden fits of weeping that would figure regularly in the next years of his life: grief for the women, the child, but for him too, he so grossly rid of his innocence that he had lost something quiescent and lyrical without which he could not even heed certain tints and groups of color. Was it worth it to be this worldly? And, if worldly were not the word, was it *spoiled*? Or *damned*? Sickert felt his was a condition beyond words, not devilish but no longer human. Whenever he was quiet, he felt something huge and slimy wallowing about at the core of him, a little Gull perhaps, and he heaved helplessly. He was going to go on painting, he knew that, but it would be painting almost void of human worry. There was nothing to worry about. One night (he could sense that night's electricity in the air around him), the thing would happen. It would not be Gull, but perhaps Netley with Slerch and Senna, come to wipe out the evidence he was, but unable to detect the evidence he had left in his paintings since 1888, at least not until a keen classics-trained mind such as Salisbury's cried *Eureka! He has blabbed it all, the baboon.* Having sold so few of them, he had them all on his hands, or in the Hampstead house; and he felt some chagrin at this, having always thought an artist should sell his stuff and start again, not add to an unmoving heap.

One day, it would all unfold linearly; he would make a narrative mural of bloodthirsty events that had sucked up women never seen again. For now, his sense of events was anthological and would remain so. They thundered through him again and again, in no clear sequence, as he tried to figure out what his role had been, how often he had played it, and what effect his presence had had. Against the mundane reality of Annie Crook in the workhouse and Alice Margaret once more adopted out, and disenfranchised from her bower of comparative bliss at Windsor Castle, he set those vignettes that had scarred him, fingering them obsessively, like an insomniac twenty-four hours a day touching with his tongue the putrid hole in his tooth. Again and again he saw that scene, which he was going to paint when he had command of his hands, in which an unwelcoming Victorian fireplace, cluttered with screens and implements, faced a young woman bearing a baby high in her arms. She seemed to be trying not to face the mirror above the mantel, and her frozen gait suggested that she was rocking the child to sleep next to a brocaded chair from which she had just risen. This sumptuous setting conflicted with her shabby clothes, as if, perhaps, she were the housemaid commanded to hold the child while the lady of the house busied herself with some importunate caller from the police or the Society of Spiritualists. Seen from certain angles the child's face seemed attached to the woman's neck, growthlike, creating an incongruous effect. High above such startling rejuvescence floated a torso leaning slightly forward as if to peer down her blouse or initiate conversation with her, no doubt using babytalk. It was clearly a bust of a high-ranking person, who wore a wig and an open-necked toga trimmed with aiguillettes. Sickert called the apparition Amphitryon: gaunt and forbidding, the genius loci of a royal house summoned into the open by some deed of unwonted unquellable lust. Or this lordly figure had come to peer right through the young woman with the indifference of death, which would explain the look of anguish she wore while one of her hands hovered nervously just past her cheek. The torso had spoken to her with drab finality. This was the inscape of rejection, to be sure, as death rejected her (having claimed too many others), with the high ceiling and the dusty-looking alcove part of the scene, yet not more than the sooty rug or the dead urns spaced at regular intervals along the mantelpiece. The only enlivening image, apart from the baby and the woman, was a bull squatting to her right, its horns seen in the drear light from a northern window. The bull was waiting to sleep. From another angle it resembled an old Masonic headdress cradled in a wide basket that held magazines about stag-hunting and heraldry. Various parts of the painting appealed to him, but what he cared about most, even as he pondered the title "X's Affiliation Order," was melding the notion of highborn indifference and lowborn dependency. It would be a parable painting, Sickert knew, the viewer's mind being prompted by the title perhaps halfway to comprehension, but it spelled nothing out. He almost smiled when he considered how the torso, naturally enough, had no lower portion from which the organs of generation might hang, as if to suggest that the poor woman in the long skirt and the cheap blouse had been impregnated by the royal head itself, a royal head being more fertile (he supposed) than a plebeian penis.

Better, he thought, to regale himself with highborn pathos than linger on scenes of assiduous butchery or such slight facts as that Marie Kelly had been the only one of the five women who had a room to herself. She would otherwise have suffered Gull's attentions in the *Crusader* if Sickert had been able to induce her to enter, which he somehow doubted; she would have cackled and told him not to be so bloody pretentious, Walt. He missed her, but in the weird transplanted sense that he might have missed something he had eaten. It was no longer on his plate, whole and enticing, but masticated and then shredded by the acids deep within him. She was like one of those "exploded" drawings or blueprints that engineers made to show the assembly of something, but only he, with his brushes and his paints, would put her cheerily back together like some Platonic bricklayer, whose mind hurt him all the time and had whole areas where nothing healthy would grow again.

He felt coming over him, like a righteous blight, the need to bear witness, never mind how covertly; but a painter had his limits, and short of veridical funk there were the limits of the medium itself. How convey in paint the mousy odor of liver failure that had hovered in Marie Kelly's breath that riotous night in Hampstead? How, with a brush, tell the exact way she had said such things as *spushally whun* (for *specially when*)? How Gull had munched raisins for his nerves would be easy to do without depicting Gull himself, and he could even show what raisins, or black grapes, had done during the Ripper's heyday. There could be a painting of himself buying grapes from a Berner Street greengrocer.

There could be a painting of anything, in fact: of Mrs. Paumier selling chestnuts on the corner of Widegate Street, not far from where Marie Kelly lived; of the greengrocer's where Alice Margaret now boarded after her Windsor rhapsody; of the infamous Netley in the act of knocking poor Alice down with the *Crusader* in Fleet Street early in October. He, who had prided himself on being able to imagine anything, had witnessed things that nobody could imagine. Yet, he thought, if you were truly imaginative, you should be able to imagine things as they are without having seen them. What a ridiculous thought. How would you ever check?

Sickert wanted to be master of both reality and invention: he wanted to be able to prove that, if he had never seen the murder and despoiling of Marie Kelly, he could have imagined and painted it just as it had happened. I imagined it, he told himself, and then it happened just so. What I painted was neither recollection prophecy, nor on-the-spot transcribing. In painting there was no such thing as time, but only something like the perpetual present of hypothesis or dictionary definition. Then there was of course the time the painter completed the work, which he signalled by writing with a brush something such as *pinxit* W.S., 31 May 1860.

Preposterous of course, but he wanted with all his heart to paint a series of throat-cut lasses from the music halls, with red scarves above their red dresses among whom might be Polly, Dark Annie, Long Liz, Eddowes and Marie Kelly, the real admixed with the imaginary, adding up to what? That was how he made the event or events his own, and no longer the Ripper's, Gull's, Netley's, the public's, the police's. Nor am I, he said with relief, anyone else's either.

He could feel an obsession gathering. His mind went from a woman with a huge square chin and an oblate unstylish hat, her name Barrett or Barnett, to a series of images in which a man sat on a bed, first wringing his hands, then clutching his brow after beating it, and finally pressing his heart with clenched fists—on his left a naked woman apparently dead or unconscious. Again and again a certain murder happened and unhappened, but the manner and mode of it varied: her head lay on a newspaper, with blood flowing from her neck across the columns; or she sat noseless in a high-backed chair, perhaps awaiting the next onslaught; or someone, a painter-murderer, raised her into the sunlight, her legs ripped off at the waist, her head missing. He had an overwhelming urge to paint Queen Victoria, and to perch a bird near her ear, a gull that actually resembled the grisly doctor himself. Hints, hints. Women with animal heads and truncated snouts sailed through his daydreams, a whole cortège of the mutilated, asking to be made whole, seemingly drained of blood. Never, however, did the scenes that passed in review include Gull in his yellow oilskins or Sickert in his painting smock, or the *Crusader,* or Netley pouncing upon poor Stride. He had somehow exorcised such horrors as these, putting his painterly parable in the place of the true or literal ones. It was a trick of imagination. Or he deflected himself at the appropriate moment, so that what he remembered he did not see. In this way he could reduce the intensity of his nights out with Gull and Netley, transferring energy from them to metaphors that, while echoing what had really happened, took him gently far afield, away from Whitechapel to Liverpool, Cardiff, Calcutta, Sierra Leone. Marie Kelly, having been mutilated until she resembled a mastiff, facially at least, came to *be* a mutilated mastiff and so vanished, much as Annie Crook, bit by bit degraded until she still had a face but no longer her own, became a piece of a conglomerate mask.

This larding and trimming of reality was a technique Sickert might have practiced on other subjects, of course, but he needed it to save his sanity now. I do not like myself, he kept thinking, I never will again. I have gone circling down the drain of Dante's Hell, but I am still alive, reporting to myself that a man can survive anything provided he keeps still. He knew now that to get rid of something you did not externalize it in a work of art, for that work of art hung around your neck. What he had to do, and did with impetuous mental agility, was to transpose things, always relating a dead individual to a class of the dead, a specific murderer to a class of murderers, and a voyeuristic painter to a class of those (many fewer, he thought, but among them Byron and Baudelaire) to whom he felt closer and closer. It was as if his life were shifting sideways; he limped along a diagonal.

He took money to the greengrocer for Alice Margaret, her face and hands covered with scabs from Netley's attack, and assured her of his continuing love in mime, but she spoke hardly at all; what little talk was left in her had been shaken out of her by the *Crusader* and its insane driver. He crouched on the rug with her, building towers with bricks of wood then knocking them down, something she herself would never attempt. He took clothes pins and mated them, wedging their two clefts together into a cross and he made paper hats that sometimes floated upside down in the sink. He felt very much in the presence of a child paralyzed by voodoo or the evil eye, and he wondered what to do with her. When would Netley strike again? The first attack, almost another murder, had served its purpose: he had gone to the execution of Marie Kelly. But Netley now had too little to do and might show up again at any moment, thundering down the street, his eye on the target.

Perhaps Sickert should track him down and kill him with the knife he had never used on Gull. What chance would he stand? Better perhaps to interfere with the *Crusader,* sawing through some piece of it so that a wheel would come off and the malevolent Netley would go spinning away to his doom. Sickert knew he could hardly invite his painter friends to help him in this caper. After all, one word in the wrong place, one hint inflated in the wrong company, and London would at last have its Ripper. Gull and Netley would cheer him on, the scapegoat smelling of turpentine and linseed oil. *How did you kill a Netley?* Sickert did not know that Netley went home nightly in a froth of homicidal fervor; and slept alone on a palliasse with both a dagger and a pistol by him, eager for someone to have a go at him. He should, he would often think before falling asleep, have had a military career, but as an officer, for which he had not had the education. He longed to be like Prince Eddy, old Collar and Cuffs, attached to the Tenth Hussars, hunting deer and shooting grouse, changing sex when he felt like it. Sickert would never have got near so light a sleeper as Netley, who held the fantasy that he was guarding a prince of the realm, who one day would reward him handsomely, and then Netley would rise in society like the little Cartesian divers in the famous experiment. Netley did as he was told, and when he was not told he did what he thought he *should* have been told.

A better idea, Sickert thought, was to remove little Alice from the danger zone; but, to pay for Dieppe, he would have to start to sell his work, inviting well-to-do boobies to his rooms to eye his canvases; yet the only people who bought anything were his painter friends, just as he had bought theirs. He began to paint serviceable portraits anyway, nothing of the murders. There was never enough money to spare, however, to set up the Dieppe ménage he dreamed of. It remained a castle in Spain, crafted from pigment thick as an Irish bog, and he began to wonder about his own safety. Just look at Gull's record, he told himself: after Stride and Eddowes he waited more than five weeks, during which he managed to fool London into believing that the Ripper had given up. He had been waiting for a 5 to follow a gap of 3 that had followed a gap of 1 week. Now, Sickert wondered, what was the mathematical puzzle that decided when he would come after his painter accomplice, polishing off Netley last of all? This was November; was he waiting for a month that had a J in it, or an L, or what? Or would it go like bloodshed chess?

> Netley takes Alice
> Sickert takes Netley
> Gull takes Sickert
> Annie remains, in the workhouse.

Would Eddy then follow, or had he now achieved exemption?

Sickert began to drink heavily in this period, some months after the butchering of Marie, and his throat was always congested, as if the drink roughened it, and the London murk was not helping.

Chapter 36

All of a sudden it was easy. He walked to 19 Cleveland Street and asked for Netley, half feeling he was asking for Prester John; but the porter recognized him and invited him in, where he marveled at the long line of bowler hats all popped on pegs in the cloakroom while their owners satisfied themselves upstairs. He was a neighbor asking about a regular. Netley, they told him, was not far away, having set up residence in Rotherhithe, where Lemuel Gulliver was supposed to have been born, not a long way from Netley, Sr.'s place in Stepney, the parish to which all children born at sea were said to belong. Perhaps it was odd, even fractionally poignant, that the Netleys homed to spots of wobbly renown, groping for something —Sickert had no idea what: an echo of tolerant myth, a nursery of fame? It would have to be done at night, he thought, and, who knew, perhaps he would come clattering home in the *Crusader,* having stolen it. Netley only rented it, he recalled, so it might well not be there, but it surely was close by. He drank sherry through the day, lamenting the change the seasons brought, and wondering what he was going to do to Netley when he found him. He reminded himself that Netley was a murderer, not on the police list, but ripe for it, and no one to trifle with. Anyone who could mount attacks on a small child in the open street was no man to be argued with.

Crossing from Wapping to Rotherhithe by the Steam Ferry, he wondered at the contraption that hydraulically transferred him from the jetty at Wapping, and from the boat's deck to Rotherhithe wharf, lowering him at the former, raising him at the latter. He stood on the elevated railed path for foot passengers and put his trust in the lift-platform, there since 1877, enjoying his pennyworth, musing that a cow would have cost three times as much, and a loaded four-horse carriage three shillings and ninepence. Beneath him, his fellow passengers (not many at this time of night), and the river, ran the Thames Tunnel, enclosing the East London Railway. He preferred to travel in fresh air, especially in view of what he thought he had come to do; and he loved the spectacle, from high above the river, of London clanking and pounding its way into the next century. He smelled sour railway smoke, horse dung, and what might have been blazing honey, all mingled in the river's noxious bouquet. He wondered if his face had the look he desired: of no misgiving whatever, no sign of self-rebuke, no shame.

Having paid off his cabbie, he began to walk along a steep lane down the center of which had been built a wall, now swathed in thistle and discarded hawsers. In the distance he could hear a sluice and a forlornly clanking donkey engine. The air smelled of oil and rotting salt. Now he saw the hulk of a two-story building that could be reached through a wide-open gateway, beyond which there was a derelict outhouse, clearly not the living quarters of anyone at all. He peered in as best he could, but got only the smell of gas. Turning, he found himself at another open gate at the top of some steps, so down he went, using an occasional match and feeling dizzy. There had been no sign in the moonlight of the *Crusader,* but that signified nothing. Then he saw a streak of light under an ill-fitting door and, just audible, heard a sigh mixed with a gasp of pain. Down he went, pausing at the door, his breath settling wet against his cheeks. His hand shook and his heart began to flutter, perhaps from the reek of gas, not from nerves at all. He listened hard for talk, but there was only a slight scrape, then the gasp-sigh of before, as if, he thought, someone were peeling a bandage away from a wound bit by bit. Or applying a poultice. So: Netley, or whoever was on the other side of that door, lived in a disused gasworks, among rust, rats, and dripping water that stank of gas. Gas it was that lit the room beyond, cellar that it must be. Without more ado, but thinking hard of Long Liz Stride in particular, Sickert shoved at the door, then realized it slid, or rather grumbled, sideways.

An intact hissing mantle lit the room, but the thing in the center was a silhouette, swinging slightly. At once Sickert thought he had entered upon a scene of suicide and for a pagan second his entire being exulted: he would not have to kill Netley, or do anything else to him, because he had already hanged himself. From a girder about ten feet high, a dark form hung at a slow twist above a small fire, whose blaze leapt to the feet of the person hanging there. If it were Netley, Sickert now saw, he was wearing yellow oilskin except for the sou'wester, but the feet were bared to the rising flames. On his head the figure wore a crown of silvery tin, like a theatrical prop, and over his eyes a black operatic mask with no eyeholes. As Sickert advanced into the cellar, half tripping over a pipe anchored into the cement, he saw that Netley, for it was indeed he, had a rose in his mouth, and that blood was leaking down his chin onto the yellow oilskin. He appeared to have noticed Sickert's arrival, but went on chewing the rose, thorns and all, in the garish yellow light, still rotating evenly on the rope about his neck. Sickert noted that the neck was upright, the head not sagging sideways.

"Netley," he whispered, then called aloud. No response. Now he stood fully in front of the weird hanging man, his mind supplying wrong analogies, mainly one from childhood, of an uncle, very tall, who had to be suspended from the ceiling on a hook to remedy a curvature of the spine. He hung there for hours, showering those beneath him with choice sarcasms, in a specially made leather harness into which his wife laced him daily. Here was no uncle, but an apparently deaf murderer, a part-Ripper indeed, punishing himself for what Sickert could only guess at. He stood, half in pity, half in amazement, almost rejoicing at the spectacle, then with a faint but imperious motion shoved the legs and feet away from the leaping tongues of flame. Now Netley made that sigh-groan-gasp he had heard before, clearly unable to bear Sickert's touch. As Sickert leaned forward, almost overbalancing from his push, both feet came up and thumped him with climactic energy, catching him square in the face. Clearly Netley could see and was able to time a vicious blow. Back Sickert tottered even as Netley, without making any attempt to remove the rose from his mouth (his hands were free and hanging by his side), made a terrible bottled, keening sound, and out of the darkness over at the other end of the cellar, an open area without a wall, leading no doubt to a vat of poisonous water, a huge mass leapt toward him, making indeed the sound of a horse, knocked him flying, then bolted through the door and tried to get up the steps. As Sickert, collecting himself, ran after the horse, the horse came back right at him, thumping him aside and trampling through the fire on the floor. During all of this, Netley continued to hang, silent after that initial loud summons to the horse, which now vanished into darkness on the far side while Netley's body did its slow twirl and sway. In his pain and panic, Sickert heard sheep and wolves, big-toothed saws and grinding iron gates. Up the stairs he stumbled, breathing hard and muttering crazed, conglomerate syllables he would never recall.

Netley had thought him worth one kick only and had then got on with his chore of torturing himself, perhaps in memory of Long Liz or even little Alice. Clearly he had done this kind of thing before, maybe to sharpen his lust for blood, and knew how to loosen himself. Sickert had seen no stepladder or box beneath or even to one side of the rope, which he now remembered as glossy, plaited perhaps from the cords of old dressing gowns. Silk? Surely not. How had Netley got up there to begin with? Then he saw it, even as he burst out of the building and headed for the gateway. *The horse:* Netley, the masochist, mounted bareback for the feast of self-immolation, sent the horse away into the darkness opposite, there to await his further calls. Then, as scales fell from his eyes, Sickert knew the horse came out of history, was the Flemish "great horse" of the Middle Ages, tampered with to produce a solid, husky carriage breed, the Percheron, eventually relegated to farm work, like the mild slogger it was. Something as heavy as the *Crusader* was its norm. Was it Netley's own? What parsimony the universe practiced. Could God have been working through a Netley? God forbid, yet Netley was a human tiger, willing to kill for sport. Some people, some days, some lives, had no redeeming features, Sickert thought, but he no sooner thought this old thought again than he began to wonder. Each day contained a fleck of good, and that was enough provided you were able to massage it, spreading it wide and ample until, transparent as gold leaf, it shone abundantly. All silver linings, he thought, are acts of will. Golden linings too. If this were true, it was no use complaining. A man could have rituals, with the mind blank in between them, all the way from the mesmerizing bouquet of dawn coffee as the east flooded vermilion to an aroma of fried trout at dusk as colours got deeper. God's ritual was not to make life too palatable: more a spoilsport than an absconded engineer. Even in the Netleys, merit or love hovered like a firefly for someone to fan it. Even in the Gulls, he whispered telegraphically.

Then, after all those good ideas, his resolve broke and he

cursed himself for not shoving his knife into Netley's belly as he spun like a marionette on the rope. It would have been easy and final, a just retaliation, but he recognized he was not the knife-plunging kind, though he might have dabbled with blades in the presence of William Withey Gull, and he had, of course. But actually killing, no: he would be death's pander, perhaps, its procurer, but no more than that; only in a blind, foaming rage would he actually do it, and this made him feel even more a coward than an accomplice murderer. Walking now, as he loved to do in London at night, he reviewed his performance and found it brainsick and wanting, the work of an amateur hero who had gone into the night after Netley without the faintest plan in his head beyond, blundering in on the man and making him feel the weight of a visitation. He wanted Netley to take heed of him, to take him seriously, as if all human response were a form of recognition: things taken in, acknowledged, and swaddled away for ever. He had not gone there to do anything much, except perhaps wet his trousers, which he was proud he had not done. But, had there been a dead woman on the floor, headless and eviscerated in the tradition Netley must have learned from Gull, would he then have tampered with it, gently eased the tip of the blade into this or that soft region until some stark longing inside him ceased its clamor and he could go home sated?

Sickert and Netley were the same age, but Netley, a virtuoso of perversion and bloodletting, was far ahead of Sickert, having a pliant mastery of the mundane arts that accompanied vile crimes: spying, identifying, marking, overhearing, accosting, lifting and lugging, dumping and arranging, not to mention the washing down and drying of affected areas. He was a good clean-up man, lacking the originality and initiative of Gull, yet willing nonetheless and as capable of an *idée fixe* as the devastating doctor his master. Sickert knew that he had been among monsters and tried to muster an appropriate shame, but he could not help thinking that he had been destined, chosen even, to do awful things for the good of his art. Having seen the flayed gargoyle of Marie Kelly, he was qualified, he felt, to undertake the worst visions in the human range, as if he had learned new colours from her liver, her shanks, her unspoiled blue-green eyes. He would never use those hues again without a certain holy nausea.

I should have killed Netley, he kept telling himself. I keep bungling things. I'm a duffer. Maybe the horse would have trampled me to death soon after, but I would have been a better corpse for having done it. Walt, oh Walt, why do you dither? What entitles you to sleepwalking your way through a butcher's shop as if it were the vale of bliss? Are you so adaptable, so elastic? He tried his Affable Arthur walk, to give himself some false jollies, but the brio would not come, the jauntiness had ripened and fallen away from his brutal, slack orbit. He was never going to be the man he wanted to be, never mind how much applause his work won over the years; he had failed to seize the horrors and paint them into something new, something he could live with, even as horrors only part-dominated, much-flinched-at. He subscribed, he saw, to the pornography of evil: reluctantly stimulated, insufficiently repelled, secretly enthralled, so long as someone else did the slaying and slashing. He half-liked having been henchman to a Ripper, and he realized he enjoyed the Netleys, the Gulls, as creatures who dared to make love to their own depravity, spending their seed in empty and rotten eye sockets because it was the spirited thing to do. He went along. He sucked up. He paid lip service. And then he recoiled, protesting that he was still the *honnête homme* he used to be, the spry almost sacerdotal friend of the down and out, the classless hail-fellow-well-met of Cleveland Street, as close to Fletcher the greengrocer as to Whistler.

Those five dead and mostly unmissed women, one of them almost loved in his perverse, unhygienic way, would have known what to do with Netley, as they had known, in a couple of instances, what to do with a Sickert. They would have, as the schoolboy phrase had it, got him down and squeezed his knackers until he hollered, but they would have gone on doing it, emptying them as if they were pimples, and slowly turning their attention, *all ten hands,* to the shaft above, quick-working it to an unhappy climax, then, with dawdling precision, rending it with their fingernails and stuffing it bit by bit up his nostrils as if that were the way to the core of his being, innovatively ignoring his mouth, but picking his nose for him in reverse until the blood poured down as the shreds went up, and they cackled like *Macbeth* hags, upping their petticoats and making water all over him in a parting shot that healed him not at all. He would have no need then of a hanging-rope or a horse's back: the women of Whitechapel would have paid him out in kind, perhaps stripping his pockets of his few miserable possessions, casually slinging his penknife, his cube of billiard chalk, his other cubes (of sugar), his picklock, his stub of pencil, his little handful of raisins, and his knuckledusters into a sump of poisonous water at the rear of his shanty-palace, where even the rats died of the gas.

Chapter 37

When Annie Crook was in the Pudding Club, Sickert had taken her some of her possessions, hoping that she would be allowed to keep them; all she owned she had kept in the kind of grip that plumbers used, consisting of strong canvas folded once, with two holes for the hands. This canvas holdall did not really close, but it served, weighted down as it was by the hobbing foot, upon which Annie or her shoemaker would repair the shoes of an entire life. A pair of slippers, an old blue candleholder with its enamel chipped to reveal black metal beneath, and a thick wooden truncheon for mashing potatoes completed the inventory of major items. Minor ones included hair clips and a bobbin into which small nails had been driven for knitting upon. There was one sentimental item, hardly a work of art, but something Sickert had painted at her request; it was a small scene of Cleveland Street that Sickert fudged to include the street name (which she could not read) next to the sweetshop at number 6. Street nameplates were usually on the buildings at the corner, and this was so on Cleveland Street; but Sickert, in some generalized attempt to get Annie started on reading, gladly rearranged the visual world for her, and indeed painted the letters so large that the final work looked like a reproduction of the street name, which blotted out the exaltedly diffuse chiaroscuro behind it. It was every bit as neat as the lettering done by the real sign painter, himself a convict in Pentonville prison. When Annie first entered Gull's vile domain, the workhouse attendants took her things away again: the hobbing foot as a dangerous weapon; the potato masher as another, and the bobbin—useful for slashing a face, perhaps—but let her keep the nameplate, the candleholder, and the hair clips, which remained in her impounded plumber's bag, shut away in a cupboard, from which someone stole the candleholder, since the cupboard was not locked. Clearly, then, if she ever got loose, she would have the makings of a not exactly luxurious life in which she would be able to squeeze the teeth of the hair clips wide open and affix them to the painted street name Sickert had done for her. Such would be the first meaningful act of her freedom, if her freedom ever came, as one day it did, she having begun to have fits, in the course of which she fell to the greasy floor and writhed. She could tell when they were coming on, as her entire body tingled and something in her head made a barely endurable buzzing sound. She also knew, pretty well, when she was not going to have an attack.

One day in late November, perhaps because she had slept uncommonly well out of total exhaustion, she decided to scream and lie on the floor to see what would happen. Things happened as usual: the attendant walked away at a pace of no discernible speed to fetch someone else, who would in turn authorize another to see to her, the main hope being that her fit would pass by the time anyone got back. Blunted and degraded she may have been, but deep within her there remained a shred of peasant sagacity: she simply had to feel well enough for it to work on her and generate some possibility of action. After all, she came from a village where the locals talked with the rough

severity of Vikings but thought like Norman farmers. All she
had to do was get up, walk through the unattended open doorway and leave by the doors through which the dust bins went.
First, though, in some bravura access of confidence, she went to
the cupboard for her plumber's grip, amazed to find it so light,
but perhaps still intent on using the last, the masher, or even the
bobbin as weapons to make her escape with. No one even
heeded her, so there she stood by the bins of potato peelings (her
frequent food), pondering as best she could, lobotomized and
fairly tranquil, the way to Sickert, whose very name made her
rummage for the street he had painted; and in her dishwater-
gray shift she began the journey from the workhouse to the
West End, the nameplate in her hand; jostled, laughed at, insulted, but for some reason unarrested, her slippered feet getting
sore and beginning to blister, her eyes scalded by the brightness
of day, her stomach full of butterflies she could not delve to and
eat. Now and then some Samaritan, thinking she was heading
back to another workhouse or the Cleveland Street Infirmary,
showed her the way, and sometimes people took her by the
hand or arm and guided her, pointing and shouting as if she
were deaf, which she was not. Thus handled toward her destination, even though wetting herself in terror at the sounds of
omnibuses she could not use, she muddled along: steered,
tripped, shoved, badgered, in the end bleeding and hopelessly
out of breath (the street name had to be her message, held aloft
while she gasped for air), and finally found herself among familiar streets and houses. She had carried her street talisman without being able to read it, confident from long ago that what it
had once said it would always say, because Sickert had told her
so. Cleveland Street had not moved away or changed its name,
or indeed its face. When she saw the umbrella-maker's and the
boot-maker's, her heart quickened even more than walking had
made it do, and when she saw Morgan's sweetshop the tears
began to fall, but she was not going there, she was aiming for
Sickert, her sponsor and saviour. If he were not home, she would
wait for him, forcing herself to resist any temptation to go and
see Mrs. Morgan (a last resort, for Annie remembered being

dragged from her basement hovel by Slerch and Senna, whose names she did not know, of course, nor Sickert's nicknames for them). She thought of Eddy, but remembered him without emotion. She wanted, in the most primitive craving lovesick way her child, last seen with Sickert, whose fate she in the whole of London knew nothing about, she and all the other inmates of this or that institution, with memories so bad and so deprived of information that they went beserk at their next sight of the forgotten moon.

Sickert saw the sign he had painted approaching him, behind it the withered ghost of somebody, surely not Annie, her eyes black-ringed, her face waxen, her hair a knot of uncombed grease, her steps awkward and uneven, but approaching him nonetheless, through the little passage beloved of the milkman (shelter for him when it rained; he stood clanking and clinking). Lordloveaduck, he thought, she's out.

"I've come," she gasped, harsh as a barker, "Mister Sickert, I'm *oam.*"

Once inside, she dropped the painted sign without watching it fall, and he began to bathe her at the sink, first peeling off her shift, at which she made no demur. Using the big brick of soap gouged by the scrubbing brush, and tinted by smaller brushes he had had to clean, he lathered her with cold water and dried her as best he could with warm air from his mouth, rubbing and puffing again and again as the pipes shuddered and bounced and the outside pipe ran black. In fifteen minutes or so he had converted her from a peripatetic scarecrow to an imitation of life, to whom he offered all he had: some stale bread, some cheese, a hunk of sausage. Annie ate with ponderous fervor, then slowed, shook her head at the wine he offered, took the apple and the orange, then the misshapen lump of chocolate. She said nothing all this time and he listened to her breath in the chew, changing her gasp to through the nose only, and then changing back to breathing through her nose and mouth. It was like watching someone being born, or giving birth, he could not be sure, and he wondered if she was going to die on her first day of life, as it were; she looked so frail and bleached, her hands a mess of chilblains and untended splits, her feet out of the slippers, a mess of blisters and scabs, her face a study in ivory and spots.

"Annie," he whispered, and she looked away to see who Annie was. His face was still sore from when Netley had kicked him. Then she was asleep and he sat there watching her slowly ease her limbs, push them out to the limits of tautness and then flex them again and again in beginning sleep. He checked her plumber's grip and laid the hair clips on his table, marveling at the nothing it contained, itself a heavy thing useful for carrying ingots in or fire irons; a loose head would roll out, a set of knives would cascade away, and books would do no better. Presumably the search for her had already started, and his studio would be one of the first places checked. Yet dare he move her now? If he waited for her to rest, the Slerches and Sennas would be upon them in ten minutes, he was sure of that; the same would be true, more or less, of the sweetshop, the house in Hampstead, and Henry Fletcher's, where Alice was. The only thing for it was to get her somehow along Cleveland Street to the male brothel and hide her there, where the goings-on were so peculiar that, although he would excite merriment, he might be able to count on some epic discretion.

After waking her with almost savage shaking, he pushed her as best he could into the first thing that came to hand: the naval officer's uniform, vast on her, of course; but like a tailor he turned up the trouser legs, tucked his red hankie into the neck of the jacket, jammed the big hat over her convolvulus of matted hair, and virtually frogmarched her out into Cleveland Street as if escorting a drunk—better a drunken captain than a helpless skivvy fugitive from so-called justice. Along the street they shuffled, some actually thinking Sickert was the captain again and Sickert himself his mysterious unknown brother with the light mustache. It was about three o'clock, and those who had washed their lunch down with ale were sleeping it off inside, so not many saw him go from number six to number nineteen, almost opposite the sweetshop. In he went, giving a little croon as if plastered, creating a great guffaw in the hallway and almost at once being ushered into the pantry, where there was a chair and, on a low table, a big roast of beef partly sliced. Nothing loth, he sat Annie in the chair, took her hat off, and began to ply her with roast beef. Ah, it was Sunday, and the frequenters of the brothel had taken some lunch and cognac on the premises instead of having three-veg-and-pud at home. Now Annie fell asleep again, almost at attention, with a slice of beef half out of her mouth like a supplementary, attenuated tongue, and he wondered about the inevitable hue and cry for her. He wondered why no Slerch, no Senna, had been at his door to intercept her; but it was Sunday, he said. They were all taking it easy, with boots off, feet up, palms at rest upon the paunch. Only on Monday would the police make a move, if at all; look how lamely they had fared with the Rippers. He stared at Annie in the dim light coming from a vent up high, asking himself how much she could stand, how many vile processes she had already put up with, what she thought had happened to her, if indeed she had a future at all. Then she addressed him, her eyes closed, the beef still in place:

"Me babby, mister."

"She is well and close, Annie." He felt as if he had said let there be light, with his mouth remaining open after the last word, *light,* then realizing his gape was that of a throat-cut woman. Annie was one of the few to whom the murders were of no import whatever, close as she had been to Kelly, to whom he himself had been close enough. He shivered and had to massage his knee where he sat on the cold dank floor to stop a muscle from throbbing along the side of his right kneecap. She seemed not to know what outfit she was wearing, and he nodded at the extreme of unselfconsciousness she had been subdued to by Gull and his brown-coated dragoons. "She is well and close, Annie. Well cared for. Just grand. Really all right." The banal phrases piled up just beyond his mouth, but she seemed not to hear, having registered the first, and her posture suggested that she was in no condition even to hug her child, just round the corner with the cabbages and cauliflowers, the lettuces and the leeks. Alice would be better off brought here to see her mother, incongruous as it was, better far than Annie exposed all over again. Besides, Annie could not walk, was not dressed for it, and had not enough emotion within her for yet another climactic encounter. Would she ever tell him how she got away, with her nameplate compass? He thanked God he had become enough of a painter to do that big souvenir postcard of Cleveland Street with fairish skill. He went back into the hallway, asked the porter about something to wear, and at once realized how much he had underestimated the place's resources. Upstairs he went and beheld a wardrobe full of ladies' attire, a bit gamy and music hall, but endearing and for him nostalgic. He selected what he thought inconspicuous: a tweed suit cut for a sturdy but not overweight woman, with brogues and blouse to match. The hat was regal and stern. Annie, if she could stand up, would look like a cadaverous lady doctor, he thought, come to auscultate her offspring's golden heart.

So it was that Sickert, in the role of magical provider, reuniter extraordinary, brought Alice Margaret along Cleveland Street to the male brothel where her mother crouched in the little pantry. Thank God he had friends in the vicinity, he thought. The mother looked spavined, done for, and the instant he appeared with her child went into the start of a new fit, which she then managed to control, telling herself that time was fiendishly short and she might never again be able to repeat this experiment, this escapade. Why, Sickert reasoned, was he not doing more for her? He never had the right plan; he had been unable to save Kelly, and now he was doing precious little to help Annie. Surely a man such as himself should be able to muster more initiative; he wasn't just dawdling around, he was cleansing and oiling the wound, but it would all lead to the same damned thing in the end. They would come and get her, they would put her back where they thought she belonged, all for having loved a prince who was still free to attend house parties, go shooting, contemplate an excursion to India or the West Indies, trot off to join his regiment.

Already, he saw, Alice Margaret had the deaf's odd mix of tautness and chubbiness in the face, the one from superhuman effort to understand what was going on around them, the other from lack of oral exercise. The child had a supernal gleam all right, as if some special benison had fallen upon her, a blight that made her face radiant from the sheer need to be expressive in a medium other than words. Was that it? He had seen the same thing in Alix, even in Eddy: a stretched, winsome poignancy that both overreached and held back, as if the person were trying to establish the exact range at which communication should happen.

He left the pantry and went for a drink in the brothel's bar, more of a lounge than anything, where several painters of his acquaintance hailed him as one back from the dead. What would they do, he thought, if they knew he was one of the Rippers? It must have been like this when Lazarus got up from his litter and made a meal on grapes. He wanted to paint Lazarus gustily chewing his portion, poised above a dish of grapes on a commonplace table. White beard unkempt. White napkin not tucked in at the neck but tied behind, making a bib for the revenant. A bottle of wine and one other plate. Lazarus ate with a spoon, reaching round in front of himself and ladling the grapes in one at a time, aiming the spoon like a spear. Alice and Annie had nothing to say to each other but a powerful amount of hugging to catch up on, even if Annie shook with fit after fit, even if Alice heard nothing of her maternal babble. Indeed, he thought, they were much alike, the child possibly stone deaf and a noncommunicant, the mother a fallible ghost with a smashed memory. What was he doing with such people? Was he even half-qualified to look after them, to minister to them, he whose hands had dipped in squandered blood? It was not that he wanted somehow to make it up to them for having botched their lives, for having brought a botched life into place where there had previously been nothing, or to the memory of Marie Kelly for having failed to put Gull and Netley off the scent for ever. He needed, with excruciated yearning, to assume a role that gave him back his dignity, to enable him to go around saying the word "righteous" as "rightuus," like good old trusting Henry Fletcher, whose cockney slang had intrusions from Latin, nobody knew why. He did not like himself, whereas once upon a time he had, with well-tempered skepticism. Nowadays he thought only of workhouses and hospitals, of grim basements and safe sewers, appalling atrocities in ill-furnished garrets and the *Crusader,* as full of blood as a bottle was of milk, thundering about London, chopping the heads off children. His brain no longer worked, but developed a tingle, a fizzle, whenever he had to think comparatively hard. He was supposed to keep watch for Slerch and Senna or their ilk, but he was wondering what Netley's horse was called; hadn't he once known and actually used the name? "Lord" or "Grace," or something derivatively splendid. Not "Eminence," but "Royal" perhaps. That would be Netley, the pretentious, maybe even changing the name with each nocturnal mission, after which he would pound home behind his grandiosely named mare and pretend to hang himself in the cellar of the gasworks. What on earth, Sickert wondered, was wrong with his life, his own? He was once a painter but now a murderous parasite of a go-between with a remarkable knack for betraying his friends. How much longer he could abide it, he had no notion, but he knew now that a removal to Dieppe would not be enough, although he would almost certainly do it, to breathe better, to walk through streets that did not accuse him all the time. Even to enter a carriage sickened him, and he had developed a profound dislike of oilskins, fires, and knives. He no longer carried a weapon of any kind, prepared to have done to him whatever Gull decided: his throat cut, his innards evicted and rearranged, or, if in Gull's eyes his offense were slight, having the mad doctor squeeze his nose and cheeks, cleaning out his pores in some weird Lilliputian ritual that blended hygiene with pain: Gull the scourge of the divine comedo.

Sickert still could smile, but the humor behind or within his smile was preternaturally twisted now; his conscience had been struck by lightning and would soon be on show at the British Museum as a curiosity, next to the Elgin marbles. Oh to have gone down aboard *The Mentor* in 1804, off the isle of Cythera, the birthplace of Venus, but, unlike the precious cargo of Greek sculptures, never to be recovered. He could see why Netley did what he did, with the crown of thorns in his mouth and the fire at his feet. It would hardly purge or purify Netley, but Sickert had begun to wonder if he, not so far immersed in blood as the other two, might find some way of cleansing his being, enough at any rate to enable him to continue as a painter. If he could only get Annie to himself for a year or two, together with Alice, making up a ménage of some kind: of altruistic self-abasement, washing Annie's feet and holding her during her fits. That would be a beginning, he thought. Something would have to happen, something of *his*, and not something passive such as standing by watching in a trance of oceanic disgust while Marie Kelly was dismembered. He would have to take the lead. Well, then, Sickert, he sighed, remove them both now to the other side of London. Take them to the coast. Borrow as much as you need from Ellen, if she will even look you in the eye. Go to Dieppe, go to Istanbul.

He had convinced himself. He went to the pantry, told Annie what he intended to do, but she stared at him in utter incomprehension, as if English were beyond her and she needed a street-name, or something such, for any meaningful dialogue to happen. He looked at the two of them, the annulled mother and the mute child, and knew he was not going to have the courage for it, to let all that was his go down the sluice for a brace of the broken as helpless as this, even though what remained of his life was crime-infested: a child's fort with soldiers and cannons, intact when seen from outside by the marauding Bedouin, but within dominated by huge roaches bigger than the lead soldiers themselves. He was still holding onto something he respected in himself, but he was unsure what it was or where: talent, perhaps, or a gossamer-frail and brainsick prophecy that, one day, he would make durable amends, after Gull and Netley had been hanged on a very high scaffold so that Netley might be attached by rope to Gull's feet, to increase the weight of Gull and have him defecate on Netley when the trap fell. Netley would die, neck snapped, beneath Gull, and they would go to different graves, Gull's full of rats, Netley's of quicklime. These social differences would persist until the end of time, but an effective partnership for murder required such violent contrasts as they three embodied: the Sir, the bon bourgeois, and the man of the people, all intent on forcing tarts to the death they had been born for. There was something sinfully redundant about killing Polly, Dark Annie, Long Liz, Eddowes, and Marie Kelly, and Sickert knew he would never come to terms with it, whereas the three of them should have polished off Queen Victoria, Salisbury, and the Prince of Wales, just, as Annie used to say, to get good changes started.

It was no use. At the door of 19 Cleveland Street there already stood a cab, not the *Crusader,* and not some toff arriving, but Slerch and Senna belatedly hoicked out on a Sunday from their boiled cabbage and sliced beets on top of Yorkshire pudding and roast mutton. Sickert saw them and knew that history could be redundant too. He rushed through the building to the back door and found there a black-draped hearse tricked out with tossing black feathers. If Annie went out by the front she would live, perhaps, but if she tried the back she would die a sudden death. Yes, she would call it a "hurst," as ever, if she survived to see it. I am making a profession, he thought, of always being too late. The workhouses of London never liked to let go, although Windsor Castle was more giving. What on earth was he thinking about? Were there no secret passages such as monks used to escape through, no false fronts, no spring-loaded chambers that led into the cellar, the sewers, and a quick ship to Belgium? He asked, but his friends in the brothel, Meral Ohonsoy and Serif Goren, about whom he never asked questions, told him no, alas, there were no other ways out, although one day they would have need of just such an escape hatch. Perhaps they should construct one, but Sickert had already gone, marching out to Slerch and Senna (the devils he did know) and asking them what they wanted. In a voice like thundering cinders, Slerch said merely "Annie Crook, a hussy," and continued to chew his sprig of hawthorn while the rotund Senna cupped her plump hands and clopped them together in parodical applause designed only to abolish time. She was warming herself while being paid to sit in the November cold, almost that of December.

"Shall we be 'aving her, then, squire?" Slerch again.

"I'll pay," Sickert said, knowing he had been a Ripper and could easily demolish these two, aided by Gull and Netley, but not alone.

All expenses had been paid already, Slerch explained with punctilious ponderousness. "We 'ave 'er welfare at 'eart, we do."

"I bet you do," Sickert said. "Where, then?"

No answer from either. Then Slerch said, as Ohonsoy appeared at the door, "Who's that bloke?"

"The *Queen*'s Man," Sickert said adventurously.

"No, that is me," Slerch growled. "Slavterfetch."

"What?"

"Bring 'er as 'as absconded *h*out, there's a good gentleman."

"Elsewise," said Senna in a voice as deep as that of Slerch, "wissslavtofetcher." In a fit of temper she slid her knitting off both needles and unraveled it all, cursing, then slung it into the gutter. As she moved, the carriage lurched and wobbled as if being heaved from underneath. Sickert felt defeated. Neither bribes nor lies would work. There was no safety hatch. They did not want the child, that was clear; she was just the quotient from some interesting piece of arithmetic. A sum of sin.

"I'll bring her," he tried, "in my own coach. Tomorrow."

"Be a good gentleman, sir, and bring her out now. Her tea will be getting cold." A blast of garlic and gravy hit Sickert full in the face and he quailed.

"I'll come with her then," he said, trying to smile, but his face was full of starch.

"Not allowed. Not *h*-allowed." Slerch.

"She'll be all right, squire." Senna.

He walked back to the door, where he found Annie, like someone drugged and already sleepwalking, ready to go, her child crammed to her side with an arm several shades of white. She was still in the naval uniform, though she had tilted the cap so far back it would fall the instant she moved. Outside, he tugged them both, the mother and the child, even as Alice began

to tip away from him and Annie began the most bestial scream
he had ever heard, a cry both feral and induced, both raucous
and splintery-tender, which went on and on as if all that was
within her was air: a clownish figure in dark blue, her mouth a
round O of howl, a pair of dead eyes that knew where she was
going for the last time: no more escapes and some kind of good
hiding when she arrived.

Chapter 38

The next thing that happened was that Gull died. Or at
least his death was announced, of Cerebral Haemorrhage/
Hemiplegia, occurring on January 27, 1890, the first onset
having been on October 10, 1887. Sickert scoffed and
trembled, knowing that Gull's Masonic masters could reach
anybody. They had either killed him (or talked him into suicide)
or spirited him away. He read the tributes, the lauds of Gull's
work on xanthoma, intermittent hematuria, treatment of tape-
worm with oil of male fern, hyperthyroidism and hypochon-
dria. Myxedema was already known as Gull's Disease. Gull
elected to use the minimum of drugs. Yes, thought Sickert:
grapes only. But Gull's real Disease was the blade.

Did it make any difference, to Annie or anyone else, exactly
where she spent her next thirty-two years, a period longer than
she was old, though it might be said that by the time she died
she had aged an enormous amount? It was as if she had been fed
into some unspeakable sump that, by dementing and degrading
people, mostly women, so unfitted them for life on earth that
they must surely have promoted themselves into the vanguard
that would one day launch to the moon, to Mars, to the next
nearest star. Annie Crook was akin to Claude Bernard's experimental dogs, not that she was baked in an oven. She rotted,
mostly, and withered, in workhouses and prisons, infirmaries

and hospitals, having her usual fits, then hallucinations, bouts of rowdy hilarity, shattering recollections of being tortured. Just one of the women of Whitechapel, she descended into the care of keepers for the workhouses of St. Marylebone, St. Pancras, Poland Street, and Fulham Road; surely, to any mind contemplating such a sojourn from the comfort of a chair, even in a rat-infested house, it was a devastating era to have to cry through, she getting dafter and lamer, more and more deluded, and gradually succumbing to cardiomyopathy from all the stress. Sacrificed to the premise: *Can a human being be broken?* she held together until the middle of the 1890s, decreasingly aware of the labels so often applied to her: inmate, patient—prisoner, even—but degenerated into a specimen, almost a cartoon, composed of generic and reputedly comic ailments such as housemaid's knee, dishwater hands, cold-floor feet, sometimes locked away in a padded cell for being too energetic in her misery, sometimes put hard to work for seeming to be too much a layabout. She was regarded as a lunatic without being put into an asylum, where of course records of her progress or lack of it would have to have been kept; as a workhouse lunatic, she lived undocumented as a hedgehog, or like a conduit to be filled up more or less at one end with stuff she vented at the other, though nobody tracked her bowels any more than they did her raving, wordless, rhythmic speeches aimed, as she alone knew, at the prince and his torturers, who had ripped her daughter from her. Between 1907 and 1913, in an enfeebled state of aphasia, she lived again on Cleveland Street, in its Infirmary; it was the longest stay she had anywhere, after which, more a parcel than a human, she went into the Hendon Infirmary and was eventually discharged to the Fulham Road Workhouse, spending her last seven years shuttled back and forth between the workhouse and the hospital next door, where she died in the Lunacy Observation Ward on February 23, 1920, having been variously diagnosed as noisy, stuporous, deluded, apathetic, and suffering from persecution mania. Time and again Sickert had tried to track her down, but since there were no records (and, when there were, no information given out), he rarely prevailed.

Those on high wanted her not to be seen, though what on earth might she have told, she who having started without writing or reading had now lost language altogether save for histrionic dumb show? He found himself, the few times he could see her, in the presence of an anonymous creature buried in a pupa. Her mind wobbled, her eyes refused to fix on him as he stood in front of her. It was one thing to try and break through the Chinese wall of silence on Annie's behalf, but quite another to try and read the mind of Netley, who either wanted to please so much or had just become involved in a murderous pattern full of murderous reflexes. Either way, Sickert was at a loss to know what was coming next. The whole Ripper affair had left him with too much to think about; he no sooner got something into focus, such as what had happened to Gull, *really,* than something else crashed into it and scattered his thoughts.

He certainly was not ready for what happened to Alice Margaret in February of 1892. Crossing Drury Lane with an elderly sister of Mrs. Fletcher, whom she would have called aunt if she had been able to speak, she was going her own slow way in a gait perfect for both of them when the egregious Netley thundered down at them, full tilt, this time almost missing his target although managing to spin Alice Margaret sideways when the corner of the *Crusader* struck her. The impact knocked the life out of her and she was carried into hospital unconscious, but released the next day, profoundly and chronically frightened and almost ready, for safety's sake, to follow her poor mother into the workhouses. After the *Crusader* hit her, it slammed into the curbstone and wrecked a wheel, upon which Netley, knowing he could not escape except on foot, jumped down, mingled with the crowd, and ran away to Westminster Bridge with several indignant, shouting witnesses after him. Perhaps his cellardom version of the garotte had made him strong of wind; he managed to outrun his pursuers but was seen to hurl himself into the Thames off Westminster Pier and was presumed drowned. He was, in fact, a strong swimmer as well as an indefatigable runner, deliberately leaving his boots and coat behind him in the waiting room (he had so much time to spare).

He allowed himself to be saved by the Pier Master, but at first put up a struggle, after which he let Pier Master Douglas take him to Westminster Hospital, where he identified himself as Nickley, of no fixed address. "I live on the river," he said defiantly.

"Ay," said the Pier Master, "and next time, young sir, you can bloody die in it."

"I've been living a terrible life," Netley said, still gasping, "with Jack the Ripper."

"Tell us another," they said. This was 1892, not 1888.

"There's no need," he flashed. "It's easily enough for a lifetime, that. I'm a careless driver, it's true, but I had a bad accident with a van six years ago, and I've never seen too well since then." He felt so ashamed of driving so poorly, he told the police, who had rather fancied taking him away for a little interrogation, that he had tried to end it all. They knew nothing of his clothes neatly folded under the seat in the waiting room at Westminster Bridge. Since Alice Margaret went more or less uninjured, and Mrs. Fletcher's sister declined to press charges, Netley was allowed to go away, not even bound over to be of good behavior. Now he was free to mount a third attack, and Sickert wondered at himself, deluging his mind with shame and guilt, unable to break the bond of silence.

Had he been on the spot, he reasoned, he would in all likelihood have pointed the finger at Netley and had him dragged through the courts for attempted murder, on either occasion. Or would he? Alas for all his good intentions: one word about Netley and attempted murder might have brought down the entire house of cards. And an assassin with an eye that good and a deadly weapon beneath his hands was no man to trifle with. No, Sickert thought, I want to be a survivor. How the mind punishes itself on the way to oblivion, only to notice that oblivion gets tempered with all kinds of mementos left behind us: letters, books, theories, paintings, deeds of blood, God knows what. If only I did not hear about things too late. He left it at that, not having had the heart to do anything too dramatic or self-advertising since January 1890, when Gull was reported as having died. Well, Sickert thought, he may indeed have had a second stroke. He could have died. Just perhaps, his corpse really was in the fancy coffin they used at his fancy funeral in the village that had the misfortune to have had him born in it, in Essex. Talk about special trains laid on from London and country folk trudging twenty miles to pay their last respects. I bet they butchered him, or smothered him, or hung him upside down, or poisoned him. One day they will do the same to me. Once Netley has murdered Alice Margaret, on Masonic orders, they will finish Netley as well. Many a time he had come this mental way, seeing everything clear and realizing he was living not on borrowed but on embezzled time. To recoup enough emotional energy to start painting seriously again, he had gone to Dieppe and had been touching up a river scene, with on his fingers some tooth powder he was thinking he might mix into his paints when, his door went *click-flap* and in strode the Prime Minister, Lord Salisbury, in from the Chalet Cecil to buy a painting, which he did, hardly looking, selecting a still life with much throat-clearing taciturnity and stunning Sickert by handing him, as if he had worked it all out beforehand, not the three pounds that Sickert might have asked, but five hundred neatly wrapped.

"Kelly-money, I suppose," he said, without even rising.

"For services rendered," Salisbury told him. "Have a lovely day, dear boy." He then breezed out. So, Sickert thought, if ever a bastard has been paid off, this bastard has. I did my job and Gull is gone, whatever they have done with *him,* and only Netley remains, their abiding threat. This is to sweeten the pill of Netley's survival and my own continuing silence, the question being: Is it a weekly, a monthly, an annual, or a one-time-only thing? A pension? A stipend? A tip? Am I a servant at heart? More importantly, when the day comes for me to pop questions at the Almighty, I am sure to ask why Salisbury and Company didn't kill me too. I could still talk, still write, still paint, still blab. Was it that they thought I somehow behaved like a gentleman? I spoke well and at least didn't look like a diehard Bohemian, therefore I was—I am—a *gent*? Am I alive because these gentleman-hooligans believe in the civilizing power of poise? Can that be it? Whatever tense I think in, am I their model civil murderer's accomplice because correctness of manners somehow imbues you with stability? Or do they think I am so enamored of my career that I would never breathe a word? I will always do better, they think, by stiffening my stiff upper lip. It must be that. They trust in my selfishness. It is not just a matter of pronouncing all aitches and dropping no terminal g's; it's their assumption that I know, and accept, their way of doing things. Britannia waives the rules. Not bad. I need a party to take it to, Sickert the wit. How awful if they're right. What kind of man am I? What kind of heathen? Roles reversed, would *I* let *them* go free for five hundred pounds? Am I that chivalrous?

The twentieth century would soon begin, making him feel lamentably ill-equipped to cope. He made a quick survey of the human wastage he had seen: Polly, Dark Annie, Long Liz and Marie. Annie and Alice were among the walking dead. Gull, apparently, was also dead and gone. It was enough, but women were still being murdered nightly in the poorer streets of London; the poor were being punished for what they were, but surely murder was not the required fillip to make the underprivileged pull up their socks and earn a decent living.

He was forgetting someone—Prince Eddy, of course, dead since January 14, no longer shooting in Scotland, celebrating his father's birthday at Sandringham, going off to Denmark as the Prince of Wales's personal representative, sailing away to Port Said and India with his wholly incompatible parents, just like a dutiful son. With syphilis or without it, Eddy had died of the flu, which had had its fling in him much as he had had one fling after another between a certain shore party in the West Indies in 1879 and his resolve to marry a certain eligible princess. On the other hand (there was always another version of these public deaths), Eddy had not died at all but had been confined on the Isle of Wight, which was perhaps only just as true as the tale that he had really died but with his fingernails gone black; Eddy had been poisoned, to clean up the scenery. Sickert longed to paint Eddy with those nails or Eddy with inch-thick bars in front of his face and his mouth gagged hard with calico, his proptotic eyes clamoring for help while paresis ate him from within. Sickert no longer felt anything for his imposter of a brother, but knew that, if he began believing all kinds of stories about Eddy, he would soon believe those about Gull, and in no time would have convinced himself that Netley had not attacked Alice twice, Gull had not sequestered and lobotomized her mother, that Marie Kelly and her accomplice tarts had all moved up to Hampstead, alive and bumptious, and on and on. The tale he would most like to have believed was the one that said Sickert had had no part in the Ripper atrocities. Surely Gull could never tell. Netley never would. So nobody would ever know. And what they did not know did not exist. Who was it, his wandering, demoralized mind prompted him, with the blackened nails? Who was the other poison victim? Mozart? No, the composer's body had only swelled up after his death.

Had Sickert known, he would have rejoiced that the Masons, after giving Gull a testimonial dinner at the King's Arms in Brook Street, Mayfair, not far from Gull's home, first stuffing him with food then quietening him with grapes, took him away to the inferior purlieus of Islington and put him in a straitjacket in a private asylum there; he was given the ironic name of Thomas Mason, otherwise known as Patient 124, hurling himself relentlessly about in his padded cell and wrecking the night with his abominable cries. Why Gull lacked the foresight to refuse grapes from his fellow Masons on a festive occasion will never be known. Clearly, Gull, caught up in the spirit of the moment—at last unwinding after a job well done, with close friends beside him extolling him to his face—lowered his ferocious guard just once. And they had him, "they" including his son-in-law, Dr. Theodore Dyke Acland. In 1896, a so-called pauper at St. Mary's insane asylum, Islington, died of natural causes, his name Thomas Mason, aged seventy-nine.

Twelve of Dr. Gull's colleagues had sat in at the confidential lunacy hearing on him, all of them Masons. Had Sickert known this, he would have been waiting for his own testimonial dinner and his own removal after it to yet another padded cell. It was too easy to remove people, to anull them, to make them into someone else, just as the murdered women had been converted into something hideous and irremediable. London seemed bent on sadistic metamorphosis, which was perhaps its way of turning Prince Albert the luxury lecher into an heir of shining rectitude and his mother the Queen into someone as loveable as her Albert had been. Could it have been the influence of Robert Louis Stevenson's *Dr. Jekyll and Mr. Hyde,* published only two years before the Ripper murders began? Had the theatrical production proved to London that all beings had two sides or two roles? Had the vision of life's insensate doubleness paralyzed the city's sense of decency and dignity? It was as if life were not complex enough when people could be depended upon to be their usual selves from day to day. By mercy yes, Sickert told himself: it used to be too easy to be Jekyll, but now it's too easy to be Hyde. And I am a man who has read his Balzac and his Dickens. I know about the lower nature of us all. I have lived it in the teeth of all the kindness there is. I have gone over to the angel of death like the most appalling traitor known, and you do not come back from that. The Jekylls who become temporary Hydes do not allow that at all. Once over there, among the tubas of depravity, you have to stay; your mind goes to hell while your external being writhes along in the customary patterns of day-to-day, and when you weep, as you always must, people think it is old age creeping up on you or the frustration of not being taken seriously by the English public or even loved by them.

Once the English public adored him as a painter, Sickert felt, they would also forgive him his part in the murders—if they ever found out; and now he was thinking that no one would ever know, there was no need for them to know, there was no need for him even to remember. It was over and done: a boil lanced and cleansed. He longed with almost childish wistfulness for the life he used to have, when there was no need to talk to anyone save the grocer and the milkman, when he could put the Ripper behind him and be the painter all in all, awaiting the tutelage of certain moments he did not mind calling vision, which was when he both saw things and saw beyond them: almost complete. In a way he envied Gull and Eddy and the women, with a final date appended to their strivings, even if stones filled Gull's coffin and Eddy was bellowing like an infected heifer on the Isle of Wight, and the women were peaceful as carbon during the first unalloyed privacy in their lives.

Chapter 39

Having been run down by the compulsive Netley at the ages of three and six, and made two miraculous recoveries, Alice Margaret finally found her way at nine into the St. Giles workhouse when Sickert was away on one of his many foreign excursions; she had wearied of the Fletchers and they of her. "Mother in prison," the admission papers said. That was in 1894. Eight years later after a stay in Dieppe, in the course of which she became accustomed to seeing Sickert wash his hair and jam his porkpie hat on top of his sopping curls like one eager to show a clean head to the world, she was back in the workhouse, this time the St. Pancras, which noted that she was "Stone deaf" and made appropriate allowances without teaching her to speak. She knew enough English, however, to decipher a wrapping-page torn from the *Marylebone Mercury and West London Gazette* of September 20, 1903. Netley, her would-be destroyer, who had flirted lifelong with suicide and had had that bad accident in 1886, on which he blamed everything else that was wrong in his life, had at last removed himself accidentally from the London scene, kicked in the head by one of the two horses he'd been driving, and killed by the wheel's passing over his throat. He had been thrown, having no strap to restrain him, when one of his van's nearside wheels struck a stone rest. He had gone down in the world somewhat, having had to surrender the *Crusader* to its owners after having given it, as he said, a lifetime's work and was then driving a two-horse van for Messrs. Thompson & McKay, carmen to the Central Railway Company. What Alice did not appreciate was that Netley's death occurred at *Clarence* Gate, Regent's Park, a gate with the same name as her father, Eddy, who had become the Duke of Clarence and Avondale in 1890. The sleepy-eyed, lascivious, mustachioed prince and his former coachman, the social-climbing automaton who had become Gull's bird of prey, had come together again in death.

Alice Margaret struggled on, becoming more inward and nervous, convinced that someone was still after her, especially in the street. She never quite recovered from her injuries and her deafness sealed her off, so that minor happenings, such as injuring her foot in 1905, magnified the furtherance of a threat as yet unfulfilled. She applied for assistance to the Relieving Officer of the Westminster Union on October 11th that year because, lame as she was, she could hardly go up and down stairs as her job required. She was then a parlormaid.

Thus did the daughter's steps sometimes repeat the mother's, not only from workhouse to workhouse, but through ledger columns headed "Cause of Distress, Temporary or Permanent." Sickert, who always needed a new garret for each painting and therefore was only a flickering presence, would have boldly written "Murderous Royalty" or something such, in the space provided, if he had had the time; but he never did, having written his fill in Goulston Street the night Dark Annie Chapman was killed. He took in Alice Margaret an interest which, for its intensity and righteous passion, came close to love both spasmodic and sublime, yet always intermittent. He watched her grow into a trembling, clumsy, sometimes eager woman who eventually married a fish-curer called Gorman, whom she married in order to keep out of the workhouses her mother knew only too well. Gorman, however, suffered from impotency, so she had little of a husband, more of a dependent to whose needs she was far from equal. The rings under her eyes, Sickert told himself, were indices to extra degrees of emotion and intensity, and the congested nasal intimacy of her voice reminded him, kept reminding him, of how secret and clandestine her making had been. Without him she would never have been. She was the catastrophic leftover from a situation too big, he thought, to have happened to just a few people. He felt overwhelmed by resentful nostalgia when he recognized that she and he were the only ones left. She gradually became his ward and, less gradually, his mistress, as he kept on remembering Marie in that role, and her prolonged silences kept him constantly in mind of the cover-up, the other silence that surrounded the Ripper affair, and would always have to, at least until he, Sickert, when he was too old to care what happened to him, told all or as much as he could.

Weary of being called a painter's painter, he slaved on, afflicted by sudden bouts of weeping, but trying to close the drawer full of blood that kept sliding open in his mind, vaguely aware that in living with Alice Margaret, the princess *manquée*, he was cleaving again to the same pain, always being tugged back into that pattern, much as Netley and Gull in their different ways had surrendered to an initially quite arbitrary design. Yet she gave Sickert a focus, a core, he would otherwise have never found, a point from which to depart toward Hogarth, Degas, and Goya. Before she went blind as well as being deaf, and became paralyzed too, Alice Margaret was going to give him a son, like some pure quotient from the disasters; not that he knew. His mind was on the work in hand, the Camden Town murder series in which the woman's face was always that of Marie Kelly alive or dead: a flash of apricot amid the dominant off-black, ruby-russet, and plum. His mind's eye was unattuned to what would happen to these works after 1908, the year he painted them, when the darks would darken even further and his knife's-edge mastery of tones would vanish into an overwhelming night amid which the highlights would develop a shriek of their own.

Chapter 40

Dragging the workman's cap low over his eyes, he set to work and painted the corpse by the light of the bull's-eye lantern, the worse to see by. Only with his red kerchief could he work on slaughter, imagining the horror and embellishing it. When he did not wear it around his neck, he knotted the corners and draped it over his head like a cap. Or he wound it around the doorknob as if to strangle the very shank. When he was stuck, he unraveled the knots and smoothed the corners out with spit, after which he stroked each corner to a damp and yielding point with which to tap either side of the bridge of his nose: a place of shocking tenderness since boyhood. The woman had had her throat cut while lying in her own bed, awake or asleep, in a cheap room in Camden Town, one of his favorite night haunts, and he wanted to do a whole series about her, either Bach-like variations or a parade of changes in which death would never come.

Sometimes, when he was very tired, he felt he must have done the ghastly thing himself. One of his problems, or one of the proofs of his genius, was that he never felt quite separate from others; in a trite and fulsome way, he loved and died with them all, ever a part of the ghoulish retinue. This particular murder had taken place in 1907, but he was really painting 1888, the year about which he thought so much and knew so much; and, calling his series as he did *The Camden Town Murder,* he was summoning up images of the five whores demolished two decades ago. Ever since then, in its heart London had winced and sickened. It was the middle of his life: he was forty-seven. Yet who knew? He might die any day, and this was the hale and hearty swansong. Sometimes when he was more than very tired, he could see clearly, as both victim and murderer and himself, and this histrionic dissipation of who he was (to others) matched his passion for disguise, for dressing up in private as "The Ripper," in his long coat. There was no dark alley that did not invite him to thrill to the hideousness of what he was doing or had done. In his studio, too, with the lantern turned down, he was the softly padding, well-spoken killer, the man of genius trying to scare himself to death, but always ending in a laugh as he tossed the disguise away and got on with his lugubrious painting instead.

It mattered little that his images of the Ripper had come from the pages of *The Illustrated Police News:* the so-called degenerate in a workingman's bowler hat or the posh fop with a fur collar. He spurned being the Eastern European Jew sometimes blamed for the Ripper atrocities; and he knew he could never pass for someone with lobeless ears and a broad nose, but he did occasionally venture forth in a top hat and with butcher knives rattling in the scratched-up leather bag. It was 1907 he was living in; he could count on time's wheel's, for most folk, as having turned. He could count on the considerable number who knew him to say, "Oh there goes Mr. Sickert, *pretending* again. Lordloveaduck, these artistic gentlemen have funny ways." Of course, he was close to the Camden Town murder inasmuch as Robert Wood, the man tried and acquitted for it, was a friend of his who had posed as a model for the series after the trial. Indeed Sickert had helped to secure the services for him of a solicitor also known for hushing up scandals in the Royal Family. All along, Sickert had known that the murderer would not be caught, but trapped in a series of paintings instead: hunched over, fondling his victim's hand, with her head twisted away from him in ultimate aversion; or having let the hand fall and fondling his own, drywashing it in a fit of severe pondering; or, as the painter's eyes had begun to see it now, hunched over like Blake's Ancient of Days, white beard streaming away from him in a gale of hatred, the very eyebrows growing fast like a corpse's, become inhuman bristles to announce atrocity to the world. Murderers, he thought, were Lazaruses who at last broke their fast, coming to life only through an act of sordid savagery, after a life of constraint and bitten lips.

Yet to ponder in this fashion was not to get the paintings done, it was only to till his mind, whereas what he really wanted were umbers and mahoganies, hues so drear that beholders would want to poison themselves. He cherished an idea filched from Fuseli: that of horrific painting, from which the viewer would recoil, nonetheless edified by having been stretched beyond customary limits. If what people truly wanted, as *The Illustrated Police News* proved, was appalling, better to have a man of taste remind them of it than some hack with a pot of India ink and a fine police pen. In a room upstairs, a murdered woman lay, her trussed and rounded hair as clean and shiny as a guardsman's boot. Horse dollop of purest ebony. I am a lover of dust, he thought. I dote on abated light, in a fold of rumpled sheet, cleft of a corpse, green rot among scuffed leather. I am the muse of the morose. Our horse's name was Clem. How did I forget such a thing as that?

He knew that what he was painting had come from his days in Venice, from tarts called La Giuseppina and Caroline dell'Acqua. Plump sluts on iron bedsteads had been his stock in trade then, all of them burning with only partly simulated lust and seeping poisons. The most horrendous nightmare of a great city stalked through his imagination and would not let go of him. Was it only twenty years since, walking home one night from a music hall, where he warmed to the glow of rotten light on the caryatids, he had encountered those girls in Copenhagen Street, on his way from Hoxton to Hampstead, and told them he was

Jack the Ripper, yes, *the* Jack the Ripper. They had fled, screaming. On other occasions, most of all when some buxom girl,
trapped between the green spot from above her and the curdled
yellow of the footlights at Gatti's, had excited him into walking
the long way home, his mind lulled itself with the thought of
Casanova's *Memoirs.* In his own edition he had written the name
of the Ripper. He had even claimed, to Sir Osbert Sitwell, that
he had lived in the same house, anxious not to be omitted from
the hideous tally, and the reckoning that was sure to follow it.
Not quite the same as being left out of an important exhibition,
this craving of his was nothing creative; on the contrary, it was
mere emulation. As a lamb in wolf's clothing he stalked the
nighttime streets, always wondering whom to accost or frighten,
and then to run from laughing as if all he ever wanted to do was
seize the very music-hall songstresses who had delighted him—
Katie and Queenie Lawrence, Vesta Victoria, Ada Lundberg—
and work on them with knives, even if only to prove what
gruesome antics a toff was capable of, once provoked. "Tramping about among the tramps," as he liked to say of himself, he
went out as a decent man fond of dropping foreign phrases
(French especially), but he also felt himself as much pushed to
extremes as an Oedipus. He minded his manners with exquisite
adroitness, but he always felt that hot and baying breath within
him, eager to maul Mesdames Lawrence, Victoria, and Lundberg, and, if not them, then their half-baked imitators, fresh
from the provinces, lured to London by some vaguely intercepted dream of a wraith-girl chirping elegantly amid the tobacco smoke, her songs purer than those actually sung, her role
harsher and more forceful than the misses from up near Bir-
mingham had dreamed. Truth was, these girls were already too
late to make their fortune on the halls, at least in Central London, with only the Hungerford and the Middlesex doing things
in good old fashion.

Imagine, he said: to have lived through all that, and still to be
hankering after the same kind of thing. How happy he was in
Mornington Crescent, brooding on the fate of one Emily Dimnock, a prostitute who had decided to reform after getting en-

gaged to a night worker on the railway. She had been found murdered in Camden Town, after first having been clasped in the murderer's arms, then thrown on the bed. Or he had found her sleeping and had raised her up. Or he had merely sat there on the end of the bed until she woke, and had then laid hold of her without a word. *Would* I, Sickert wondered, *what would I do?* Slowly the old murders faded from his mind's eye and their echo in this new century began to fill him up, making him hunch this way or that, and move his arms and hands with canny abruptness. He stood and removed the red handkerchief from the doorknob, wadding it up between his palms.

Then he unfolded it, used it to mop his face, and began to nibble a corner, gently tugging the hem against his front teeth while he whistled. He wet it with his tongue and peered through it. Then he laid it on his knee and tried to make it into animal forms: a basket; a doll in a long nightdress. When he inhaled it, after unfolding it, he smelled wet laundry on the line on Monday (Tuesday in the north), and all the dankness in the world seemed to hover beneath his nostrils. It was a red of the music hall, to be sure, but most of all his own red, the flash he liked beneath his chin when he roamed the streets of London, Venice, and Dieppe. Neat on his kneecap again, he made the bed with its tiny red sheet, trying to imagine Emily Dimnock asleep alive, then dead, flailing about with trapped legs as her murderer, breaking his fast, used all his weight against her, yet not without letting her have a last look at the lamplight, resolved to make her see what she was losing. Who could the man have been?

He, Sickert, was not going to make another name for himself by going around saying he knew who the Camden Town murderer was, and he was not going to impersonate him. He was going to strike him dead in pigment. Why, he already had, stunning him for all eternity with the arbitrary finality of an unpondered pose. No lamplight for him, either, or only a glimpse as the brush came down across the eyes, lidding them, aiming them down, beyond all looks.

He was torn between painting what was identifiably present, which he could do well, and heaping up a mass of emotions, all olive black, from a subdued palette. He could not forget visiting Degas and seeing his collection in the rue Victor-Massé by candlelight. There was the painting of a woman playing the piano, and some musician, Degas told him with delight, had recognized the score in the picture: *"Du Beethoven!"* Well, he wanted to leave hints in his work, but he wanted to do something more feral, something between mud and terminal moraine. The colors in his paintings of Emily Dimnock should typify a world in which such a thing could happen; not *make* it happen, but seem congruous after the event, as if the killer's mind had flooded out all over the counterpane: a sludge of misery and malevolence, upon which, nonetheless, what light there was obligingly continued to play, like the guttering candle in Degas's apartment while the two of them wove their way through the thicket of easels, each bearing a Corot or an Ingres. It was all the same light, unkillable and inopportune.

At his core, he knew, something liberal insisted that an artist—or anyone—could not love people without loving their pain; yet how could anyone in his right mind love it, even relish it? It was hardly enough merely to observe it, to heed it. He had to go farther than that, and he often caught himself in reversals of common sense, insisting that he had to bear the pain of others, or even *inflict* it. Just so long as he was not out of it, on the legendary outside, looking in. That, he told himself with a disconsolate smirk, would kill him. Yet how to do it? The way was not through pain of his own, but through some prodigious empathy that made him into what he painted, even something as vague as quivering protoplasm stranded in a brown froth. To do the Camden Town series properly, he would have to be both the victim and the murderer, so he imagined the one intensely, certain he could feel the blade and the flood, and quizzed the other in the person of the painter accused and eventually acquitted of the crime. "What did it *feel* like," he asked him, "to be accused? Did you ever wish at any moment that you had indeed done it? We have all been at that point, have we not—the forbidden irrevocable."

Anyone, Sickert thought, who's lingered on such an act of

blood has in a way also committed it, is guilty of it, and God knows I am guilty, of much more than anyone might guess. He resented the way in which the Camden Town Murder had lit up his imagination again, making 1888 come back with more than obsessive force, dragging him into a past buried but active in the grave. Couldn't the Camden Town murderer have waited until 1935, say? Obviously not. His need was urgent. Her sum of days was final. The squalid little bedroom in Camden Town, where Sickert himself had wandered, looking for subjects, would have waited for ever, until demolished, but the death-wish in both the slain and the slayer had come to the boil. Derisive of his own mixed metaphors (were they metaphors or just muddled hues?), Sickert rapidly sketched out a sequence of events: frames for a motion picture to come, in which all that was missing was the very thing he craved: the mental interior, the why and the repining, the almost complete mental blank during the act, followed by realization's spate. He had to know everything, but his problem, even after that, was how to insinu-ate thought processes into pigment. It was not enough, not quite, to suggest lugubriousness or shame, as he well might through judicious chiaroscuro; he wanted the paint to track the mind from A to B, and so forth. He wanted his to be an art superior to that of words, communicating through bare vibra-tion in some part of the spectrum the birth of a wormhole in slime. Lord knew, the murderer had expressed himself, although the cutthroat at once joined thousands of others, serving merely to punctuate with a stop the complex process that had led to it. I like what's ugly, he told himself, but only in a quest for knowledge. I take no pleasure in it, I. Well, I did once. He was thinking back to when he had achieved what he sometimes called climactic vicariousness; in that year the rapt observer had been indistinguishable from the sleepwalking participant. Since no one had been caught, there was no one to hang, and therefore the perfect murder, made up of five murders, had taken place, and thousands of Londoners had thrilled at the very thought. It had been almost Roman. They all wanted blood provided they were not splashed. Who gave a fig about five prostitutes cut up and disemboweled? He for one did, but he had been close to the five in a way that most Londoners had not; and he often felt he had run his now thriving career with his little finger while using the other nine to thrust back down the rising lump of degraded emotion that threatened to raise him high and dry and expose him. *Seaweed rising,* he called this phenomenon, bound one day to engulf him, never mind how famous he'd become.

The more he worked on the Camden Town Murder, the more his mind betrayed him, sidling back to those other murders, and then, as if for some needed counterpoint to the appalling savagery, to the tender if fatuous love story that started the whole thing off. These tender emotions had no place in his Camden Town series, so they surfaced, came to the fore, and took him over, almost cheering him as he toiled grim and stertorous, as if Juliet might replace Cordelia. Who had she been? If only she had never been. If only she had stayed put. But forces as strong as those that have impelled the human race to totter to its hind legs impelled her to break loose from what she was born into. She languished for want of a golden city.

Now he took the red kerchief, arranged it into a blindfold and covered his eyes, after which he went on painting again, almost by finger feel, to see what might happen in the dark. That was where things usually happened, and not acts of darkness only. He the painter was willing to go blind so long as his mind went blank as well, and he wondered with a deep intrinsic shudder if the blind man, obliged to forage forward with his lips and nose, could tell the difference between dead and crawling flesh lifted from the grave and the deceitful flesh of the newly murdered victim. No, that's not it, he said, but I am getting warm.

ABOUT THE AUTHOR

PAUL WEST has published a dozen novels, among them *Rat Man of Paris, The Very Rich Hours of Count von Stauffenberg, Gala, The Place in Flowers Where Pollen Rests* and *Lord Byron's Doctor*, which became a bestseller in France and was shortlisted for both the Médicis and Fémina prizes. His numerous works of nonfiction include the best-selling *Words for a Deaf Daughter* and, most recently, *Portable People*, a collection of biographical sketches. His short stories have been collected under the title *The Universe, and Other Fictions,* and his second volume of criticism, *Sheer Fiction II*, was published recently. He is at work on a new novel and a nonfiction book about living with illness.

Paul West is a Guggenheim Fellow, and has received the Arts and Letters Award from the American Academy and Institute of Arts and Letters, the Hazlett Award for Excellence in the Arts, and other honors. He was a judge for the 1990 National Book Award in Fiction. Educated at Oxford and Columbia universities, he was recently appointed a Literary Lion of the New York Public Library.